The Wanting

by

Christina Strigas

The Wanting

Cover Art by *Diana Carlile*

The Wild Rose Press, Inc.
PO Box 708
Adams Basin, NY 14410-0708
Visit us at www.thewildrosepress.com

Publishing History
First Edition, 2021
Trade Paperback ISBN 978-1-5092-3898-9
Digital ISBN 978-1-5092-3899-6

Previously Published Muse It Up Publishing 2018
Published in the United States of America

You think loving me is easy, but my kisses can turn into punches. Ironing bores me. Not that caring about that is relevant, the truth is…romance is killing us. We live in a "brave new world," a world in which making love to loveless people every night, is meaningless. You don't know how much I would rather watch Moulin Rouge. I'll watch it over and over again until a man is fed up with all of me.

I'll smoke under the fan and write on anything available. I'll have pens in every corner of a room. You'll never have to search for one again. Yes, I'm quite loud and messy. My underwear is sometimes just kicked aside.

When you'll want to kiss me, I'll wrap my arms around your neck. I'll love hard and reckless. I'll ignore your faults and make our bed. Remember this: I'll hate watching the news.

If your wanting is strong, then leave a book by your bed. Even if you don't read it, every once in a while, read me a line. I'll get so horny that I'll kiss you madly.

These are just a few of my secrets that I'll never tell you because you don't even exist.

I'll wait with scented candles, and your old T-shirts will hang loosely to my mid-thighs. I'll drink wine and announce the years that fly by because my sensitivity to time rivals no one's.

You'll start wondering why your attraction to me is worth your while. Is it because we have not kissed yet? Or perhaps we have made no confessions to each other. I have your soul close to mine, caressing it, talking to it. When you are far, I can hear

Praise for Christina Strigas

"This is a beautifully crafted erotic romance, an unconventional journey of seeking desire, and learning that desire without soul leaves one wanting for the person who embodies both. An incredibly sexy book with intriguing characters and a lot of intense passion."

~Dorothy Kollat, author of HEATED

"*The Wanting* is still a complete page-turner filled with romance, sex, and the mystery of unexplained connections between souls who have barely met. As a lover of Strigas' poetry books, *The Wanting* proves that she knows how to bring the characters in her poems to life in her novels as well!"

~Chrissi Sepe, author of BLISS, BLISS, BLISS

Dedication

This book is dedicated to all the soul mates who find
each other
all the ones that keep searching
and all the others that can never be together.

This book is for you.

Part One

Souls meet…
Love at first sight and other love bites.

Serena
I love your soul…

You think loving me is easy, but my kisses can turn into punches. Ironing bores me. Not that caring about that is relevant, the truth is…romance is killing us. We live in a "brave new world," a world in which making love to loveless people every night, is meaningless. You don't know how much I would rather watch *Moulin Rouge*. I'll watch it over and over again until a man is fed up with all of me.

I'll smoke under the fan and write on anything available. I'll have pens in every corner of a room. You'll never have to search for one again. Yes, I'm quite loud and messy. My underwear is sometimes just kicked aside.

When you'll want to kiss me, I'll wrap my arms around your neck. I'll love hard and reckless. I'll ignore your faults and make our bed. Remember this: I'll hate watching the news.

If your wanting is strong, then leave a book by your bed. Even if you don't read it, every once in a while, read me a line. I'll get so horny that I'll kiss you madly.

These are just a few of my secrets that I'll never tell you because *you* don't even exist.

I'll wait with scented candles, and your old T-shirts will hang loosely to my mid-thighs. I'll drink wine and announce the years that fly by because my sensitivity to

1

time rivals no one's.

You'll start wondering why your attraction to me is worth your while. Is it because we have not kissed yet? Or perhaps we have made no confessions to each other. I have your soul close to mine, caressing it, talking to it. When you are far, I can hear you…from miles away.

I think our first kiss should be up against a wall. Perhaps a brick wall, but most definitely *a wall*. Maybe I'm wrong. I've been known to be *very* wrong.

I want our first kiss to be a long French kiss, with my back on your warm comforter—duvet, to be exact—and absolutely *no* flowers on the duvet. A dark colour.

I mix up my fantasies and yours. Perhaps yours are quite different or don't have any—of me, that is. I hope you would love me endlessly, leave me love notes and make me coffee.

You already know how your soul is precious to me; how your heart erupts with pain, and there is nothing to be done, but watch the lava flow. I'm scared of getting burned. I'm scared of thunder. I'm scared of sleeping alone. I'm scared of the way your eyes look at me. I'm scared of your loneliness. I'm scared of your mouth that beckons me.

I know your soul would be magnetic.

I would walk right into it and sit inside it for a while. You would open up to me, and my breath would be stable in your scent. Today *is the day I'll tell him that I love his soul*. But instead, we would talk incessantly about nothing in particular.

My soul would be closed till your hands pound at my door and I let you walk inside it for a while. Your legs stop at the STOP sign and look at my wall of fears, and then your wheels drive right into me. You're in until my excuses for you to leave pile up. Your legs walked inside me for way too long. My panic that your eyes might have seen my wall made just for you…with wicked love words and flowing adjectives.

I will make sure you can read my eyes when I find you.

I want your soul to wrap me up in a handmade blanket. When will I find you?

My confession…

I like to eat a big lunch, popping out of bed instantly in the morning. Rarely do I remember my dreams, but notebooks are close by to write down every detail and then analyze my life, researching every detail of my dream until its symbolism is understood.

I hate crowds. Books are for inhaling. The past occupies my mind. I love to smell clothes at every opportunity. Every fabric softener smells good to me. There are soul mates out there I've never met. Some lyrics are written just for me. The sound of birds calms me down immediately. Horses grab my attention and make me feel—free, wild to roam the earth and feel the wind caress my hair. I vent and curse like a sailor with extreme pleasure. One day, my children will be born. Writing is my disease. My heart is sensitive. When I cry, a well empties. My legs are my best asset. There was that competition in grade six—the "best legs" competition—that my legs won, my mind got so flustered that I stuck a pencil in my forehead by accident. It turned out to be my most embarrassing moment.

I love to walk barefoot. If someone wants to love me, it's not so hard. Pleasing me is not that complicated. I want to take more bubble baths and stop rambling on and on, but it's that voice in my head taking control and whispering to me to keep going. Sand and seashells are my weaknesses. My deep breaths help. It really fuckin' works. I have to swear sometimes.

I'm restless. Cleaning is my pet peeve. Wine is like sugar to me. Jim Morrison is my first poet crush. I retyped all his poems in typewriting class and got an A. Museums feel like home and antiques my comfort.

I stare at candle flames, waiting for spirits. I'm only twenty-three, but feel one hundred years old.

Teddy
Bad hair day…

When I wake up, I yearn to see her beautiful violet eyes. I call her my little Liz Taylor in my head, yearning to rub my hands up and down her long legs and examine her for any moles I could memorize. These are my fantasies. Other men fantasize about porn stars, while I'm fantasizing about my non-existent soul mate. I feel ready, so ready to meet someone right now. I keep searching, but nothing.

I have this hole in the pit of my stomach, like this woman I imagine, was once mine, perhaps in a past life or era, like the Renaissance. I see her walking down a white spiral staircase, surrounded by marble walls. Her step is slow, graceful, and she carefully scans the room, looking only for me. I miss her and I haven't even met her yet. How pathetic am I? My friends would laugh at my thoughts.

Do soul mates exist? No sign of one yet, and I'm twenty-seven.

She will have the power to crack my heart in two and watch it fall into tiny pieces at her feet. My life is so empty right now. I just need her to fill up this sadness.

I look at myself in the rearview mirror. Fuck, my face is a mess. I better not meet her today. I scan the parking lot as I always do and park.

She probably does not even exist.

I have a confession for you...

Words come back to haunt you, it's true. My pointy-nosed eleventh-grade teacher prophesized my future. *"Teddy, you will become a teacher one day. Mark my words,"* she said, looking at me with her big, brown eyes. *"Because a teacher is someone who is not able to do, to pursue, to attract, to embrace...A teacher is what you become when you give up."* I thought she was stupid for insulting herself, till exactly six years later there my future smacked me in my own classroom and it hit me like a ton of bricks: I *had given* up on my future—graduate studies, writing a book—and my life had just begun. It was like a self-fulfilled prophecy. My life not feeling any more satisfied than now. I was smart, twenty-two, and starting a teaching career in my favourite field: history. Yet, the emptiness surrounded me more and more.

I turned the corner to enter the school parking lot, and there *you* were. Getting out of my car, there was this kinetic energy pulling me toward you.

You were in the parking lot. Your long, brown hair just above your waist, engaged in a conversation with a woman about something, or maybe nothing important, because you suddenly turned your whole body around and looked at me. Once your gaze met mine, your mouth ceased talking. I stared at you until my breath halted, yet my legs continued walking. Your eyes waited for that split second for me to say something—anything, but my legs kept on going into a trance. I memorized your beautiful face and your exquisite eyes.

That was five years ago. It was August 30th, 2007.

Serena
The moment it happened…

I had an hour and a half to myself. I was sitting in front of Lake of Two Mountains, and then I saw it: a willow tree. It somehow spoke to me, keeping me company. Teenagers were tossing rocks into the lake and texting at the same time. How did they do that? Being a few years older than them felt like decades; texting was my pet peeve. It was so antisocial, so "let's get down to business and cut the small talk." Whatever happened to small talk? People were coming and going; a slight breeze tousled my hair, chilling me for a while. Sunlight was streaming through the trees. It was my time to reflect, to look up at the beautiful blue sky, to look at the lake, and not be distracted.

My manuscript was finished. But was it ever really finished? Who would even want to read it? Writers should put their manuscript aside for a few weeks and then read it again with a critical eye. The problem was editing my own work was torturous and unthinkable. My ability to edit was nil. Zero. No talent there.

I had to study for my exam.

When I was eighteen, I had to go back to my old high school to get a letter of recommendation for my application into the communications program at Concordia University. Getting off the bus, my old drama teacher appeared in front of me.

"Miss Moss!" I shouted, out of breath. "Just the

person I wanted to see!" She turned around and gave me the biggest smile.

"Serena Photine! It's so lovely to see you." She hugged me, emphasizing my last name like she'd never forget me.

"It's great to see you too!" She had been one of my favorite teachers. She had taught me so much.

"Where are you studying now?" she asked.

"I'm at Dawson, and I'm putting together my portfolio for Concordia."

She gave me a knowing smile. "Communications?"

"Yes! How did you know?"

"Serena, you were one of the best students I've ever had. I know you will go far."

"Thanks, Miss. Can I ask a favour of you?"

"What can I do for you?" Her gentle eyes were inquisitive as always. All around us the hustle and bustle of teenagers walking by filled the September air. "You do know today is the first day of classes?"

I suddenly got distracted by this weird feeling to turn toward an approaching car. I kept my eyes on Miss Moss, but when I heard the car door slam, I did turn around.

"Oh, is it? I…I…" I froze. There *he* was, walking toward me. He had a slow stride. His shoulders were broad, his walk confident and purposeful. He looked exactly as I had imagined. He was looking straight ahead, but then I saw his head turn, and our gazes locked. He stopped walking. His eyes made me forget everything, when he neared—it looked like he was coming straight for me. I waited for…something, but he didn't stop to tell me he was The One. Our eyes spoke to each other's. And then he was gone.

"Serena? Are you okay?"

"Oh, sorry…." Feeling totally fucked up, I mumbled on for a while, and then I handed her the form and explained what I needed. She smiled again and said she would mail it to the university, and I thanked her.

My thoughts wandered. Who was *he*? Why didn't he stop and say something? Perhaps I looked too desperate. I scared him away with my scary witch eyes and needy aura.

The electricity between us had been palpable. He must have felt it too. My whole body reacted to his look, made me feel alive, and full of desire.

Still, I've thought about him from time to time and wondered "What if?" Perhaps it was ridiculous to think of someone after five years when I'd seen him for only a few seconds—twenty-two seconds, to be exact. I have replayed the scenario in my head so often that I count the seconds as I replay it in my mind. I'm really fucked up. That was 2007.

I replayed it again. He had been wearing navy blue slacks and a white shirt with one button left open at the collar. He had brown hair with a slight wave. It wasn't too short—just above his ears—and it was messy looking. I concentrated on what he was holding. He had been holding something…My gaze was too focused on his face. I heard some rocks splashing into the lake, and I turned to look at who was throwing them.

A young couple was sitting on the sand, and the man was tossing rocks across the water while smiling at the woman. A brown satchel mailbag lay behind him on the sand. I stared at it, and then suddenly I remembered.

He had been carrying exactly the same bag.

Teddy
Scenarios…

I fidgeted, unsure how to occupy myself for a full hour. Finally, I turned on the TV and watched other people's lives. Reality shows drew me in like a drug, wasting away precious hours instead of doing something productive, like writing my novel. There must be a book inside me somewhere, but there was nothing to write from complete boredom. My life was a serious dull ache.

I flipped the channels and watched a movie with unrecognizable actors. Somehow, their unfamiliarity soothed me, and nothing was written down. My intention was to apply for graduate studies, but my B average was never good enough to get into the program. I needed to forget that rejection.

Who was that girl Miss Moss was talking to five years ago? Every time I wanted to ask Miss Moss about her, something stopped me; my shyness? No. It was probably the ridiculous idea of pining over some girl I'd seen for a mere few seconds, and felt like an idiot to ask about her. Miss Moss would probably look at me as if to say, *Are you serious? It took you five years to ask?* Besides, I did have a few girlfriends during these past five years, so to ask about some other woman—someone I'd caught only a glimpse of—would have seemed so preposterous.

I'd forgotten about her for a while, until recently. I guess the lack of meeting anyone worthwhile always brought me back to her, that beautiful girl who had taken my breath away. I'd never looked at a girl like that before. In those few seconds, I saw the possibilities but did nothing about it. Heat enveloped my body the moment my gaze met hers, this insatiable thirst to have her and to feel her close to me.

I've played out several scenarios in my head on how that could have actually happened:

Scenario Number One:

"Excuse me for interrupting, but can I ask you a question?"

She looks at me and responds, "Sure." Then she looks at Miss Moss and says, "Excuse me, will you?"

Miss Moss nods.

"Yes?" her lovely voice sings to me.

"I couldn't help but notice how beautiful you are. What's your name?" She would be Aphrodite, or Belinda, or Cassandra, or Samantha or…

"Jasmine."

"I'm Teddy. Can I have your number? I would love to take you out on a date."

She gives me a dazzling smile and recites her phone number. I memorize it. No need to write it down. No need to type it into my phone. It would be engraved on my heart forever. "Don't you want to write it down?"

"I have a great memory."

She grins and then excuses herself to go back to her conversation with Miss Moss, who is standing by calmly.

Scenario Number Two:

She grabs my arm. "Sorry, I thought you were someone else," she says with a smile.

"I can be anyone you want me to be," I reply, smiling back.

She laughs, stepping away from Miss Moss, who seems to understand the seriousness of this first meeting and leaves us alone.

All the sounds of the day disappear as I look into her light violet eyes and study her cute button nose and full lower lip. Her brown hair blows wildly in the wind, and she has no reply. She stares at me and then asks, "Did you go to this high school?"

"No, I'm a teacher here. Actually, it's my first day."

"Oh! That's great."

"What's your name?"

"Naomi," she says in a sexy voice. "You?"

"I'm Theodore, but everyone calls me Teddy."

Her gaze shifts slowly to give my body a thorough look-over. I try to make out the image of a woman's profile on her grey shirt. Naomi's leggings outline the shape of her legs. Her heavy eyeliner adds to her beauty, and my thought is lost in hers. My eyes travel from top to bottom. She's wearing tan-colour booties. Her outfit is well coordinated.

"Can I call you sometime?" I ask.

Of course, the scenario ends with me memorizing her number, but even in this one, I still have no clue why she was at that spot at that precise moment.

Scenario Number Three:

As I stop walking, she stops talking. My smile reaches her and she reciprocates. I bravely walk up to her. Miss Moss remains still, glancing from me to her.

"Hi," I say to Miss Moss, not remembering her name. I continue smiling at the girl.

"You're a new teacher here, aren't you?" Miss Moss asks. "I saw you at the staff meeting, but we haven't been formally introduced. I'm Arianne."

"I'm Theodore Neros."

Throughout this exchange, *she* remains quiet.

Miss Moss looks at both of us again. "Theodore, this is Katrina, your soul mate." Arianne smiles. "I have to go," she says to Katrina, and then whispers something in her ear.

I turn to Katrina and say, "Hi."

"Hi," she replies in a sweet voice. "What is she talking about? Soul mate…? Where did she get that idea?"

"I have no clue, but can I have your number so we can find out?" I quickly ask. She looks at me for a split second, and I don't know if she'll say yes or no, so I add, "I would love to take you out on a date."

She looks shy, and then responds, "Okay."

Pulling out a piece of paper and a pen from her purse, she writes it down before I can memorize it. I take it and hold on to it tightly.

"I have to catch my bus," she says and begins to quickly walk away.

"I'll call you," I shout after her, and we wave good-bye to each other.

And that is the beginning of the affair.

I could go on and on with other scenarios, but they'd end up being more like sexual fantasies.

This kind of connection had never happened before. I was so in tune with my wants that I automatically knew if I liked or disliked a girl when I met her. My first reaction was instinctive and trustworthy. I was still waiting to have that same feeling I'd gotten when I'd seen *that* girl, and what scared the fuck out of me was that I wouldn't ever again. Perhaps that was why my thoughts traveled to her more and more lately.

What kind of guy pines for a girl for five years just because of one look? Dan poked fun at me all the time. Heck, *I* even laughed at my pitiful love life.

Serena
My angel tattoo

The angel was for my daddy, who died when I was seven. He died from lung disease; basically, he drank himself to death at the age of thirty-four. Mom said he had demons in his soul and empty pockets. She'd seen a sadness in him that had attracted her like a moth to a flame. My mom loved him passionately, and though my mother moved on—after all, she was a widow at thirty with two young kids to take care of—she'd never gotten over his death. My little sister, Elsa, has said Mom sees ghosts, but how Daddy had become part of her *raison d'être* and this was still questionable. According to Elsa, she talked to him every night. The only problem was that Elsa too was an alcoholic as well as a substance abuser, and half the time I didn't know whether she was high or low—high on drugs and self-loathing or low on love and cash.

Elsa's favourite pastimes were skipping school, drinking, and doing drugs. I lived alone now because of all the Hollywood drama at home, although Mom either called or texted each day to tell me every act in Elsa's life. Still, despite all the melodrama, I missed them.

I don't want to tell you too much about Elsa, because then this book would be about her, and she would take over my life again—with her late-night phone calls, her pills, her reading my diary…

Let's just say she took me to the tattoo parlor…

"I have a buddy who is fucking amazing! He can draw anything on skin. He has so much talent. Eddie says he should be on *Ink*," Elsa said, her dark eyes shining with excitement.

How could she know people like that? She was only seventeen but knew all of Montreal—where to get cheap ciggies, where to drink underage, where to party till six o'clock in the morning, who to call for "organic" marijuana… She had "connections."

"I know nothing about this guy, Elsa. How do I know if I can trust him? Does he sterilize his needles?"

"Serena, really. Get your fuckin' head out of *Pride and Prejudice* and join us in the fuckin' twenty-first century! Of course, he does! Eddie has five awesome tattoos. His sleeves are masterpieces."

"Eddie has sleeves?"

"Yeah, I tell him to wear jackets when he comes over so Mom doesn't have a heart attack."

"How come I didn't know this?"

"You can't know everything. What the fuck, Serena? Do you want me to call Matt or not?"

"Matt? That's the guy? What nationality is he? How long has he been tattooing?"

"He's Irish or Scottish or Eng—who cares? I don't know his fucking resume! Seriously, get your head out of your ass, sis."

She looked at me like *I* was crazy while she sat there, playing with a nail file and insulting me. I didn't feel my questions were so unreasonable.

"I'm just careful. That's all. It's a big decision."

"No, it's not. Just do it. Stop analyzing and thinking so much. You really should get out more." She looked around my room. "You and your books. You should live more and read less!"

"Are you serious? I'm going to take advice from *you*?"

She was dressed from head to toe in solid black, and she had these awful cherry-red streaks on the ends of her hair. Looking at her, I couldn't believe how she dressed on a daily basis.

"Yes, you are. On this shit, you most definitely are. And I'm coming with you. There are some strange people around that area of town."

I rolled my eyes. "Whatever. Just make the appointment for me one night next week. And don't tell Mom!"

"Finally, a secret we can share," she joked, leaving the nail file on my bed and scouring my room. "Hey, where's that Clash CD?"

"I don't know, and I really don't care," I said.

I was twenty-one. It was right after my birthday, and I had declared myself "ready" for a tattoo. It was the last thing I wanted to do before I moved out.

"I'm moving out July 1st," I confessed.

"What? Why? You're leaving me?"

With that, Elsa made me feel like I was abandoning her, and the guilt would settle in soon. But that was a responsibility I shouldn't have had. She was my younger sister, not my daughter.

"I want to do my graduate studies next year, and need to be close to the university. It has nothing to do with you." I lied. It had everything to do with her. She invaded my space, my time, and my life. I needed to be free and on my own. My mom was going to hit the roof, but I'd been slowly preparing her. She understood too.

She realized.

"Yeah, okay. Maybe you could finally get laid," Elsa said with a laugh.

I gave her a dirty look. "Get out of my room, and just make my appointment," I shouted, pushing her through the door while she laughed hysterically. She had serious problems I don't want to delve into.

"And for your information, I *have* gotten laid!" I added as I slammed the door shut. Granted, it had been a long time ago, but at least I wasn't a virgin. I had made sure of that.

The following week, Elsa and Eddie took me to this tattoo parlor on Ontario Street that scared the living daylights out of me. It looked like all the bikers of Montreal had gone there by the looks of this place and the pictures on the wall as well as the people inside. But when I looked at Matt's portfolio, I immediately loved his work.

"Wow! He does have talent," I said to Elsa.

"Of course, he does. Would I steer you wrong?" She nudged my elbow as we sat on this decrepit couch that I refused to place my back against.

"Serena, he's fuckin' awesome. Look at this." For the billionth time that day, Eddie lifted his sleeves to show me his tattoos again. As if I could ignore them.

"I know," I said. "It's really incredible." Eddie had a green serpent running all along his arm, entwined with vines and some Chinese characters, but it was all the detailing and shading in the colours that blew me away. The tattoo had taken about six months to complete.

"I told you," Elsa hollered, stepping closer to Eddie and caressing his arm. Standing together like that, they looked like Sid and Nancy. I turned back to the portfolio, thinking how crazy they were acting.

"So?" Matt came over and sat across from me. He had tattoos on every visible inch of his body. He was ugly as hell, and he didn't smile. This was the guy who was going to graze a needle across my skin? *I'm fucked.* He looked scary, unpleasant, and that did nothing to make me feel at ease.

"You have some creative work here," I said politely. I felt stupid speaking to him as though talking to a professor. I changed my tone. "It's fuckin' incredible!"

Elsa looked at me and smiled. "My sis wants an angel tattoo." She beat me to it. "Our dad died when we were young. I was only three, and I can't remember anything about him. I know he was a fuckin' drunk, though."

I knew Elsa loved shocking people, but this time I wanted to punch her in the face. She used shock value as a defense mechanism to keep people at a distance, to show she was a badass. But I knew the truth; she was hurt and fearful. She wanted to breathe the same air as he had. She wanted to paint his empty canvas. She spoke to him all the time, but no matter how she tried to pretend his death wasn't relevant, I could read her like an open book. Her pain was apparent to me. She wanted to place him in a box and stay close to him. But I needed to fly and to speak my truth. I wanted to show the world my dad meant *something* to me, though I didn't know what that something was. Yes, he had been a drunk, but underneath the booze there had been a man who begged for the truth.

I looked at Elsa angrily. "Can I speak now? This is my tattoo, not *yours*."

Matt smiled—finally. "Come over to my desk, and

let's see what you want. Elsa, Eddie, relax on the couch."

I got up and followed him to the other side of the tattoo parlor. It wasn't that far, but at least there I could speak for myself.

"So, Serena, right?"

"Yes."

"Tell me what you want."

And that was how it happened. The angel on my back had flowing hair, a little like my natural brown hair, and only her back could be seen. I hoped Daddy would have liked it. She was placed on my right shoulder because the mole on my left was too big and awkward to work with. I requested the first letter of his name in Greek lettering around the halo.

I loved my tattoo. Elsa and Eddie had stayed with me the whole time, asking if I was in pain or if I needed anything. When they left to get me coffee, Matt looked at me. "You're lucky you have such a caring sister. She can never stop talking about how smart you are and how you will be a great writer one day. She adores you."

I almost fell off my chair, but just smiled at him. I felt like crying because I actually was leaving her. She had been right once again.

Returning with my coffee, Elsa kissed the top of my head. "It's our little secret," she whispered.

The funny thing was, I liked having this secret between us.

Teddy
I always wanted a tattoo

I'd thought about getting a tattoo for years. I didn't know why it excited me so. Perhaps a tattoo would tell the world I was different. The problem was that having a tattoo had now become mainstream. Even my Aunt Kathy had one on her ankle, and that was what had stopped me from even walking into a tattoo parlor. It was as common as a cup of coffee. Which flavor? Roses or butterflies? Skulls or dragons? Chinese characters or Indian?

I didn't have a tattoo story. I wish I had.

I did see this pretty cool tattoo about two years ago at Foufounes Électriques, my friend Dan's favourite venue to watch live music that wrecked your ears. I went with him just to see the craziness there. We had gone to see some band from around here. Dan was all gung-ho and hyped about it.

"They're so good. I think you'll like them. They even sing a few ballads."

"Ballads? Do I look like someone who likes *ballads*?"

"Kind of. You *are* a school teacher."

"Fuck you!" I put on my cool jeans and a tight black T-shirt that night. "I'm ready to rock!"

"I know, bro," he said. "Why do you think I like to go with you?"

We smoked a few joints before the show, and everything seemed super bright that night. A couple came up next to me, and the guy accidentally brushed his shoulder against mine.

"Sorry," the guy said.

"It's cool," I said and then noticed his arms. "Wow! Nice tattoo."

He had a green serpent all along his arm, intertwined with Chinese characters and vines. It was unique, and I still remembered it for some strange reason.

"Thanks. I designed it myself." His girlfriend looked in my direction and gave me a dirty look. The guy was about to say something more, but she pulled him away toward the dance floor.

"Let's go dance, Eddie," she said, completely ignoring me.

That was my tattoo story. Not much there.

What I thought I always wanted turned out to be something I didn't want anymore. I didn't want to give my skin over to art. Plus, I could think of nothing interesting to ink into my skin.

But I couldn't say that about the mystery girl. The more I thought about her, the more I wanted her.

Serena
I kind of have a plan…

"He's a teacher," I said to my friend Connie.

"Who? That guy you're still pining for five years later? It's *not* normal." She glared at me while measuring the coffee. "Can't you forget about him? Life is going on around you, and you're still thinking about some guy you never even spoke to."

"I know, I know. It's stupid… But I finally realized he must be a teacher at Comedy High." That was what everyone called our old high school before they changed the name about a gazillion times.

"How can you be so sure?" She grabbed two mugs and placed them in front of her.

"I'm sure because I remembered something very important," I said with conviction.

"What?" Connie looked slightly irritated.

"He had a mailbag," I said as though I had solved a puzzle.

"A what? What's a mailbag? Isn't that what postmen carry?" She looked confused, her big, brown eyes inquisitive. She wore her hair up in a bun and had on sweatpants and no makeup. I loved Connie's *laissez-faire* attitude with everything. I wished I was more like her.

"Mail carriers." I corrected her. "Yes and no. Teachers carry them too."

"So if he had a mailbag, he could also work at the

school in some other position, right? Maybe as a guidance counselor or something?" She placed the sugar and cream next to the hot coffee.

"I guess so." I hadn't thought of that.

"Why don't you go visit Miss Moss again?" she suggested, adding jokingly, "Since you were her pet."

"I don't know…"

"C'mon. Just go tomorrow."

"You think that's a good idea?"

"Yes." Connie placed the mugs on the table. "What else are you going to do besides wallow in self-pity? I'm fed up of hearing about it."

"Thanks a lot." I was hurt. "I know I sound like a pain, but for some strange reason I can't get him out of my mind, Connie."

"Then go surprise Miss Moss and take a walk around to see if he's there. She'll be thrilled to see you anyway, especially when you tell her you'll be applying for the M.A. program."

"Okay, okay. I'll go tomorrow." The idea made me nervous, so I changed the subject. "Hey, remember when we were in Mr. B's class in secondary two, and he would have us sit outside in the courtyard while he lectured us on life, spitting all over us?" I laughed.

"How could I forget?"

We laughed about that and shared some other funny stories about our good times. We had memories that would last a lifetime. I loved Connie so much. She understood me like no one else. I met her in sec one, and we had been best friends ever since. She is an engineer now and working for a prestigious company downtown. She said she didn't love her job, but I knew she got a kick out of being the only female engineer in her company.

She was my idol.

"When I grow up, I want to be just like you!" I teased.

"That's what you always say, but you'll be going to school your whole life, and you'll never grow up." She laughed back. "Stay where you are, Serena. The real world isn't so appealing."

The next day I went to see Miss Moss.

Teddy
Sick as a dog...

I woke up and vomited all over the toilet, sick since two a.m. I knew it was gastro. My sister's kids had been sick all weekend, and I had passed by for a quick visit on Sunday. She'd told me to stay away, but that had been the only day I could touch base with her and talk.

"It's airborne," Stephanie had said.

"I'm as strong as an ox," I replied.

"C'mon, Teddy. You know how much I love you. I really don't want to see you sick."

My sister and I were inseparable. We were only fourteen months apart in age. One school year. Her friends were my friends, and my friends were her friends. She actually married one of my good friends, Roberto, who was in the restaurant business and often worked late.

I called Stephanie that morning. "I'm sick as a dog. I got the gastro!"

"I'm so sorry. I told you to stay away," she said sympathetically.

"How long does it last?"

"A few days."

"A few days? Fuck."

"What's wrong? You do have sick days."

"I do, it's just that I have tickets to see Jack White."

"What? And you weren't going to tell me?"

"I was going to surprise you for your birthday."

"Oh my God! I love you! Isn't the show this Friday?"

"Yes."

"Okay, listen up." Her tone changed to a motherly one. "You are going to eat only chicken soup for two days. No meat, no solid food. Drink plenty of water, and sleep all day." She paused. "Did I ever tell you that you are the best brother?"

"Not really, but I'm listening," I joked.

"You're the best!" she shouted. "I'm so excited. I have to tell Roberto…" She started to make her plans, and then we hung up.

I called the school and told the secretary I was sick and couldn't come in for the next two days.

As luck would have it, I picked the wrong day to be sick.

Serena
Disappointment gets me down…

"Oh, Serena! I'm so happy for you!"

"I haven't been accepted yet," I said.

"You will. Do you need another reference letter from me?"

"No, thanks. These reference letters have to be written by my university professors. I've already asked my Shakespeare and modern drama professors to write one. I had the highest mark in their classes."

I looked around Miss Moss's office and realized nothing had really changed. The same desks, the same prints of William Shakespeare on the wall, the same diplomas marking all the teachers' accomplishments so all students knew they were the "experts." Every time I walked into this office, I felt like I was home. I liked the smell of the old wooden desks the most.

Miss Moss was crammed into the office, sitting alone. The other three English teachers weren't in the room at the moment.

How was I going to bring up the subject about that guy?

"So, any new teachers?" I asked.

"Well, this year they hired one new math teacher. Everyone else is back from previous years."

"How about in the last five years? Any new teachers since then?"

"Of course, my dear. There are always teachers for hire. Why? Are you thinking of teaching? Not high school. You should teach university."

Shit, this conversation was twisting around, away from where I wanted to take it.

"No, I was just curious as to the qualifications. Who have they hired recently?" I prodded on.

"Well"—she became all serious—"the last couple of years…? There was Mrs. Tessier, who started last year. She's the French teacher. Then there was Miss Di Malo, who teaches English. And then a few years ago there was Mr. Neros. We all call him Teddy Bear because he has a cute smile…" Looking off into space, she thought some more.

"What does Mr. Neros teach?"

"He's the history teacher." She looked across the hallway. Kids were hustling about to get to their classes. She continued. "I think he's over there."

I turned around to see who she was looking at, and across the room was a young man in a plaid jacket, engaged in an intense conversation with one of his male students. I knew immediately it wasn't him.

"Sorry, that's not him," Miss Moss said. "That's Mr. Beauchemin. He's quite handsome, though, in an old-fashioned, Dickens kind of way." She smiled at me.

I wasn't sure what she saw in him that was appealing.

"So that's not Mr. Neros?"

"No, but why are you so curious?"

"It's nothing." I looked down.

"What is it?" she probed.

"I *am* thinking of becoming a high school teacher." I lied so I wouldn't have to tell her my stupid story. I suddenly felt so ridiculous. "I'm going to take this year to think about it." I didn't think that made any sense, considering I wanted to apply to the M.A. program, but continued with that story, illustrating it with my serious face and tone.

Miss Moss studied me, a look I knew all too well. "Dear, you have your whole life ahead of you. Do your master's, and then see what you want to do. You are such a good writer. Don't limit yourself. The world is your oyster." She was full of wisdom and good advice, but then she glanced at her watch and quickly stood up. "I hate to cut this short, Serena, but I must do some photocopying downstairs and prepare a quick quiz for my next period." She looked at her watch again. "And I have only thirty minutes."

I got up. "That's fine, Miss Moss. I enjoyed our visit. Thanks for your advice."

"Come by anytime, and please keep me posted," she said with a warm smile.

We hugged each other, and then I left. Stepping into the hallway, I saw that the history office was empty. Peeking inside and counting three desks…three history teachers… Maybe he was one of them. I peered at each desk to see if their names were on them, but no such luck. Then, the nameplates on the door caught my attention. Of course! How stupid of me. I should have looked at the most obvious place. *Mr. Theodore Neros, Mr. David Beauchemin, Mr. Paul Tate.*

Hanging on one of the walls was a bulletin board and a few diplomas. The names were not easy to make out from this distance. The office was pretty messy, with books all over the place.

"Can I help you?"

I turned around and stared directly at the teacher Miss Moss had spoken of, who was across the hall a moment ago. He startled me.

"Oh, no. I was just looking for someone," I said nervously. *What did I just say?*

"Who?" He looked at me peculiarly. He *did* look like someone out of a Dickens novel. "I would be glad to help you, young lady."

"I don't know." I looked around for the quickest escape. "I have to go. He's not here," I mustered enough courage to say and then quickly said good-bye.

He took a good look at me before I hurried off.

Well, that was a bloody waste of time, I thought. Or was it?

I had a photographic memory. I was sure there was something in that office that would help me find my mystery man.

Or maybe he wasn't even there anymore. After all, teachers changed schools all the time.

I stopped off at the front desk to sign out and overheard a conversation behind the secretary.

"Teddy has the gastro today."

"Oh yeah? I didn't know it was going around."

"Apparently it is."

So Teddy was absent today. He *could* be the one— or not.

Teddy
I missed her…

"A girl came by here the other day when you were sick," Dave said, shuffling through his papers. He was chewing gum and looked like the Mad Hatter today. No wonder all the kids made fun of him. He chewed and spoke at the same time—an annoying combination.

I was getting my handouts ready, barely paying attention until this point.

"What girl?" I asked, looking up.

"I'd never seen her before. She said she was looking for someone but wouldn't tell me who. She was a little hottie too. The type that would make you sing 'Don't Stand So Close to Me.'" He chuckled, a gleam in his eyes.

"Really?" I wondered who it could have been. "What did she look like?"

"She had long brown hair, beautiful eyes, about this tall"—he lifted his hand to just below his shoulder—"probably about five-feet-five. She was something."

The gleam in his eyes looked almost manic now, and the whole time he spoke, I wanted to clobber him. His attitude was annoying the fuckin' hell out of me but I wanted to remain calm, appear unaffected.

"Do you know her?" he asked with a raised brow. "Because you should know her."

"Maybe. Describe her again." I didn't know why,

32

but I needed to make sure I'd heard every detail.

"She had loooong brooown haaaair down to her waist, kind of wavy, not straight." He paused to remember, then continued to speak slowly. "She was wearing jeans and a black top, I think."

"What exactly did she say, Dave?" I asked, wondering if I was hallucinating. Brown hair down to her waist… Could it have been her?

"I told you, she was searching for someone. I found her looking around in the office." Dave gathered his things and got up to leave.

"Hold on. Did she talk to anyone?"

"Let me think…" He stared off into space. My patience was wearing thin. "Oh yeah. Before I went to my class, I was here, talking to Gerald. You know. The kid I told you about who got an F on his test? He was telling me how he wanted to rewrite the test. Can you believe that? He said he'd forgotten there was a test. Kids these days… Did he take me for a fool? I asked him. 'No way,' I said. 'I don't give rewrites.' But Gerald continued to argue the point."

Fuck! I didn't want to hear all this.

"Dave, did you see her talking to anyone?" I asked again, ready to pounce on him.

"That's what I was getting at. While talking to Gerald, I saw her from across the office, sitting in the English department, her back turned to me. She had been talking to Arianne."

"Are you sure?"

"Yeah, yeah. I told Gerald, 'No way,' and he said— get this—that he was going to 'talk to the principal.' Do these kids think the principal actually gives a shit? I got angry and told him, 'Go ahead. Talk to the principal. I'm not changing my mind.' And I looked across and noticed her. I didn't think anything of it—I thought she was a student or something—but when I saw her up close, I knew she was no student. She must have been about twenty-two or three."

I wondered if it could be her. But how could that be possible? Just because I had been thinking about her didn't mean *she* remembered *me*. "Anything else?"

He shook his head. "Nope, sorry. But why are you so interested? An ex?"

"Just curious," I replied, trying to sound nonchalant.

"Well, that's all I got. Can you believe Gerald's nerve?" Dave placed his books in the crook of his elbow and checked his watch. "I have to get to class. He's going to see the principal…" he mumbled, mimicking the student and rolling his eyes.

I looked around the empty office. Could she have been looking for me? My mind reeled and raced a hundred miles an hour in a marathon of questions and answers. Why had she come here? Perhaps she couldn't get me off of her mind as well… And when had she chosen to come? On the day I was sick.

I knew the only way to find her was through Arianne Moss.

I had to ask her.

Serena
Getting closer…

I kept going over and over the conversation I had with Miss Moss in my head to make sure I hadn't missed anything she'd said. Could "Teddy Bear" be him? It had to be. I was so close.

I knew his name now.

I rolled it around on my tongue and liked its feeling, like a new song or lyric. I felt butterflies when I said it out loud as if he would rush through my front door and reply, *"Yes? You called me?"*

My phone rang.

"Well?"

"I know his name," I said.

"Did you meet him?" Connie sounded more excited than I was. "C'mon, speak up!"

"I didn't meet him. He was off sick."

"What's his name?"

"Theodore Neros, but he's known as Teddy."

"I like the sound of that. I've never known a Teddy before," she said.

"Me too."

"I know, silly. We've known pretty much the same people since high school."

I laughed. "I'm so nervous."

"You haven't even met him yet, Serena."

"I know."
"And what's the next move?"
"I have no fuckin' idea."

Teddy
Closer and closer…

I had to speak to Arianne. As soon as I had a free period, I would walk across to her office and just ask her. It would be as simple as that. Today's schedule showed I was free at third period. After second, I heard the bell ring and went straight to her office. I peeked in, but no one was there. *Fuck.*

I went downstairs to the cafeteria to get a cup of coffee. I had been a wreck since Friday, wondering how I would approach this. I was a fuckin' moron; I would just ask her, plain and simple. Why did I have to make it so complicated?

I sat down at my desk with my coffee and about sixty-four term assignments to correct. I read one and then read it again. Nothing was computing today. I looked across the hallway again to see if there was any movement in the English department. Nothing.

I rubbed my eyes and tried to focus. I had peace and quiet. Dave was teaching a class. I reread the assignment and gave it a C. It was nothing great, little effort put into it. Next. This one was even worse than the first. I gave it a D. Too many grammatical mistakes. Didn't they use a spell-checker? There was movement across the hallway and, jumping up out of my chair, practically dropped all the papers.

She was sitting at her desk.

"Hi, Arianne," I said, maybe a little too excitedly. I smiled and leaned against the door.

"Hey, Teddy. I heard you were sick. Feeling better?"

"Yes, thanks for asking. Caught the gastro from my sister's kids."

"That's too bad. Everything good besides that?" Looking distracted, she picked up some papers.

"Yeah, not bad." I peered down the hallway to make sure no one was around before I continued. "I want to ask you something, though, if you have a minute." My heart pounded.

"Sure, fire away."

"Well, you know the young lady who was here yesterday? She came to visit you," I said in an overly friendly tone, looking directly at her.

"Of course. Serena. She was one of my brightest students."

She looked at me curiously, so I walked into her office and sat down in front of her. I looked around again to make certain no one was nearby, listening.

She noticed I was acting funny. "How do you know Serena?" she asked.

"Actually, I don't know her." I looked down at my hands in my lap. "I would like to get to know her." There, I said it. The ball was in her court. I looked up at her again.

Her eyes lit up. "You like her!" Then she appeared confused. "Wait, you don't know her. And you were sick yesterday. How did you know she was here?"

"Yes, I was sick, but Dave told me a young woman came by our office, and she was looking for someone…"

"So, you *do* know each other." She shook her head. "This is getting weird. What is it you aren't telling me?

I knew she was acting a little strange."

I started to sweat. I was honest, but I didn't know how to tell Arianne the truth without getting her involved, and I wanted her to cooperate with me. I had to find out about that girl.

"She was acting strange?" That made me even more curious.

"Oh no you don't." She smiled. "First tell me how you know Serena."

At the sound of her name again, I felt a flutter. That was a perfect name for her. S-e-r-e-n-a. I spelled out the letters in my head as if I were in grade one. And then I sat there, staring into space.

"Teddy, what is it?" Arianne looked concerned.

Well, here goes nothing. I would just tell her the truth and see where that got me. Probably nowhere.

"This is going to sound crazy, but I saw her here at this school a few years ago, and I never forgot her face. I've never spoken to her. I don't have a relationship with her, but I want to meet her." I looked at Arianne as if she had all the answers.

"Really?" She appeared to be trying to remember. "I think that was a long time ago." She looked odd now as if she remembered something, "Teddy, I don't know if I can help you. I don't have her phone number, but I do know which school she goes to and what she will be studying. But I don't feel comfortable telling you any of this without her permission." She was intense now. "There is a lot of crazy stuff that goes on, Teddy. I don't want to be responsible for any of it." She looked down at her papers and lifted her pen.

I didn't know what to say. How could I respond to that? Did I sound like a raving lunatic? A psycho? A stalker? Most definitely. I'd really botched this up.

"But, Arianne, I'm not crazy. I just want her number," I blurted out. Why did I use the word "crazy"? I was burying myself over here. "I like her," I finally said, sighing. I felt so stupid.

"I'm sorry, Teddy. I really can't help you." She cast her eyes down on her corrections again and, just like that, ignored me.

How the heck had I fucked this up? My only way of finding her, and here I was fucking it up.

"Can you at least tell me where she is studying?" The desperation in my voice was awful.

Arianne looked at me pitifully and changed her tone. "How about if she calls me or visits me again, I'll mention you to her, and if she is interested, then I will give you any information she wants to give you? I can't just give you private information about my ex-students." She eyed me closely. "I hope you understand why."

I shifted in my seat and then quickly stood up. What else could I say? Of course, I understood.

"Arianne, I'm just a guy who finds a girl pretty." There, that was plain and simple.

"Regardless, I can't give you what you're asking for. Now, if you'll excuse me"—she pointed to her pile of papers—"I have a lot of work waiting for me."

"Sure, sure," I said, fumbling for words, adjectives, nouns, verbs—anything remotely intelligent. Instead, I said nothing and left the one person who could help me meet my soul mate thinking I was a bloody rapist, stalker or, even worse, in love.

I needed a drink tonight. I texted Dan.

Bro, The Spidernuts are playing at Foufounes! he wrote back.

I don't care who the fuck is playing, as long as you're driving, I replied.

As I drove home, I wondered what Arianne had meant by Serena acting strange. I spoke her name out loud over and over again, loving the sound of it. She was searching me out.

I had to find her.

"Serena, I will find you. I will meet you, and I will kiss you." I was getting hard just at the mere thought of seeing her again.

Part Two

Souls Part
Love is not shaken by others. It stays strong and carries
you through storms.

Serena
I know some places we can go…

"Sis, you have to come!" Elsa sat on my couch, texting non-stop with Eddie. She came over to hang out, and now all she did was try to find an excuse to leave.

"If you want, we'll hang here. If not, then go. I want to watch a movie." What I really wanted to do was absolutely nothing.

"Eddie says this band is the new Arcade Fire."

"Who is Arcade Fire?"

"Come out of your cave. Seriously? You don't know who Arcade Fire is?" She jiggled her leg nervously. "Get dressed. Please? Pretty please? With a cherry on top?" She placed her hands together as though praying.

"I'm already dressed." I was wearing my jeans and a T-shirt. How dressy did she want me to be? Besides, going out with Elsa was not my thing. It always ended ugly.

"Look, Serena, I want to be with you, but Eddie is on his way. It'll be fun. He wants you to come too. Let's have a few drinks and unwind. You'll hear some great music."

I smirked. "Your idea of great music and my idea of great music are not the same."

"If you even remotely loved me, you would come." Elsa sulked as if she were two.

"Why do you want me to go out with you so badly?"

45

"I told you, I was going to hang with you, but now Eddie wants me to go out with him. I'm torn here. Can't you see that?" She pouted, just like when we were kids and she wanted me to play outside with her.

"I don't fit in at that place," I said. I wouldn't have minded going for a drink, but at Foufounes? I hated that place.

"I have a great idea." She bounded off the couch, her hair flying everywhere, and stood in front of me. "If you come with us and you absolutely hate it, I promise, cross my heart"—she made a little sign of the cross over her heart—"we will go anywhere else you choose. Even that awful Crescent Street." She rolled her eyes.

"Okay, okay." I always gave in to her. What was my problem? "But you promise, if I don't like it, we leave?" I eyed her closely.

"I just fuckin' told you so! Now, let's see what you could wear." She ran into my bedroom and threw open my closet door. "This is awful, sis. Shit, I have to get creative."

"Get out of my room!"

Elsa had already flung two outfits onto the bed, rearranged them, and was looking through my scarf collection. "Actually, this isn't too shabby." She picked up an electric blue scarf with silver threads. "This will do quite well. Now for the pants…" She looked at both pairs of jeans on the bed and nodded. Then she checked out the ones I was wearing. "You know, those are nice. They make your legs look good. I love the straight-leg look on you." She smiled.

"I'm keeping these jeans on whether you like them or not."

"How about this top?" She held up a black top with

a print of a dragon on it. God only knew how she'd found that. It had been at the back of my closet. I think I'd worn it one Halloween, when I dressed up as a Chinese New Year Girl. Not one of my most memorable evenings.

"That's a Halloween outfit."

"You could have fooled me. It's so cool. If you don't want it, then I'll keep it." She started to fold it into a tiny square.

"What are you doing? I didn't say I was giving it to you. Give it back to me!"

I took off my T-shirt and put on the top. Elsa wrapped the scarf around my neck in this weird way that made the two lengths equal.

"How did you do that?" I asked, walking to the mirror to see my reflection.

"I watch way too many fashion shows." She smirked as she looked me up and down. "I like it, sis. It makes you look tough. Not that your sense of fashion is bad. Actually, Eddie thinks you're the perfect girl, with all your well-coordinated clothes. You know, you don't have to match *everything*."

She had said that jokingly, but deep down it bothered Elsa, being compared to me her whole life.

"I'm by far the perfect girl!" I said, exasperated.

"That's what I told him, but he said it in a respectful way, Serena. I'm not fuckin' jealous. Seriously."

"I didn't say that!"

"He just admires that you have it all together. He wouldn't be caught dead with someone like you."

I looked at the blue scarf, ignoring her criticism. I loved the way she complimented me and then insulted me. That was the Elsa Special. "But blue? Why blue?"

"Why not? Why the fuck not? All you need now are

boots. No high heels shit. Black boots. Do you have any?" She was texting with one hand now.

"Of course. What girl doesn't have a pair of black boots?"

"You'd be surprised at what I see on TV," she replied with a laugh. Her phone beeped for the umpteenth time.

I bent down in my closet and found the black boots I'd worn only once because I found them to be too sleazy. They would be perfect for the occasion. I put them on.

Before I could look in the mirror, Elsa whistled at me. "Sexy and tough. I think this should be your new look."

I peered into the mirror and wanted to change immediately. I looked like I belonged onstage with Steven Tyler.

"I don't know."

"I know. And I love it! Now go freshen up your face, and let's get the fuck out of here." The whole time Elsa was texting Eddie, probably giving him a blow-by-blow description of my wardrobe collection.

"Could you put the phone down for one minute?"

"No. Now go to the washroom and put on some makeup."

I did as I was told, wondering why I was actually listening to my foolish sister.

Although she pissed me off, Elsa was tough and knew exactly what she wanted when it came to her needs. I knew what I wanted in my life and career as opposed to her, but her bossy attitude always shocked me. I could never understand how she got away with acting that way.

Tonight, all I wanted was to have a relaxing evening, and now I was heading to the worst place possible, in my opinion.

I looked at my book on the night table and whispered, "I'll be back."

Elsa stood at the door, laughing at me as she glanced at the book like it was a disease. "C'mon. You look fuckin' hot. Forget your books for one night."

"Okay, okay." I looked at her clothes, which she probably bought at some thrift shop, and felt a pang of jealousy at how she could pull it off and look so cool. I'd be scared if I saw her coming toward me.

"You look pretty good yourself, Elsa." I smiled.

"Oh, I can't believe I got a compliment from you. I'm putting it on my social page." She started pressing all kinds of buttons on her phone, moving her thumbs quickly. When I spotted her social page icon, I almost died.

"Are you serious? Are you fuckin' crazy? Elsa, you have to stop this!"

"Done, big sis. Your sexiness and kindness are viral."

I grabbed the phone. "What did you write?"

"Only that my big sister rocks." She hugged me. "You know I love you. Now let's go."

"I hate the way you manipulate me into doing what you want." I wished I was more like her. How did she do it? We had the same parents, but we were so completely and utterly different.

"I take after Dad's side of the family. Lucky me. Maybe one day I'll be a drunk too."

I didn't say anything. What was there to say? I just prayed to God I would arrive home in one piece. The last time I had gone out with my sister, it was a pretty messy affair…

As soon as we walked into Foufounes Electrique, I wanted to leave. Elsa spotted Eddie immediately, like he had some kind of sign on the top of his head.

"Baby!" she screamed from across the bar. Eddie waved at us and approached with a big smile, clutching two beer bottles.

"Hi, Serena." He kissed me on the cheek. "You look different…really cool." He checked out my boots. The music was blaring and deafening me. I could hardly hear what he was saying.

"I know," Elsa said. "Isn't she hot? I dressed her, thank you very much." She took a bow and giggled. Eddie grabbed her and kissed her on the lips. They were so secure with each other, never showing any signs of jealousy. I did envy that.

"You are a genius, baby. A hot genius." He lowered his hands down to her waist and cupped her bum.

Laughing, she slapped his hands away. He whispered something into her ear, and she shook her head. "No, she doesn't do that shit," I heard her say over the music.

"Elsa." I gestured for her to come to me. When she reached me, I leaned over, put my arm around her shoulder, and said in a low voice, "You better not do any drugs."

Eddie grabbed her out of my arms and shouted, "C'mon babe, the band is going on in five." He looked over at me. "Order what you want. I have a tab."

"We'll be right back, Serengeti. Don't do anything I wouldn't do." Elsa winked at me. Ha-ha. She thought she was funny as she grabbed the beer bottle from Eddie's hand and started to drink while walking away.

I took a seat at the bar, and when a young barmaid with bright orange hair came over to my area, I ordered a beer. "Put it on Eddie's tab," I said.

"Eddie doesn't have a tab." She looked around. "Nor will he ever have one again." She gave me a nasty look.

It figured he didn't really have a tab. I'd found it odd to begin with, but I'd fallen for it anyway, like he knew I would. I was the older sister. I was the gullible one.

I opened my purse. "How much?" I asked.

"Six dollars," the barmaid said.

I tried to concentrate on the money, but her hair and makeup were completely out of control, distracting me. Finally, I pulled out a twenty and handed it her, asking for only ten dollars back. She gave me a sideways smile to show her appreciation for the tip. Didn't anybody say "thank you" anymore?

I looked around the bar/club/hellhole to take in my environment, then took a sip of my beer just to do something instead of looking like a complete loner. I was going to kill my sister for leaving me here like this while she was off doing God-knew-what drugs. I had to have another talk with her. I felt so totally out of place.

Then I noticed a guy with a shaved head staring right at me from across the bar. He made it quite obvious. *Oh, fuck.* I turned away quickly to not give him any funny ideas. I had no intention of speaking with freaks tonight. He looked intimidating. I turned my back to him and faced the barmaid again, watching as she poured glass of draft beer after glass of draft beer. I was sure her hand got so tired at night... It seemed like there were way more guys than girls here. Usually in clubs it was the opposite.

At the sound of a microphone being installed and a loud, annoying, beeping noise, I turned toward the stage. Sure enough, the band was getting ready to play. The guitarist had no shirt on, and tattoos covered every part of his chest. I turned my stool completely around to watch the band set up; it was better than watching Carrot Orange Girl pouring beers. I didn't think people drank mixed drinks in a place like this.

"Great band tonight," I heard a male voice with a distinct English accent say. I turned to my left, and there stood the bald guy. Up close he was really good-looking. His features impressed me.

"I guess so. That's what my sister says."

"You don't know them?" He inched closer to me while I tried to push my stool away. He noticed my movement and stopped dead in his tracks.

"Not particularly interested," I said, moving the top part of my body away from his.

"I don't bite," he said and smiled.

"How do I know that?"

He was holding a foreign beer in his hand and took a swig out of it like he'd been doing it for years. He didn't reply to my reference to vampirism but instead asked me a bizarre question. "What are you doing here?"

"I have no idea." That made him smile again.

"What's your name?"

I liked his accent. "Serena."

"Beautiful name for a beautiful girl."

"Whatever."

"I'm Ben." He politely extended his hand and shook mine. "Nice to meet you, Serena," he said, ignoring my previous comment. Perhaps I had been too harsh.

"Nice to meet you too, Ben."

I stared at the band still preparing their equipment. I had no intention of continuing this conversation, even though he seemed easy and fun to talk to. He just didn't seem to be my type of guy. I felt uncomfortable, although he had loads of sex appeal.

"Serena, may I ask you a question?"

I had to give it to him—he used proper English and grammar. I liked that. "If you must," I said.

"I must." He stood up. "Do you want me to leave?" His dark eyes gazed into mine with honesty.

"Yes, I do." My answer was curt, but I didn't know if I really wanted him to leave. He just scared me for some reason.

"Why?" he asked.

"I'm not interested," I replied, hoping he would just go away. Yet another part of me wanted to continue this conversation.

He probed on. "Don't you want to know where I'm from?"

Actually, I was dying to find out the moment I heard his accent. Not because I liked him, though. I was just curious. Whenever someone spoke with an English accent, I wanted to know from where they came.

"No." I lied, playing some kind of game with him that I myself couldn't understand

He didn't move. I continued looking straight ahead, and could feel his eyes on me. When I finally turned to him again, he was smiling at me. I couldn't help myself—I smiled back, and that was when I noticed he had the cutest dimples.

"Do I amuse you?" he asked.

"Your line of questioning amuses me." I turned my whole body toward him. "Look, Ben, I'm just here because I was dragged here. I hate this place. I wanted to spend a quiet night at home, doing nothing but watching a movie, but *no*. My sister wanted to meet her boyfriend, and she dumped me here all alone. I hate the music, and I'm not remotely interested in picking up anyone—or being picked up, for that matter. So why don't you go on your merry way and find a pretty, young, freaky girl, with earrings all over her face and body? Someone who will swoon all over you and your English accent. Sorry, but you're not my type."

There, that should have done the trick.

He looked at me, expressionless, and took a sip of his beer, his gaze not leaving mine. He placed the beer on the bar and said, "Wow. Not the response I was hoping for."

"Serena!" I heard my sister's voice a few feet away in the other direction. Ben and I both turned, and she smiled. "You met Ben!"

"This is your sister?" Ben looked from me to Elsa and back again with a shocked expression. "I never would have guessed. But now, come to think of it, you do have a lot in common—namely, the attitude."

"Are you crazy?" Elsa's eyes were bloodshot. "My sister is a goody-two-shoes. Don't drink, don't smoke, what do you do?" she sang.

"I can't believe you're quoting that stupid Adam Ant song again!" I shouted at her.

"Uncle Bill loved to say that to her when she was a teenager." Elsa laughed at the private joke, thrown out into the air and in front of Ben, whom I had just met. She was stoned, and I had just embarrassed myself by my criticism and sarcasm. I blushed, but it was so dark in there, I was sure no one noticed. I looked down at my boots and nervously crossed my legs.

"I wouldn't throw your sister under the bus so firmly, my dear," Ben stated with authority. He glanced at me and winked. "She has a quick and lovely mouth on her."

I pressed my lips together as his gaze traveled right to my mouth. I turned away slightly, uncomfortable with my sister's laughter and Ben's compliment. I wanted to look at him again without being too obvious, so I took a quick glance. He was wearing tight blue jeans and a black T-shirt with holes in it, his dark chest hair peeking through. He was muscular, but not like the type that works out at the gym. I stopped at his boots. Of course, they were black.

"Give him a shot," Elsa whispered into my ear. "He's a good guy, a bit of a badass. Don't be such a square." Then she wrapped her arms around Eddie, whose eyes were droopy and utterly glazed over.

Pissed, I turned away from both of them. She was only nineteen. I'd hoped she would someday stop acting so immaturely, but that time hadn't come yet, and somehow I knew it wouldn't come for a long time.

Next to me, Ben shifted his weight from one leg to another, trying to get comfortable, I guessed. I was still sitting on my stool, and he towered over me. I stood up to see exactly how tall he was. I was five-feet-five, so considering my heels, he must have been about six-feet-three. He stared at me, and this time I didn't look away.

"So, Ben, where exactly are you from?" I brushed my hair away from my face. Why not have some fun? I was bored anyway and he was attractive. A second bottle of beer was in front of me on the bar.

He smiled. "I thought you'd never ask. I'm from Liverpool, or better known to Londoners as 'Cesspool.'" He chuckled.

"Are you visiting?"

"No, I've been living in Montreal for seven years now."

The band members shuffled around on the stage and then the lead singer turned on the microphone and spoke closely to it. "Hello, everyone! We are the Spidernuts, and we're gonna rock the mother fuckin' house tonight!"

Loud cheers exploded around us, and everyone clapped.

"I love this band," Ben said.

Elsa and Eddie cheered, their hands circled around their mouths. I didn't say anything. I knew I would hate the band's music. It started to play, and the crowd got even louder. Eddie and Elsa disappeared again. This time she didn't even tell me she would be back.

"Your sister is a wild one," Ben shouted into my ear. "She should take it a bit more slowly."

"You're telling me," I said sarcastically. "I know. Trust me, I know."

"I'm just saying. I've been around."

Ben appeared to be a nice guy, as Elsa had pointed out, but I wasn't sold just yet. He wore two diamond studs in each earlobe. I quickly turned away, but then my gaze was back on his face again. The two tiny piercings on his nose completely caught my full attention. He merely enjoyed the band, letting me gawk at him.

"Do you dance, Serena?" he asked, not looking at me.

"Not to this," I said, watching the band members

jump around onstage and make noise, not music.

"Then to what, pray tell?" He bobbed his head in time to the beat of the noise, then turned and waited for an answer.

"I have to feel like dancing in order to dance. I'm not in a dancing mood. This music makes me want to bolt."

"Would you like to come outside with me for a cigarette?" He asked the question as if he had taken me to a ball or something.

"I don't smoke." Although the idea of leaving— even for a few minutes—was tempting.

He looked disappointed. "Well, I'm going for a smoke."

"And miss all the fun?"

He took my joke as his opening and grabbed my hand. "Join me anyway."

Join him? I liked that verb. I saw it written in my mind. J-O-I-N. Not *c'mon, let's go,* but *join.*

"Okay."

I held onto my tiny purse tightly as we walked toward the bar's door. Once outside, he pulled out a crumpled pack of cigarettes from his back pocket and offered me one. I said no.

"Are you certain?"

"Yes. I'm not that drunk yet." I smirked.

"Oh, so you *do* let loose. There's hope for you yet." Ben smirked back at me, and I felt a tingling sensation on the edge of my skin.

What the fuck?

He lit his cigarette. The area in front of the club was crowded with people smoking all around us. I felt like an oddball. It was a nice night too—not too cold, but a crisp autumn night. I stood in front of him with my arms folded across my chest. He blew out the first puff of smoke and then eyed me.

"So, tell me about yourself." He stared straight into my eyes.

I tightened my hold. "There's really not much to tell." Too many ears around us.

"Let's move over," he said, and led me a few feet away from the crowd.

"There's always something to tell, even in silence." He took two quick puffs of his cigarette.

I liked the sound of that. I smiled to myself and placed my hands in my jeans' pockets. *Here goes nothing.*

"I'm a student."

"What are you studying?"

"English literature."

"Now that is really going to get you places," he said sarcastically. "That's what my mum told me when I left England."

"I'm used to that comment. I hear it often." I watched Ben smoke and contemplate his next thought carefully. He bit his lip first and then took a deep breath. He definitely had a sensual mouth that called out to be kissed. Why was I thinking such erotic thoughts?

"I have a confession to make. Elsa told me a few things about you a while back when we met here. I don't know her very well—I've known Eddie longer—but I knew who you were the moment I saw you. You stick out like a sore thumb in this dive, but honestly, not in a bad way." He smiled and rubbed the back of his bald head. He seemed nervous now. It was kind of cute and innocent. I liked his hands. "Definitely in a good way."

His gaze lingered on my boots.

"What did she tell you?" What was he going to say?

"She told me that you will be published soon by a publisher in the States and that you are an exceptional writer."

"Published?" My sister needed help; she was delusional. "I have to *find* a publisher first." I rolled my eyes.

"You are very similar to your sister."

"No, I'm not." I was nothing like her. I felt flushed again. "What do *you* do, Ben?" I was curious as hell and ready to change the topic. No one had ever told me that my sister and I were similar.

"Ah yes… That dreaded question, the answer to which indicates my worth in the 'good-provider role,' as coined by sociologist Jessie Bernard." He shuffled his feet, took another quick puff, blew out the smoke, and flicked his cigarette to the ground in front of him. "I'm a writer," he said calmly. He didn't wait for my reply but stepped back and gestured for me to go ahead of him. "Shall we? The band awaits us. I'm sure you are eager to hear the rest of its repertoire."

Speechless, I simply nodded and stepped in front of him. *A writer? He's a fuckin' writer?* I walked into the bar and didn't know which way to go. Ben moved in front of me and said something like "follow me" or "I'll lead the way." Staring at his strong-looking back, I was ready to ask him a million questions. I stumbled and he turned, grabbing my hand as I almost hit a pole. What the hell was a pole doing in the middle of the club anyway? The music was loud, but as my racing thoughts started to subside, I realized the band was performing a slow song, and the singer's voice was soothing.

When we got to the bar, I spotted Eddie and Elsa. They were swaying in each other's arms to the beat of the music. I reached over the bar top to take a sip of the beer I'd left there. My throat was dry, and my mind was reeling. *A writer? Really?*

"Wait! Don't drink that!" Ben yanked the bottle out of my hand. "You never leave your drink unattended at a club—especially *this* club."

He placed the bottle back on the bar and signaled the barmaid. With a quick hand gesture, he ordered two more beers. His actions seemed so protective. I stared at him and wondered how he would move that tremendous body of his in bed. He was ultra-super-sexy. He took out some money from his wallet and quickly paid for the two beers.

He handed me my drink and smiled.

"Thank you," I said.

"My pleasure. You never know what some creep might do to get a woman, including spiking their drink." He looked me up and down. "And you are not just any woman."

His expression sent a strangely pleasant sensation straight to my belly. While his last statement permeated my thoughts, he sipped his beer and watched the band. The song it was playing sounded good, so I paid close attention to the lyrics. Something about "five seconds to a broken heart if you leave me like this, wanting you more and more each day… I would die inside every five seconds of my life." As soon as the song ended, everyone clapped, including me.

Ben peeked at me from the corner of his eye. "So, did you like the song?"

"Actually, Ben, I loved it."

"I like the sound of my name on your lips." He leaned in close to me, and a surge of energy drew me toward him. I was definitely attracted to him. I'd have to be *gay* to not be captivated.

A few girls glanced his way, trying to get his attention, but he had his eyes on my neck. "I like your scarf," he said, reaching out and touching it gently. "It's really funky."

As he felt my scarf, his gaze swept up my neck and landed on my lips. He looked as if he was imagining…something, and it gave me shivers—the good kind. I wasn't sure what he was thinking, but I knew it wasn't innocent thoughts or Bible stories. His eyes spoke of something…

"I don't usually dress like this," I said, all sober and proper, dizzy from his words. "But thanks."

"It wouldn't matter to me how you dressed. I look past the superficiality of designers, brands, and all that other phony shit. It really is not important to me."

One of the lights above the bar was directly above him, and as I stared into his eyes, I noticed tiny, light brown speckles in them. Dark brown eyes with dark eyebrows looked back at me, waiting for a reply. He leaned back and took a sip of his beer. He had a long neck with a little bit of stubble. I finished my beer and pushed it toward the barmaid, indicating I wanted another one.

"Why are you bald?" *Did I just ask that?* It was the alcohol talking.

Choking, Ben spit beer all over himself. "Now we're talking!" He laughed. "Why am I bald?" He thought about the question as if it was the first time he'd been asked it. "When my mum asked me that same question,

I replied, 'Why the fuck not?'"

"You say 'fuck' to your mom?"

"It's the English way. 'Fuck' is to the English as 'eh' is to Canadians."

I nodded in understanding. "Getting back to my question, then… You don't have an answer?"

"If I told you that girls liked it, would that suffice?"

There were those dimples again. I shifted uncomfortably while sweeping the hair out of my face. "I thought you weren't superficial?"

"You got me there." And then his face turned serious. "The answer is plain and simple. I like it. Do you like it?" He stared into my eyes.

"I don't know." I tried hard not to stare at his luscious lips. "At first, I didn't, but now I've gotten used to it, so I guess so."

"Don't guess. Speak the truth. Yes or no?"

I didn't want to say yes and give him the impression that I liked his baldness and therefore liked him, but I didn't want to say no and hurt his feelings.

"It is not a yes-or-no question," I replied curtly.

"Funny, I thought it was, but if you need more time to think about it, then by all means"—he looked at his watch—"take all the time in the world. The night is still young."

I glanced at my watch. It was only twelve thirty.

"Tell me, what do you write?" I asked, changing the subject and thus avoiding giving him an answer—for now. I had been dying to ask that question from the moment he had said he was a writer.

"I write erotic fiction for an e-publisher." He winked at me slyly, which set my body on edge. I hadn't expected that answer. I got this flash of that actor from

Transporter. "I have a pseudonym." He smiled as if he were pulling a prank.

"Why?"

"Why? Why do you think?" He laughed. "My mum wouldn't be too proud of my writing 'pornography,' as she calls it."

"It's kind of cute how you think of your 'mum.'" I smiled. "But seriously, what is your pseudonym?"

"First of all, I think of my 'mum' because she saved my life by sending me to Montreal, and secondly, if I tell you my pseudonym, will you promise not to laugh?" Wearing a humorous expression, he leaned closer to me and looked directly into my eyes.

"I won't laugh if you don't," I promised and smiled, thinking about his mom saving his life.

"Domenic S. Amour," he said with authority, enunciating each syllable.

I giggled. "That sounds so sexy. What's the S for?"

"What else? Sex."

We looked at each other and burst out laughing.

"I know, it's ridiculous," he said after a couple of seconds. "But, Serena, I need to make a living, and using my real name… Well, it gets complicated. Did you know Anne Rice wrote erotica, and she had not only one pseudonym, but two? Anne Rampling and A.N. Roquelaure. Have you ever read those books of hers?"

"No. I have read *Interview with the Vampire*, which I loved very much, but you know, I still can't believe you're a writer." The closest I'd ever gotten to erotic fiction was an essay I'd written in college on pornography versus erotica.

"Why not? Do you think you're the only writer in town?" he jested. "We're everywhere."

"I don't know… I just feel like I'm all alone sometimes, like there's no one to talk to about my ideas, and there truly isn't. When I try to talk to my sister, she rolls her eyes after *one minute* and says I should be talking to more intellectual types who understand the meaning of 'alliteration.' She understands the meaning of 'alliteration.' She is smart, but she won't give me feedback."

I sat on the bar stool. My legs were starting to kill me, and my feet ached in my boots. Ben gestured to the barmaid for more beer and paid for them when they arrived.

"You *are* all alone with your writing. That's the honest truth," Ben said. He stood next to me and placed his elbows on the bar, leaning toward it and slightly toward me. I got a whiff of his musky cologne and inhaled it in. He handed me a beer, and I thanked him.

"How many books have you published?" I was eager to find out more about Ben and his writing.

"Fifteen e-books," he replied. "That would be around two real books, if the author was, say, Jonathan Franzen. Do you know the book *The Corrections*?"

I nodded. I had heard something about Oprah wanting it for her book club, but the author had declined. It was a scandal at the time, but not much more came of it.

"Of course, you have. You would have to be living under a rock to not have heard about it. That book has a two-hundred-thousand-word count. To give you a better understanding, my books are about thirty thousand words long. Hence, two of Franzen's books equals fifteen of mine, approximately."

"Oh." I had no idea what he was talking about. I

needed a paper and pen to do the math. My mental math skills had ended in grade five.

"Trust me, the way the publishing business is going, you're better off finding a real job and working on your 'real' manuscript. I'm just making a living, and a bare minimal one at that. Luckily, I don't pay rent—that's another story I don't want to get into right now—but the money I make is enough. For food, clothes, razors"—he jokingly gestured to his head—"and whatever other garbage I require to survive. Serena, at two ninety-nine an e-book, how much money do you think I make?" He shook his head, appalled at his situation. "You don't even want to know."

What did he mean by not paying rent?

He must have seen my puzzled expression because his tone changed. "I'm just grateful to my mum's family, who have given me the monetary support to write."

"This sounds very discouraging." I drank my beer, wondering how his mom's family helped him. Too many questions were rolling around in my head. I glanced about for my sister and Eddie, who had disappeared, and realized the music was getting louder.

"The publishing business has changed drastically," Ben continued in a serious tone. "You think it was hard to publish before? Now it's ten times tougher. There are publishers, e-publishers, self-publishers, agents who want to screw you over, publishing houses that don't accept unsolicited manuscripts, ones that do but won't like yours anyway because the competition is too fierce. It's fuckin' overwhelming." Ben rubbed the back of his head, his gaze never leaving my face. "My e-books are selling. I write every day. I am producing what the market wants. I can't stop writing. It's a compulsion in me. I have to get it out. I find pleasure and pain in writing. Plus, I love writing about sex." Then he smiled at me and lifted his empty bottle. "Cheers, to writing."

"Cheers," I repeated.

We each took a sip of our beers, and a million more questions came to me. "Are you working on another manuscript?" I wondered if all he wanted to do was write erotica.

"What do you mean?"

I guess I had been too tactful, not wanting to offend him. "I mean…is erotica the only genre you want to write in?"

"For the moment." Averting my gaze, he took another swig of his beer, and then he looked directly at me. "That's what is on my mind."

I knew there was more to the answer than that, but the way he looked at me gave me a flutter. His eyes narrowed in on mine, and I quickly changed the subject.

"So, how old are you?" I felt flushed.

"I'm twenty-nine, just a couple of months shy of thirty." He smiled provocatively, seemingly comfortable with the change of topic. "And you?"

"Twenty-three." I calculated that he was almost seven years older than me. I hadn't thought he was *that* much older. I looked around anxiously to see if Eddie and Elsa were anywhere to be seen. I spotted them, all over each other, on the dance floor.

Ben followed my gaze and said, "They are really into it."

"I need some fresh air." I stood. The music was making me feel like I had a drum set in my brain. I couldn't think straight.

"Perfect. I've been dying for a smoke. Wait, that

didn't sound right. I want a cigarette right now." He chuckled. I smiled back at him and followed his cute behind, my eyes on his back, completely focused on this marvelous body in front of me.

I followed him like a soldier, my eyes only on him, and almost fell flat on my face when I turned my head for a second to look for the exit sign. That was when my world tilted for the second time that evening. I was no longer lost on Ben's island of beauty. Bam! There I stood, face to face with Teddy.

I stopped dead in my tracks. Ben continued straight ahead and outside.

It couldn't be. I didn't move. I stood still as Teddy's green eyes lit up my soul, just like they had done the very first time I'd looked upon them. I thought I wouldn't feel this way again. It had been such a long time ago. I thought our souls wouldn't even remember, but they did. Man, did they ever.

He looked at me and stilled. His friend nudged him, but he didn't speak. Seconds flew by. It seemed like our souls were communicating while our bodies stood there like surrogate mothers. *Can you two get this over, already? Don't you see?*

I knew those eyes, knew them intimately, perhaps from another lifetime.

My thoughts raced. My heart pounded.

Finally, he opened his mouth and spoke. "Serena, I've been looking for you for five years."

I heard what he said, but I couldn't speak. I froze, looking at his luscious lips and not thinking straight.

"I know," I somehow managed to mumble.

Our souls were having a deep, silent exchange. Somehow, they knew, even while we stood there, trying to figure out what was transpiring between us. The loud music faded away, and the song *Amen* by Leonard Cohen began to play inside my twisted mind. His voice was rough, singing over and over, *tell me again, tell me again... Amen...*

"Serena?"

Ben's voice shook me out of my reverie. He had come back and was standing next to me, looking confused. I sensed Ben's gaze darting from me to Teddy, but our eyes were locked. Ben didn't ask any questions. With a cigarette sticking out of his mouth and his lighter in his right hand, he continued giving me and Teddy the once-over. I felt Ben's presence like a background beat of a song.

I turned to Ben and, gathering all the willpower, said, "I'll be with you in a minute."

Ben simply turned and left. I looked at Teddy and gave him a smile. It was a forced smile, one that showed I was a respectful, responsible, young woman who had been taught to not be rude. Why *that* smile? I wasn't sure.

"I know who you are," Teddy said, his eyes revealing *everything*.

I felt my insides weaken. He knew who I was? What did he mean? I knew he had been thinking about me the same way I had been thinking about him all these years. Otherwise, we would not have stopped dead in our tracks like this.

Even after five years, I felt the attraction. It was instinctual. I couldn't talk myself out of it. We were facing each other and blocking the second entrance to the club. The intensity of the energy between us blew into a bubble, surrounding us in a state of awe.

"You have really shitty timing," I said.

"Why?" he asked, his eyes full of intent, persuasion, love, sorrow.

"Because I met someone tonight," was what I said, but what I was thinking was, what were the chances of meeting someone who was a writer and a gentleman, a punk rocker and a romantic, bald yet attractive? Someone I finally felt a connection with after having just one conversation—a stimulating conversation, at that?

Teddy's face dropped; I had just stabbed him with my words.

"Do you want to see me again?" he asked with that look of love on his face that I could never escape from. It had been in my dreams for five years. "I need to see you again."

"Yes," I said quietly, almost in a whisper. I needed to see him again too. "I know exactly where to find you," I said and took a step back. "I have to go. My friend is waiting." *Friend? Ben is my friend now?*

"But I don't know where to find *you*," Teddy said after I turned around. I knew he'd meant for me to turn back, to change my path, but it was beyond me now. It was out of my reach.

I stepped outside into the fresh air, knowing I had control now. If I wanted to find Teddy, I knew exactly where to go.

I met Ben's gaze. His eyes were questioning, curious, understanding, and captivating—the complete opposite of Teddy's. I smiled at him, my first relaxed, authentic smile of the night.

"Are you ready for a cigarette now?" he asked.

"As ready as I'll ever be." I extended my hand as he reached into his pocket to pull out his pack. "Don't make fun of me if I don't inhale."

"On the contrary. I'll admire that you don't."

I gave him a flirty smile. A sexy smile. A smile I had kept hidden for a long time. Ben made me look deep into my closet of smiles for the best one to use. He held the lighter in front of me and flicked it, placing one hand around my cigarette, gently touching my hand as he did. Electric volts stormed through me.

What was going on? I had finally found Teddy, and I had turned my back on him. But I had to go with my gut, and that led me to Ben, who had this magnetic pull I couldn't resist. There was something about him that attracted me more than the possibility of knowing Teddy at last. I needed to explore it further.

If I had turned around, I would have seen Teddy staring at us with complete hatred, but the truth was I was meant to meet Ben that night.

Teddy
Now I do the watching…

"We'll probably miss the first set," Dan said, pissed off.

"I know, I know. I was exhausted. I'm just getting over my cold. I passed out on the couch, so sue me," I said to him, just as annoyed as he quickly swerved to the left to grab a parking spot on Saint Catherine Street. "Calm down, Dan."

"I'm lucky I just found this spot, bro. You'll be okay, especially after your beauty sleep." He laughed. "You're such a wimp sometimes. No, make that a pussy."

"And you're such an asshole," I retorted.

He placed the car in Park and opened the door before the key was out of the ignition. "C'mon, wimp," he joked.

"I'm coming, asshole," I shouted as two young kids walked by Dan's car and gave us a weird look. Teenagers and their looks—you didn't know if they wanted to punch you out or tap you on the shoulder and say, 'Cool, bro.'

"Okay, knock it off now," Dan said, checking out two girls standing outside the club and smoking. "Act civilized," he whispered.

"In this joint? You've got to be kidding me." I looked at him like he was nuts. Those girls seemed like they were ready to slap us out if we even spoke to them. "This band better be good."

"Do you really care? You really need to get laid." Dan gestured to the two girls, and I gave him the look again.

"Seriously, they are not my type."

"Oh yeah, I forgot. Your type is the one you wallow over for five years," he said sarcastically and moved up ahead of me. The girls completely ignored us as we walked by. Dan gawked at them for a moment, waiting for an in, and then he looked at me. "You are so fucked. You could have at least looked their way. I want to get laid."

"They are not looking for a guy like you," I said matter-of-factly. "And definitely not a school teacher, like me. They'd probably go running the other way if they heard I taught teenagers and that I'm a responsible human being."

"Don't stereotype them. For all we know those girls could be teachers too."

Was he serious? "They're young enough to be my students!"

"Whatever." Dan opened the front doors, and we walked into the club. We paid an entrance fee to see the band and passed the second set of doors. The music was blaring, and the place was packed. I put my money back into my pocket and then lifted my head to go toward the bar.

That's when I saw her at the same moment she saw me. Our eyes locked.

Her blue-violet eyes… It was her. Serena. Everyone else disappeared. My world fell apart, and she appeared like Venus out of the ocean. I barely noticed a bald guy just ahead of her, walking past me.

She stopped in front of me, and he continued walking. I couldn't speak.

One. Two. Three.

Our eyes spoke to each other's. Our souls met once again, and they were communicating. We waited. For what, I don't know, but I knew I had to say something. I thought my voice was going to give out on me, like in those dreams where you're screaming but there's no sound. I wanted to throw my arms around her and say "welcome back."

"Serena, I've been looking for you for five years," I finally said, staring deeply into her eyes. She was beautiful. "Moondance" by Van Morrison started to play in my head as the sound of the punk rock music disappeared. I *wanna make love to you tonight* echoed in the back of my mind.

"I know," she said. She knew what I was talking about.

Out of nowhere, Bald Guy came back. He stood next to Serena and said her name. He looked from me to her for a few seconds, a cigarette sticking out of his mouth. She looked at him and told him she would be outside in a minute. She would? She wanted to go outside with Bald Guy and not talk to me? Fuck, he was good-looking, that prick.

"I know who you are," I said, not wanting to break the magical spell my soul was under. I didn't know what else to say. *"I know who you are"* just came out, like a mantra in my head. What an idiotic thing to say. My eyes took in all of her—her movements, her voice, her words—and I felt a stirring deep within me.

"You have really shitty timing." She smiled, and my

heart skipped a beat.

"Why?" I asked, trying to understand her as my body reacted to every word coming out of her mouth.

The answer I got wasn't what I'd expected at all. "Because I met someone tonight."

Was she serious? I guess she was. I felt a kick to my stomach along with an ache throughout my body to have her.

"Do you want to see me again?" I asked, cursing my luck, and wanting to stab Bald Guy. "I need to see you again," I confessed before she could answer, knowing I was affecting her in some way. She didn't move; she just stared at me with those magical eyes of hers. They fluttered and twinkled at me as I glanced at her full lips—lips I wanted to kiss passionately.

"Yes," she said quietly. It was almost a whisper. A hot, exotic whisper that made my insides explode with fervor. "I know exactly where to find you." Then she took a step back and looked down, averting my gaze. "I have to go. My friend is waiting."

"But I don't know where to find *you*," I said desperately as she turned to go outside.

I wanted her to come back to tell me she wanted to stay with me all night long. To talk, to whisper sexy words into each other's ears, to discuss the years that had gone by and how many times we'd thought of that moment that had passed between us. I wanted her to forget about the fuckin' bald guy who looked as if he could charm the pants off her and every other girl in here. He seriously looked like a badass.

I couldn't help it—my feet were walking toward the door, walking toward her. She stood a little too far off to be able to see me. Her hand reached over to take a cigarette from Baldy and smiled at him. It was a smile that made me crazy green with envy. I felt rage and the frustration of so much built-up sexual tension. I wanted to go over there and knock him out and take her away from his smoke-infested cancer society. She smoked and liked Foufounes? She'd just met him? Her clothes and his matched as if they belonged together. I hated him.

"Buddy, are you okay? You look like you're going to kill that guy. Who was that?" Dan asked. I had completely forgotten about him. "What's going on? I didn't want to interrupt. There was an awful lot of attraction between you and that rocker chick."

"That rocker chick? Shut the fuck up, Dan!" I turned away from them and walked back into the club.

Dan followed, and when we stopped near the bar, he leaned over to get the barmaid's attention. He literally had to flag her down. She had all the piercings and tattoos any barmaid would need to have as a prerequisite to work in this place. Dan ordered two beers, and I glanced around, searching for Serena. She was probably still outside with Bald Guy.

Dan interrupted my thoughts. "Earth to Teddy. Earth to Teddy," he repeated like an immature ten-year-old.

Irritated, I frowned in his direction. "What? What do you want from me?"

"Looking for that rocker chick? She's way out of your league, bro. I don't care what kind of googly eyes you were making at each other. I know—even if you say, *'she's that girl,'*" he said as he scanned the bar. He was always on the lookout for girls. "There's rocker chick, nine o'clock. Don't look now. She's walking straight by here. She's with that freak-head."

I couldn't figure out which way to not look, so I just

stared straight ahead at the band and downed my beer. I waited for her to pass by or at least to notice me, but she didn't. Bald Guy gave me a dirty look, and she peeked at me shyly.

"So, what's her story, morning glory?" Dan asked as he peered at her and then studied me for my reaction. Dan *had* to interject lyrics from a song in most sentences. He was obsessed with music in a crazy, unhealthy way. He thought it was cool to quote lyrics. I wondered whoever told him that. It got stale after a few years, but I was so used to it that I felt like I knew what he was going to refer to before he actually did.

"It's her. She's 'the one,' idiot! Her name is Serena, not rocker chick, and she *just* met a guy. Don't I have great timing?"

"Is that what she said to you earlier?" Dan asked with wide eyes.

"Among other things."

"I really think you need to get over her." He patted my back. "Let's listen to the band." Although he appeared to shrug it off for my sake, he kept on glancing at Serena too.

The band was playing, and it got so loud I couldn't hear myself think. I looked around the club and spotted Serena. She was talking to some girl, and Baldy was talking to a guy with tattoos all along his arms, kind of like that guy I'd seen a while back and admired for his tattoos. Come to think of it, they looked like the couple… I couldn't remember how long ago that was. Serena was talking closely to the girl. They were probably best friends; they looked like best friends. Funny, but I'd never taken her for this type of girl. Five years ago, she had seemed completely different—less intimidating.

Now she appeared unapproachable, though she was still stunning. That hadn't changed.

I caught the two of them looking at me, and I quickly turned away. I felt like I was in high school again and that my crush had just looked at me. How sappy. How pathetic. I took a swig of my second beer. Dan was ordering them so fast. The band was too fuckin' loud, and Dan stared at the band, bopping his head. The music was horrible. A bunch of noise.

"Cool, eh?" Dan asked, leaning in toward me but still facing the stage.

"I can't hear a fuckin' thing but noise. If I'm not deaf after the show, I will be tomorrow."

Then the band started to play a ballad that was easier to listen to.

Dan smirked and took a sip of his beer. "Stop busting my balls, and stop wallowing. It's embarrassing." He struck my bottle with his. "Cheers, to wallowing fools like you. To The Wallflowers." What was he talking about?

"To pricks like you, who don't make any sense."

"I love you, man," Dan said, reciting the commercial.

"Yeah, suck it."

He messed up my hair. "Only fools fall in love."

Baldy said something in Serena's ear. Her friend kissed Tattoo Guy madly on the mouth. No doubt that was her boyfriend. It seemed like the four of them were close friends, although Serena had said she had just met Baldy. I studied him intently. He looked like he was intelligent. My problem was that I pigeonholed everyone into a certain type: the intellectual type, the rocker chick type, the badass type, the goody two-shoes type… On and on, my brain processed people by stereotyping them, as if they could be neatly placed into categories. As if they weren't complex individuals. I saw everything too black and white…

Dan nudged my elbow. "Stop gawking, fool. You look like a psycho. You won't score any brownie points with her if you come across as a stalker."

"Stop exaggerating. A stalker," I mocked. "Right!" Angry, I turned away. "Okay, okay, settle down."

He laughed. "Settle down? Hey, I'm not one of your students."

"Dan, get a life." I tried to concentrate on the band and not listen to his annoying banter.

"I think we need some shots. Some whiskey, some scotch and some beer." He sang off cue, as if the too-loud music wasn't irritating enough.

"The guitarist isn't too bad," I said, trying to get into the mood just the same.

"I told you they were awesome."

I felt her staring at me. Turning my head, I caught her glance. It was for just a split second, but I saw it—that same look she had given me five years ago. Then she looked upset, as if I had done something to her. I couldn't believe she was here in the same room with me and that I had to pretend she wasn't. Now that I'd gotten a good look at her, I didn't even think she was my type. *Here we go again with types.* I wanted to smash the illusions of "types" all across the dance floor. She was here at the same club as me, listening to the same band, and I couldn't do anything to change the fact that she *just met a guy*. I chuckled to myself. What kind of luck did I have?

"What's so funny? You like laughing to yourself?"

"I'm just looking at Serena over there and I'm thinking I don't think she's my type at all. I don't know... All these years I had this ideal in my head, and now it's been shattered."

"Bro, take it easy. You don't even know anything about her. You know, they're all the same in the end." Dan smirked and nudged me again. "Smile."

"Words of advice from a guy who hasn't had a decent relationship since two thousand seven."

"Hey, I've had many relationships. More than I can say about you." He laughed.

"I said *decent*. With someone you can take out to a public place."

"Why do you think I come to this joint?" Dan laughed again and went off on a rambling tangent. "I spy with my little eye a blonde hottie in a black miniskirt, black leather jacket, black shoes, and black stockings." His eyes twinkled.

"That describes just about every girl in here," I said, rolling my eyes.

Dan's attitude toward women stemmed mostly from the fact that he was good-looking and charming. He always made the ladies smile, no matter their age—from young, adolescent girls to older women to grandmas. He loved to give compliments, and he had a way of finding the nicest attribute about a woman and pointing it out in a humorous way but without being offensive.

He gestured for me to look at the two girls ahead of us, standing to our left. They seemed slightly out of place. The blonde girl he'd referred to was dressed as if she were at an office party. The other girl was a brunette and taller than her friend. They were talking to each other, and as they spoke, I could tell they were first-timers. They both looked around awkwardly.

"I see her," I said.

"She has a friend."

"I can see that too," I replied sarcastically.

"Okay, let's go."

"Hold on. Serena's here."

"And? Clearly she is *not* interested."

"She never said that. She said she knows where to find me."

"And if she wants to find you, she will, but right now, tonight, she is dallying with Vin Diesel, and by the looks of it, she is really into him—minus the few glances she's thrown your pathetic way."

With that last bit, I got excited. "She's looking at me?"

"A few glances do not remotely equate to 'looking at me.'" Dan sounded annoyed, and then he challenged me. "If she can play the game, why can't you?"

I guess he had a point. It was ridiculous to sit here and hope she would come over so we could catch up like old friends when we weren't even acquaintances. It was also ridiculous to think she would leave Baldy's side, walk over to me, and talk to me all night long. That was wishful thinking.

I shrugged my shoulders. "Okay, then. Let's go talk to your blonde and her friend."

Dan walked ahead of me toward the two girls, and I followed, fully aware Serena was watching me. I didn't look her way, but I knew it, and then Dan confirmed it.

"Don't look now, but baby doll, who dissed you, is staring right at you."

My body tensed up, and I nervously scratched my head, then ran my fingers through my hair.

We stood next to the two girls and watched the band for a few seconds. I looked at them from up close and noticed the brunette was pretty, but no sparks were flying. She wasn't even looking my way. Dan moved in for the kill immediately, charming his way in there with his sweet talk and charismatic ways.

He turned back toward me and introduced me to them. "This is Jenny. Jenny, this is Teddy."

I shook the blonde's hand. She had lovely eyes, a cute little nose, and a warm smile. "Nice to meet you," I said.

Then he turned to the other girl and introduced me to her.

"Melina, this is Teddy. Teddy, Melina."

I nodded at her, and she repeated the gesture, appearing uninterested. Jenny gave Dan that smile that spoke a million words, and Melina just stared at the band. Dan moved away from me and closer to Jenny, leaving me standing next to Melina. I glanced at him. He was already making his moves, flirting and whispering into Jenny's ear.

I was preoccupied with thoughts of Serena and Baldy, and I quickly peeked over at them, trying to not make it too obvious. They appeared to be in a deep conversation, and my jealousy reached new levels. I imagined taking out a seraph blade—like I even had one—and using it to threaten Baldy's life. I envisioned the blood and mayhem, Serena standing by and becoming enchanted by my superhuman strength and skill at wielding mythological weapons of legend, when suddenly I realized I'd been asked a question.

"Well?"

Light eyes looked into mine inquisitively, and I tried

to see what color they were.

"Uh... Sorry. I didn't hear you. Pardon me?" I sounded like an uneducated fool. *Pardon me* must have saved me. At least I didn't say *what?*

"Do you like the music?" Melina shouted, and up close and personal like this, I saw that she was really, *really* pretty. Her eyes looked to be light blue, but I couldn't be sure.

"Uh...not really," I stammered, distracted by her eyes, Baldy, Serena, and the blaring noise she called music. She waited for me to say something more, but I was too into my imagined heroic acts of legendary proportion to impress Serena that I didn't have a better response. I sounded so pathetically adolescent and ignorant.

"You?" I asked, shouting louder than she had. She winced and lifted her hand to cover her ear. "Sorry."

"Me what?" she shouted back, looking annoyed. Maybe she had realized I wasn't at all interested in talking with her.

"Sorry. I mean... Let me start over." I cleared my mind. "I'm sorry if I seem rude. I'm just a little distracted."

"By what?" She eyed me closely as if she were trying to figure me out. Her straight brown hair fell to her shoulders, and she had bangs. I never knew a girl with bangs before. She had a clear complexion and a brown mole on the side of her chin that was damn sexy. She would think I was crazy if I told her about Serena.

"How about we talk about something else?"

"Okay." She seemed surprised by my reply but at the same time relieved.

"What do you do for a living?" I asked.

"I'm a school teacher."

"What? Me too!"

"Really?" She gave me a once-over. "You don't strike me as a school teacher."

"I don't wear these clothes to work." I laughed. "I gather you don't wear miniskirts and those high-heeled shoes to school. You're not dressed like a teacher either."

"Actually, I do."

That answer intrigued me. "Which grade do you teach?"

"Grade six."

"That explains it. If you taught high school dressed like this, you would drive all the young guys crazy," I joked while looking closely at her body. It was absolutely perfect.

"Look at that… And here I thought you were a complete asshole by ignoring me." She gave me another once-over from top to bottom. *Did she just insult me?* "I gather you teach high school and not elementary. That clarifies it," she said coldly.

"Hold on. Firstly, I'm not ignoring you. I'm talking to you right now. And secondly, that *clarifies* what?"

"Your attitude and disinterest."

"Who said I wasn't interested?" Actually, with *her* attitude, I wasn't interested.

"Okay, forget it, will you?" she nagged as if we'd known each other for years. She wasn't even facing me.

"You look like *you're* not interested," I said to irritate her even more.

"I'm not. I'm glad you realize that."

And that was my first smile of the evening. She actually made me grin.

"So, Melina, where do you teach?" I asked,

changing the topic.

"Downtown," she replied robotically. After seeming to hesitate, she continued. "At Montreal Elementary, where the energy flows in another direction than the rest of Quebec. You?"

She turned to me while holding onto her drink for dear life, not even taking a sip. Why did she speak in riddles?

"In Laval, at The Laval Freedom High School," I replied, trying my best not to look at Serena. *Fuck, there I go again! I just glanced at her!* I was sure her conversation with Baldy was going better than mine was with this standoffish woman.

"Why does the name of that high school keep changing?" Melina eyed me like a reporter, waiting for a reply, all eyes and ears on me.

Who gave a fuck? I took a deep breath. "Well, it gives the administration a topic to discuss at meetings." I smiled at a rigid face, her expression as if to say, *that's your answer?* I stared into her eyes and realized they were as light as the sky on a sunny day. What a strange thought.

"What color are your eyes? In this light it's hard to tell," I said, keeping my distance and changing the subject once again.

She went with the flow of conversation without a hitch. "My mom says they're blue; my dad says they're green. I've heard it all. On my driver's license, I had to write blue. It's open for discussion, and it wouldn't be the first time, but a lot of people say my eyes look a witch's." She spoke as if she had answered the question a thousand times before and was bored to death of it. She seemed comfortable with her self-awareness.

I laughed at her quirkiness and then shot a glance at Serena. She stood really close to Baldy now, her back completely turned to me. *Oh yeah? Two can play that game.* But was she playing a game, trying to make me jealous? I sounded delusional now. Why would she be remotely interested in my conversation with Melina? And just what *was* I doing with Melina? Not much, except quickly losing her with my apparent disinterest.

"A witch, huh?" I turned completely toward Melina, trying my ultimate best to concentrate on the color of her eyes again, while in my mind I was lost in Serena's.

"Is that the only word you retained from that answer? It doesn't surprise me." Obviously irritated, she turned away and looked straight ahead at the band.

"Excuse me?" Why was she angry at me?

"Well, if you could stop *staring* at your ex-girlfriend for one second, maybe you could listen to what *I* have to say. Why are you even pretending to listen to me when you didn't hear a word I said?" She gave me another angry look and then stared at the band again. She was fuming mad.

I peeked over at Dan to save me—as if he could— but he had eyes only for Jenny, and they appeared to be involved in an intimate conversation.

"My ex-girlfriend?" I blurted out at Melina. I sounded like some kind of moron with my one-word answers.

Maybe she had a point. I suddenly felt like a heel, acting like a jerk, and now Melina was giving me the cold shoulder. I had been trying to be polite but hadn't succeeded. My gawking at Serena had obviously infuriated her. Where was this conversation going? My head was spinning.

Get it together, Teddy.

I glanced at her and then actually *looked* at her for the very first time. Melina had spunk and quite the attitude. Standing next to her, I could see she was just an inch shorter than me. She was curvaceous too. Underneath that skirt and top was definitely a body that would make me crazy with lust—that would make *any* man hot. I caught a glimpse of her neck. It was so sexy how it curved gracefully into her shoulder, and I felt a flutter—not butterflies, but dragonflies—in my stomach. *Carpe diem, Teddy,* a tiny voice said inside me.

She knew I was staring at her. She felt it. She slowly turned her head.

"If I tell you the truth, will you promise to not laugh or make fun of me?" I asked as I turned toward her and leaned in a little too close, inhaling some kind of apple scent that managed to arouse me. I had this image of a juicy green apple, the kind I would find in my lunch bag in elementary school.

She turned to me, and I instantly pulled back so her face wouldn't be mere inches from mine. I then looked at her lips—I couldn't help it—and she caught me. There was a sexual allure to Melina that drew me in, and a toughness about her that pushed me away at the same time. I was confused and unsure of everything about her.

"Look, Teddy, I'm not here looking for Mr. Right. God knows I won't find him at Foufounes Électriques. I'm here because I just broke up with my boyfriend, who cheated on me after four years with my friend. No, not Jenny."

As I listened to her, I thought how she had this presence that was beginning to draw me in. I knew for certain that she must be a fantastic teacher. She paused, and I stared at her, dumbfounded. I'd thought I was going to tell her *my* story…

"And he said it was a mistake," she continued. "Can you believe he used that exact word? *Mistake.* He said he loved me. He fucked my friend. Actually, she is no longer our friend." She pointed her index finger at Jenny and then herself. "But you know what? It's really him who is at fault. I won't say his name. It's him I'm extremely mad at. And guess what! Don't they get to live happily ever after—after my misery."

I followed her gaze as she looked around and then back at me as if she wanted to kill me. Anger blazed in her eyes.

"They are together, prancing around the city, making love—excuse me, fucking—while I sit here at this fucking ugly place, slowly dying inside." The expression in her eyes changed to pain, and for a split second I thought she was going to cry, but she then looked straight ahead and erased all her emotions from her face. "Fuck it." She blinked a few times to stop the tears, and I felt so bad for her. "Sorry, I don't know why I just told a complete stranger about my sorrowful love life." She stopped talking and studied the band, seeming determined to not look at me. Then after a minute, she faced me. "You were going to say?"

What *could* I say after that confession? I shrugged my shoulders. "Nothing."

Serena
Girl meets boy...

After running into Teddy, I felt off-balance, distracted. He was right there in the same club as me, but I felt this tug toward Ben, this sexual attraction I couldn't deny. Teddy must have felt the connection between Ben and me as well, and that look in his eyes scared me shitless. No one had ever looked at me the way Teddy did. A part of me wanted to run over to him. Another part wanted to be with Ben. I decided to stay where I was.

It should have felt right. It should have felt like I had no choice but to go talk to Teddy. I should have walked on over to him, pushed aside the gorgeous brunette with those scary eyes he was talking to, and said, *"Let's get out of here."* Especially since he'd pretty much confessed that after five years he still couldn't stop thinking about me. Five years? I had felt the same way— up until tonight. Ben sent sexual shivers through me that I wanted to explore further.

Ben grinned. "Do you want to dance?"

Why wouldn't Ben give up on dancing with me? Amongst the partygoers dancing, Elsa and Eddie were all over each other. It was more like dirty dancing. I was not in the mood.

"Uh, no thanks."

He saw where my line of vision went and smirked. "Not like them."

"I told you earlier, I don't dance to this music."

"If you let yourself go, maybe you could."

"I do not let myself go," I said, but I didn't really believe that, and the uncertainty came out in my voice.

Ben smiled and, moving like a jaguar, came closer to me. "I'd like to see you letting go."

A deep frisson skittered from the bottom of my spine up to my nape. It was Ben's accent that completely got me. I didn't move. We were standing so close now, and the music was too loud. We had to practically shout into each other's ears to be heard, but his last sentence was said low, and his lips almost touched my earlobe.

"I don't know if you would like that side of me," I said.

"So there is another side to you. I knew it." He pulled back to look at me. A gleam danced in his eyes, and his dimples were pronounced.

"Isn't there to everyone?" I asked, trying to conceal my embarrassment at what I'd just said to him.

"Not so sure about that. With me, what you see is what you get. I don't hide any part of myself, because I really don't give a fuck what people think, except my mum." He winked, and then his tone sharply changed. "Serena, we live in a world where we have to continuously put up a front. A front for your boss, a front for your mother, father, lover, sister, friends… What are people so fuckin' scared of?"

"Getting hurt," I replied, exhaling a breath.

He remained silent, mulling over my response, then said, "I suppose you're right. Getting hurt is a major motivation for not telling the truth, for putting up a front, for pretending to not be looking at that guy across the room, who can't stop staring at you. I get it. He's an ex.

I could tell there was something there."

Ben looked directly at me as I took a swig of my beer and then sputtered it all over my top.

"You okay?" His eyes were full of concern. "I'll get you a napkin." He quickly caught the barmaid's attention and within seconds produced some napkins.

I tried to digest what he had said. He had noticed. Shit! That had been so rude of me. I suspected he was offended, but he was so sweet for getting me a napkin so fast, so quick to attend to my needs. I liked the way that made me feel.

"Thanks." I wiped the beer off my top, then eyed him closely wondering what he thinks of this situation. "An ex?"

"Yes. That or a ghost, given the look on your face when you were talking to him."

"He's not an ex. I hardly know him." My gaze focused on my wet top, doing my best to clean off the stain.

"It didn't look that way to me." He withdrew from me a bit.

What could I tell him? That I'd met Teddy once, and not even? That would sound so stupid and immature. I had to stop looking at Teddy.

"Ben, are you interested in me?" *Why did I just ask that?*

"Very much so." He came closer again and looked deep into my eyes. "From the moment I first saw you, you excited me. I would really like to see you again," he said bluntly and so comfortably.

I did want to see him again. The more I looked at him, the better-looking he became. The more words we exchanged, the more his gaze entrapped mine. He had eyes only for me. He made me feel secure, wanted, needed. He made me feel as if there were no other girls around.

"Oh," I said in a low voice, averting his gaze and my emotions at the same time. He was so forthcoming, so willing to tell me how he felt… No man had ever spoken to me so openly.

"You're not so sure, are you now?" he said, and a tingling sensation whipped through me.

"It's not that. I just didn't expect to meet anybody tonight, especially here, and I meet you. And I do like you, despite everything." What the heck did I say? Did that even make sense? Why couldn't I just say yes? Why did I have to complicate matters?

"Despite everything?" He cocked an eyebrow. "What is that supposed to mean?"

"I don't know what I mean. Despite the fact that you are different from any man I've ever met." That sounded smart. "In a good way, in an inviting way," I added, brushing the hair out of my face. "I guess what I'm saying is, I *would* like to see you again." There, I had made my decision.

"That came out in a roundabout way," Ben said, grinning. "You had me scared there for a second." He spoke a little loudly in my ear now. "Serena, I'm not as tough as I appear. I'm just a guy talking to a beautiful, stunning woman. It's plain and simple." He moved in even closer. "Plus, I'm dying to find out what your manuscript is about."

"It's not erotica." I laughed, loving the way he managed to get that part in. "It's a love story in an urban fantasy setting," I said reluctantly.

"Wow! That took me by surprise. Vampires?"

"And werewolves, shifters, fairies, and other surprises."

"Incredible! I love that!" He looked excited. I guessed that was a genre he really liked. "Can I read it?"

"No!"

"Why not?"

"I'm not ready to show it to anyone yet."

"Serena, you have to if you ever want to publish it." He took a sip of his beer, examining me. "Can you do me a favor?"

"What?" I started to feel more at ease.

"Go to my website, and read some excerpts from my books. Then email me what you think."

"What's your website?" Now I got excited.

"It's my pen name dot com."

I giggled. "Amour?" The beer was starting to affect me.

"Yes. Amour. Check out my writing, and then you can decide if you'd like to share your writing with me." His gaze rested on my lips for a few seconds.

"What's your real last name?" I asked.

"It's Dunstan. Ben Dunstan. Now, doesn't Domenic S. Amour sound more glamorous?" He grinned. "What's your last name?"

"Photine, with a 'ph,' which I pretty much have had to explain to people my whole life. Everyone writes it with an 'f.' My dad was Greek, and my mom is English."

"Cool. Serena Photine. It sounds French."

"I know. It's easy to pronounce in French."

"So, promise me you will check out my website, Serena Photine."

I nodded. "I will." *As soon as I get home*, I wanted to say, but kept my mouth shut.

"Thanks. It gets pretty raunchy, so prepare yourself."

I smiled. "I'm not as innocent as I look."

"I never said you looked innocent, especially with those boots you're wearing. You have no idea what I've been thinking about—in terms of your boots, that is."

Ben's gaze traveled up and down my body, and I took a quick breath as I noticed his biceps under the sleeves of his T-shirt and his strong legs through his jeans. *He must work out. His body is so perfect.*

I gave him a seductive smile. "And to think I didn't want to go out tonight…"

"Aren't you glad you did?"

"Yes, but—" I felt a slap on my back.

"So, you two, I see you're getting along famously." Eddie slurred his words and almost fell between us. His eyes were bloodshot and his breath smelled of beer and cigarettes. I pulled back.

"Hey, sis! Still here?" Elsa came stumbling over, all sweaty from dancing. Did she actually think I'd left? "So, I guess we're not going to Crescent Street?" she joked.

"Crescent Street?" Ben smirked, looking from Elsa to Eddie to me, his dark eyes inquisitive. He didn't miss a beat.

"Yes, my sister said that if she was bored, we would have to go to a bar on Crescent, but since she hasn't been complaining, I guess we're staying."

Her drunkenness was quite evident to me by now. Elsa looked at Ben and winked.

"So, Elsa, you really *did* have to drag her here?" Ben asked while not taking his eyes off me.

"Drag? You don't know the half of it! Beg is more

the word. And don't forget, I had to dress her!"

Turning away from Ben's intense stare to exhale, I gave Elsa a dirty look, and she covered her mouth, realizing how what she'd said sounded. Just then Eddie popped into the conversation. I hadn't realized he'd been following it.

"Elsa, babe, I don't think your sister needs any help in the fashion department. She has her own distinct style." Eddie to the rescue.

Ben watched for my reaction the whole time. I knew because I felt his gaze on me, but I didn't turn back to him until he said, "I do so love her boots."

He was grinning, obviously sensing my uncomfortable state. I caught his gaze lingering on my legs, and a wave of dizziness came over me. It was probably the beer. I had lost count of how many I'd had, and with the way Ben was looking at me right now, I had to escape his intense stare.

"Excuse me. I have to go to the ladies' room." My body was reacting to Ben. His stare was making me weak. I wanted to wrap my arms around him and pull him close. My body wasn't ready for this. I hadn't even thought about Teddy. Ben had managed to get my mind off him.

"Would you like me to accompany you?" Ben asked all serious, every ounce of flirtatiousness gone. Accompany? I liked that word.

"No, thank you. I'm quite capable of getting there by myself," I said, trying to look steady on my feet. Eddie and Elsa were already back on the dance floor. I spun on my heels and walked toward the Toilet sign, trying with all my might to keep a straight line. Shit. I was tipsy.

I went to the washroom, and as soon as I came out, I felt a strong hand on my shoulder.

"Are you all right?" It was Ben. His eyes were full of concern.

"I'm fine," I lied. "I think I'm ready to go home now. I have to find my sister."

"Your sister won't want to leave. I'll take you home," he said, his voice insistent and dominating.

"You?"

"Yes, me. I promise I won't do anything you don't want me to." He studied me.

"Okay, take me home." The room was spinning. Suddenly it hit me—I was drunk. Shit. Ben was taking me home. I had to get it together.

As we said our good-byes to Elsa and Eddie and walked toward the club's exit, I saw that Teddy was deep in conversation with the witchy brunette. He didn't even notice me leaving, and that immediately angered me. Here I was, leaving with Ben, and there he was with another woman. She was more of a brunette bombshell. She caught my eye, looked at me as if she knew who I was, and then glared at me territorially.

I quickly grabbed Ben's arm in case I fell into a wall. I liked the way his arm felt. It made me feel safe, a feeling I had long forgotten. I couldn't remember ever feeling this way next to a man.

Teddy
Boy meets girl…

After Melina told me about her ex-boyfriend hooking up with her best friend, I wasn't about to reveal my story of being in love with someone I didn't even know and who was standing in the same room, falling for a guy right before my very eyes. Had all these years of waiting for Serena been some crazy fantasy? Was I just a fuckin' hopeless romantic?

Melina looked at me. "Are you sure you have nothing to say? It sure seemed to me you had something to say about you and"—she pointed toward Serena—"her."

I couldn't believe she actually pointed at her. Hadn't Melina's parents ever taught her it was impolite to point?

"Actually, there is no story to tell. I only just met her tonight. I saw her once before a few years ago, but it doesn't matter."

Melina studied me. I felt like a complete buffoon, swaying nervously from one foot to the other, trying to hide the attraction I had for Serena.

"I think it matters to *you*. I think it matters a whole hell of a lot more than you're willing to admit. I don't know you. Actually, I don't think I want to get to know any man for a very long time. I've lost all my trust in men because of Fucker. That's what I call him. Capital 'F.'"

She looked truly pissed now. Her anger was so evident, and for some unknown reason, it excited me.

"I don't ever say his name," she went on. "As for my so-called friend, she's known to me as Cunt with a capital 'C.'"

I burst out laughing. I'd never met a woman who spoke or swore like that. And she was a grade school teacher! Her bluntness was refreshing, and I liked it, but above all, her sexy body was enticing me more and more.

"I hate men," she continued. "If I were you, Teddy, I would end this conversation now."

I glanced at Dan and Jenny. They were laughing, having a blast. Their arms were on each other's shoulders, and they looked pretty intimate.

"My friend Jenny loves men. Do you know why?" Venom laced Melina's voice.

"Why?" I anticipated another crazy answer, but I was captivated by her attitude and the way she expressed herself.

"Because she doesn't trust them long enough to go on a third date. She says two dates are enough, and she doesn't want to be with a guy long enough to break his heart. She says she loves them so much that she needs to protect them from her."

"Wait." I laughed. "She stops after *two* dates so she doesn't break *their* hearts? That's ingenious. She and Dan will get along very well. He's exactly the same way."

Melina peered over at them and smiled mischievously. "Perhaps."

For the second time that evening, I looked closely at Melina. She had a long, classical nose and a full lower lip, and there was an air about her, an energy I was drawn to. I was definitely attracted to her. She was a great conversationalist—she said exactly what was on her mind—and she was a spunky girl. Granted, an angry one too, but that made her even sexier. Sexy was definitely the word for her. When she did give me the occasional smile, I felt something stir inside me.

"You know that all men are not like Fucker." I grinned at the name.

She chuckled. "Oh, so *you* are the exception? Did you know that every boyfriend I've ever had has cheated on me? I always found out after the fact, but they all had that in common. I may only be twenty-five, but…" She counted on her fingers. "First, Joey, Italian Fucker number one, from sixteen to twenty. He was my first pathetic love. Cheated on me three times. Every time, I forgave him. Do you want to know what he told me when I broke up with him?"

I nodded. She was going to tell me anyway.

"We were parked in front of my house, where he made me feel like a piece of shit because he didn't know anything about what I wanted. He said I was a total bitch and that I'd deserved it!" She raised two fingers. "Number two two-timer. I went out with him from twenty-one till twenty-two. Two years of following him around, waiting in front of his house with Jenny to see if he was lying to me. Following him downtown and then losing him somehow. He drove me crazy! I would cry all the way home because I could never trust him, till finally, I caught him lying one too many times. And then Fucker." She held up three fingers. "Third one is a charm." She paused and looked straight ahead. "Fucker and Cunt broke my heart, and that, in a nutshell, is the story of my miserable love life."

No wonder she was so angry at men.

"If I were you," she continued, "I would seriously get as far away from me as possible. I don't like men at this point, and you are a man. Hence, I don't like you."

Well, there was my luck. I kept quiet. How could I reply to that? My thoughts were to tell her that my record with women sucked, but I was definitely not a cheater. I could have asked her why she'd picked these guys. There were so many things to say and ask her, but my mouth kept shut. She scared me a bit. As good-looking and smart as she was, her pain pushed me away. By sitting there quietly, she pretty much ignored me. Jenny and Dan were having the time of their lives, and across the room, Serena and Bald Guy were—heck, they weren't there anymore. I looked around for them. During my exchange with Melina, I'd lost track of them. I'd gotten lost in her story.

"Looking for your ex?" Melina asked me with a raised eyebrow.

"She's not my ex."

"Yeah right, she's not. I saw her leave with that gorgeous bald guy." Gorgeous? My heart pounded. She *left* with him? I thought she had just met him tonight. "I'm surprised you didn't notice," she added, raising her eyebrow again, and aggravation got the better of me.

"Look, I was actually listening to you, okay? I couldn't believe your luck with guys, and I felt bad for you, so yes, I lost track of everything else while being politely attentive to you and hearing all about *your* hatred of men."

Her eyebrows frowned. "I'm sorry to have ruined your night," she said, a wounded expression on her beautiful face.

"I didn't say that." I felt bad again. "Why are you putting words in my mouth?" Her distress was apparent. Was she fuckin' crazy?

"Teddy, you seem like a nice guy. If I were you, I would stay away from Good Girl and I'll-Rock-Your-World-Tonight Bad Boy. Stop moping over someone you've 'just met.'" She gave me an indignant look, then stood and nudged Jenny's shoulder. "Jen, I'm leaving," she said, avoiding my gaze.

She was leaving? Why didn't that surprise me?

"Hold on, Mel. I'm driving," Jenny said. "Let's stay a little longer. Come on." She pleaded with her eyes.

"Look, I really want to go. I'm not taking a fuckin' cab. It's going to cost me a fortune." Melina raised both hands in frustration. "I just want to go home," she said breathlessly, sounding as if she were giving up on everything.

I couldn't believe how she made me feel—frustrated one moment and sympathetic the next. She was getting under my skin in more ways than one. I was drawn to her and pissed at her the same time. I had never felt this way about a woman. I wanted to jump her bones, yet I wanted to run as far away as possible.

I stood and said to Jenny, "Look, why don't you and Dan stay, and I'll take Melina home? I'm ready to leave too. It all works out." I saw the twinkle of excitement in Dan's and Jenny's eyes, and I smiled to acknowledge it. "You two just enjoy your night."

I turned to Melina, who was tapping her foot and giving Jenny a dirty look. "I don't know…"

"I'm just offering," I said, honestly trying to be nice and to make up for being an asshole earlier.

Jenny interrupted us. "Excuse us one second."

She took Melina to the side and said something to her. Whatever it was, Melina seemed to put up a good argument. She was waving her hands around, and then she shot me a dirty look. Here I was, trying to be chivalrous, and she just looked irritated with me. Finally, she shrugged her shoulders and walked back to me.

"Let's go, Ted," she said with disdain. "I'll let you drive me home, but no funny business, got it?"

"It's Teddy."

"I like Ted better," she said, and walked off ahead of me.

I was beginning to think she was some kind of control freak.

Serena

Something strange happened on the way to my house…

"You want me to get onto *this*?"

I gaped in astonishment at the motorcycle and hesitated. I'd never been on one before. Ben looked amused as I stared at his legs straddling the bike. He seemed perfectly comfortable on it, but the outline of his muscular thighs in those tight jeans scared the living shit out of me. I wanted to touch them. Fuck! *Get a grip, Serena.* The booze had made me horny, but my inexperience in bed made me feel insecure. Ben appeared to know what he was doing. He could charm the pants off me with one lustful look. I also still felt off-balance from running into Teddy at the bar.

Ben had his hands on the handlebars, and he kick-started the bike in one sweeping motion that was so hot. He reached behind and grabbed two helmets, placing one on his head and handed me the other one.

"Snap it on. Let's go," he said, completely ignoring my reluctance.

"I don't know…"

"The fresh air will do you some good. Trust me."

"I've never been on a motorcycle before," I confessed shyly, trying to push my hair out of my face. The wind was gentle but constant.

He smiled, seeming to understand my hesitation

now. "Come here."

I took a step closer to the bike and bent down as he held out the helmet. He gently brushed the hair away from my face, and our eyes locked. Then, without even looking, he placed the helmet on my head and snapped it shut, jolting me out of my trance. His dark eyes enchanted me, and those lips…He was so gorgeous.

"Sit behind me, and hold on tight. Don't worry. I'll go slow."

His voice was pure seduction. I sat down behind him, straddling the seat but careful not to touch him. He took my arms and placed them around his waist.

"I don't want you to fall off," he said with concern as a bolt of electricity rushed through my veins.

Oh fuck. I was so close to him. I smelled his leather jacket and his cologne, the scent of a certain flower I couldn't quite place with a hint of wood. It was so masculine.

"Are you okay?" he asked, looking straight ahead, before adjusting his mirrors.

"Yes," I mumbled close to his ear.

"Where to?"

"The corner of Sherbrooke and Jeanne Mance, turn left, second apartment building on the right-hand side."

His two feet were on the road, and then he lifted one to the pedal. "Okay, here we go, love."

I inhaled his scent deeply to calm my nerves, but that didn't seem to help. Instead, it aroused a sensual stir inside of me. My dizziness was slowly fading, being replaced by horniness, as the wind hit my face and my body pressed against his.

We rode up a side street with no cars ahead. It felt like the street was all ours. Ben wasn't going too fast.

"Serena, are you sure you're fine?" he shouted over the roar of the bike. I hadn't realized how loud it could be.

"Yes," I shouted back.

We rode the rest of the way without speaking till we reached the lights at the corner of Sherbrooke Street. I felt so free and alive. I had always wanted to ride on a motorcycle. Ben turned and glanced at me

"Enjoying the ride?" he asked.

"Yes, I really am." The wind was helping to ease my dizziness.

"Do you want to go for a ride first and then I could drop you off? Are you up for it?" His eyes twinkled again like a young teenager's.

"Okay." I didn't want to let go of him or let the night end.

"Hold on, Serena. I'm going to go a little faster." We passed by my apartment building and headed down Park Avenue. "I love this city," he shouted.

The mountain was on our left. The autumn air chilled me a bit, but Ben's body heat was warming me up.

"I know," I shouted breathlessly, my mouth near his neck. I felt his body react to my words.

He turned left at the lights and headed toward Mount Royal's summit, where one could get a panoramic view of the city. I knew the spot. There were cars parked in every parking spot, but he found a place to park his bike. The sky was filled with stars, and the cool breeze surrounded us. He turned off the ignition, but I still held on to him tightly.

Ben laughed. "You can let go now. Were you scared?"

He gestured for me to get off first. I instantly let go of his waist and quickly dismounted, almost losing my balance. Still seated, he grabbed me and pulled me close to him.

"Are you okay?" he asked for what sounded like the tenth time.

"Why do you keep asking me that?" I said with annoyance. "I'm not drunk."

He kept his arm around my waist, giving no indication that he was going to let me go. I didn't move.

"Well, I want to make sure you're fine. You were wobbling in the club. I told you the fresh air would help."

Holding me tightly, he gazed at my lips. I pulled away, and he let go of me and got off his bike, casually swinging his leg over the motorcycle, not realizing how sexy he looked.

He was beautiful. A few girls turned their heads to look at him. He had such a perfect face. His nose was classically shaped, and his high cheekbones made him look Native American. His olive complexion was smooth, and those brown eyes were deadly. I tried to imagine him with hair but couldn't. The baldness made him look like a badass and a man who knew what he wanted. His height was what I liked the most. He looked around six feet tall. I was wearing my boots and he was still slightly taller.

"You can take off your helmet now." He smirked. He had a sense of humour—I gave him that. He took off his, and when I fumbled with mine, in one fluid motion he was in front of me, unsnapping it and carefully taking it off my head. "Watch your hair. I don't want to snag it," he said thoughtfully. He took the helmets and clipped them to the side of his bike. "Let's go see the beautiful city you come from," he said, turning toward me. "Beautiful girl, beautiful city." He narrowed his eyes, and I felt a surge of arousal, as if he had said *"let's go to bed"* or something like that. His voice was so intoxicating.

Ben took a step toward the lookout point, and I followed. At the first glimpse of Montreal, I let out a sigh. "Wow, I rarely come here."

"I always come here." He placed his hands in his jeans' pockets, looking for change, and pulled out a few coins. "Up close and personal," he said as he inserted the coins into the slot and rotated the binoculars into position. "You go first, Serena."

I bent to look into the eyepiece and placed my hands on the handles to shift it from left to right.

"See anything?"

"The Big O—the money pit," I joked.

"My turn." I stepped away from the binoculars and watched as he shifted them from left to right. I was thrilled that it gave me the chance to gawk at him without him knowing. The shape of his ass, sticking out like that, and the way he held the handles turned me on.

"See anything?" I asked, repeating his question.

He let go of the binoculars and looked directly at me. "Yes, Serena, I see something so amazing it makes the city lights seem dull. I see someone who takes my breath away. I'd much rather look at you."

He stepped closer to me and reached out to touch my hair. He tucked a few strands behind my ear, then rubbed my earlobe gently with his right hand. Tremors ran through my body upon his words and then his touch.

"I have to kiss you right now," Ben said, and he bent slightly.

I lifted my face toward his, powerless at this attraction and need to be kissed by him. He tilted his head to the left, and then I felt his lips ever so gently kiss mine. It was a brief kiss, but it spoke of many more to come, like the birthday wishes you'd get as a child. I wanted more, but it seemed like he didn't. A slight shiver rippled through me, and I took a quick step back.

"That was so nice. I love the feel of your lips." His eyes filled with passion, and I knew he wanted me. "Can I do that again?" he asked in a husky voice.

"Yes," I managed to say weakly as I felt a surge of adrenaline between my legs.

This time he opened his mouth, and I opened mine in return to feel his sweet tongue flicker urgently against mine. His hands brushed my hair aside as he cupped my face closer to his. I wrapped my arms around his neck and immediately felt his energy. My pussy quivered, and blood rushed through my veins. I said his name over and over in my head. *Ben. Ben. Ben.* It was a never-ending kiss—we couldn't stop. Then, in unison, we closed our lips and opened our eyes. Fire filled with sexuality danced in his, and he must have seen the same in mine. He bent to kiss my neck.

"I want you so much." His voice was hoarse, needy.

His breath against my skin sent bolts of excitement up and down my hungry body. I hadn't had sex in so long that I thought I was going to explode right there.

"I want to take you home…" He spoke into my neck, this time in a sultry voice. "I want to be inside you."

"Take me home," I said breathlessly. "Let's go."

Ben quickly grabbed my hand and led me to his bike. The houses and streets whizzed by us, and all the while I felt the heat generating from our bodies. *"I want to be inside you."* The way he'd said those words drove me crazy. Nobody had ever said that to me before.

I'd just met him. I'd never had sex with guys like this before. What if I was no good at it? He would know I'm inexperienced. Plus, he wrote erotica, so he was probably great in bed. Was I still drunk? Probably somewhat, yet I was still sober enough to let him come over and fuck me all night long—or at least I thought I was.

"We're here," he said, placing his feet on the pavement and shutting off the ignition.

I got off his motorcycle, and insane thoughts ran through my mind. *He's too hot for me. I can't possibly sleep with this gorgeous man...* I was flustered—and weak, dizzy, definitely drunk—as I planted my feet unsteadily onto the pavement. Oh yes, I knew I wasn't thinking straight. He waited for me to say something. I couldn't speak. He got off his motorcycle and stood before me, his tall, beautiful body an invitation, his dark eyes examining me, arousing me.

"Serena, shall we end the night like this? It's up to you. I've told you what I want."

I had to say something. I wanted him, but felt intimidated by him. He leaned in close to me and seemed to understand my ambivalence.

"Ben, I've never done this before. I've never brought home a man I've just met. I'm not the one-night stand type of girl. I don't think I'm ready. As much as I want to, I can't."

He nodded. "I know. I can see you're hesitant, but I can also see that your body is reacting to me." He leaned on one leg and spoke slowly, taking me in with every core of his body, arousing me with just one look. "Can I have your number? I need to see you again."

Need. *He* needs *to see me again.*

"431-262-5555."

He repeated the number a few times." Thank you for the ride. I really had a good time."

"It was such a pleasure to meet you," he said, looking me up and down. I felt this pounding in my sex. "I loved every moment I spent with you, Serena. This was a memorable night because I met you."

He gave me a kiss on each cheek. Catching a whiff of his musky cologne, I almost wrapped my arms around his neck. Instead, I kissed his cheeks too and felt his rough skin against my lips. In that brief moment, I knew I had to see him again. Like a perfect gentleman, he pulled back, and then he got onto his bike and started the engine.

"I'll watch that you get safely to the door," he said, showing no emotion on his face. He was serious, his desire no longer apparent.

"Goodnight," I said quietly, a stirring erupting inside of me. I walked to the front door, fumbling for the keys. As soon as I inserted the key, I turned around to wave. He waved back and sped off. He was smiling, radiant like a star. I wanted to shout *wait, come back,* but he was gone.

That night, I dreamed of Ben kissing me till dawn, kissing me deeply while I lay on my bed. I felt his tongue inside my mouth, on my neck, on my nipples. My body responded to his touch, and when I awoke, I was wet. Oddly enough, though, the first person I thought of was Teddy.

I didn't understand. I *couldn't* understand. Maybe my soul mate wasn't my soul mate after all, but someone from my past life. Like in that movie *Café de Flo-re*, with Vanessa Paradis, who fell in love with her son from a past life, and then her son met his true soul mate, and he left Vanessa's character heartbroken. I cried like a baby watching that movie. Maybe Teddy had been my son in a past life and Ben was my soul mate. Or maybe vice versa.

Snap out of it, Serena. I was overanalyzing things again.

I couldn't wait to hear Ben's voice again. He made me believe in more than just soul mates. He made me feel alive. I wanted to be naked with him. I wanted to feel his body next to mine and have his scent linger on me. I wanted him to touch me. I wanted him deep inside me. I wanted to discover what real sex was all about.

My time of awakening was now. I felt it.

Teddy
Sweet as sugar, tough as nails…

My sister once had a black T-shirt that read "Sweet as Sugar" on the front in cute pink writing and "Tough as Nails" on the back in white gothic script. Melina reminded me of that T-shirt. She was the epitome of that expression.

"Don't get any funny ideas," she said as I opened my jeep door for her. Candy wrappers littered the back seat, empty squeeze juice boxes occupied the coffee holders, and crumbs speckled the floor mats. She peered at me suspiciously, as if to say, *Do you drink from those?* And then worse, *Do you have kids?*

"Melina, lighten up. Excuse the mess," I said, huffing. Her distrustful looks and defensive attitude were really beginning to aggravate me.

"I know what you're thinking. Just because I'm in your car, you might think I'm easy, but I'm not. So don't think it's because of your good looks." All this before I had put the key in the ignition.

Hold on, did she just say good looks? I didn't react, pretending that girls always called me good looking. I started the car and turned to sneak a quick peek at her. She was looking out the window with what appeared to be a frustrated expression on her face. Why? All these guessing games were making me apprehensive.

I stared at her profile. Her dark hair curled into her

cheek, and suddenly, this urge came over me to touch her on the exact spot where her hair met her face. Looking straight ahead, in case she caught me looking at her, and I shook my head slightly, telling myself to focus on driving. Even if I wanted to sleep with her, she'd made it quite clear she wasn't interested. Taking her home and never seeing her again was in the cards.

I turned to look at her again and noticed how her breasts were just the perfect size for my hands. *Oh shit.* Blood rushed to my cock and fucking her was the only thing on my mind at that moment. I wanted to hear her moan and see her writhe in ecstasy. Somehow, she managed to excite me and piss me off at the same time. I had never met anybody like her, and my emotions were confusing me. I wanted her sex right in the palm of my hand.

She turned to me with a questioning look. "Why are you shaking your head like that?" Her gaze darted everywhere in the car.

At the start of the car engine, the radio turned on as well. Playing was Van Morrison's "Someone Like You," a song that got to me every time with its heart-wrenching lyrics.

"I'm just tired," I replied, trying to focus on the road and ignore my cock. It settled down as the music played, and I instantly thought of Serena. The clock on my dashboard read two-thirty in the morning.

"It's her, right? Your ex?" Melina blurted.

Why would she ask me that? Why would she care my thoughts were on Serena? Unless…*unless* she was actually jealous and she did want me to fuck her. Before I could answer, she continued her interrogation.

"Do you have kids?"

112

I was floored. How the fuck did her mind work? Then she gave me a stern look and pondered which question to answer. I ran my hands through my hair and burst out laughing.

"Melina, before I shift gears to drive, let me make myself clear."

She turned her whole body toward me and crossed her legs, showing me a glimpse of her thighs. The view threw me completely off balance, and I stopped talking as the blood rushed straight to my cock again. *Oh fuck!*

"Yes? I'm waiting, Ted."

"I am not married, nor do I have a girlfriend. I am neither a liar nor a cheater. Hence, I am probably not your type."

I should have kept my mouth shut, but it was too late. The words just came out—loudly. She was getting the better of me, and I couldn't help the irritation from slipping into my voice.

"These juice boxes belong to my nieces, just for your information. And I am driving you home because I offered to, to make sure you get there safe and sound, not to get in your pants. When I do get you there, I will say goodnight—without trying to kiss you. And no, she is not my ex."

I wondered if I'd answered all her questions. My annoyance rose. That last remark about Serena was clear that I was available but not interested in her. Although my cock was thinking otherwise. That constant fucking battle between my two heads.

Melina listened quietly to everything, the tension in the air. From the corner of my eye, I could see she was looking straight ahead. My indifference and overreaction was my defense mechanism. I just wanted to get her home, out of my car, and then go home to whack off.

"Are you actually speechless?" I asked incredulously.

She didn't say another word, and when I finally pulled out and onto the road, she just robotically guided me to her apartment building while Van Morrison sang on in the background. I was angry at her for being so hostile, and angry at myself for behaving the same way. I'd never been so rude to a girl I had just met.

She opened the window slightly and took in a breath of fresh air. "Ted, I think I might owe you an apology." She seemed nervous now, playing with her fingers, as my eyes glanced at her from the side, tilting my head a tad and then swiftly looking back at the road. "I hate men right now," she continued, "and since you're a man, you're bearing the brunt of that. I don't believe in exceptions. I've been hurt too often."

She bent her head down and looked at her hands, and I felt a pull toward her vulnerability. Her body language said it all—no matter how tough she sounded, it was clear that inside she was in pain.

"Melina, those assholes give good guys like me a bad name. If Dan were here, he would say you give love a bad name." I chuckled, trying to make light of the situation.

She still looked serious but lifted her head and grinned.

"Did I just see the beginnings of a smile?"

"Turn here." She pointed to a side street. "Hold on! You're going to miss it!"

I swerved the car and just barely managed to make the turn. We both swayed to the left along with the car.

"That's my place. Two twenty-seven. I almost

missed it!"

"Where?" I asked, slowing down.

"The ugly brown door."

"Circa 1970?" I joked.

"Yes, that's the one. My thoughts exactly, but I think it gives the building character."

"Wow. I think that's the most positive thing you've said all night."

I parked the car in front of her building. As she laughed at my comment, feeling like the walls around her was suddenly coming down. *Maybe I* do *have a chance with her.* She unfastened her seat belt. *What should I say now?* She grabbed her purse and held it tightly on her lap but showed no sign of getting ready to leave. The DJ was talking, and we sat there listening.

"I like this DJ," she said. "He has a relaxing voice."

"Yeah, me too. When I can't sleep, I listen to the radio." I leaned back against the head-rest.

"Why can't you sleep?"

I turned and looked at her, trying to understand why she would even care. She seemed to really want to know. She had her seatbelt off, but wasn't leaving. Was she trying to get to know me? *I can't sleep because I'm always so horny,* I wanted to say, but didn't. I had thought we were just going to say our goodbyes and fuck-offs, but her attitude seemed to have changed, and again my eyes wandered all over her body, visions of her naked in my car. She caught my look but didn't turn away.

"Because I think too much in the middle of the night," I finally replied. My cock swelled.

Then *the song* came on—"Crazy on You" by Heart.

"I love this song!" we said in unison.

"Have you seen *The Virgin Suicides*?" she asked, her eyes gleaming with excitement. She bent one leg under herself and turned toward me. At the sight of her legs again, my body reacted, and I unbuckled my seatbelt, my erection growing by the second.

"I read the book, but the movie was much better. I know which scene you're referring to." The air in the car grew a little thick as I looked at her lips.

"I've always wanted to replay that scene," she said in a low voice.

With me? I wanted to ask. Obviously with me. There was no one else in the car. I remembered the exact part of the song when Josh Hartnett and Kirsten Dunst had kissed. We listened quietly to the song for a few seconds, staring at each other.

This was my chance. I *actually* had a shot with her, and here I'd thought I had no chance in hell. I was sure she hated me. Though Melina was a distraction from Serena, I wanted her badly, imagining her sweet pussy on my throbbing cock. Her mixed signals were killing me.

I looked at her, and she looked at me. We waited. The sexual tension between us was palpable. Her breasts heaved up and down with every breath as she seductively licked her lips—slowly, deliberately, invitingly— tempting my manhood. And that was it. Before I knew it, I had pulled her to me, my hands entangled in her hair, and my lips on her mouth. It was a kiss full of anger and need, our tongues in a duel. She was on my lap, her hands in my hair too, and kissing me hard.

The song went on and on as long as our kiss did, and when it ended, we slowly pulled away from each other, panting for air. Oxygen. My blood was boiling for her, and my mouth was sore from the kiss.

"Oh my God." I tried to catch my breath.

Melina leaned over and opened her door. I shut off the car engine, jerked the keys out of the ignition, and then opened my door too. I got out of the car and ran across to the passenger side to help her out.

"I don't know what came over me," she said, her eyes still full of lust and want.

"This." I kissed her again, up against my car, with the door wide open. I wrapped my hands around her waist to steady her—it was a tiny waist too—and she placed her knee on the car seat to hold herself up.

Then she pulled away. "Come inside," she whispered authoritatively.

I moved back, and she stepped in front of me. Slamming the car door with my foot, I pulled her toward me to kiss her again. I felt her heat through my jeans and rubbed my body against hers. She moaned, and I thought I'd explode right there. I was so hot for her. Still kissing, we took a few steps together toward her front door, doing a sort of dance and stumbling over our feet. She reached into her purse and pulled out keys.

When Melina turned to her front door, I pressed my body behind her and pushed my full-blown erection against her ass. She thrust her ass out toward my cock while fumbling with her keys.

"Oh, that feels so good," I whispered into her ear. Pulling her hair to the side, I kissed the back of her neck. She shivered slightly and, moaning, leaned back on me. She smelled like strawberries.

"Yes, Ted, that feels so fucking good."

Like a vulture, my hands around her waist again while she unlocked the door. We stepped inside a tiny foyer, and she fit another key into the lock of a second door. I continued kissing her neck, this time flicking my tongue into her ear. She let out another moan that went straight to my cock.

We stepped into the hallway, and the glass door shut behind us. She pointed toward the elevator. Stepping inside, she pressed the button to go up. Patience went out the window. I pulled her close, kissed her, and then pushed her against the wall with my body. At the sound of the elevator ringing, I placed my hands on her skirt to lift it up.

"I want to see you naked." I was almost delirious with desire.

The door opened.

"Soon enough, big boy." She smiled and pulled me out of the elevator.

In her quiet hallway, I backed her into the wall again and nudged her legs open with my knee. My fingers traveled high up her thigh in search of her panties, but all I felt was soft skin and then a firm ass with no underwear. My hard-on throbbed, and all I could think of was fucking her madly.

"You're not wearing any underwear." I got even harder, if that were possible, and could have come right there and then.

She gave me a sultry look and grabbed my cock through my jeans. "Good observation, teach." She smiled again. "We're here," she whispered and pulled away. "Follow me."

Her boldness coupled with her suggestive tone unleashed something inside me—a mad desire to instantly be inside her. She was so fucking sexy my mind was dizzy as her ass wiggled seductively, all I wanted to do was fill her up with my cock.

Holding her keys, she led me down a long corridor and then turned left. My erection was so hard, walking was difficult. She stopped in front of door number 107. Reaching from behind her, I hungrily caressed her breasts through her blouse. She let out a slight moan while unlocking the door, and then we stepped into her apartment, the both of us breathless.

"Don't move," Melina whispered and shut her front door. She slowly pulled down her skirt and then her blouse and bra, while my legs stood motionless. She left her shoes on. "Do you like what you see?" she asked, tilting her head slightly, making sure I got a good, clear view of her stark nakedness.

"Yes, I do. I want you so badly."

"Then what are you waiting for?"

I quickly removed my shoes and socks, then pulled off my pants, T-shirt, and underwear. We both stood there, completely naked and utterly horny, at the entrance of her living room.

"Follow me." Melina turned to her right.

I looked in that direction and saw her bedroom at the end of a short passageway. I slowly followed but didn't touch her at first—the way she purposely swayed her firm, round, naked ass had me mesmerized. Then I took a few quick steps, grabbed her from behind, and held on to her the rest of the way into her bedroom.

She stopped two feet from her bed. Everything in the room was dark—the walls, the bedspread, the furniture. Just one tiny lit lamp gave the room an exotic ambiance. Caressing her body from top to bottom, and then, as if reading each other's minds, we took a giant leap and landed on the bed, her facedown beneath me. I cupped her gorgeous ass, kissing her nape, and then slowly turned her over.

She spread her legs in invitation. Her pussy was a work of art, and when my hand touched it, her wetness all but shot another pang of lust through me. Without even thinking, my fingers pounded inside her.

"Does that feel good, baby?" I asked as my tongue flicked around her taut, pink nipples. Eyes closed, she moved her head from side to side, slowing down my pace, plunging my fingers in and out of her creamy pussy while sucking hard on her nipples.

She thrust her hips up and down. "Don't stop, teach. That's it. Feel my pussy. Suck my nipples harder," she said through stuttered breaths.

Her words drove me crazy. I did exactly as she said and sucked those nipples like I'd never sucked before.

"Harder!"

I sucked even harder, and felt her pussy contract around my fingers. Shit, she was going to come.

"I want to fuck you now," I mumbled into her breasts, and she lifted my head. She kicked off her shoes as my mouth continued licking them while looking deep into her sexy eyes. "You taste delicious."

"I've been ready to fuck you since our first kiss in the car," she said in a low, raspy voice.

"Yes." I pushed my hair out of my face, then teased her pussy with my cock, placing it at her opening, slowly rubbing it against her clit. At the feel of her wetness, my dick wanted to ram right into her, but held back. Her moans grew louder as her body writhed against mine. The way she was loving it made me hornier; how she wanted it so badly, how she wanted to just get fucked. She wrapped her arms around me. I had her pinned under me, one forearm on each side of her, and we ground our hips against each other's.

In ecstasy, she closed her eyes, laid her head back, and groaned. "I think I'm in heaven."

I grinned. "Open your eyes, Melina." When she did, they were a wicked blue and sexually charged. "Your eyes are out of this world"—I moaned—"just like your body." I continued to thrust my cock against her slit, her wetness driving me nuts.

"That feels…so fuckin'…*good*."

"I've only just begun."

My mouth found her nipples again and languidly kissed them, making her cry out in a desperate moan. I reached down between her legs and pumped two fingers in and out of her wet lips. She writhed and sighed loudly. My body moved down even lower, spread her diamond-shaped pussy with both my hands and leaned in. Blowing on it, my cock throbbed harder when she groaned even louder, flicking my tongue through her sweet juices. She was delirious by now, shouting. Did the whole apartment building hear her? Not caring who heard, my hands reached over and grabbed her ass, pulled her closer to me, and plunged my tongue deep inside her. Her breathing quickened, and again, realizing she was going to come, I came up for air and pulled myself up to her open mouth. I wanted her to come while we fucked—hard—but she suddenly, violently, grabbed me and flipped me over.

"I'm not ready to come, teach. I'll tell you when I'm ready. Now it's my turn. Don't move," she said authoritatively.

She went straight for my dick. She licked the head a few times and then, with her mouth wide open, swallowed it. As she moved her mouth up and down, I let out a wild moan. She took me in so deep, feeling the back of her throat. She was incredible. Obviously, she wanted to be the boss, and it was easy to let her. She wanted to wait for her orgasm, and that excited me even more.

"Oh fuck, you're driving me crazy," I said, losing control.

Melina lifted her head to peek up at me. Her tousled hair fell all around her face, her breasts pressed against my legs, and her glorious ass sticking up in the air.

"I've only just begun." She repeated my words with a wicked grin, and the look of lust in her eyes pierced through me. She rubbed her wet pussy on my thigh, pushing me to my limit.

"I can't take it. I want you."

She immediately stopped moving. "Me too. Hold on." She leaned toward her night table, opened the drawer, and pulled out a foil packet with the word *One* on it. "Protection," she said matter-of-factly and pulled out a condom.

I thought of U2's song "One," and suddenly my thoughts were all fucked up, thinking of songs and music.

She ripped open the packet and placed the condom onto my cock. Then, as quick as a racehorse, Melina climbed on top of me and glided my dick inside her. She thrust down on me hard and moaned loudly, holding on to her hips, loving the sensation.

She began to fuck me faster and faster, and then she took my hands in hers. "Squeeze my nipples," she said.

She's a wild one! Like a real-life porn star. I'm fucking a porn star!

As I squeezed her nipples as hard as I could, I felt I was going to come. I guessed she'd sensed it too, because then she asked, "You're ready?"

"Yes!" I shouted.

"Yes. Yes! Harder!" she yelled and then moaned, "I'm coming…"

My cock reacted strongly, throbbing as she thrust herself vigorously on me, I did the same, meeting her movements halfway, and I exploded along with her.

"Oh my God." I was still squeezing her nipples while I shouted, "Yes! Yes, baby…"

She tore herself off my cock and landed next to me on the mattress. "Don't call me baby, Ted." Her voice had instantly returned to normal.

"Don't call me Ted," I replied, out of breath, annoyed at her sudden coldness.

Melina immediately got off the bed and looked around as if in search of her clothes, which were still in the entrance of her apartment. She stomped out of the bedroom.

I felt so uncomfortable lying naked on her bed. I had just come, so I couldn't move. It was three thirty in the morning, and all I wanted to do was close my eyes and sleep, not fight. I heard her in the living room, and then she stormed back into the bedroom. With fire in her eyes, she threw my clothes next to me on the bed.

"Teddy, can you get dressed, please? I don't cuddle," she said flatly, her blue eyes devoid of emotion in the dim light.

"Are you serious?" Feeling weak, I got up and grabbed my clothes.

"Do I look like I'm joking?" The anger rose in her voice once again.

"You're throwing me *out*?" I couldn't believe it. Hadn't we just had hot sex? It was the best sex *I'd* ever had.

She was fully dressed, wearing the same pencil skirt and black blouse, but now barefoot. I pulled on my jeans, wanting to run out of her apartment, and scanned the room. Everything was so organized. I zipped up my jeans. Her delicate-looking perfume bottles were placed neatly on a mirrored tray with intricate detailing. I put on my T-shirt and noticed how immaculate the room was. No sign of dust or messiness anywhere. I put on my socks and couldn't get the image of Melina without underwear out of my head. One minute she was so hot and warm, and the next minute she was cold and aloof. What had triggered such a reaction? Was it because I said *baby* in a moment of passion? Had her exes called her *baby*? Of course, they had. Everyone said *baby*.

"Can I at least use your washroom before I leave?" I really had to go and couldn't hold it.

"Through there." She pointed to the hallway, not even looking at me. "Second door."

"Okay."

I opened the second door on my right and walked into the cleanest bathroom I'd ever seen. It was old-fashioned, with tiny tiles from the sixties, but Melina had added a bronze finish to the walls to match the beige color. I peed right away and instinctively wanted to open all her drawers and cupboards to see if I could figure her out. But that would have been intrusive; plus, it would have made too much noise. What if the cabinet doors creaked?

I smelled my hands. Her scent was still on me, and right away I was hard again. *Fuck!* Turning on the faucet and washing my hands with the vanilla soap on the vanity, and then drying my hands with her beige towel, the sound of the door shutting made me realize how quiet it had become. The apartment was silent.

I walked into the living room, and there she was. Melina was sitting on the couch, eating an apple and bobbing her leg. She looked at me but said nothing. Her eyes revealed nothing.

"I guess this is good-bye, then," I said. "Melina, how was I offensive?"

She sat there staring at me, taking a bite out of her Granny Smith. "Would you like an apple?" she asked, completely ignoring my two statements.

Did she want me to stay or leave? "Um, no thanks."

"It's really juicy." She licked her lips while checking out my fully dressed body. What the fuck? Was she crazy?

Melina stood, holding the apple in one hand and chewing slowly. "You didn't offend me. Fucker called me baby while we had sex, and I *never* want *anyone* to call me baby again. That's all." Her eyes remained cold, expressionless, unreadable. "Now you know."

I didn't move, trying to figure her out, but it would probably take a long, long time to figure out someone like Melina. She was definitely intriguing, and the way she just sat there excited me in the strangest way. *Crunch. Crunch.* I watched her mouth as she chewed and imagined those lips on my cock again. She must have seen it in my eyes. I was fully erect now, the blood rushing straight to my dick. She glanced at my crotch and gave me a wicked smile. All I could think about was fucking her again. Even if she seemed to be a crazy bitch, why not fuck her one more time, I thought. It wasn't like

I was going to see her again.

"Teddy, if you want out, you should leave now. My door is unlocked. But if you want more of what I have…" She stretched her legs out on the couch, and as she began touching her breasts, she gestured for me to take a bite of her apple. "Would you like an apple now?"

She looked like a goddess. My body went from angry to wanting in one moment. My cock shouted, *Yes! Yes!* while my mind said, *Get the fuck out. She's a crazy bitch.*

Once again, my cock won the argument.

I walked over to her and took a bite of the apple. "What are you doing to me, Melina?" I asked as I swallowed the sweet-tart fruit. "I want you again."

"So come and get it, Teddy," she mouthed.

I watched her lips move, and before I knew it, I was all over her again. Shoving my hand between her legs, spreading them apart, an instant rush of heat came over me. She took another bite of her apple and leaned toward me.

"Open your mouth," she commanded, and I obeyed, tasting the apple in her mouth and kissing her madly.

"Is this really juicy?" My voice up against her ear, referring to her pussy while I finger-fucked her.

She understood and moaned. "Yes. Yes, it is. Do you know what you're getting yourself into?" she whispered back.

"You. I'm getting into you." Her breathing quickened with every thrust of my finger. "I've never met anyone like you."

Melina abruptly pushed away my hands and got up. She looked upset.

"I want you to leave, Ted," she said, adjusting her

shirt and hair, her face back to that blank expression.

"What did I say? Are we playing that game again?" I ran my hands through my hair, looking at her standing in front of me while sitting on the couch, my hard-on unwilling to die down.

"You are so gorgeous, Melina. You're going to drive me completely insane with lust."

My erection poked out at both of us through my pants, but my decision to leave was based on her erratic behaviour swinging from one extreme to the other. *I should leave,* I kept repeating in my head, but my body did not move, my eyes gazing at her body, wanting to fuck her again.

Flushed, she looked at me. "Really, teach?"

"Really."

"Really?" She came closer now.

"Really," I repeated.

She raised one leg and placed her foot beside me on the couch, and then grabbed my hand and pushed it under her skirt. "Finger-fuck me again, and don't feed me any trashy lines."

I was feeding her trashy lines?

Man, she was complicated. My fingers plunged deep inside her. And it was a fact I knew—I *knew*—I was in deep fuckin' trouble because for sure one night with her would not be enough.

Serena
Do you see me?

"So?"

Elsa called me bright and early the next morning. I had a splitting headache, and my mouth felt dry. She had texted me at least five times, and I had ignored each one.

"Elsa, I'm sleeping. What do you want?" I snapped, knowing full well why she'd called.

"Did Ben make the moves on you?"

Not even a *hello, how are you?*

"How do you know I didn't make the moves on *him*?" I retorted, now really annoyed with her calling.

"Because I know you, Serengeti." She sounded slightly exasperated. Elsa's way of being affectionate was calling me Serengeti.

"You were really wasted last night, Elsa. How did you get home?"

"Don't you know Eddie takes good care of me?"

That, he did. He knew her limits as well as his own. He was the only one who could pull Elsa out of her downward spiral. They were meant for each other. He'd even convinced her to go to hairdressing school, which she was presently pursuing.

"How did Mom react when she saw you?"

"She was sleeping. She gave up waiting up for me a long time ago."

Poor Mom. She had it rough with Elsa. "Just be

careful, sis. You know how addictive drugs are—and how you can get when you're on them."

"I'm not the same person, okay? Now, let's talk about you! Isn't Ben hot?"

"Yes," I admitted.

"Don't you want to jump his bones?"

Jump his bones? I smirked. "We went to the mountain, and we kissed." I waited for her reaction.

"What? Good for you, sis. Take a chance."

"We'll see. I gave Ben my number."

"He'll call."

"By the way, why did you tell him I had published my book? Are you serious? I haven't even sent it out yet!"

"Well, it will be published. You're brilliant, even if you're innocent as hell. You need a man like Ben to rock your world."

"I have to let you go. My headache is intense, my homework is piling up and my assignment is due soon."

"How can you do homework at a time like this?"

"Bye, Elsa!" I hung up.

I took two Advil and drank two glasses of water. The homework could wait. I turned on my laptop and waited for it to start. I entered my password and then clicked the Internet Explorer button. *Here goes nothing…*

I typed in Domenic S. Amour. His website popped up, and I clicked the link.

At the top of his site's homepage were different headings: Home. Author. Excerpts. On the black background of the page was a pair of handcuffs. Slender, feminine arms held them, while a man's hand, his arm extended, held the key. I found it sexy, erotic. I clicked on Excerpts and read the cover of his latest book.

Darkest Angel, Volume Three. A half-naked blonde was embraced by a beautiful, dark-haired man. *How typical.* I clicked Book Excerpt, and the page popped up.

Christopher took out his metal handcuffs and roughly placed them around Isabella's tiny wrists. She had them raised above her head as she lay, bare and exposed, on his bed. His insides rumbled.

"Oh, that's so cold." She sighed.

"Soon you'll be hot, Izzy." He called her that only when they made love. Feeling intense lust, he stared into her dark eyes, and he saw the same desire reflected back at him.

"I'm already hot and wet," Isabella whispered, her blonde hair tied in a tight bun.

He kissed her neck, then licked her slowly. He was on a voyage, exploring her luxurious body with his tongue. He had to consume all of her. She had been playing a cat-and-mouse game with him for the past two weeks. He twirled his tongue around her nipples, first from left to right, and then right to left. She let out a moan.

"Do you like that, Izzy?" he asked between licks. He knew his husky voice sent shivers down Isabella's spine. She wanted him like she never wanted another human being. She had told him that so many times. His dominance drove her mad. with desire.

"Yes." She moaned again.

"Don't make a sound," he commanded in a cold voice, the one he used only when disciplining Isabella. "Or else." She knew she would get spanked if she moaned, but sometimes she couldn't help it. "I'll tell you when to moan," he continued, knowing it wouldn't take

long for her to lose control.

"Yes."

"Yes what, Izzy?"

"Yes, Mr. Christopher Hawk."

"That's a good girl."

He loved to arouse Isabella. She was the first woman he was compelled to pursue. He had to control women, and he liked to make them beg for his sex. But he aimed to bring Isabella to the point of no return. He had been hard as a rock for her since she broke up with him seven days ago, and he hadn't slept a single night. The image of her body was imprinted in his mind and had driven him wild with lust. He had to possess her in all ways possible, body and soul.

He rammed his finger into her wet pussy. "You're almost there."

Isabella let out a slight moan.

"Don't moan or I'll stop."

Christopher wanted to play the game, so he taunted her.

"No, Mr. Christopher Hawk. Don't stop."

"Good girl, Izzy."

He bent down and quickly darted his tongue in and out of her pussy. Her body quivered, and he knew she wouldn't be able to take it much longer. After all the suffering he endured these days after the breakup, he wanted to torture her a bit longer. He eased his way up the bed and lay next to her.

"Now that your hands are tied up"—he grinned— "how do you think you could please me further, Izzy?" he asked roughly. He traced her body with the tips of his fingers and felt her shake under him. She was biting her lips to control her moans, and that created a fresh

fervour of desire in him. His cock throbbed as he fell under her spell again.

Isabella had limits. Any second now, she would come wildly if he didn't fuck her, but she couldn't ask him until he told her. She had to wait for his instructions.

"Say it," he said.

"I'm ready for your cock," she replied quickly.

"Say it again more slowly." He tilted her body to the side and slid his cock inside her sex, then grabbed her ass with one hand and her nipple with the other. "You can moan now."

"I'm...ready...for...your...cock."

He thrust inside her, and she let out a guttural moan.

A moan that was just the first of many. Christopher fucked her in all the positions he had imagined these past few days. He made her come three times before he finally let it all out and wildly spilled his cum on her beautiful breasts.

He gently unclasped her hands and then lay next to her, but she turned over, leaving her back exposed to him.

"Izzy, what are you doing?" he asked as he caressed her body.

"I need to sleep. I'm exhausted."

"I don't think you'll be sleeping quite yet."

Was that it? Fuck. This was good stuff. *Hot* stuff. I wanted to read more. Ben was really good at writing erotica. No wonder he was a published author.

When you're a writer, you write, and not from experience all the time... I knew that. The heroine of my story was a drug addict, and I'd smoked up only that one time and vomited all over the bathroom.

The truth was that I was sexually inexperienced but needed to get laid. Elsa was absolutely right. I'd been with only two guys, and the experiences had left much to be desired. I brushed the memories away and how they made me feel. I'd never even had an orgasm. I faked them. The only orgasms I'd ever had were on my own with my good friend Vibrator, which was tucked away in my panty drawer.

I clicked back to the homepage and then on Author.

Domenic S. Amour has been with Hot Sex Publishing for five years now. As a highly talented novelist, his captivating writing style has made him one of our top authors. He is presently working on volume three in the series Darkest Angel, *about Isabella Venizia, a young, submissive secretary, and Christopher Hawk, her gorgeous boss who pursues her in a mad, passionate, roller coaster ride. He will do anything to have her, but will he let his volatile past catch up with him and threaten his feelings for Isabella? Volume three promises to knock you off your feet with its torrid love scenes and grand finale to this tumultuous relationship. Coming soon.*

That night I dreamed about sex. Fucking *hot* sex. Probably because of those sex scenes from Ben's excerpts. They had stayed on my mind all day. Monday was a short day and classes bored me, luckily noon came around and I was home. My thoughts were preoccupied with ordering Ben's books and as soon as I got home, I did just that.

I sat in front of the monitor and reread everything. My need to read them surpassed all my other needs. I clicked on Buy Books, charged my credit card and was downloading Ben's novels to my e-reader.

My cell phone rang. The screen showed a number I didn't recognize.

"Hello?"

"Hi, Serena."

It was Ben. My insides fluttered at another excerpt, and feeling very turned on.

"Hi, Ben."

"How are you feeling?"

"Fine, thanks. Just got back from school." *I'm horny as hell*, I wanted to say.

"I had a great time Saturday night."

"Me too." It was the truth.

"Would you like to go for a cup of coffee today?"

Well, that was straight to the point. I loved the way he said cup of coffee instead of just coffee.

"Uh, I have homework."

"When will you be finished? I can't concentrate on writing today. I keep thinking about Saturday night."

"Um, I'll be finished in a few hours."

"How about five?" He was insistent. I hadn't even said yes yet. I paused. "Are you there?"

"Yes, I'm here. I don't know…"

"I'll pick you up at five."

"Okay, five it is," I replied, excited by his voice and the urgency in it.

"See you soon. I can't wait." And he hung up.

I shut down the computer and made myself a quick toast and cup of coffee. Taking out my assignment and staring at the outline, my thousand-word paper on how Virginia Woolf used stream of consciousness in her novel *To the Lighthouse* and how effective it is. Staring at the question, my mind wandered. Glancing at my alarm clock, I had four and a half hours to go. I shut my eyes, and before I knew it…

My eyes opened and I bolted out of bed. Shit! It was four thirty. Half an hour to get ready. The mirror reflected back my messy hair. Muttering under my breath, I grabbed a towel.

I took the fastest shower ever and quickly got dressed, pulling on a pair of jeans, as usual, and a snug, brown, cotton blouse with tiny buttons on the sleeves and down the front. I unbuttoned the ones in front to leave my neck exposed and then put on a leather strap necklace. I slipped into my flat brown booties and examined myself in the mirror. Not bad. My look was casual but cool.

Ben's kiss and tongue popped into my thoughts. Would he like my clothes? Probably.

Putting on a pair of hoop earrings, I let my hair air dry. I imagined Ben touching it, and goosebumps invaded my body. My mind wandered to how he would grab my hair and kiss me again. My hair was scrunched up so the natural waviness would come out, and allowed it to fall down to my waist. He had said it was soft. Parting it on the side, letting one side fall on my cheek and tucking the other side behind my ear, I then applied some light brown eyeshadow, eyeliner, and added some white frosty eyeshadow on top of the brown, my plum blush and a fruity lip gloss. My face looked great.

I glanced at my clock. Five minutes left. The thought of riding his motorcycle again made me giddy, just like a schoolgirl. I went to the bathroom and splashed on my favorite floral scented perfume.

I looked different from the other night, looking

raunchier and had this rock star vibe going on. Tonight, my look was softer, more natural—my usual look. I wanted Ben to see me in my everyday style, not how Elsa dressed me.

My self-esteem was in shambles, but a last quick look in the mirror confirmed to me that my best look was this, and that had to be enough for him.

My phone rang. I picked it up, anticipating hearing Ben's voice.

"I'm downstairs," he said. "And bring your sunglasses."

Teddy
Heat lightning and love and danger

When I left Melina's place, I couldn't walk, and my cock was sore. A good sore. A sore I had never experienced before. Could this have been my sexual awakening, starring Melina the sex goddess? She had asked me to do things to her I hadn't ever imagined myself doing in real life, only in my fantasyland while masturbating. My porn collection consisted of films that Dan didn't want anymore. Hence, scratched DVDs and unattractive women with even worse-looking men. They got me off a few times, but it was really low-quality, shit porn that came out of my closet during desolate and desperate times.

I drove home in a daze as the sun rose. She had wanted to sleep. "And I can't sleep with strangers in my bed" were her exact words. She had had six orgasms, and I had come three times. At least the last round I'd stayed hard longer than the first two, which made her so crazy she moaned like a wild animal. Just remembering the sounds she made gave me a chubby. I patted my dick. *C'mon, fella. You really need to rest.*

At the door, she gave me a tiny fluorescent pink paper. "Call me, teach. I had a great time." And I kissed her goodbye on both cheeks while clutching the paper tightly. I left her apartment on a complete sexual high, craving shut-eye myself. "Drive safe." She stuck her finger in her pussy, and before I knew it, her finger was in my mouth. "Something to remember me by," she said. Then she quickly removed her finger from my mouth and kicked me out the door.

What the fuck? I wasn't going to call her. Her manic behaviour was too fucking strange. I would need a manual to figure out her quirks.

I could still taste her, though, and a jolt of pleasure shot through me at the thought of her naked body and how she knew exactly how to use her tongue on my cock.

When I parked my car, the sun was in the sky, and its brightness blinded me.

I kicked my front door shut, stripped, and stayed in bed until noon. I woke up with a hard-on, thinking about my night with her.

She had wanted me to fuck her standing up. "Don't sit down, or I'll kick you out," she'd said huskily. "Fuck me from behind as deeply as you can, teach." She turned her ass to me and pressed her sex against my cock. Her wetness had my cock twitching all sorts. She grabbed it and started to rub it with her left hand. Then she spread her legs wider. "I'm ready, teach." And she handed me a foil packet. I quickly ripped it open with my mouth and put on the condom.

"You sure are," I said, overcome with lust.

My body was ready to explode. How could this be happening again? I had just come on the couch ten minutes ago. There she'd wanted us to sixty-nine each other. I was delirious. I entered her sex and felt her quiver.

"Fuck me, teach. Fuck me hard."

As soon as she said *hard*, I lost it. I pounded her with all my might, uttering nonsense and asking her over and over if she liked it. She told me to shut up and just fuck her.

"Listen to me, teach. You're going too fast. Take it slow. I want it slow. *Slooow*."

But I couldn't stop. She pulled away and turned around. My dick was standing out, saluting her. She grabbed it.

"Now, teach, you're going to have to slow it down." She stroked me unhurriedly. "I'll tell you how I want it."

What the fuck was she saying? She was going to tell me how to fuck her?

"Agreed?" Her tone turned serious, and her blue eyes were cold again.

My cock wilted slightly at her attitude. One minute she was on fire, reciting porn lines, and the other, she was the fucking Ice Queen. But in my horny stupor, I agreed, and she stroked me again till I was hard.

"Now, where were we?" she asked.

I shoved her back down a little roughly, figuring she'd like that, and she let out a moan. "Right here," I mumbled, and I fucked her slowly. "Slow, slow, slow," I repeated as I thrust as slowly as possible, when what I really wanted to do was bang the fuck out of her fast and hard.

"Yes, teach. Slow. Take it slow." And then she screamed, "Fast! Faster! Faster! I'm coming!"

Well, that was it for me. At the sound of her high and low moans of orgasm, I came right away, grabbing her hips and pulling her toward me.

My phone buzzed, startling me out of my memory. It was a text from Dan: *R u awake? Call me ASAP.*

I dialed his number.

"So?" he said after picking up the phone.

"Last night was insane." I heard the grogginess in my voice.

"What happened?"

"What *happened?* Where do I begin?" I figured I'd make the description quick for Dan. "We fucked like rabbits."

"Bro, can I pick them or what?"

"And you?" I asked, ignoring his question.

"Well, Jenny and I got along famously. We got to first base." First base? I couldn't believe how he still spoke like a fourteen-year-old. "But Jenny told me that Melina…how do I say this…is a man-eater." He laughed.

"I can believe that. She has a voracious sexual appetite."

"What the fuck? Voracious?"

"Yes, voracious. As in insatiably horny," I said, annoyed. "We did it three times." I might as well boast. I hadn't bragged about sex in what seemed like years.

"In one night?" He whistled. "Lucky dog, you sack-licker!"

"You're a sack-licker, whatever that is supposed to mean."

"I want details, man."

"Another time. I just woke up, and I need a cup of coffee."

"I'll swing by with some coffee. I'm not doing anything."

"Okay." I hung up.

I jumped into the shower, and by the time I got out, my front door was buzzing. I wrapped a towel around my waist and buzzed Dan upstairs.

He held two Mezzo cappuccinos and two biscotti

from Starbucks and had a stupid grin plastered on his face. "So, you finally got laid properly, bro," he screamed from the front door.

"Sh! Shut up! My neighbours!"

"All right, all right. Keep your socks on," he said, still grinning. "What god-awful song is this now?"

I was blasting Icky Blossom's new song, "Heat Lightning," over and over again and thinking of Melina. I was a complete and utter sap. I was hopeless.

"Fuck off."

Serena
He's too sexy for me…

"Oh, I'll be right down."

I looked at my clock. It was five on the nose. Ben was a punctual guy. I put on my sunglasses, thoughts of Christopher Hawk reeling through my mind. Even if the story was fictional, it was so bloody hot.

I snatched my jacket, still lying on my couch from last night.

The first thing I noticed when I saw Ben outside were his legs, strong and muscular, straddling his bike. Oh fuck, he was unbelievably beautiful! His profile in perfect view, I wanted to turn back around and go hide. He was way too hot for me. He was way too cool for me. When the glass door of my apartment building shut behind me, he turned toward me. He was wearing sunglasses, so I couldn't see his eyes through the dark tint, but I felt his gaze. He had this invisible string pulling me toward him. His hands were on the handlebars, and he was leaning forward. His long, lean body presented itself to me in ways I hadn't noticed yesterday.

"Hi, gorgeous." He smiled.

"Hi, Ben." I smiled back.

Suddenly my stomach rumbled. I was sure he heard it, and I felt like hiding under a rock. I should have been the one to call *him* gorgeous. He looked like he was posing for an ad. He could have sold just about anything with the way he looked.

"I don't know about you, but I'm starving," he said. Meanwhile, my stomach continued to misbehave, uncontrollably making all kinds of weird noises. "And by the sound of it, I think your stomach is trying to tell me something."

He laughed, and when I saw those dimples, I laughed too.

"I haven't had a decent meal all day," I said. "I fell asleep and just woke up half an hour ago."

"Ah, so you've had your beauty rest and are ready for round two," he joked, handing me the helmet. I took it confidently, knowing exactly what to do with it this time, although I wouldn't have minded if he had put it on me again.

"I was zonked. I'm not used to drinking, so I don't think there will be around two," I said seriously.

"I wasn't talking about the *drinking*," he said in a serious tone.

He's talking about the kissing. Shit!

"Well, I've made it a point in my life to not drink." Where had that come from? My voice was a little shaky, and I was babbling again. "I'm not used to drinking, and I abhor it." He wanted to kiss me again? I was so nervous, I didn't move.

"That's a good thing, Serena." Ben smiled. He leaned over and made some space for me, then patted the plush seat behind him, gesturing for me to sit. "Alcohol is a killer. I've seen many families destroyed by it."

There was something in his voice, something I couldn't quite put my finger on.

You're telling me. My father died from it, I wanted to shout, but that would have killed the mood. I was already killing the mood. Stop, I told myself. I didn't know how much he knew about my father. Elsa had a big mouth. I lifted my left leg to sit, and suddenly my phone buzzed. I put my leg back down.

"Excuse me one moment, Ben."

I pulled my phone out of my purse and flipped it open. It was a text from Elsa. Actually, there were five texts from her. She must have sent them while I was sleeping. I hadn't checked my phone when I woke up.

Text number one was sent at 2:00 p.m., when I was in my REM state: *Ben has been texting Eddie all day. He wants 2 know everything about u. E told B u r a slut xoxo lol.*

Text number two, 2:20 p.m.: *B asked about some guy at the club. Which guy? I told E there is no guy. U r such a loser sis xoxo*

Text number three, 2:45 p.m.: *B likes u. xoxox*

Text number four, 3:00 p.m.: *Where the fuck r u?*

Text number five, 4:00 p.m.: *B told E he can't eat. He can't wait till 5. Have fun and I know u r ignoring me. Call me later. Live dangerously b a slut. xoxo*

It took me a few seconds to read all that and compose myself. My sister was such an annoying freak. I should have checked my messages and asked Elsa about Ben. I set my phone on vibrate and shoved it back into my purse. I sat behind Ben, who had been eyeing me the whole time. My heart fluttered at the thought that Ben had said he liked me and wanted to know more about me, and here he was in front of me, magnificent, gorgeous, and interested in little old me, while I kept on thinking about a guy I'd never probably ever see again.

"So, where do you want to eat?" I asked, trying to act nonchalant. He started the engine, and the roar of it went through me.

"You better wrap your arms around me if you don't want to fall off. You'll see where we're going," he said in a hard tone and took off.

Our coffee date had just become a real date. I tightened my arms around his waist and held on with all my might. He rode a little faster than the night before, and it felt more thrilling.

When we reached the traffic lights on Saint Laurent Street, Ben shouted over the noise of the bike, "Check out the sky. It's breathtaking."

I looked up. I had been so preoccupied with breathing in Ben's scent and keeping my arms around him that I hadn't noticed.

"It is." After a few minutes, it occurred to me that we weren't budging, but Ben's broad shoulders blocked my view. "A lot of traffic?"

"It's always like this on this street. Construction, cars, and tons of people," he replied. "I'm enjoying this ride, though," he added. My throat went dry, and my stomach rumbled again, embarrassing me. He was so close to my body.

"This traffic better start moving. Hungry girl on the road," he joked.

I chuckled at that, realizing my sex was mere inches away from his behind and generating the heat of an oven. My chest was up against his back, and my nipples popped to rock hard. Fuck. Did he feel that? Shit, how horny was I? It could have just been my overactive imagination, but I could swear he leaned back right at that moment for a split second. We remained quiet as he snaked through the traffic with ease. That turned me on even more. I had to think about something else, and then

I remembered my last sexual encounter and immediately dried up…

His name was Kenneth, and I had met him at Concordia in one of my English Lit classes, modern drama. From the first day of class, he followed me around, waited to see where I would sit, switched seats with other students to be near me, pretended he hadn't taken proper notes, walked with me to the metro… Suddenly I was going out for drinks and having sex with him. It was awful.

He was a nice guy from the West Island who grew up with a big family. His mother was a stay-at-home mom, and his father was part of the corporate world. Kenneth was the kind of guy you married. You knew he would do something grand with his life and follow in his father's footsteps. *"Imagine, I just took this class as an elective, and I meet the girl of my dreams"* was his favorite line to say to anyone who cared to listen. My mom adored him. What mom wouldn't? He was cute, reliable, and came from money. Yet there was always that *but* at the back of my mind. He just didn't do it for me. We were having sex two times a week, and it was boring and predictable. I knew what married life with Kenneth would be like.

One day while at his apartment, we'd had sex in our usual position—he'd never kissed or licked my sex or done anything else my sister and Connie had experienced—and I knew I had to end our relationship. I couldn't continue with the awful sex, and after our sixteenth *alien encounter*, as I called them, I said, "It's over. I don't feel anything for you." What surprised me the most was how he cried; he'd actually thought I was *the one…*

My stomach flip-flopped as the memory of Kenneth made me emotionally sick, and I accidentally let out a small burp. Fuck. Thank God, I wasn't facing Ben. I would have died right then of embarrassment.

"Excuse me," I mumbled, feeling my face flush.

"That's okay, Serena. I love a girl who burps or farts on the first date. It gets all that formality out of the way." He laughed.

He made me smile, but my mind raced back in time…

I was seventeen. It was grad night, and I had sex with Gery—spelled with one R—a boy who'd had a crush on me since elementary school.

I was with a group of classmates—seven girls and five boys. Some of us were coupled off, and some of us, like me and Gery, were just friends. We had booked a room at a hotel, and everyone was either entering or leaving the room. Somehow Gery and I ended up in the hotel room alone.

"Why don't we try on the bathrobes in the bathroom and pretend we're rich folk?" he asked. Then he pulled out a joint. "Look what I have."

"Okay, why not?" I said. "It's grad night, and I've never done it before. Let's do it."

We smoked up while wearing the bathrobes, and then he kissed me—sloppily. His tongue was all over my mouth, and I kept thinking how this must be what it was like to kiss a lizard. He touched my sex, then awkwardly put his penis inside me, and in thirty seconds it was over. It had hurt like hell, and I vomited in the bathroom.

That was how I lost my virginity, and that was the first and last time I smoked up…

"We're here."

Ben's announcement bounced me out of my reverie. "Schwartz's?"

"Yes, is that okay? Only the best smoked meat for you."

"I love smoked meat. It's just that I used to come here with my dad." I quickly looked away, biting my lip. Talking about Dad wasn't cool. Why did I open that door? "He died when I was seven."

"I'm so sorry. Elsa had told me that."

Obviously, she had. No surprise there.

He got off the bike first, then helped me with my helmet. As we walked toward the restaurant, memories flooded me like a tsunami.

"No doubt, there's a lineup," he said.

"What else is new?"

We waited in line about ten minutes, making small talk and watching the hustle and bustle inside the restaurant. When we got inside and reached our table, we sat down, and Ben placed his sunglasses on top of his head. I noticed it had some stubble and thought it looked really good. He looked at me from across the table.

"If it's any consolation, I never even met my dad. I grew up with a single mum," he said, rubbing the back of his head and looking uncomfortable.

"I'm sorry." I didn't know what else to say.

"Don't be sorry. He was a fuckin' prick. He left my mum as soon as he found out she was pregnant. He didn't want anything to do with me." He stared at me.

"Do you know who he is?"

"I knew his family well. It was a small community. He skipped town and moved to London."

The waitress came to our table and greeted us. She had a pretty face. "Hello, how are you today?"

"Great, thanks," Ben replied, and I smiled back, but I could tell he was upset discussing his father.

"Can I get you something to drink?" she asked, placing two menus on the table.

"Serena?"

"I'll have a 7 Up," I said to the waitress.

"Make that two, please," Ben said, lifting a menu and handing it to me.

The waitress nodded and walked away.

"Have you been here since your dad died?" He held the closed menu in his hands.

I opened mine and examined it. "A few times," I replied, not looking at him. "I try to avoid it. Right about now, my dad would be complaining to the waiter that they should have a liquor license and how he would have one if he owned this joint," I said, reading the menu and recalling how he drank more than he ate.

"That's shitty. Bloody hell, do you want to leave?" Ben quickly got up, his eyes full of concern.

That was a little dramatic. His genuine concern touched me, but why would I want to leave? I looked up at him and couldn't help admiring his body and loving the fact that he was ready to jet out of there.

"Leave? No. Sit down, Ben." My father wouldn't get the better of me again. It was bad enough that I'd drunk too much the night before, which went against my grain; he wouldn't make me run out on my date.

Ben sat again, and I felt slightly embarrassed.

He remained silent while reading his menu, and then

he peeked over at me. "Serena, what would you like?"

"Small plate smoked meat," I replied quietly.

As soon as we closed our menus, the waitress came over with our soft drinks and took our orders.

"Lean or fat?" she asked me.

"Fat."

"And for you?"

"I'll have the large plate smoked meat, and bring on the fat," Ben joked.

She smiled and gave him a quick, admiring look. "I love your accent."

"Thank you," he replied.

She jotted down the orders and took off.

"If you're going to have smoked meat, you have to have it with fat." He chuckled.

"I agree."

He lifted his glass. "Cheers, Serena. To dads. To the fucked-up ones like ours, and to the good ones like theirs." Smiling, he gestured around the restaurant at the clients.

I giggled, and we clinked our glasses together. "Cheers to that."

He placed his elbows on the table. "So, did you go to my website?"

"Yes," I mumbled. *Shit.*

"And?" His eyes sparkled with curiosity. "What did you think?"

"I thought it was good…really good. I read an excerpt of one of your books." I must have blushed because he gave me a wicked smile. "It was pretty damn hot," I admitted. "How do you write like that?"

"Like what?" He watched my every movement.

"So…so…I don't know. Descriptively."

"The words come out. I imagine these characters in my head and go with it." He leaned in closer, pressing his elbows on the table. "What's your book about?"

I wasn't ready to divulge that information. "It's complicated."

"Spill the beans. You read mine. At least tell me the blurb." He sounded excited.

"It's a love story. It's about a girl who falls head over heels in love with her soul mate, and then he mysteriously disappears, and she falls for his best friend, who's a vampire." That sounded awful. I couldn't think straight with his gaze penetrating into mine so intensely like that. "I haven't written a blurb yet." I looked down.

"That's okay. I'd love to read it. It sounds very cool."

"I'll think about it."

"That's an improvement from 'no.' I'll convince you *yet*." He grinned. "I have my ways."

I got a tingling sensation straight to my pussy when he said he had *his ways*. I'd bet he did. I thought of handcuffs and instantly felt anxious. I took a sip of my drink, then mimicked an awkward smile.

"I can't wait till you say 'yes,'" he said in a low voice that sent more shivers up my spine. He gazed at my lips, and I couldn't take my eyes off his beautiful face. His dark brown eyes pierced mine, and I wanted to say *yes, yes*, right there and then.

"We'll see," I murmured.

He leaned back in his chair and placed his hands on his thighs. "We'll see," he repeated. He wore a T-shirt that read NANOWRIMO. He caught me studying it and smiled. "Have you done it too?"

"Done what?"

"Participated in NaNoWriMo?"

"I don't know what that is." Should I have known? Did not knowing make me look bad?

"It's a writing competition. You have to write a fifty-thousand-word novel during the month of November. I did it in 2009 for the fun of it. Eyes closed."

"Did you publish it?"

"That one? No. It wasn't erotica." He laughed.

Wow! I was impressed by his cool, nonchalant attitude.

The waitress brought our plates to the table. "Here you go." She placed the small smoked meat sandwich in front of me and the large one in front of Ben. "Enjoy your meal."

I added some ketchup and pepper to my fries, then took a bite and savoured the taste for all of one second. I was already on my third bite, enjoying my food and not even looking at Ben, when I glanced at his plate and saw that he too was enjoying his meal.

"Delicious," he said after swallowing.

I nodded, not wanting to talk with my mouth full.

"You have a good appetite." He smiled.

I had finished my sandwich in record time.

"I don't think I've ever seen a girl so thin eat a sandwich so fast." He smirked. "Shit, you even beat me."

I dug into the fries. "You heard my stomach rumbling earlier. I was hungry." I smiled.

"Are you going to eat your pickle?" he asked, eyeing it.

"No, I hate pickles."

I gave it to him, and our fingers touched. I instantly felt the electricity run through me, and his expression became serious. He placed the tip of pickle in his mouth and took a bite of it, his gaze on me the whole time.

"Your pickle tastes better than mine did." He grinned, crunching down on it, clearly savoring the taste. As he put the rest of it in his mouth, chewed it, and swallowed it, I stared at him while thinking about Christopher Hawk and Isabella in bed together. I had even stopped eating the fries.

"Are you done?" he asked, wiping his mouth.

I felt my cheeks flush at my thoughts. My imagination was going wild. I was imagining him naked and doing delicious things to me with that mouth of his.

"Excuse me?" I asked, still gazing at his lips.

He smiled, a wide grin from ear to ear. "I said, are you done?"

No, I'm not done. "Yes, I'm finished. If you'll excuse me, I have to go to the washroom."

"Go ahead. Just don't take too long, or I'll have to come after you," he joked, referring to his coming to get me at Foufounes…when I was drunk. I hated being drunk. I couldn't believe I'd let myself get to that place. I pushed my chair away and got up.

Once in the bathroom, I texted Elsa: *Why didn't you tell me he wrote erotica?*

She immediately texted me back: *I didn't want 2 scare u.*

Me: *Why is he single?*

Elsa: *He was engaged. Who cares anyway? He's into u.*

Me: *He intimidates me.*

Elsa: *U r a smart, beautiful pain in the butt! Be cool & have fun cu later xoxo*

He was once engaged? As I walked toward the table and his strong back, I regretted texting Elsa. I was such an idiot. Now I knew something about him I wasn't supposed to know, and it was going to gnaw at me.

Teddy
You can't escape what's meant to happen…

"After you guys left, Jenny told me something. She said that Melina is a man-eater." Dan sat down on the couch, sipping his coffee, and then he looked at me, grinning. "Boy, can I pick 'em, eh?"

"You already told me that, you spaz," I said, sitting across from him in my armchair. "What else did she tell you?"

"That Melina chews men up, spits them out, and leaves them wanting more. This is her revenge phase, she said."

"Revenge?" As soon as I asked the question, I knew the answer. Of course. It made sense in a demented way.

"Her last boyfriend cheated on her with her friend, and she slashed his tires in the middle of the night. Jenny went with her and tried to talk her out of it the whole time." He placed his legs on my coffee table and leaned back. "She's *Fatal Attraction* Girl come to life," he said with a smirk.

"What the fuck?" *Slashing tires*? *Did she forget to mention that part*? "She told me that all her boyfriends have cheated on her. She hates men, and I thought she hated me too. Then, all of a sudden, I'm dropping her off and about to say 'Bye, nice to have met you,' when the fucking song comes on." I took a sip of my coffee, remembering last night and getting aroused all over

155

again. "You know, Hearts' 'Crazy on You'?"

Dan nodded, looking clueless.

"I know you haven't seen The Virgin Suicides—"

"The what? Bro, I don't know what kind of movies you're watching—"

"Shut up and listen, you fucktard."

Dan gestured zipping his mouth shut.

"There's a part in the movie when Kirsten Dunst runs into the car Josh Hartnett is sitting in and is about to take off, and she jumps on top of him, and the song 'Crazy on You' is playing, and they're kissing in the car so passionately, so fuckin' sexy and crazy, and then she runs back into her house."

"That's it?" Dan looked disappointed.

"Search it, you schmuck."

"I'm not going to do an online search for a love scene. You gotta be kidding me, bro. If it was porn, yes, but this movie sounds lame." He liked to bug me about my taste in movies.

"Pass me your iPhone." He had it next to him on the couch, so I got up and grabbed it before he even realized what I'd asked him.

Dan smirked. "You're such a pussy. I don't get how you're not married by now with a bunch of kids, living the dream."

I went to YouTube and found the scene, then sat down next to him. "Just watch." I pressed play. We watched the scene intently.

"That's fuckin' hot!" Dan exclaimed. "Well, my advice to you, Teddy boy, is to have fun!"

"I did!"

"At least one of us got action last night." He took another sip of his coffee, then put it down on the table.

"Well, are you going to see her again?"

"I don't think so. She's fucking nuts."

"Whatever… Hey, remember that time I was going out with Rachel the designer and Anne the fitness trainer? It was fuckin' exhausting, bro. I would have a date with one, and then the next night with the other. They looked alike too. They didn't care that I dated other girls, but after a month, I had had enough. One girlfriend is bad enough, but two? I needed my space."

"Dan, you're something else," I said, laughing. I couldn't understand how his warped mind jumped from one topic to another.

"A woman like that will eat innocent you alive," he joked.

"I'm not that innocent."

"I can't believe you're quoting Britney, bitch."

We laughed. I didn't want Melina as a girlfriend, just as a fuck. She didn't strike me as the type I would get along with. Her domineering ways and erratic behaviour really didn't do it for me. Perhaps in the bedroom, but that was where it ended.

"And how was the sex?" Dan asked, suddenly serious. "C'mon, details, man." Then he made a face. "Oh my God. I think I found my soul mate…" He laughed after mimicking me.

I couldn't compare Serena and Melina. I'd thought Serena was the one for me, but given the company she kept, I was starting to wonder whether all this time I'd been under some kind of illusion that Serena was the perfect woman for me. Melina was just a fun night. I knew it wouldn't go any further.

"By the way, last night Melina told me that Jenny doesn't go on third dates, and this is a direct quote." I lifted two fingers on each hand, quoting her. "Two dates are enough. She doesn't want to be with a guy long enough to break his heart, so she needs to protect them from her." It was my turn to smirk. "Seems like you may have met your match, Danny boy."

"Whatever. Don't worry your ugly ass about me. Tell me more about the sex with Mad Melina." He waved his hand in irritation, then bent forward to pick up his coffee.

"It was fuckin' awesome. The best sex of my life."

"Serena who?" Dan teased.

"Actually, I did think about her a few times. At Foufounes, Melina thought she was my ex."

"Give up on that dream, Teddy." Dan picked up the brown bag with the biscotto and opened it. He reached inside and handed me one. "Serena is this fantasy girl you've created in your head. Did you see her last night with that bald model?"

Yes, I saw her. "Model?"

"I'm sorry to burst your bubble, but he looked like a fuckin' model, and you know I don't dig talking about other guys." He removed the lid from his paper cup, dunked the biscotto into the coffee, then opened his mouth wide, and bit into it.

I held on to mine, thinking of the model. He probably *was* a model. "Fuck, she'd just met him too!" I was so pissed off. How would I ever see her again?

"Do you seriously think you will see her again?" Dan asked with his mouth full, reading my mind.

"She said she knew where to find me. That means she knows where I work, but it doesn't mean she's coming tomorrow. Besides, right now I'm so preoccupied with Melina and hot sex with her that all I can think about is the number she jotted down on a piece of pink paper." I didn't want to call her, but the idea of having sex with her again had tremendous appeal.

"Only you would notice the color of the paper. Fuck, you should have been born a girl." Rolling his eyes, he shoved the last piece of cookie into his mouth. "Listen, call Melina, fuck her brains out till you get all your sexual frustration out, and if Serena comes by, you keep your options open. You know what I mean?" He winked at me.

First, he tells me to stay away from her, then he tells me to fuck her. I was taking advice from Dan? I took a bite of the biscotto.

"Delicious," I said, savoring the taste of the chocolate swirl and ignoring his pathetic so-called advice.

"I knew I should have bought more." He sat up straight on the couch and got a serious look in his eyes. "Do what you feel is right, but just be careful."

"She's a school teacher. Can you believe it?"

"That's fuckin' hot."

I thought of Melina's body and started to get hard. "She really knows what she wants," I said hoarsely. I had to change the subject, or I'd have to call her right then. "Tell me about Jenny."

"She appears to be normal."

"And you would know about normalcy," I said sarcastically. Dan thought he knew everything, but he was mostly annoying as hell.

Dan smirked. "I've had my share of whack jobs. I got her number, and I'm calling her later today."

"What happened to your three-day waiting period?" I grinned.

"That was in college, nimrod. I stopped that long ago. Girls hated that. They like to be chased. So, are you calling her or what?"

"I don't know if I'll call." I didn't know what I wanted. I couldn't just hold out for Serena. That was ridiculous. I was a hot-blooded man, and Melina was willing...

"Maybe we can go on a double date." Dan laughed.

Everything was a joke to Dan. He was always messing around and acting immature, unless it was about work.

"Whatever," I said, rolling my eyes.

"I'm just kidding! What...? Are we in high school?" His eyes twinkled with mischief.

"With you, I think so."

Dan got up, looking serious once again. "I gotta go. I work at three." Then he turned all responsible on me. "I can't be late."

"Okay, at least it's Sunday."

"Thank God." Dan worked in the pharmacy department at the hospital, preparing medications. The weekend was always less busy than the weekdays. "It'll definitely be quieter."

"I'll keep you posted on what happens."

"You better."

As soon as Dan left, I put on my sweatpants and a T-shirt, strapped on my iPod, hit my running playlist, grabbed a water bottle, and went outside for a cool run to clear my head. I ran straight to the mountain. It was only five minutes away, and I loved to run through the paths.

It was a beautiful autumn day. The leaves had begun to fall, and their vivid colours brightened up everything around. Running to Young Galaxy's "Swing Your Heartache," which was not a really peppy song, yet had tight lyrics between a man and a woman, had me feeling all fucked up again.

I thought of Serena. How the fuck could we ever be together? Waiting for her was part of my plan, whether it was realistic or not. What if she never came to see me? From the look on her face at Foufounes, it felt as if she wanted to see me again, but how can I ever be sure?

The magic between us was undeniable. That kinetic energy must have filled up the whole god damn room.

Then I thought of Melina. Could the attraction be just sexual? Obviously. My attraction to Melina was sexual there was no doubt about it. The best thing would be to stay away from Melina and not call her. It would get complicated. What if she wanted a relationship? I didn't want one with her. Not the normal boyfriend-girlfriend type, anyway. She struck me as someone who would want too much from me.

The song changed to Stars' "Personal." As I ran, feeling the rustling of leaves under my feet and listening to the two voices intertwined, relating a story, the feeling came over me that this song was written for me and Selena. She probably knew the song. After all, she was my fantasy girl. If I wanted her to like this band, then she did.

"It wasn't meant to be." The singers kept on singing, and this heaviness crept into my heart, like someone had smashed it with a jackhammer. I stopped running and walked instead. I picked up my iPod and put on Arcade Fire's "Rebellion." That song always got me pumped while running. Walking a little faster, and picking up my pace, my body got right back on track as

my feet hit the ground at a fast pace, pushing myself to the limit.

I wanted Serena so badly. Even after all these years, wanting to get to know her intrigued me. My cock hardened just imagining kissing her sweet lips and spreading her legs...

I just wanted to *not* think.

My feet hit the gravel pavement to the beat of the music, and *"every time you close your eyes"* echoed in the background. My head was clearer now. My heart was pumping, the sweat trickling down, I was so thirsty. Still running, I opened my water bottle to take a sip. Following the curved road, and lifting my head to drink, Dave Matthews Band's "Crash into Me" had just begun, and right then, bam, my body smashed head-on into the girl ahead of me, running straight toward me with full force.

"I'm so sorry," I said, my voice short of breath. And then I saw a familiar-looking face and body, wet from my water bottle, sprawled in front of me on the gravel. When she lifted her head, she was wearing a mischievous smile, and my body weakened.

"Funny bumping into you like this, teach, and you making me all wet *again*," she said.

Serena

Don't let your blood run cold, I'm turning into a lizard

And, what if he had been engaged? I was cross-legged, trying to hide my thoughts, but Ben looked at me puzzled.

"I thought for a second I'd have to come after you, like last night," emphasizing the night and sending some shivers down my spine again as thoughts of kissing him sent my brain reeling, and set my body on alert.

"Would you like to go get some dessert?" he asked as the waitress cleared our table.

"Sure." Why not? I didn't want the date to end.

"I know the perfect place." He stood and put on his jacket.

"Hold on." I was still sitting, my hand in my purse, looking for my wallet.

"I already paid the bill, Serena." He came around the table and stood behind me, then elegantly lifted my jacket off the chair. "Here you go." He held open my jacket, and I got up and spread my arms so he could help me into it. As he did, my arms gently brushed his hands, and that tingling sensation rushed through my body again. He patted my arms and back. "You look great," he said, still standing behind me.

I didn't look at him, my body frozen, sensing his every movement around me. Forcing myself to walk ahead of him toward the exit, while he followed close behind, had me feeling restless. The waitress thanked us at the door and smiled at Ben, checking him out from head to toe.

Yes, he's hot, and he's with me. Why was he with me again? He liked me. He seemed to really like me. My tongue was tied around Ben, wanting to impress him, but my brain kept telling me I couldn't.

As we left the restaurant, I sensed Ben's gaze on my back and probably my ass too. I turned around, and sure enough, he had a hot look in his eyes as they swept my body from head to toe. He looked flushed, but he didn't turn away. He held my gaze without flinching.

"Do you like chocolate?" he asked with that look that had sex written all over his face.

My body instantly reacted. "Yes," I replied calmly.

"Great. Let's go."

As we approached his bike, he took out his key from his jacket pocket. He unclipped the helmets and passed me mine. We put on our helmets, checking each other quietly. He sat first, and I placed myself snugly behind him.

"Getting used to the bike, I see."

I couldn't see him smile, but I knew he was. "I really love the feeling."

"What's not to like?"

He started the motorcycle, let go of the handlebar, and shifted gears. I had no idea what he was doing, but his self-assurance and well-built, robust body gave me the impression he knew exactly what he wanted, which simultaneously scared the shit out of me and thrilled me. Yet the scent of his leather jacket combined with his cologne made me feel content, relaxed in all my tangled thoughts.

He parked in front of Juliette et Chocolat.

"I always walk by here but never go inside," I said.

"The first time I saw it open, I had to try the desserts. They looked so tempting. How can you deny yourself such pleasures?" He shut off the engine and turned his head to me. "You really need to enjoy yourself a little, Serena."

He was absolutely right. I had thought about the sugar intake, the calories, and all the reasons to not walk in, but I'd never let myself be guided by the reasons I should walk in.

He must have seen from my expression that I was thinking about what he said because then he chuckled. "Don't worry. Stick with me, kid, and I'll show you the way."

He got off the bike and extended his hand to help me off. I smiled but said nothing. I was sure he could show me things I had only imagined. The image of the handcuffs on his website flashed across my mind.

"Are you like…Christopher Hawk?" My words sounded jumbled to my ears, my disorganized thoughts controlling them. I couldn't believe I'd just asked him that.

"Christopher Hawk?" He burst out laughing. "You're so funny," he said, not answering my question.

We walked toward the front door of the café-patisserie, and he placed his hand on the door handle, then stopped. I almost bumped into him, our bodies touching slightly, and he turned to me, his face a few inches from mine, and he said in a coarse voice, "I could be whoever you want me to be, Serena."

I thought he was going to kiss me, but instead, he

opened the door, and I had to take a step back. I almost fell into the person behind me, a man, who gave me a dirty look.

Ben caught the look and asked him, "Is there a problem?"

Hearing Ben's English accent and intimidating voice, the man quickly stepped back and replied, "No problem, no problem," while looking down.

I loved Ben's authoritative tone and protective ways. I smiled shyly at him.

As soon as I walked in, I was drawn to the display of mouth-watering sweets, from chocolate cakes to any flavour and design of dessert imaginable.

"Amazing display," Ben said, watching me, and then he bent toward my ear. "That guy was a fuckin' prick."

I giggled. "I know." I turned back to the desserts. "Wow. Everything looks so good."

"Let's sit and look at a menu."

He held my hand and found an empty table near the window, overlooking Saint Laurent Street, giving us a view of the passersby.

We sat down, and a young French waitress approached us. "*Bonsoir*." She smiled and handed us each a menu, then walked away.

It was such a detailed menu for a coffee shop. I eyed everything, from *Drinks* to *Savory Meals* to *The Chocolate Bar*, and then the last page, *Desserts*, which caught my attention.

"I love everything on the menu."

"Me too, but I already know what I'm having." He hadn't even glanced at his. He was watching the people outside walking by while waiting for me to choose a dessert.

"I can't decide."

"Between what?"

"The chocolate and banana crepe and the white chocolate raspberry cheesecake."

"That's a tough one." Still watching the foot traffic, he scratched his head. "It depends what you're in the mood for, chocolate or sex." His eyes widened. "Uh, sorry. I meant cheesecake. I don't know where my mind is at…" He turned to look at me. "Chocolate or cheesecake."

I burst out laughing. "Well, with the cheesecake I would get chocolate as well. It's white chocolate, so technically if I order my second choice, I'll get the best of both worlds."

"Yes," he agreed, composing himself but clearly still alert to everything I said. "But I have to tell you, the crepe is outstanding here. I'll have it, and you can try mine. Usually I have the Juliette tiramisu, but now that you said chocolate and banana crepe, I feel like having one. That has to be one of the best combinations." He smiled. "How about a coffee? Or a chocolate drink?"

"I'd like a *café au lait*, please."

I placed my menu on the table, and we glanced outside. A bunch of teenagers were walking by, shoving each other and laughing. The waitress came over and asked us in French if we had made our choices.

"*Oui*," Ben said with a Parisian accent. "*Un cappuccino, un café au lait, une crêpe aux chocolat et bananes, et un gâteau au fromage au chocolat blanc et à la framboise, s'il vous plaît.*"

"*Merci*," she said, quickly writing down the order.

The tables were really tiny compared to the ones at

Schwartz's. I felt the tips of Ben's knees on mine and tried to pull my legs back, but there was really no room. He didn't pull his legs away at all. He seemed to like the fact that they were touching mine.

"Serena, can I answer your question seriously now?" He rested his elbows on the table and leaned in close to me as if he didn't want anyone around to hear.

I placed my elbows on the table too and waited for his answer.

"I'm not Christopher Hawk, but we have some similarities."

Teddy
Take me into the dark

Melina stared up at me suggestively, as if she wanted me right there and then. I was still thinking about her double entendre.

I extended my hand graciously. "I'm so sorry. I was drinking water and didn't see you in front of me."

"I noticed that, teach," she said, smiling.

At the sound of "teach," my whole body reacted. I felt a rush of blood to my groin area and had to talk myself out of a hard-on. She turned to get up onto her knees, eyeing my crotch provocatively. Meanwhile, I was talking to Dick. *Calm the fuck down. Go back to sleep.* But no. He wanted sex. He had his own memories of last night. He wouldn't let up or down.

Melina stood inches away from me. "So, why haven't you called?"

"I was going to call you after my run," I lied, losing my nerve as she stared me down with those hard-blue eyes.

"Do you actually think I believe you?" She grabbed the bottle of water out of my hand and finished it, tipping her head back and sucking down the last drop, looking sexy as hell as she did.

I had to have her again. *He* was ready. I couldn't talk *him* out of anything. *He* definitely had a mind of his own. Even if my mind didn't have any intention of calling her, my cock still wanted to fuck her. I said nothing, looking at her, trying to remain calm.

"My place, eight o'clock sharp. BYOB." And she threw the empty bottle at me. Thanks to my quick reflexes, my hand reached out and caught it, while my dick felt a semi-erection and the other hand held an empty bottle of water.

I still had my iPod's earbuds in, and Maximo Park was singing "Hips and Lips." Perfect fuckin' song, I thought. *"The way you stick out your lips, and keep your hands on your hips, and I'm supposed to know what that means."* I ran all the way home and took a cold shower, then sat in front of the television at six o'clock and watched the news. My stomach started to growl, and I made a ham and cheese sandwich with some mayo, Dijon, marble cheese, and lettuce. I ate it and then made another one. My only meal all day had been the coffee and biscotti Dan had brought to me.

I thought of Melina sprawled on the gravel, her brown hair in a high ponytail, wearing no makeup, and dressed in black tight leotards and a neon orange hoodie with Reebok written on the front.

I couldn't believe I ran into her. Another double entendre. She was so fuckin' hot. The way she spoke and behaved like she knew exactly what she wanted. My body couldn't say no to her. Some kind of spell had enchanted me with those wicked eyes of hers. My body responded to her almost instantly. She was different from any other woman I'd ever had sex with. Usually my initiative was more pronounced with women, and it was enjoyable to have that power turning on a woman, but with Melina, it was the complete opposite; *she* was telling *me* what to do, and it really turned me on.

I walked over to my wine collection, which consisted of ten bottles next to a tight cupboard that didn't fit any plates. Picking the Woodbridge Cabernet Sauvignon and placing the bottle on the kitchen counter, I headed to my bedroom closet, and after examining my wardrobe, my black Diesel jeans were my best bet, and light blue polo shirt, leaving the first three buttons undone. I strapped on my watch—a gift from my sister for my twenty-fifth birthday—my ring and my chain with a cross. Splashing some Giorgio Armani cologne on my cheeks and neck, my body anticipated a night of hot sex. My hair was still wet, combing it out and working in a little gel to tame the frizz. My bangs were long and shouting out "please cut me".

When my hair was cut short, I looked like a teacher, but when it was longer, it looked rougher and not like a typical teacher. Longer hair was my preference, it was less predictable. Being a teacher, people thought you were either boring, or super smart, or underpaid, or a struggling writer, or talented with kids. I'd heard it all, but I'd always known that teaching was in me. Those high school kids were my life. Year after year, teachers played a part in creating a new generation, teaching young minds history, and why people did what they did, and how it related to today. It was about memorizing dates, theories, treaties, laws, governments, and wars. It was about acknowledging hatred, survival, Indians, slavery, the Renaissance, Greek civilization, the Romans, and on and on the list went. Some students loved it, most hated it, but when those moments of understanding occurred and were appreciated by those teenagers, that was when I loved my job.

When a student told me to fuck off, or to get a life,

my reply remained the same: "I am a teacher, and I am here to teach. You are a student, and you are here to learn. You need me to mark your papers and to give you a grade at the end of the year so you can pass this class and continue on to your next grade. That's who I am." The student usually sat back down and nodded. After all, in plain and simple terms, they needed me more than I needed them. If I made that clear, they understood. Kids were smarter than society gave them credit for.

I added some more gel to my hair to brush my bangs away from my face. My watch read 6:20. There was still an hour and forty minutes to go. Time was passing slowly.

I turned on my computer and checked my emails. A few from some disgruntled parents, wanting to know why their son or daughter got an F in History. Skimming through them, I scrolled down. Nothing interesting. My mouse clicked iTunes, selected Awolnation's "Kill Your Heroes," and listened to the song as I surfed the net, visited some of my favourite bloggers, and read some great articles. Then I visited a music blog and clicked a new song by Alex Clare called "Too Close." It was a great song.

I thought about Serena again, feeling too close to love her. Not knowing what that meant, it made sense in a senseless kind of way. In a song, everything made sense, but living it was abrupt, cold, non-lyrical.

I put the computer in sleep mode as Mumford & Sons sang "I Will Wait." Again, I thought of Serena. What the fuck was wrong with me? I was about to go fuck the brains out of Melina, a woman who knew how to fuck, how to suck, how to move... But her personality was horrendous. Why should this matter? Being used is what my body needed, being her booty call is what my cock needed.

The silence of my apartment had me at a standstill. Usually music got me thinking, day-dreaming, wanting, horny, sad, depressed, nostalgic—something. But now emptiness entered me like a quick shot of whiskey. It now crept to 7:20. Let me see what the online philosophers were writing tonight. Posting on social sites gave me rashes. The only reason I go on is to spy on my ex-girlfriends.

I clicked on Lilianne and looked at her profile picture. It was still the same one from a year ago, when we had dated. "When it says 'profile picture,'" she had said, "it means profile picture. What do you think?" It was a shot of her profile as she looked out into the ocean, from one of her vacation trips with her friends.

Lilianne had an insane social life. She was part of every organization created. She was into every cancer research fund. She volunteered for security during the Jazz Festival, the Literary Festival, the Arab Festival…not knowing myself there were so many festivals in the city. She was always in a rush, and she was addicted to her BlackBerry, to emails, updates, and tweets, to social networks I didn't even know existed.

In the beginning, her lifestyle took me in, and my company was her date to all the functions. After a while she treated me like her puppy dog. At all these events, no names were remembered, because no one cared about me, and the feeling was mutual. That was all fine and dandy. We had a social life that kept us so occupied we barely had time for sex, and when we had sex, we were like an old, married couple. Then she broke up with me because she needed space, and I left that restaurant skipping and whistling. Today she was "at the World Film Festival." Why did she feel the need to tell everyone where she was? And why the fuck was I reading this shit?

I went on to ex number two, Aurelie Manon Tremblay, who was my one and only French-Canadian girlfriend. Everything with Aurelie was easy—sex, friendship, love, eating in restaurants, drinking, smoking, listening to music, hanging with friends. She was the buddy I never had; she was my best friend.

She had been living on her own since the age of eighteen, and she knew every nook and cranny of the city. She took me to bars and restaurants around the city that were obscure and well hidden from human eyes. Rolling my eyes was part of the restaurant experience. She loved going to Foufounes Electriques, while my preference was for Café Campus at the time. We would pick up the *Mirror* and look for new bands. Every weekend, we watched a live show and critiqued the music, the audience, the musicians, the lead singer, the sound, the feedback. We would sit at a cafe on Saint Laurent and talk non-stop. We'd switch from French to English easily—she more than I—and then we'd end the night with sex.

Her profile was updated almost weekly. Her photo was one of her sitting in front of her apartment building, smiling at the camera. She looked sweet and innocent, her blue eyes twinkling and her blond hair loose around her face. The problem with Aurelie was that I was never sexually attracted to her. I loved her mind. I loved her ideas and her energy. She knew I couldn't love her the way she wanted to be loved. Our conversations were enjoyable and looking back, my mind missed the exciting debates, but she was more of a best friend than a girlfriend. Kissing her was boring as fuck. My thoughts would wander, thinking of other women to get off. That wasn't fuckin' normal, although when I told Dan, he'd said, "It's perfectly normal, bro. We need some fantasy in our sex lives. Even Dr. Phil says so." I told him to please not quote Dr. Phil to me and to fuck off.

I clicked on ex number three, Enna Texson. Her mom literally named her after the number one in Greek, *enna*. Just because of that, I knew she was different.

The first time I saw her was during orientation at university. She had long blond hair to her waist. She wore tight jeans and a green tie-dyed top with beads on it. She stuck out like a sore thumb. She was a throwback hippie, and I was instantly drawn to her.

I sat behind her in the auditorium, and watched as she pulled out a notebook and a black pen. After the orientation, she ran out of there like a bat out of hell. A few days later, classes started, and she happened to be in two of my four classes that first semester. I played it cool with her. I watched her and noticed she didn't talk much in class. She took down a lot of notes, but kept to herself. Guys sat next to her and tried to start a conversation, but she didn't seem interested. She had these cat eyes that intrigued the fuck out of me.

On exam day for adolescent psychology, she sat next to me. The aroma of her lime-coconut perfume—it was something like that—stopped me from concentrating. I kept looking at her, and she was writing madly on the paper with such force and passion. What the fuck was she writing? My mind couldn't focus on the exam. Enna's name was playing like a bad record in my brain, completely distracting me. Suddenly she got up and handed in her paper. It was only an hour and a half into the exam.

I handed in my exam after two and a half hours, and as I left the classroom, there she was, sitting at one of the picnic tables near some vending machines. She was reading *Anna Karenina* and seemed to be in deep concentration.

"Enjoying the book?" I asked.

She looked up at me. "Extremely."

"How did you find the exam?" I asked as she looked at my hair oddly.

"I thought it was easy." She placed her bookmark into her book and gestured for me to sit.

And so, began the most tumultuous relationship of my life. She was a brilliant girl with many problems, the first being that she had suicidal tendencies due to an abusive father and a mother who had abandoned her. She had grown up in foster homes, and she was emotionally wrecked.

I looked at her profile picture. She had none. It was the blue background. I clicked on her page and read her status. "Dead is my soul, dead is my love." She had poetry notes with every date from the last couple of years. I exited her profile right away. I didn't want to go down that dark road.

I glanced at my watch. 7:50. Fuck. I had to leave. I shut down the computer, grabbed my coat, keys, wallet, and wine, and quickly left.

I was at Melina's house by 8:10. I rang her bell, nervous like a teenager on his first date.

"Teach?" she asked through the intercom.

"Yes," I replied. Why did she insist on calling me that?

I wondered if I'd ever find a "normal" kind of girl. Could Serena be that normal girl? Did one even exist? Serena struck me as normal. My attraction to Selena was energetic, as crazy as that sounded. It was a feeling, a connection that was undeniable. I believed in that spiritual shit.

Melina was wearing a brown trench coat, tied snugly around her waist, with the collar of her white chemise sticking out. Her cleavage peeked out at me, and her bare neck was exposed. She had on brown high heels with straps, and her toenails were painted a dark, ruby red. Her makeup was dark too, her eyes accentuated with dark purple eyeshadow and eyeliner. She looked like a movie star. Her brown hair was pin straight, and her bangs covered half her eyes. I cleared my head of all thoughts of Serena. Melina looked beautiful, and I smiled at her.

"Hello," I said.

She smiled back. "Come in," she said, giving me the once-over from head to toe. "You look delicious."

Still feeling woozy from the rush of driving fast and running up three flights of stairs instead of waiting for the elevator, I handed her the bottle of wine, wondering what was under her trench coat. Did she just say *delicious*?

My first sensation arose within me like a dormant volcano waiting to erupt. She went to the kitchen, pulled open a drawer, and took out a wine bottle opener. She opened the sides and twisted it up while looking at me. Then she roughly shoved the opener into the cork and turned it around.

"Would you like me…to help?"

She stopped what she was doing, and her eyes

sparkled. "Yes, please."

I walked into the kitchen, which was spotless, and she stepped aside, still holding the opener.

"I think I might need that." I pointed to the bottle.

"Oh, of course."

She handed it to me, along with the opener and our hands touching briefly. I took it and twisted the opener in the cork. She moved away and opened a cupboard, then I heard the clinking of glasses. She placed them gently onto the counter. Twisting and turning the cork, it popped out and we were ready to rock and roll.

"You do that well," she said, watching my hands. I pulled out the cork from the opener and placed it on the counter, then lifted the bottle and poured our drinks into the wine glasses.

I passed her one wine glass, then lifted mine toward her. "Cheers."

I waited. She finally lifted her glass too and said "cheers" or "fears" or something like that, then grinned. We stood in her kitchen, awkwardly drinking and not talking. She took a sip. I took a sip. Back and forth we went, finishing the first glass in record time.

"I was thirsty," I said, feeling the warm effect of the wine.

"And here I thought you were horny." She poured more wine into our glasses and turned away.

"You are absolutely right." I took the glass and sipped some more wine.

She leaned back against the counter and rested her elbows on it, her trench coat slightly open, and I caught a glimpse of a black lace bra. My insides rumbled. Not moving, she watched me closely, eyeing my body up and down. I felt this surge of energy from her, and I walked over to her.

"Not yet, big boy. Let's finish the wine. I have another surprise for you," she said with a wicked smile.

Deciding to play her game, I pulled back and leaned against the opposite counter. Resting my elbows on the countertop, I pushed my chest outward, emphasizing it, and her gaze moved straight to it. I pushed my erection forward so she could see it too, and sure enough, she did.

She took another sip of wine. "Drink, teach. Drink up."

I took a long sip but left a little wine in the glass. We had this lockdown stare going on. Neither of us budged. We drank and stared at each other. My instinct was to bend her over the counter and ram my cock into her, but it seemed she had other tortures on her mind right now. She wanted to draw out the sexual tension that was driving me insane.

Suddenly she jumped up and sat her ass on the counter, and as if she were sitting on a park bench, she swung her legs while leaning forward, her palms flat on the countertop. Her trench coat fell open slightly, and the belt slowly loosened, revealing the strap of a black garter belt on her left leg. She crossed her legs to bring attention to the garter strap and then uncrossed them and stuck out her long, lean legs. She placed her hand behind her back and must have pressed a button, because then a song came on, loud and clear. It was a soulful voice, no one I had ever heard before.

"Who is this?"

"'Next To Me' by Emeli Sandé," she said in a sultry voice.

We listened to the song play until the end. Then she bent her index finger and gestured for me to come over.

I took two quick steps and lifted my polo shirt over my head, placing my hands on her thighs like I had been dying to do from the second she opened the door.

She brushed them away. "Not yet. I go first."

She yanked the shirt from my hand and threw it on the counter. She was slightly hunched over, sitting on the counter, her hair falling on my face as I inhaled some cherry blossom scent. "Your hair smells so good."

She caressed my chest, which had some hair on it. My chest was built too—more like a runner, since running every day kept me in shape. I felt myself get harder.

"I really like your upper body. Were you all sweaty today? Fancy, bumping into you again after last night." she asked while massaging my chest and my shoulders, running her hands through my hair and then back down again. It was so sensual, and her voice made me dizzy. Her eyes were full of desire. "You are so very…very…delightful to look at," she said in a low tone.

I couldn't take it, placing my hands on her thighs, slowly stroking them up and down, and opening her trench coat a little more, my mind was all fuzzy with desire. I pulled her robe slightly off her shoulder while she continued massaging my chest. I breathed in her scent; my cock wanted to fuck her right there, fast and hard.

She wrapped her legs around my waist. I undid the belt completely to open her trench coat. She bent down as my mouth found hers to kiss. She met my lips, and aggressively yet sensually, plunged her tongue into my mouth. Her fingers were still in my hair, and my hands slid inside her coat to feel the warmth of her body. Her pussy was against my abdomen, as her warm heat pressed up against mine emanating intense need to be possessed.

She thrust her sex toward my groin. I cupped her ass, then slipped my hands inside her panties—well, her thong, actually, because her ass cheeks were bare. And what an ass it was! Perfect! My cock pressed against the counter, too low for her to feel it, so lifting her up in the air, still kissing her, and squeezing our bodies together, we both let out a low sensual moan.

I wanted to taste her, laying her flat on her back on the table. She spread her legs wide open. "Are you hungry, teach?" she asked in that seductive voice that would drive any man to the brink of desire. She still had on her trench coat, but her black lace bra holding up her gorgeous breasts, peeked up at me, so full and tempting. She was also wearing her black lace thong and garter belt. She extended her leg and strapped it into a chair with her high-heeled shoe.

Her hair was beautifully spread out on the rectangular table, and there we were, shirtless but still in my jeans, Melina, half-naked.

"Time to undress you," she said, smiling. Undoing my top button and then slowly pulling down my zipper, she exposed the rest of my body gradually while looking directly into my eyes.

Before any words escaped my mouth, she lifted her head slightly. "Leave your jeans on for now," she said, and then, "Well? Are you hungry?"

I gazed at her pussy with true hunger now. "Very much so."

I reached out and moved her thong to the side. Lo and behold, her pussy swollen and glistening wet, and I bent down to taste her sweetness. Flicking my tongue in and out of her sex her moans filled the room. She tasted out of this world and sounded like porn star Traci Lords. I felt her groans all the way to the tip of my cock, and I wasn't even inside her yet.

Suddenly she shoved me away. "No, not yet." She seemed pissed. "I didn't say I was ready to come." She pushed herself up and off the table. "Let's go to my bed. My ass is killing me."

As she walked in front of me, she let the trench coat drop to the floor. I almost tripped on it. She didn't stop; she continued on to her bedroom, her bare ass swaying and her high heels clicking on her wooden floor. Her long hair was all over the place. I loved every single movement she made. She screamed of sex. Every single curve of her body turned me on.

As soon as we entered her bedroom, she turned to me, a slight coldness in her eyes that wasn't there before.

"Lie down, teach. I'm taking you places you've never been before."

She turned around and left the room. I lay down on the bed, wondering what she was up to. My dick saluted the room, but then it suddenly went limp. I heard her opening and closing cupboards, and then a minute later, she came back into the bedroom, holding a joint and a lighter. She lay down to my left and placed the joint between her lips.

"Have you ever fucked while stoned?" She asked the question as casually as if she had asked whether I preferred fish or steak.

"Yes." *With Enna*. This was going to be fun.

"Well, you've never fucked *me* while stoned." She lit the joint, then blew out smoke rings.

"What kind of teacher smokes up?" I asked jokingly.

"The real kind." She reached over and grabbed my cock with one hand while holding the joint in the other. She took one quick drag and then placed the joint between my lips. "Inhale," she said, her blue eyes twinkling. I did. "Take another. C'mon, you look like you could fuck me to death while stoned," she said hoarsely.

I took the joint from her hand and inhaled three tokes, holding the smoke in for a few seconds. I coughed it out. "It's been a while." I coughed again, sitting up.

"Well, we're going to have to change that." She sat up too, and I handed her the joint. "No, hold it, and open your mouth," she said and I held it between her lips.

I watched her mouth closely. She inhaled like an expert and then, looking directly into my eyes, slowly blew the smoke into my mouth. I inhaled the smoke, and my insides started to feel warm and fuzzy. My eyes grew heavy from lust, euphoria and felt a mad rush to my sex. Back and forth we passed the joint, till we felt the effects on every nerve ending of our bodies. We lay there.

She put her hands behind her head and propped herself up on a pillow. "I'd like you to touch me now. I'm on fire." She gave me a come-hither look.

I was so stoned that my body felt on fire too. Using my legs, I removed my jeans and kicked them to the floor, then did the same with my underwear. As she watched, she tilted her head to the side, taking in every movement. She spread her legs wide apart. Her pussy was swollen, and she was breathing heavily. I slowly undressed her, starting with her shoes, but didn't remove the garter belt or stockings. I wanted to fuck her with those on. I ran my hands along her body and up to her breasts, and unclipped the lace bra. She let out a slight moan as my lips met her belly button and my hand tugged off her thong, ever so slowly.

I kissed her calves while gently tracing the outline of her body with my hands. As my lips traveled higher and higher, she shivered. She let out another sigh and closed her eyes, thrusting her sex upward. Naked and hard, I sat up on the bed now, caressing her body. Taking her breasts in my hands, I stroked the nipples with the tips of my fingers. I outlined her areolas and then pulled hard on her nipples. She stuck out her breasts and mumbled something like "again" or "c'mon," and I pulled her nipples slowly and then harder, over and over again, till she couldn't stop moaning.

Then she violently pushed away my hands. "Stop!" And she shoved me onto my back so my cock, fully erect, stood up.

With both hands, she grabbed and then stroked my dick up and down. My eyes closed, lost in the sensation. The weed was taking full effect now, my needs wanting to feel the heat of her mouth. She flicked her tongue up and down my sex, plunging it deep into her mouth, while she accepted it, moaning.

She sucked my cock for a time, then stopped, slid her body up toward me, and kissed my lips before placing her pussy directly above my cock, her slit ready to devour me. I thrust at her opening, feeling her wetness, and moaned as she jerked her tongue in and out of my mouth. Breathless, I watched as she bent to the side of the bed to get a condom. She quickly rolled it onto my dick, then straddled me again. I kissed her and squeezed her ass, then slid my hands between our legs and guided my cock into her, a gentle shove that made her moan.

"I'm ready," she said, opening her eyes and revealing a look of abandonment and desire.

"I know," I mumbled. "I can't take it anymore." I was delirious, with an ache that made me crazy.

As soon as I was inside her warm, wet channel, some kind of frenzy took control over me, and with all my strength, my cock pounded her hard, my hands holding her hips with a craving I wasn't sure could be satisfied. My cock deep inside her, I didn't want to leave any inch of her inner walls untouched. Hardcore fucking. She moaned and accepted all of me.

Melina slammed down onto my dick, rubbing her clit against me and shouting, "I'm coming for you, teach! I'm coming!"

She sounded like a howling madwoman, arousing me further, until my voice shouted back, "I'm coming too!" And it was done with quick thrusts. "Don't move," I said as the last of my cum spurted out.

She sat on top of me, staring down with a funny look on her face.

"What is it?" I asked, trying to catch my breath. Although the act didn't take long, it was fuckin' intense—hot as hell inside her. I smiled. "That was fucking incredible." Placing one hand under my head and keeping the other on her hip, she stared down at me for a few seconds and smiled back.

"Not bad, teach." She smirked. "Do you have the munchies?"

She giggled as she gently pulled herself off my dick. She removed the condom and threw it into her wastebasket with perfect precision. She did everything so flawlessly. She stood straight and tall, naked and self-assured. Most women went running to get dressed after sex, but she was comfortable with her sexuality and body like no woman I'd ever met before.

"Yes, I certainly do, Miss… What's your last name again?"

"Orfeo." She placed her hands on her hips, looking for her shoes. Was she actually going to put them on again?

"Melina Orfeo," I repeated. "You have a lovely name."

She put on her high heels and turned to me. "Thanks, Teddy. What's your last name? Since we're sharing."

I lay on the bed, both hands propped behind the pillow. She had an exceptionally comfortable mattress. "My full name is Theodore Neros."

"I love that. Why the fuck do people call you Teddy? That's awful. Theodore is much better. I'm calling you Theodore from now on, and there is absolutely nothing you can do about it."

"What if I told you that I hate that name?" I asked, sitting up.

I had flashbacks of elementary school and the kids bugging me about my Greek name, rhyming it with "whore." When my sister found out, she told my mom, and my mom spoke to the principal. But it made no difference because that was how kids were. My mom and dad divorced when I was ten, and my mom fought all my battles, while my dad had a different girlfriend every couple of months.

"No one has called me Theodore since grade six. When I went to high school, I switched to Ted." I got up, clearing my mind. "I'm starved." I slapped her ass. "Let's eat, sexy."

She looked at me crossly. "Don't slap me unless I

ask you to." She headed off, and I followed.

She opened the fridge door and stood in front of it. What the fuck? Was she crazy? Slap her when she asked? A chuckle crept up on me.

She turned to me and smiled. "Good stuff, right?"

"Yes, very." And I laughed.

She giggled. "What's so funny?"

"Don't slap me unless I ask you too," I repeated, laughing some more.

She started to laugh too, and soon she was holding her stomach. "Stop! I can't breathe!" she said, laughing even louder and holding onto the fridge. Then she shut the fridge door. "I don't even know why I'm laughing." There was a soft urgency in her eyes I hadn't noticed before.

"Because you don't want me to slap you unless you ask me to." I laughed even harder.

Her expression changed, and she became serious, all laughter gone from her eyes. "You find that funny, then?"

"What?" What just happened? Why was she so serious now? I tried to stop laughing but couldn't. "Yes," I replied, slowly catching my breath and becoming serious as the coldness in her blue eyes returned.

"I will make some pasta and marinara sauce," she said. "We need to eat because the night has just begun, and the spanking will take up a lot of your energy, Theodore."

Serena
The truth will set you free—or tie you up...

"What kind of similarities?"

"The kind I don't feel comfortable discussing on our first date," Ben replied, but then he looked at me, his expression thoughtful, as if he was considering telling me something. "I will be honest with you, though, because I want you to know something about me." He leaned in even closer. "I am completely and utterly monogamous, and I don't take any lies or bullshit."

"Okay." The way he said that had me perched on the edge of my seat. "Do you like rough sex?"

I had to be direct. I may have asked the question a little too loudly because a few heads turned, and at that moment, the waitress came over with our coffees and desserts. I looked down shyly and waited for her to set down the plates. Shit. Why did I ask that?

Once the waitress walked away, Ben smirked. "Are you always this blunt?"

"No, I don't know what's gotten into me. I apologize. You don't have to answer that."

"But I do have to answer that. Only it's not a yes or no answer, and our coffees are waiting." He lifted his spoon and twirled it into his cup, not adding any sugar or cream to it. *He's definitely sweet enough.* "Let's eat dessert first. Try the cake."

Everything looked yummy. I bit into the cake right

away. "Wow! This is scrumptious," I said, my mouth full. The combination of cheesecake, chocolate and raspberry was heavenly.

Ben smiled. "I told you."

He took his fork and knife and sliced the crêpe into precise, even pieces. He offered me a bite first, which was so polite, while I was already on my second bite of cheesecake. *What is wrong with me today?* I had no manners with Ben. I was asking him pointed questions and was eating like a pig.

I nodded, still chewing my cake. He placed a piece of crêpe onto his fork. "Here, try it." He held the fork in front of my mouth, waiting patiently until I swallowed my bite. He had a silly grin on his face.

"Usually girls never eat when I go on a date with them," he said. "This is so refreshing. Finally, a woman with an appetite."

They don't eat because you are so delectable to gaze at. I smiled back and opened my mouth to taste the crêpe.

"Mmmm… That is yummy," I said after swallowing it.

"Yes, it is yummy," he repeated, smiling, his dimples tantalizing me again.

"You have cute dimples," I said.

"Thank you."

Ben looked like something serious was on his mind. I wanted to tell him I had no idea what rough sex meant. The thought of Christopher Hawk scared the living hell out of me but at the same time struck something inside, awakening a part of me I hadn't even known existed. I'd never read erotica; I read those Nora Roberts novels, but they weren't even close to Ben's writing.

"Look, Serena, don't let it freak you out. Don't think

I write about everything I want to happen. I know what people want to read. My books are about the Dominant-submissive relationship, with twenty percent bondage and eighty percent vanilla sex. I add in the handcuffs, scarves, vibrators, ropes, chains, blindfolds…for excitement, so the reader keeps reading. None of that turns me on, except for…" He looked around.

Completely enthralled, I listened to him. I had never met anyone who spoke about sex toys so openly. I took another bite of my cake and sip of my coffee, averting his gaze.

"Go on." I swallowed my bite, waiting.

"Except for scarves. All shapes and sizes," he said in a low, husky voice, his eyes gleaming.

Scarves? I hadn't expected that.

"You should read my book." He looked serious again.

"I ordered both. I will as soon as they arrive," I promised.

"Call me when you finish them. Anytime. I want your feedback."

"How many copies have you sold?"

"Last time I checked, forty thousand of book one and thirty-four thousand of book two. The other nine, a little less. My publisher seems to think that with the third one I'll sell over one hundred thousand copies."

"Too bad they're not in paper book format."

"I know. I would love to hold copies of my books."

"Do you think one day you will?"

"If I sell over two hundred thousand copies, then I'm going to get an agent."

"Why?"

"Why the fuck not? I figure an agent will help

promote my book or get the series published." He looked agitated. "It's such a competitive field, and it is so subjective." He looked discouraged. "Before I opted for an e-publisher, I tried to publish through the traditional ways, and received one rejection letter after another." He gave me a weary smile. "That's not to say that some e-publishers didn't reject me—trust me, a lot did—so when Hot Sex Publishing accepted my novel, I was thrilled. I could stop wasting my time chasing after publishers and focus on writing. They loved my style and said my writing voice was unique and exactly what they were looking for. Plus, I really suck at editing my own work."

"I suck at that too," I said.

My cake and coffee were almost finished. Ben took a few more bites of his crêpe and then offered me some more.

"No, thanks. I'm full."

"Okay."

He finished his crêpe and then leaned back in his chair. "Now I can't breathe," he said as he spread his legs slightly. He looked so tall, dwarfing the tiny table we occupied. "I think we need to take a long walk," he suggested.

I glanced at my watch. It was almost eight o'clock, still early. I looked across at Ben, so sexy, gazing at me pensively.

"That sounds like a good idea," I said. "We've been sitting for hours."

"It doesn't feel like hours…" He had that warm look in his brown eyes that drew me like a magnet. He looked around for the waitress and flagged her down, gesturing for the bill.

"I got dessert," I said, unzipping my purse.

"Not on my watch," he said firmly, standing up and reaching into his front jeans pocket.

Two girls behind him eyed each other and then Ben's lean body. I stared at his long legs and the subtle outline of his sex, but he caught me and smirked again. I immediately looked behind him and noticed the girls ogling now. How could they not?

He pulled out his money and then glanced at me. I tried to concentrate on not looking like a pervert staring at his perfect body.

"I don't know what it is about you, Serena, but you're making me all fucked up."

Not taking his eyes off me, he counted and did some mental calculations while I tried to figure out what shade of brown his eyes were—chestnut, chocolate, hazelnut… He left the cash on the table.

"I'd like to pay too," I offered, wondering how, exactly, I was *making him all fucked up*.

"Forget about it. Look, Serena, number one, I'm old-fashioned. Number two, you're a student. Number three, my mum told me to always pay for a girl on a date. She said it made her feel special. And in case you're thinking about how you fuck me up, it's simple: You do it for me." His gaze never left mine.

"*Un moment. L'addition, monsieur*," the waitress said, holding the bill in her hand and looking at the money on the table. She'd overheard the last part of the sentence and looked at me as if she wanted to be me. I just stood there, speechless.

He turned to her. "*Je sais. Vingt-quatre et quarante-trois.*" He smiled at her as he said, "*Merci.*"

She looked from the bill to him and then to the table.

He had left thirty dollars under his coffee mug. She was just as surprised as I was. "*Merci beaucoup*," she said and picked up the money, the empty plates and coffee cups.

Ben put on his jacket, and I put on mine, pondering how smart he was.

"It's no big deal," he said as if he had just read my mind. "I have a mathematical mind." He shrugged. The two girls were still openly staring at him, and I gave them a dirty look. They turned away and concentrated on their coffee." I also have a photographic memory," he added.

I thought, *you're fuckin' steaming, rocking hot, with your perfect body and face,* but all I said was, "So, Ben, what you are telling me is that you are a genius?" A *beautiful* genius.

He stepped behind me and placed his hand on the small of my back to guide me out the café. My mind spun. So, I was with a man who not only could model for Calvin Klein underwear and was gorgeous with his three-day-stubble head, but who was a mathematical genius who wrote erotica and liked rough sex. Sweat trickled between my breasts. I was in way over my head. Now his mind excited me too. Nothing was more of a turn-on than a smart man.

The fresh air felt great against my skin. Ben bent his head down and said, "I hope I'm not scaring you away." He paused just outside the entrance of the café, reached for his cigarettes inside his jacket pocket, and took one out.

"Scare me?" More like frighten the pants off of me. The sexiness he exuded made me nervous. "Not at all," I lied, watching his every move. His hands and fingertips as he gestured, his lips as he spoke, his chest as he breathed—everything about him set my senses on fire. And yes, that did frighten me, because the sexual urge to be with him was so strong. Plus, he was utterly charming and, above all, brilliant.

"Let's walk," he said after he lit his cigarette.

"You do it for me" echoed in my mind, and my head was reeling.

As he walked, he exhaled the smoke away from my direction. "What I mean is…" He seemed to be struggling to find his words. "I love sex."

"Oh," was all I said. Didn't all men love sex? I couldn't comment because my sexual experience didn't remotely come close to his. Ben appeared to be so sure of himself. He was an incredible kisser, and he knew what and how he liked sex. He had preferences, used sex toys, liked scarves… He wrote erotica, for Christ's sake! I felt dizzy.

He saw what must have been a what-the-fuck expression on my face, and I looked down and kicked a tiny pebble.

"Let's not talk about sex," he said. "Let's window-shop, and if you want to go into a store to browse, then by all means…I'll follow." He took another drag of his cigarette and exhaled the smoke.

Too many *let's*, I thought. *He* seemed nervous now. I was a little intimidated, but I wasn't afraid to talk about sex. Despite my confusion—and desperation—I wasn't a fuckin' virgin! He flicked his cigarette butt toward the street.

We continued to walk side by side, and then I turned to him. "Ben?"

"Yes?"

"You don't scare me," I said in the strongest, sexiest

voice I could muster.

I decided then and there that I wanted to sleep with him, to feel his body and touch him all over. I wanted to explore this side of me that he was arousing. I wanted to be driven wild by him. I wanted to feel his tongue all over my body, making all my fantasies come alive.

He stopped dead in his tracks, and I did the same. We faced each other.

"If you ever get scared, you can use a safe word," he said, his voice full of concern, his eyes serious.

"A what?" What was he talking about?

Ben smiled, and his eyes gleamed with excitement. My insides knotted up. "I'll explain in due time. For now, let's just walk, Serena."

He extended his arm as if we were going to a ball. I linked my arm through his, and his body heat warmed me in the cool night air. His forearm felt strong.

A safe word? What was I getting myself into? Excitement flooded my body at the thought of Ben touching me.

Teddy
I'm crazy for you but for how long...

Melina opened the pantry door and took out a glass jar of tomato sauce, some garlic, and basil, and then she pressed her iPod buttons again. "Catch," she said, throwing me an onion. She pulled out a cutting board as Alicia Keys sang loud and clear, "No One" echoing in the kitchen. Melina started to move her body seductively to the beat while she chopped the garlic.

I took the onion to the sink, ran some cold water on it like my mother used to do, and placed it next to her. I opened the drawer where she kept her knives and silently started to chop next to her, listening to the song and wondering how much energy I needed for the next tumble in bed. I peeked at her, and she suddenly burst out laughing.

I grabbed my glass of wine, which was still on the counter, and downed it. "I was so thirsty," I said, laughing at nothing in particular.

"Can you pass me my glass, please?" she asked, still giggling.

I held it out toward her, but she was still chopping the garlic, so she opened her mouth, gesturing for me to hold it for her while she drank. I placed the edge of the wine glass between her lips and gently lifted it upward. This needed some concentration. "Stop laughing. I don't want to spill it all over you."

"Why not?" she asked, purposely tilting her head forward and letting the wine spill down her neck. I instantly went for it, licking it up as she giggled.

One thing led to another, and I was fucking her again, this time from behind, and she insisted I not stop. She placed her hands on the counter, thrust her ass outward, and I bent my knees to drive into her quickly and fervently. She wanted it hard but then pushed me back.

"Stop!" she shouted.

I pulled out of her.

"What the fuck?" I asked angrily, huffing and puffing, my erect cock throbbing. She looked at it and started to laugh again. "What's so funny?"

"You are!" she said, laughing hysterically now. Then, turning all serious, she said, "I have to finish the sauce." And she continued chopping the ingredients. It seemed her powerful sex drive could be switched on and off at the drop of a hat.

I stood there, not moving. Was she serious? She was going to change her mind right in the middle of fucking? I couldn't even try to understand her anymore. She was so unpredictable. No, make that manic.

She glanced at me. "I'm not ready to come yet, Theodore. I have to finish the sauce." Her voice had turned cold.

"You're the one who told me to fuck you from behind—now. Those were your exact words." I was so pissed off at her. "I don't want blue balls," I added and then regretted it.

I should have fucking left. Who needed this shit? I certainly didn't. But I had a hard-on that wouldn't quit, and she was drawing me in like a magnet. All I could think of was pounding her hard. My legs didn't want to move; they wanted to be right behind her round, firm ass.

She burst out laughing yet again. "Trust me, you'll be satisfied."

And then I started to laugh too. What else was there to do? "I need some water." I walked toward the fridge, my dick saluting her. The effect of the weed had made me wild with an insatiable need to be inside her warm pussy.

"In the fridge."

We cooked the rest of the sauce and pasta, enjoying her selection of music. I'd never cooked naked in a kitchen with anyone before, so the experience was quite erotic and stimulating. Plus, my cock was still hard, and I was still feeling the buzz from smoking the joint. Melina took out a strainer, put it into the sink, and dumped in the boiled pasta as I poured us two more glasses of wine. Practically ignoring me, she quickly set the table.

I took a sip of wine, watching her every move. She was a perfect *naked* hostess. I leaned against the kitchen counter, purposely displaying my hard cock, wanting some kind of reaction from her. She looked at me and quickly looked back to what she was doing. She took out two white plates, placed the penne on them, and then added the marinara sauce. It smelled delicious. *I may as well satisfy one appetite at least.* What the fuck was she thinking? I couldn't think straight. Between the drugs and her killer body, all I wanted to do was come.

"Sit down, Theodore," she said, walking toward the table with the two plates in her hand.

"That smells amazing." I sat and tried to relax.

"Let's see what we created." She sat next to me.

"*Bon appetit,*" she said.

"*Bon appetit,*" I repeated, settling in and replacing my hunger for sex with food.

The smell of garlic invaded my senses as I took my first bite. "Mmm… This is fantastic."

She took a bite and agreed, and then we ate pretty much in silence while Amy Winehouse sang in the background. I don't even think we chewed our food; we finished so quickly. We were famished.

She got up, picked up both empty plates, ran some water on them, and placed them into the sink. She turned around and finally acknowledged me with a wicked smile.

"It's time," she announced with a slight coldness in her tone.

"Time for what?" My dick reacted to her words before my mind could.

"The spanking," she replied and walked toward her bedroom. I got up and followed.

"I want you to use your hand," she called out from the bedroom since I was still in the hallway.

In the bedroom, she was on her hands and knees on the bed, her voluptuous ass in the air and her breasts swaying. My reaction was probably a little shock on my face, feeling slightly taken aback. Was this a porno shoot?

How do I spank her? How hard? She wasn't even looking at me. Did she think my knowledge on spanking was vast?

But seeing Melina in that position excited the fuck out of me, and despite my confusion about how to do it, my desire to smack that inviting ass overcame me. The sight of her generous curves gave me a high that had nothing to do with the drugs. I was ready to do this shit.

I walked over to her and stood next to the bed, admiring her body in that tempting position. She tilted her head and saw the look on my face. Did she realize how confusing this was? Not thinking she cared a rat's ass about my state of mind, she smiled.

"You're so good-looking, Theodore. It's a shame you don't realize it." She had that wicked gleam in her eyes again. "If you knew what a gorgeous cock you have and what you can make it do, you would be even sexier…" Her voice trailed off, but then she said roughly, "Spank my ass like a dirty little boy, teach." At the sound of her words, my cock pulsed. There was no control over my body when my cock was around Melina. She looked directly at my sex. "Slow it down, cowboy. We have all night. Now listen, raise your right hand, and spank my ass. Come closer."

I lifted my hand and aimed to slap her ass cheek, but I was awkwardly positioned, so I ended up tapping it instead.

"I didn't feel a thing," she said impatiently.

I moved and spanked her a little harder.

"Use your strength, Theodore. I can take it." Her voice was harsh, powerful. I slapped her hard on the buttock, and she let out a tiny sigh. "A little harder and quicker," she instructed.

I spanked her right ass cheek at least ten times straight, till my arm started to throb and the palm of my hand burned.

"Now the other cheek."

I spanked her left ass cheek as many times as the other cheek and with the same strength. My concentration on the spanking was so intense that

Melina's voice wasn't even registering between moans. She was saying something about slaps and cocks and pain and pleasure. Her words were mumbled and her sentences interrupted with her moaning. My excitement was due to her excitement. Spanking her didn't do anything for me sexually. If anything, it was tough work. It took a lot of my energy—she had been right about that part—and she wanted me to go on and on. This was exhausting. How the hell was my stamina going to keep up with her? Luckily, my running comes in handy with a sex-fiend girl.

"Stop!" she shouted, and I did just that. "Are you a fuckin' idiot? I said stop, like, five times!"

My dick quickly shrank. "Look, Melina, I didn't hear you. Sorry."

She eyed me as I stepped back from the bed. "Where do you think you're going?" She turned over and sat on the bed, flashing me her angry eyes. "Theodore, if you can't handle me, then leave, and don't come back. *Ever*."

My gaze traveled down to her breasts with their perfect-sized nipples that I wanted to suck and then to the triangle of her sex, which was slightly open, revealing her swollen clit. Daring to walk a few steps forward. She took in a deep breath, waiting to see what I would do.

"Melina, I can handle you." I sat on the bed. "But can you take it easy on me? I'm not your boy toy."

She smiled, but it wasn't genuine. It was a sly smile, one that revealed she had many skeletons in her closet. "You have to know by now that I need sex. That I crave it. That I want it like a glass of water when thirsty. I can't live without sex. I find you so sexy and hot, Theodore. I want you inside me. I want to have you, but I want all of you. I don't want you with anyone else when you're with me. Promise me. *Promise me*."

"I'm not ready for a relationship right now," I said.

"To be fair to you, let me be clear," she continued, ignoring my statement.

"What do you mean?" I became concerned because her demeanor had changed. She was quiet and seemed vulnerable—yet still tough.

"It's probably obvious that I like to tell you what to do during sex." She looked directly into my eyes as if waiting for me to say something about that.

"Yes, it certainly is," I responded.

"I'm a Dominant."

"A what? I know you like control, but what exactly does the term 'Dominant' mean?" She wanted to dominate me?

"C'mon. You know. Why are you acting stupid, teach? I like to tell men what to do to me. I want to be in control. I don't fake orgasms. I don't fake sex. I like it, and I want you to do as I say."

I shrugged. "Can't we just fuck?" I couldn't think straight. She was fucking confusing me with all this shit about Doms. Did I really want to get into kinky sex? I really just wanted to fuck her.

Before I could even think of a response, she looked at me with a glimmer in her eye. "Did spanking me turn you on?"

"Not really. It's you who turns me on."

Actually, it was her sexual prowess that turned me on. The way she wanted it so badly. The way she turned into a porn star once we got going. Though spanking her wasn't too bad, it was her reaction to it that aroused me. I liked it after a while too, but when I saw how hot it made Melina, it got me rock hard as well.

She took my hand and placed it on her pussy. "Let's stop all this small talk." She kissed me hard on the mouth. "You drive me crazy," she whispered into my ear, then took my fingers and placed them inside her— alongside her own.

She was going to drive *me* crazy.

Serena
Safe words and safe sex tales

I knew what he meant, but it was too soon. We hadn't even had sex yet, and already Ben was talking about safe words, as if things were going to get out of control.

"Ben, I've had the most boring sex life ever," I said as we continued walking up Saint Laurent Street.

Where did that come from? Without knowing why, and for some bizarre reason, telling Ben the truth about my idle sex life, felt great. It was like confessing, suddenly the stories about Gery and Kenneth poured out, and what sex had been like with them. Trusting Ben felt natural.

He listened attentively, nodding, sometimes rolling his eyes. His one comment made me think more about what *he* would be like in bed.

"Those punks don't know a thing about a woman and what she needs."

It was getting chilly, so we turned around and headed back toward the motorcycle. Ben wasn't as open to sharing his past sexual experiences. His list was probably as long as his books, and that made my heart heavy. He was more interested in my sex life.

"So, you're telling me you have never had great sex or good sex or mind-blowing sex. You're telling me you have never had an orgasm during sex." He looked directly into my eyes and gave me a sly grin. "I have my work cut out for me. I think I can please you, Serena. I think I can make you come the first time." His gaze traveled the length of my body, and my sex stirred.

I think you can too.

"Here we are," he said as we approached his motorcycle. "So, where to now?" His eyes were dark, with a devilish gleam.

"Home. I have homework to finish for tomorrow morning," I said grumpily.

"I'll help you do it, and then we can move on to more exciting things." He traced the outline of my lips with his fingertip, and a shudder whipped through me. "I really want you, Serena," he said, feeling the insides of my lips now. I swallowed nervously, a tingling sensation all over my body, especially inside my belly.

"If you want to help me, sure," I said. Of course, he wanted to. I was so stupid. "Okay, yes," I said with conviction.

"Hop on." He bent to grab the helmets, then placed mine on my head and snapped it shut. He came very close to my face—so close I thought he was going to kiss me—but he pulled back and said, "Your perfume is really nice."

My throat felt so dry, swallowing hard, imagining those lips all over me. "Thank you," I whispered, keeping my eyes on his gorgeous face.

We sat on the bike, and he leaned his body back toward me a little closer than he had before. My sex heated up as my arms wrapped snugly around his solid frame. The two girls from before were just leaving the café, and they glanced at Ben, giving him a smile and completely ignoring me. The nerve of some girls! They whispered to each other and glanced back at us again. My muscles tensed up and loosened my grip around his waist slightly.

"Don't fret," he said, feeling my disconnection. "I only have eyes for you."

The ride home was quick—no traffic this time. After parking the bike, Ben followed me wordlessly to my building's front door. As soon as the front door opened, I realized my place was a disaster.

"Ben, excuse the mess."

He looked around. "What mess?" He hadn't taken his eyes off me. "I don't see any mess."

He took off his shoes and then his jacket, placing it on the couch while I was still removing my boots. He sat on the couch and spread his arms along the top, then crossed one leg over the other, watching me take off my coat, open my closet, and hang it up. He quickly got up and passed me his jacket. He was lightning fast—one second he was on the couch, the next he was by my side.

"Let me help you." He took the hanger from my hand and helped me place his coat on it, touching my knuckles gently. A current slithered through me. He looked around my apartment and smiled. "Nice place. I love the colors."

I had painted the living room burgundy red and placed gold mirrors found in a used furniture store on one wall. My couch was burgundy velvet and had belonged to my mother. There was a wooden, glass-top coffee table in front of the couch, and a black leather armchair off to the side. It was on special at The Brick for two hundred dollars because of a discoloration on the back so my sister had coloured over with a permanent marker. That had actually been Elsa's idea. That was it for furniture. In my white kitchen was a small, natural wood colour breakfast table my mom bought me as a gift from Ikea along with a couple of high stools. All my books were on a long bookshelf between the kitchen and the living room. Ben went straight to the shelf and started to look at them without picking any books up.

"Thanks," I said, feeling nervous as I watched him move around my apartment so comfortably. "What can I offer you?"

"What do you have?" he asked from the bookcase, creating a distance between us.

Another tingle ran through my body. Perhaps I wasn't ready for this. *Well, get ready*, a little voice inside me said. *Seize the moment. Carpe fucking diem.* Wasn't that what all the literature professors spoke of? All the love stories…

"I have coffee, herbal tea, or fresh sage." I didn't want to offer any alcohol, and God knew if the one or two bottles I had were even drinkable. No way was I going down that road again.

"Fresh sage sounds appealing," he said, still looking at my books. "I see you have a thing for Canadian literature."

"Not really. I had to read thirteen books in two months for a six-credit course and present my review of the authors. I didn't really get into those—the books you're referring to—except for Margaret Laurence."

"She was an exceptional writer," he agreed.

In the kitchen, I placed some water into a small pot and added the sage to it. I took out two brown mugs with *café* written on them and placed them on the counter. Turning my head, he was right behind me and my breath caught. How did he move so fast? His presence made my heart pound.

"Hmm, you have homework?" He reached into my loose hair with his hand and gently shook it out. "I've wanted to do that all day. Sorry." He smiled and pulled back.

The hairs on the back of my neck stood as another tingle erupted deep in my belly and shot all the way down to my sex.

"Uh…yes, I have to write a paper on *To the Lighthouse*," I said in a low voice, trying to pretend Ben's hands in my hair hadn't affected me at all.

He stood tall in front of me. "Virginia Woolf, huh?" He grinned as if he had a secret. "I'm sure we can find other ways to amuse ourselves for a couple of hours besides writing about a lighthouse…" He took a step near me. "Of course, if you want to work on it right away, I'll understand." He took another step closer, his eyes gleaming. Leaning against the counter, I heard the sound of the water heating up. The apartment was quiet, silent, except for our breathing, which was getting heavier and heavier. "So, Serena, what if I told you I really wanted to fuck you right now?" he said calmly, his gaze burning into mine, waiting for my reaction.

An involuntary gasp escaped me. My pussy was instantly wet, and my throat felt parched. I licked my lips from nervousness, and his gaze went straight to my mouth. I couldn't even respond with words, but Ben could see I was answering him without speaking, and he didn't wait for a verbal reply. He came closer, and once his chest was against mine, my nipples immediately hardened at his body heat. He pulled away, took a step toward the stove, and shut it off.

"I want to put out all fires—especially *yours*," he

said and lifted me up.

I giggled because it was so unexpected and romantic but at the same time so masculine. I placed my arms around his neck, wrapped my legs around his waist as he walked me toward the bedroom, which was pink—fuchsia hot pink. I loved the colour because it made me feel so girly-girly. Ben held me tightly, walking effortlessly as if I weighed ten pounds.

He let out a tiny laugh as we entered my room. "I love a pink room," he said, looking around and taking in the pink curtains and the zebra-print bedspread. "It makes me wild." He looked deeply into my eyes. "If it gets too much, Serena, promise me you'll use a safe word. Pick a word." His tone was serious and his dark eyes even darker.

My heart pounded with every word he spoke. I needed to feel him close to me. No fear came over me—just a heady sexual charge that left me breathless.

"Pink," I mumbled.

"Pink it is," he said. The way he said that simple word was so hot.

He kissed me, pulling me closer to him. I held on to his neck, sliding my tongue between his lips and feeling his warm, delicious tongue entering my mouth. He twirled his tongue around mine, over and over again, sucking and weaving it with his until it felt like they were one. He didn't break the kiss as he lay me on the bed, but then he pulled back. "I'm going to take my time with you, Serena."

I was speechless. I just stared at him as if he were an alien—a fucking gorgeous alien in my pink bedroom. He lay down next to me and unbuttoned my blouse without even looking at what he was doing. He stared at my lips and kissed them after undoing each button. And with each undone button, my excitement grew, until I was panting. He hadn't even touched me yet, and I thought, *put out my fire*. I closed my eyes for a second.

"Open your eyes," he said in a firm voice. "I want to watch you."

I obeyed, intimidated by the tone of his voice. He undid the last button and removed my blouse. I was wearing my peach bra, and he smiled. He caressed my breasts through my bra, then slid his hand behind my back to unsnap the hook. I arched my back to give him some space, which caused my chest to thrust forward, and he took that as an opportunity. He kissed my breasts—again, through my bra—and a tingling sensation zipped through my body as he pulled the bra off with his teeth, savagely tossing it aside as if he were a lion about to eat his prey. It was a violent thought, but I felt like he was going to devour me, and I was powerless, like a helpless animal.

He fastened his mouth to my nipple, and then pulled it with his teeth. "Does that hurt?" he asked with a muffled breath.

"No." But I wasn't sure whether it felt good or bad. It felt weird. Then he sucked it really hard, and there was an instant tug right in my sex, as if the two were connected. Yes, it was a good feeling, as a moan escaped my lips. He did it again and again. *Oh. Wow!*

As soon as Ben heard me moan, he moved on to the other nipple and repeated the same meticulous process. It left me feeling delirious. He slowly moved his lips downward, licking and kissing my stomach, until he reached my jeans. He undid the top button, and then looked up at me.

"How do you like it thus far?"

Thus far? Now his vocabulary was arousing me, especially with that pronounced English accent.

"I…like…it," I stammered.

His gaze met mine as he stood and pulled off my pants in one sweeping motion, then threw them on the floor. He dug his teeth into the side string of my underwear and slowly tugged them down my legs, leaving a trail of feverish kisses and transporting me to seventh heaven.

"Where's that blue scarf you were wearing last night?" he asked once he came back up on the bed.

He leaned on his elbow and lay there as if he'd just asked me what time it was. There I was, completely naked, while he was completely dressed, and now he wanted me to get the scarf? He had a thing for scarves… What the fuck did he want to do with it? I swallowed hard, and I knew he sensed my hesitation as I self-consciously sat up, trying to remember where I'd thrown the scarf last night. Oh yeah, it was at the bottom of my closet.

"I'll get it." He popped out of bed and waited for me to gesture to where it is.

Already emotionally spent and dizzy in anticipation of what he was going to do with the scarf, I pointed to my closet.

"On the floor," I said, and he opened the closet, bent down, and picked it up.

He placed it around his neck, smelled it, and gave me a dark look of longing. A deep breath came out of my lungs when he reached for his shirt with both hands and pulled it over his head. He removed his jeans, and then, ever so slowly, taunting me, he slid his underwear down his legs, then flung them across the room with one kick. His cock sprang forth, beautifully erect. Oh God, he was so big! He looked like a fucking Greek god. He saw how focused I was on him, and he smiled.

Right across his chest, from side to side, was a tattoo of a bird with immense wings. It was superb, with exquisite lines and colours. He stood naked before me, my blue scarf wrapped around his neck, a devilish grin on his face, and the wide bird wings on his chest calling to me.

"I love your tattoo," I said. *And I love your cock.*

"Thank you. I had it done when I was eighteen, in London."

He glanced down at it, appeared to think of something, and then quickly looked back at me. I was lying flat on my back, so he couldn't see my tattoo, and then what he had just said hit me…

"Aren't you from Liverpool?"

"Moved to London to study English. I got involved with someone, and my mum wanted me to get the fuck out of London. Hence,"—he lifted both hands in the air and gestured to his body—"here I am. Mum thought I'd be some kind of doctor. I had the potential, plus I got accepted to med school on a scholarship, but I liked women and writing more than numbers and science." He took a step closer. "I don't really want to talk about that period in my life."

I tried to concentrate on what he was saying, but it was difficult with him standing completely naked before me. I knew now wasn't the time to delve into his past, but I wondered why he had to leave London. He could have been a doctor. His mum was overprotective…and he is…hot… He likes women… My mind continued to wander for a few seconds as my gaze traveled lower again to stare at his massive cock. Lust continued to build, my pussy as wet as can be.

He took the scarf off his neck and placed it on the bed. He seemed preoccupied for a second, and then he turned to me, wearing a gentle expression. "If you don't want to do this, I won't push you."

I glanced at the scarf and then back at him a little fearfully. Need flared through me, the thought of being with him excited me so much—a man who had so much desire for me. For some strange reason, trusting Ben was natural as well…but what did he want to do to me? And when he said *women*, hundreds of women passed through my mind and made me insecure and nervous…wondering just how many women he had pleased.

"You're looking at me like you're going to freak out."

I *was* freaking out. "It's okay," I said, calming myself down. "I want to do this." *As long as Ben touched me soon, everything would be alright.*

He wrapped the scarf around his neck again. Then he took the two ends and slowly caressed my entire naked body with them, sending my nerve endings in a frenzy.

"Oh, Serena, baby girl," he said. "Relax, I won't hurt you. Close your eyes."

And the last thing I saw before he covered my eyes with the scarf was Ben hovering over me, his expression sly and his dark eyes full of excitement. There was something in them not seen before. It made me a bit nervous again thinking if this is what I wanted to do anymore.

Everything went black.

I felt Ben near me, but he didn't touch me. What was going on? *Pink* was on the tip of my tongue, when, through the darkness, his voice carried me back to reality.

"Serena, just let yourself go…"

I had never been blindfolded. Ben kissed my shoulders and then moved down my arms. My heart was pounding. He must have felt it too, because he securely clasped my hands with his, and that calmed me down.

"Serena, your body is my treasure, and I will take good care of it. Don't be nervous." He kissed my neck, then lower till he reached my breasts. "Although, I do like that you're nervous." He placed my free hand on his beating heart. "I'm nervous too…" And then he gently placed both my hands back on the bed and resumed licking and kissing of my breasts, sucking my nipples, making my body squirm under his touch.

My body is his treasure. I repeated those words in my mind, letting out a low moan. Heat rose from inside and traveled to every nerve ending in my body. He was nervous too? Somehow, I found that hard to believe.

He left a trail of perfect kisses on my stomach, and then he reached my belly button. "Oh, you have an innie, just like me." He buried his tongue in it.

Did his tongue and lips just travel to places on my body *nobody* had ever been? Yes, it had. Instantly my body relaxed. The darkness no longer bothered me. In fact, it made all my senses come alive as his tongue invaded every inch of my body, making me more aware of the sensations deep in my sex. His hands slid down my legs, slowly spreading them apart, and then he plunged his tongue into me with rapid, feverish thrusts that sent spasms of pleasure to every part of my mind and body. I moaned restlessly, passionately, crazily. My state of pleasure was quickly rising and reaching a state of ecstasy felt only with my vibrator, and that didn't even come close to Ben's tongue work.

He abruptly stopped. "I feel you ready to come, Serena, I feel you. But I'm not quite ready yet."

I thought of his book's excerpt and Christopher Hawk. The fact that my blindfold was on my eyes was such a high; my rationale was gone. Somehow, in my mind I had taken on the role of Izzy.

"Ben, I'll make you ready," I heard myself say, and I had no idea who that girl was. Did *I* just say that? I felt his surprise and sensed his smile.

"Open your mouth for me, Serena, baby girl," he said hotly, his voice hoarse.

Suddenly, the need to see him overpowered my senses. I reached up to pull off the scarf, but he stopped me. "Pink?" he asked, jumping off me and waiting.

No, fuck! No pink! "No," I said, putting my hands back down to my sides where he had gently placed them.

"Then open up," he said.

What had just come over me was unbeknownst to me; his seductive voice made me feel as if a trance had overpowered me—a sizzling-hot sexual trance.

I felt his body on top of mine. His cock swung just over my lips as he spread his legs wide and balanced himself on his knees, next to my shoulders. I opened my mouth, waiting, anticipating, but unsure whether I could do this blindfolded and in this awkward position. He was so fucking big I wondered if my mouth would gag. Could I do it? The men I'd been with before him seemed miniscule in comparison.

He outlined my lips with his fingertips. His cock was on my neck. Oh shit. *Double* shit! The darkness scared me and turned me on simultaneously. *Pink* was on the tip of my tongue, but suddenly his cock was between my lips, and I drew him in, sucking so hard, his taste so sweet. My hands reached up and grasped his hips when he started to moan and thrust gently into my mouth. This was all new to me. His balls were under my neck, warming me, as my mouth moved quickly, taking him in deeper.

He pulled his cock out, lifted himself off me, and caressed my face. "You're so beautiful, Serena. You have a beautiful mouth and a magical body I will bring you to the edge very soon," he said, kissing my neck, my jawline, and again my nipples, now swollen and hard under his tongue.

He placed his hand on my sex, whispering, "You're very wet," and he eased two fingers inside quick then slow then a quick twirling motion going around and around. *Oh.*

"Ahhh!" I moaned as Ben palmed my clit. I couldn't keep my body in place.

"Serena, I love your pussy."

He penetrated me further with his fingers while playing with my clit, and the stimulation had me reeling. On the verge of coming, I moaned.

"Not yet." And he was no longer on me.

My pleasure was escalating, and I repeatedly moaned, twisting my body. My orgasm was ready to explode right then without him even touching me. His hard breathing close to my ear once he lay down next to me. His musky, woodsy scent, invaded my sense as my body moved toward him, needing to feel him inside me.

"I just want to look at your naked, gorgeous body before I enter you. I will enter you, and it will be hard. Is that okay?" His voice was gentle as he traced my nipples with the tips of his fingers, driving me absolutely mad.

"Yes," I managed to say, gasping in anticipation.

"She speaks," he said jokingly, and then he sat up. "I want to see your eyes now. I want to see you when I fuck you."

His words excited me even further, and I felt all the blood rush to my pussy.

He took the scarf off my eyes, and the light blinded me till I focused on Ben. His wanting gaze, full of animal lust, drove me wild. Before I realized what he was doing, he'd sat me up and had tied the scarf around my waist and then to his. We were entwined. He sat down on the bed, his legs wrapped around me and my legs wrapped around him. Our arms were on each other's backs, and the scarf bound us together. His face was inches from mine. His eyes were slightly hooded, hard to read, but locked with mine.

He bit my lower lip and then my top lip. "Give me your tongue," he said, breathing into my mouth.

I stuck out my tongue, and he captured it with his teeth, gently biting, then licking it, opening my mouth as wide as he could as he played incessantly with my tongue using his. I stroked his back and slid my hands up onto his rigid shoulders, then down to his biceps, loving the feel of them under my fingers. *Oh, he's built like a brick.*

I caressed his neck and felt the stubble on his head. It was rough, unfamiliar. All the while, our tongues did things together that I didn't know could affect my body so…so…completely. My pussy swelled upon the touch of his firm cock. It spoke to me in a secret language. *Can*

217

I come in? I wanted to laugh at my stupid thoughts, but my sex seemed to swell even more. It throbbed, ready— so ready for the knocking. His cock was knocking on my door. *Knock, knock, knocking on Serena's door...* Then I thought of *To the Lighthouse* and the paper I had to do. Why am I thinking of this now? I placed that stupid thought out of my head.

Ben kissed my neck and then thrust the tip of his cock into my opening. I actually sensed my pussy opening up for him; they were having their own conversation. I had never felt this kind of sexual connection before.

"I can't take it anymore. I have to fuck you now," Ben said desperately, but then his expression changed. "I want to drive you crazier," he said in a serious tone, and he came closer, holding on tightly to my hips as he guided his cock inside me a centimetre more. He closed his eyes for a second, and when he opened them again, they seemed darker, wilder. "I need to feel you. *Now.*" His tone was hard, then slowly slid his cock inside, his gaze never leaving mine.

I sucked in air. It felt sensational, but then suddenly his expression changed to absolute horror, and he pulled out.

"Shit! How could I fuckin' forget?"

"What?" Forget what? That I wasn't his type? Why did he pull out of me in a panic?

"I forgot my fuckin' safe. I *never* forget. Do you have any?" He looked positively desperate, no longer horrified.

Did *I* have any? Was he kidding me? "No."

"Fuck. We can't have sex." He sat back, frowning, clearly pissed off.

Wow. It seemed he could leap from one emotion to another within a second. I was still open and ready for him—I had been since the moment I saw him on his motorcycle. He looked at me and the scarf binding us together, and then he reacted to the expression on my face.

"I'm sorry." He came closer and kissed me hard, then whispered, "I'm not going to fuck you tonight, but that doesn't mean I'm not going to make you come for me, Serena."

Come for him? Oh. My body quivered.

He placed his hand directly onto my clit and squeezed it tenderly, and then he slid two fingers deep inside. With his fingers in my pussy, his palm rubbing my clit, his lips on mine, and his tongue flicking in and out of my mouth, my body started to spasm. I felt it rise…my insides reacting quickly to his touch…and bam! I exploded like a bomb under his touch.

"There you go," he whispered through his kisses, and I let out another moan—loud and long—while my body convulsed in aftershocks of deep pleasure. "Keep your eyes open. Look at me, Serena." He untied the scarf around his waist. "Lie down and spread your legs wide."

Ben kissed my left inner thigh. *Oh.* Instead of moving up, he went down, down, down, kissing my knee, my calf and—oh my!—my toes. He knew all the erogenous zones of my body, caressing my skin in between his feather-light kisses. Then he did the same to my right leg, but this time going up. He kissed my toes, my calf, my knee, and he even caressed the sensitive area behind my knee. The closer Ben came to my pussy, the more I writhed, and the more he kissed.

"Don't move, baby," he said, his breath hot on my

skin. From my right inner thigh to my left, he licked my flesh, igniting the fire.

"Oh my God." I exhaled heavily, my body responding to him, climbing toward another climax again. Could it be possible? Could I have another orgasm so quickly? I felt it coming again…*Oh shit.*

He stopped. "Not yet," Ben said, "even though you're ready."

While gazing into each other's eyes, he came closer to me and thrust his cock, so big and so needy, against the side of my leg. I hated that we didn't have a condom. I had felt him inside me for one brief second, and it was so hot and thrilling, I really wanted to know how all of him would feel and what he would do to me.

"Oh my God!" I shouted, coming at the mere thought of him fucking me while he lapped my pussy and played with my clit.

"That's a good girl," he said, unraveling the scarf from behind his back and lying down next to me.

He was still hard, his gorgeous cock sticking out and tempting me. But no. We couldn't without a safe. Breathing heavily and without looking at me, he reached out, grabbed my nipple, and squeezed it hard.

"It wasn't meant to happen today, but I gave you a taste of what it could be with me."

He squeezed the other nipple—harder—and I felt a quickening in my loins again. Then he turned over, propped his elbow up against a pillow, and rested his head on one hand.

"I want you to make me come, Serena. I need you. If I can't fuck you, then I want you to put my cock in your mouth." He caressed my face. "Will you do that for me? I'm not really asking you. I'm telling you."

Fuck! Nobody had ever spoken to me that way. His telling me what to do excited me so much, gave me thrills all over my body. And his voice, his words—shit, I wanted to feel him inside me so badly.

"Yes, I can do that." I reached over and took his cock in my hand. He turned flat on his back. *Well, if he can make me crazy, then why can't I do the same to him?* I released his cock and reached across him to grab the scarf and place it over his eyes.

He popped his head up and glared at me. "What do you think you're doing?"

"I was going to use the…scarf…" My insides went numb.

"No." He took my hand and placed it back onto his cock, then angrily threw the scarf on the floor. "Sorry," he quickly said. "I want to see your face while you suck me—all of me—into your mouth, swallowing me…" Desire had returned to his eyes.

I felt a tickle of hesitation for a split second. I don't even know this guy from a fly on the wall and I'm trusting him like this. What the hell? My logical voice responded, but he reminded me of Hawk from his book and the sound of his voice got me all hot again. I bent down and kissed the tip of his cock, then licked the sides before devouring him. In perfect sync, he drove his cock in and out of my mouth, matching my own movements. His taste and unique scent of soap combined with sex made me want him even more. Glancing up, he was watching me, pleasure written on his face while he groaned.

He pulled my face up to look at him. "Serena, you're lucky I don't have a safe with me because I would fuck your brains out. You would be so sore you wouldn't be able to walk for days."

He placed my mouth back onto his cock, thrust one time, and let out a moan as he spurted his salty cum down my throat.

"Yes, Serena, taste all of me," he said hoarsely. He held my head against him while he thrust the last drops into my mouth. I swallowed, enjoying his taste. It was gratifying to have satisfied Ben as he had satisfied me.

"Come here," he said. I lay next to him, and he looked at me, smiling, his eyes full of excitement and his face flushed. "That was fuckin' amazing. You are fuckin' amazing."

"Sorry about the condoms." I didn't know what else to say. That he was fuckin' God's gift to women? I was too shy to talk to him so openly.

"Don't be sorry." He placed my hand on his cock again. "There are other ways of pleasing each other, my dear, *without* condoms." He didn't let go of my hand while I stroked his cock, and it became immense again. "You see?" he said, lust filling his eyes once more. "You have no idea what I could do to you."

"I think I have an idea *now*," I replied, smiling.

"No, you don't." He let go of my hand and pulled away. "I am really smitten with you, Serena."

Did he just say smitten? Why did he pull away?

He was hot one minute and cold the next. What the fuck? That was what bothered me. He was so hard to read. Unpredictable. I was attracted to him—that was evident—but was I ready for more? Something in his eyes scared me, intimidated me. We weren't on even ground. My inexperience when it came to sex, and obviously his experience was maybe a recipe for disaster. Who was he really? Even though my body wanted him, half my mind kept hollering, *do you know what you're getting yourself into, girl?*

"Ben, I like you too," I said, trying to figure out what he wanted from me.

"No, I don't just like you. I like ice cream. I like the Montreal Canadians. I like ketchup with my fries. Do you get my point?" He lay there staring at me like I was stupid or something. "I want you to be mine." His dark eyes reflected nothing of the intimacy we had just shared.

"What do you mean *mine*?"

He sat up, rubbed his hands up and down my legs and arms, and gave me a look I couldn't decipher. "It's time I explain some things to you, Serena. And then you can tell me if you want to be mine."

I wondered, was now a good time to say *pink*?

Teddy
The day after the night before…

When that first morning bell rang and I had to be in history class to begin the discussion on the Renaissance, I wanted not only the one cup of coffee I was holding onto for dear life but also a coffee pot next to me to get me through the day. My cock was painfully raw from all the sex, and all *it* could think about was Melina.

"What's wrong with your hair this morning?" Dave asked, his in perfect place as usual. It was blow-dried and gelled back like the geeky history professor he embodied. "You look like you haven't slept a wink." He smirked. That was his idea of a dirty comment, sounding like one of his lectures. I couldn't share my hot sex story with Dave. And I couldn't wait till lunch to call Dan.

"Just tired." I didn't look up as I scoured my desk for my Renaissance sheets with the vocabulary I needed to teach and the topic outline for the week. Luckily it was one of my favorite eras, so I gave up and decided to wing it. The second bell was going to ring soon, and I still hadn't made my way to class. "Gotta go." With my coffee cup in hand, I was out the door, leaving poor Dave to look at me strangely.

I tried to arrange my hair with my free hand and ended up almost knocking a student in the teeth as everyone, including me, hurried to their classes before the second bell rang.

"Pardon me," I hollered, the light blue lockers leaving us only about four tight metres to rush through. Another student bumped into me, and the first thing I gripped more tightly was my coffee.

"Sorry, sir," the kid mumbled.

Room 225. Next classroom, and I would be there. As soon as class started, the second bell rang. My usual routine of being prompt was a daily habit, sitting with a pencil in my hand and counting to thirty before taking attendance was the way my class was run. Counting in my head as I approached my desk, I tried to fix my hair.

The girls in the front row smiled and checked me out, whispering into each other's ears. Not again, I thought. It was this group the teachers in the staff room referred to as the Mean Girls. They were wickedly hot—something I would never admit out loud—and they were bitterly cruel. They thought they deserved everything they had, and they outright flirted with the male teachers, believing we all wanted to fuck them. That definitely wasn't my thing; underage teenagers didn't turn me on. Then I thought of Melina and last night, and I felt a chubby coming on. *Fuck. Not now.*

After the sex, the spanking, and the food, we actually slept till about five in the morning, when Melina woke me up with my sex in her mouth. She told me I had to get my ass out of there soon because she had to get ready for work, as did I…

"But at five a.m.?" I asked.

She said she had some papers to finish correcting, and she wanted to take a morning run.

"What energy you have," I said, half asleep, needing to rest some more, but my dick had woken up and was saluting her.

She sucked me hard and deep, and I lost all control when she popped up her head and said, "Tell me you want it." She tickled my balls with both hands, her naked body slithering its way up to me.

"I want it." Fuck, she talked a lot. "I want it," I repeated, and wondered what she was going to do next. I'd realized by then that she had to take the lead or she would jump off me, give me a nasty, get-the-fuck-out look, and I would be left ignorant as to what to do and feel stupid.

"Fuck me with your fingers, Theodore."

Before I could even move it, she had taken my right hand and roughly shoved my fingers into her as if I didn't know what to do. I knew what to do. I knew how to fuck. I finger-fucked her like a madman, pleasuring her like the well-skilled lover I knew I was, till she writhed and sighed and threw her head back, shouting, "More, you fuckin' asshole! Harder! Fuck me with your fingers!" Or something vulgar and erotic like that, which made my cock throb. I wanted my dick to be sliding in and out of her wet, delicious pussy.

I pulled my fingers out. "You're ready. I can feel you."

She sat up, her blue eyes cold. "Did I tell you I'm ready? I want to come now. I said put your fingers inside me, and do as I say, or get the fuck out!" She spread her legs and waited, her long hair spilling out on the bed, her big tits swollen, her clit awaiting my touch.

That was it. I was pissed now. "You want me to finger-fuck you, Melina?" I said roughly. "Say it again." *Let's see how she responds to that.*

She climbed on top of me with a wild look in her eyes. "Theodore, don't move, big boy."

She held me down with her arms, positioned her hot, wet pussy over my cock, and instructed me to *"not fuckin' move"* again. She inched her pussy down and then ever so slowly moved up and down. I couldn't help it—I had to meet her thrusts. But every time I did, she yelled, "I told you not to move!" Then she fuckin' pinched and pulled her nipples, which drove me completely insane with lust…

"Sir, are you okay?" Mean Girl number one asked. She studied my eyes for a trace of interest as she thrust her breasts outward, and I had to concentrate hard on not looking at them. My chubby was getting a little out of control. I had to stop thinking about Melina *right now*, or I'd be in big fuckin' trouble—big teacher-student harassment trouble, the Lolita kind.

"Yes, I am, Chantal."

I counted to thirty. Done. I said good morning to the class and started to write the forty vocabulary words they needed to memorize on the blackboard. As I wrote, I thought of how Melina fucked me. She knew exactly how to make herself come, and once she did, I came right away…

"You will have to learn to control yourself better," she said, laughing and grabbing my limp, post-orgasm dick.

"Control myself?"

"Not come so fast, Theodore. It's something you haven't mastered at all, but you will with me." She flashed me a winning smile.

Why did I have to learn to not come so fast? I couldn't hold on forever. I wasn't one of those guys who could last for hours. She lightly caressed my cock; it was so tender.

"Be here at seven tonight," she said quickly, glancing at the clock. She climbed off me and headed for the bathroom. "I'm going to take a shower and get ready for work." She turned back around, and her eyes were blank. "I really need you to leave." She blew me a kiss.

It was five thirty. Wasn't half an hour of sex good enough for her? Apparently not. She was a raving sex fiend…

"Sir, what does that say?" Tom asked.

I'd written "fresco" without the R. Fuck.

"Oops. Sorry. I forgot the R."

I'd never misspelled a word on the blackboard before. Shit. I continued writing out the words, but my mind kept on wandering to last night…

"Are you still here?" she called out as I was just about to leave.

"I'm at the door," I called back.

She walked into the living room with a towel wrapped around her body and another one tied on top of her head. Her skin was glowing and still a bit wet, and she held a comb in her hand.

"What's taking you so long?" She looked at me as if I'd been spying on her or something. What did she think I was up to? Her gaze scanned the room and then me.

"I was just lying on your bed, and I closed my eyes for a few seconds." I was guilty of relaxing?

She smiled and let down her hair, then started to detangle her hair. She watched me closely while I stood at the door, as if she was waiting for something. The tension in the air was hot. I looked at her body glistening with water droplets. She smelled like peaches or something. I took a step toward her, thinking maybe she wanted a quickie.

"Too bad you're dressed," she said and walked back into her bedroom. "Plus, there's not enough time for what I have planned for next time," she called out.

Next time? That would be tonight at seven…

"Sir?"

I quickly turned around and looked at my class. I'd finished writing everything on the board, but my mind was definitely not there. I ran my fingers through my hair, approached my desk, downed my now-cold coffee, and set to work, erasing all thoughts of Melina and her sexy body out of my mind—for now.

At lunch, I went outside and called Dan. I told him everything.

"Bro, how the fuck does this shit happen to a pretty boy like you? Can you handle this sex shit?"

I could just see him, laughing and enjoying poking fun at me. "The reason it's happening is *because* I'm a pretty boy, asshole. She wants me badly."

"Serena who?" Dan joked.

"Fuck you! This has nothing to do with Serena."

"Do you still want to see Serena again?"

"Of course I do, dip-shit." But I wasn't even thinking about her right now.

"Who are you trying to kid? Who cares? Have a good fuckin' time. Jenny and I are seeing each other Friday night. Maybe we'll get to second base. Guess what she told me last night?"

"What?"

"She said Melina thinks you're hot and that sex with you is fantastic."

"Find out more about Melina for me, bro. Anything you can. Call Jenny today, and ask her some questions about her past, whatever." I practically begged him.

"I don't know…I'll see what I can do, Romeo. Got to get back to work." He yawned.

Oh sure. *He* was *tired*. With all his union-sanctioned breaks, his lunch hour, a set number of hours in his shift… He had it too easy at the hospital.

"Remember, get me some info."

"Okay, okay. Later." Dan hung up.

Somehow, I made it through the day and then went straight home for a quick nap. I was physically and emotionally spent. The alarm on my phone was set for six o'clock, but at five thirty my phone buzzed. It was Dan. I opened my eyes and scanned his text.

I think you are in deep, deep shit. Call me ASAP.

My heart thumping, I dialed his number.

"Hello?" he answered calmly, knowing full well it was me on the other end.

"What the fuck do you mean by your text?" I was damn near hysterical.

"Calm down, lover boy. You sound awful. Were you sleeping?"

"Yes, I was sleeping! Now tell me what's up!"

"Well, Jenny loves to talk, and you know how girls can spill the beans on their best friend and then they make you promise not to say anything…"

"Make a long story short, Dan!"

"Melina's a control freak. A sexual deviant. A sex addict. Jenny says every man she's ever been with ends up cheating on her. And get this, Jenny seems to think they do it on purpose. They cheat on Melina in order to break up with her because she wants to control everything they do. Twisted, no?"

"So, you're telling me she's absolutely addicted to sex, she controls men… What else? I know there's more."

"Jenny says Melina is a Dominant. You do know what that is, right?"

"Fuck, Dan. A Dominant? Like a Dominatrix?"

"Guess so. She likes to dominate in sex. She wants you to be her submissive, which pretty much means you have to obey her commands." He cleared his throat, then chuckled. "Her *sexual* commands, pretty boy."

"I figured that part out," I replied. "Listen, I gotta go, I got a text from someone."

"Maybe it's Miss Dominant…" He laughed.

"Fuck off." I quickly hung up, but then my phone buzzed again. It was a text from my sister, Stephanie.

Hey bro, what's up? Wanna come by 4 Mexican night? The girls are asking about u.

Can't little sis. I'm tied up tonight.

Little did I realize it was a double entendre I was texting her, and that a few hours later, Melina would take out a rope and want to tie me up.

Serena
Will I be completely his?

"I want you to be my submissive," Ben said, his dark, serious eyes penetrating mine but showing no emotion. He got up and reached for his underwear. "Let's go get some water or something else to drink."

I stood and put on my bra and underwear. *Should I put on my jeans too?* Fuck it. If he was going to walk around in his underwear, then I would in mine. Besides, I had a more pressing matter on my mind—the word s*ubmissive* blaring in my head.

He was already in the kitchen, opening the fridge and getting comfortable. He sure knew how to take control. He opened up a few cupboards to find my glasses, took out two, and poured water from the Brita. He handed me a glass, and we drank in silence, his gaze, pondering and thoughtful, on mine. He looked around my tiny kitchen. On my counter, I had a set of coffee, tea, and sugar containers—a gift from my mom—in this terra cotta color that reminded me of Mexico. I wondered what he was thinking. The blender, coffeemaker, and toaster were lined up next to one another, and a small radio with a CD player was plugged in on the other side of the counter, next to the kitchen sink. Luckily no dirty dishes were in the sink, which was rare, since I had no dishwasher and had to wash everything by hand.

"You have such a cozy place, Serena. It's really

warm and friendly, like you." He gazed at me from my toes to my head, making me feel vulnerable in just my undergarments.

He looked over at the kitchen table and gestured for us to sit. I went first, and then he went to the radio and pressed Play on the CD player. When I heard Duffy's voice blare loud and clear, I smiled.

"Nice. I really like her. Plus, she's British." He sat down across from me, his chest bare, his legs dangling down. I sat with my legs crossed and placed my feet on the second bar of the stool's legs. "So, as I was saying earlier, I want you to be my submissive," he said in a casual tone. "Which basically means you have to do what I ask you to do. Let me rephrase that—what I *tell* you to do." His eyes gleamed.

I didn't quite like the sound of that. I had a mind of my own, and I didn't want any man to tell me what to do, much less *have* to do it. His tone scared the shit out of me. What reaction did he want from me? What kind of relationship was he looking for? For sure, my thoughts were scattered right now, telling myself to wait and to not get into anything with Ben right away.

"I don't know if I want to do whatever you want me to do."

"You already have. Did you like what I did to you?" His gaze ran up and down my body. "Because it was pretty clear to me that you did like what I was doing to you. If you follow my lead, we'll be fine."

I didn't like the way he said that. It was too forceful, like I had to do whatever he wanted. What about my needs? What if my body didn't want to do what he demanded? Yes, my body did like what he had done to me in bed, but I had no clue what else was entailed in being his submissive. This was a whole new world for me.

"And if I don't?"

"You can say 'pink,' and everything immediately stops. I'll never hurt you." His tone had changed, and he took my hand in his. "I just want to possess you fully and completely. I will be completely yours too."

"Could I be in danger?" My mind raced a mile a minute, imagining scenarios…

"Trust me, I would never hurt you. We will take it slow. I repeat, I will be completely yours." His dark eyes penetrated mine, inviting me in.

He will be completely mine? I looked at his body and felt flushed already. My mind was so caught up in his scent and his looks, but a part of me wasn't so sure about what he was asking. He made it sound so easy. Should I just try it out? What was there to lose? If my answer was no, I would probably think about the what-if for the rest of my life. *Be adventurous. Try it.* Then, if my body couldn't go through with it, I could always say no or use the safe word… I bit my lip, thinking. He watched me intently, waiting for a reply. His gaze lingered on my lips.

Fuck it.

I could trust him. He'd made me feel safe from the moment we met—even if that was just over twenty-four hours ago. He made me feel great in bed too, meeting my needs, and desired to please me more than any other man I'd known. Why not? It was a risk my mind and body was willing to take, because despite my uneasy feeling, the desire I felt for Ben was real, and my sexual desire shouted, *Yes! Yes!*

"Okay. Let's just take it slow, and we'll see how it

goes. I don't know if I like the words you're using. They kind of make it feel cold, don't you think, Ben?"

"No, I don't think so." He spoke firmly, no longer warm and intimate. "I want to make myself understood, Serena. I'm not your regular boyfriend. I'm not your regular lover. I'm not your normal fuck." He swayed back on the stool, and I caught a glimpse of his sex.

No, you most surely aren't.

"Not every guy you meet is a dominant man. In fact, most are weak and immature and know nothing about pleasing a woman."

Ain't that the truth.

Suddenly, my thoughts turned to Teddy. Did he too make these kinds of sexual arrangements? Somehow, my instinct told me no. Would Teddy be a "normal" fuck? What exactly was a normal fuck? Would that be Gery and Kenneth, my only two experiences, which had been so horrible for me? I had to agree with Ben—he was anything but normal or regular.

"Are you there, Serena?" He studied my face. "Did you hear what I just said?"

"Yes. Every single word. I was just thinking, if you're not a normal fuck, as you put it, then what would a normal fuck be? Because frankly, I've only had horrible fucks, and if I had to choose between that and you, well then, Ben, I choose you."

I confidently said, without a doubt. I knew my words had made an impression on Ben, for his brown eyes sparkled with awe. He got off his stool and came toward me like a stealthy animal about to snatch its prey. He grabbed me by the waist, flung me over his shoulder, and said jokingly, "Me, Tarzan. You, Jane." Then he walked with me on his back to my bedroom. Laughing, I landed on my bed, and then his body and lips crushed mine in a suffocating, intoxicating kiss that made my insides go to jelly and bananas.

He looked at my clock radio and stood. "I'll be back." He had a determined look in his eyes.

"Where are you going?"

"I have to get inside your pussy tonight, or I won't make it. Where is the closest pharmacy or *dépanneur*? It's only ten forty-five." Before I knew it, he had his pants and shirt on.

Shit. He was going out for condoms. This was going to happen tonight! "Two blocks down on my side of the street. There's a *dépanneur* that has absolutely everything anyone could need in the middle of the night or day. You can't miss it."

"Would you like anything?" he asked before leaving my bedroom.

I was still lying on the bed, amazed at how quickly he thought and moved. "No, thanks."

"Do me a favour." He gave my body an admiring once-over.

"Yes?"

"Don't move. Give me your key. I want you to stay like that till I get back."

I wasn't comfortable with that idea. "No, I don't think I want to give you my key. Not yet." I'd just met him yesterday. Hello? Was he serious?

"Okay, that's fine." He looked down, his eyes and emotion hidden from me, and then he turned to leave.

When the door shut, I got up and ran to the bathroom. Shit. Shit. There was some serious sex with Ben happening tonight. My nervousness, anxiousness flustered me, equally, it aroused me—all at the same time. We were going to have sex! He was too incredible for me. Too fuckin' hot.

A Dominant and submissive... Was this good for me? I'd said yes, but now, returning to my bed and lying down, staring at my ceiling, my decision plagued me. I was a grown woman. Granted, not one with a lot of sexual experience, but it was obvious my attraction to Ben was strong. When we were out, he made me feel like I was the only woman in the room, and he showed me nothing but respect. He was dominating, and I liked that about him.

Ben wanted to tell me what to do. My body wanted him to tell me what to do *in bed*. It had felt good before... Thinking he would be back very soon, my chest tightened. My thoughts raced to Teddy—as always—and how that connection with him was still there, regardless of what was going to happen within the next little while.

The sound of the buzzer startled me out of my thoughts. My legs ran to it, not hesitating for even a second. I had made up my mind, buzzing Ben up, and he walked into my apartment, breathless, wet, and holding a plastic bag with a box of condoms inside.

"Is it raining?" Not realizing it was raining outside. Duffy still sang away, muffling out-door sounds.

He didn't speak. He took off his jacket, rubbed the top of his head with wet hands, then kicked off his shoes and opened the bag. He pulled a condom from the box, took my hand, and led me straight to the bedroom. His eyes seemed darker, intense, deliberately avoiding mine.

"I can't think of anything but fucking you. I have to get it out of my system. Right. Now. I ran all the way here." He stopped in front of my bedroom doorway, took my hand, and placed it on his heart. "Feel this," he said, still out of breath.

His heart thumped hard against my palm, covered tightly by his cold, wet hand. When he finally looked at me, it was hungrily, and he held my gaze as he slowly lowered my hand to his powerful cock, eager for me to touch it, eager for me to feel the hardness waiting for me, eager for me to want him too. I squeezed it gently, and he let out a small sigh.

"Now, please resume your position before I left. I can't get the vision of you lying on the bed out of my mind."

He let go of my hand, and I did exactly as he said, his command having such an effect on me. It was as if he was touching me with his words. They were the best foreplay I had ever had. He hypnotized me with his wicked, rough voice. I had never heard a man speak so plainly, so demandingly, so harshly, and above all, so shockingly.

I lay on the bed, admiring Ben's body. He tossed the condom next to me and started to undress. First he took off his socks, then his jeans, his underwear, and lastly, his shirt. He seemed to have no sense of how sexy he looked removing his clothes. He did it so naturally. His movements were seductive, his eyes lit with intense fire. With an indecent appraisal of my body, he licked his lips, placed his knees on the bed, and stuck out his perfect chest. He rubbed the top of his head with both hands—the two-day-old stubble looked exceptionally sexy tonight—then displayed his full, solid cock.

"Serena, get ready to get fucked like you've never been fucked before."

I gulped, and my breath quickened at his words. With his left hand still on his head, he lifted my left leg with his right hand, blew on it, and then licked it. He then brought down his left hand and cupped my sex with it, quickly slipping two fingers inside me. With the tip of his thumb, he rubbed my clit in a circular motion, sending shivers and shakes from the top of my head down to the tips of my toes.

Oh. My. Oh. My.

He shifted a bit, and his cock nudged the side of my leg. It felt so big. I lifted my head and found him looking at me with red-hot desire. He snatched up the condom and put it on in one swift motion.

Here it comes. Brace yourself.

I spread my legs wide, anticipating his body over mine, but instead he grabbed my ankles and positioned them high up near my shoulders.

"Bend your knees, Serena."

I did and felt instant relief on my back. On his knees and firmly holding my ankles, he rubbed his cock against my sex, driving me absolutely irrational with desire. I had never craved anyone this much before, nor had I ever beheld such a striking specimen so eager to have me.

I let out a loud groan.

"You want to get fucked hard?" he asked lasciviously, his voice unforgiving, his eyes full of hunger.

Back and forth he brushed his dick against my pussy, squeezing my ankles tight. He bent forward, and I thought he was going to kiss me, but instead he flicked his tongue into my mouth without touching my lips. I was overwhelmed with desire and lust as he slowly nudged the tip of his hard cock into me, and I let out a wild moan I didn't even know I had in me.

"That's it, Serena, baby girl. Let it all out." He

teased me some more with his cock, then said, "Say it, or I won't fuck you."

What am I supposed to say?

I looked at him, and he repeated, "Say it, or I won't fuck you, Serena."

Ben inched his cock in and out of my pussy, shocking my body with spasms of ecstasy. It was crude and arousing all at once. I couldn't stop staring at his physique. With my feet so close to my head, my pussy was completely exposed, open to him, visible. I felt like I was being consumed by him, drowning in his sex, trying hard to catch my breath.

"Say it." This time his voice was firmer, his eyes raging at me.

He rammed his cock fully, deeply inside me and kept it there. Our bodies were locked. My pussy and his cock were meeting for the first time. I felt my pussy opening up and welcoming him, singing that line from Rihanna's song—*where have you been all my life?* I was ready to explode. Without wanting to, I rocked my hips back—it felt so natural to do it.

Ben did that thing with his tongue again, without touching my lips, and then he whispered, "Say you want me to fuck you."

I guess he realized he had to spell it out for me.

"I can't." I really couldn't, but then I tried saying it in my head. *I want you to fuck me.* Okay, maybe I could say it to him.

"Yes, you can." He pulled his cock out from me, his eyes stormy. "Say it, or I can't fuck you." He kissed my neck. "And he really loved being inside you." He breathed on my skin, continuing the lament. "He wants it again."

My skin was on fire, my nipples hard against his chest, and he let go of my ankles to pinch them. I wrapped my legs around his neck and drew him in close to kiss him. While we explored each other's mouths, his sex poked at my opening and teased my clit, driving me wild and making me writhe uncontrollably.

"Say it, and we can end this torture." Ben's eyes, full of longing, had turned a dark chocolate color—his pupils dilated with lust.

"I want…you…to fuck me," I said breathlessly, gazing at him, both embarrassed and proud of myself. *I did it!*

Ben gave a wicked smile, a smile that deepened his dimples. "I want to fuck you." And he slammed into me with one quick motion. "Open up for me, baby. Don't be shy."

He pounded into my pussy hard, hurting me slightly but also sending jolts of pleasure all through my body, feeling like a virgin with him. His face tensed up as he thrust harder and harder, so deep inside me, the pleasure intensifying.

"Say my name. I can't take it anymore." He stopped moving for a second and just looked at me.

"What?" Why did he stop? I couldn't read his eyes at all.

"Nothing." And he continued to thrust into me as he had before—hard and fast. "Say my name," he instructed, his tone rough.

"Ben," I said in a low voice, getting a weird vibe from him.

"Say it like you mean it." He thrust harder now, making my nerve endings scream his name.

"Ben!" I shouted.

"Like that." He slammed into me, watching my face with a need I couldn't place.

"Oh Ben," I said in a lower voice, from a natural place inside me, and he grabbed my hair with both his hands, rubbed my clitoris in quick, tiny motions with his cock, and that was it.

"Ben!" I shouted, coming in a violent rush as he fucked me hard.

"Serena!" And his quick thrusting slowed down. I realized he had come too. His gaze never left mine as he pulled my hair, and I squeezed the bed sheets tightly.

He shut his eyes for a few seconds to compose himself, and I did the same, my hands limp on the bed. He pulled out of me, and I heard him walking away as he said, "I'm going to the bathroom."

I heard the rain on the windowsill and became more alert to the sounds around me. The flushing of the toilet bowl, the water running... Still I kept my eyes closed, unable to move from my position. My sex was hot and sore.

I heard Ben walk back into the room and stand at the foot of my bed. I opened my eyes. He was fully dressed, looking at me greedily.

When did he get dressed—and why?

"Serena, I'm sorry I didn't take my time with you and pleasure you. I know it was a little quick, but I couldn't control myself." He cleared his throat. "That is the first and last time that's going to happen." His expression became hard. "We're going to be great together." He looked at my naked body, and I felt a coldness from him that made me feel vulnerable. But then his expression softened. "Don't be afraid of me. The only person who should be afraid of me is me."

What the fuck did that mean?

"Do you really have to leave?" That was the thing that concerned me. He was dressed and leaving. "Why?" And why was he afraid of himself?

"If I stay, I'll want to fuck you over and over, and I think you have to do your assignment. Unless, of course, you want some more…" He smiled and rubbed my toes in a way that made my insides rumble and tumble.

His gaze went straight to my sex. "My, my Serena, I think I'm not going anywhere. And you are in luck."

"How so?"

"I did my dissertation on Virginia Woolf."

Aha! So that was why he'd looked at me like that earlier. Was this man ever going to stop shocking me—body and mind?

"I usually don't stay after sex," he said, removing his shirt and jeans, "but I guess this time I'll make an exception, since you might need my *expertise*."

I smiled at him. "What was it you wanted me to say to you again?" I asked, teasing him.

"Serena, I think you clearly remember," he replied in a scolding voice.

"I want you…to…fuck me now."

"You're a quick learner." A devilish grin appeared as his dark-eyed gaze hovered over mine. He reached down and lightly rubbed my nipples. "Now, let's start with lesson number one: how to make yourself come without my touch."

Teddy
To stay or flee? That is the question

I rang Melina's doorbell at exactly seven o'clock, then stood outside her apartment building, examining the door. It wasn't that ugly. My face felt flushed and my body excited just imagining what her next move might be. What Dan had said about her being a Dominatrix didn't intimidate me at all. Heck, her being in control did excite me, it was different from other women I'd been with, but it was her erratic behaviour that bothered me, plus giving up control all the time was definitely not my thing. Giving women all the power in bed was not my idea of being sexually satisfied. I preferred to drive a woman to the edge, that power excited me more. Why did it have to be one or the other with Melina? Why couldn't it be both? If she wanted it only one way, we wouldn't be able to continue this relationship.

I had never had a woman do the things she'd done to me before, and maybe that was the main reason my body reacted to her and there was this sexual attraction there.

She buzzed me in, taking the elevator up to her apartment, remembering Saturday night, it was hard to believe that only two days had passes. It was only Monday today. Two days of non-stop sex. I immediately became hard walking to her door and knocked on it once.

She opened it and pulled me inside, taking the wine

without looking at it, not even a "thank you."

"Hi," I said, feeling goofy for no reason, really. It was just the way she dragged me in, as if she wasn't sure whether my legs were going to bolt right out of there. Did she sense my apprehension?

When my eyes looked upon her, I almost fell over my feet. She was striking. She had on a tight black mini-dress with spaghetti straps, no bra; her nipples peeking at me through the see-through material, making me weak at the knees, her black suede stilettos were sexy, my imagination already running amuck…imagining fucking her with just those shoes on, and then my gaze went directly to her neck. She wore no necklace, no earrings. Her hair flowed down her back, and her eye makeup was done up as if she were going to a club.

"Hi back." My adrenaline spiked as she stared at me closely. She looked hungrily at my dark blue fitted jeans, my burgundy shirt with suspenders, which showed off my broad shoulders, and my stylish black shoes from Aldo. If he'd seen me, Dan would have smirked and said, *You look like one of those gay guys in the village. You're such a metrosexual. It shows you shop at Simons.*

"You look…gorgeous," I stammered.

"You look yummy," she said, extending her arm for my coat.

The table was already set for two, with a bottle of wine opened and poured into a decanter.

I took off my coat, and she hung it in her closet. My eyes turned to her and as she walking it was quite obvious she wasn't wearing any underwear. Her ass was plump and provocative, and all my cock wanted to do was lift her dress from behind and grab it. I swallowed and waited for her.

"Go ahead and have a seat," she said, closing the closet door.

Everything in the apartment was immaculate. I walked to the table and sat.

"Do you know what a scene is?" she asked as she sat across from me, smirking, immediately getting down to business, her blue eyes hooded.

"Like in a movie?" My mouth felt dry.

"Exactly. Can you pour the wine, Theodore?"

"Certainly."

"You are the waiter, and I am the client." she said, giving me a wanton look. "Now, stand up, and pour me the wine." Her eyes were serious and cold. "And address me as Miss Bella."

I stood and poured the wine, swallowing my saliva. Did that mean I couldn't drink? I was dying for a sip; my nerves were seriously on edge.

"Here you go, Miss Bella," I said, trying to immerse myself into the role. My job as a waiter during the summer of my first year at university, came in handy.

Melina crossed her legs and looked at me. "Thank you, Theodore." She took a sip while I waited for her approval of the wine, like waiters usually do at restaurants. "I don't think this is good," she said disapprovingly.

"What seems to be the problem with it, Miss Bella?" I asked, wondering where she was going with this and starting to feel ridiculous.

"Well, I ordered a cabernet sauvignon, and this is a merlot."

"Oh." Now what? Who gave a fuck?

She looked around the apartment as if we were in a real restaurant. "Why don't you try it for yourself,

Theodore?"

"I don't think my boss would allow that," I said, even though I was thirsty as hell and wanted to down the whole bottle. But I figured I might as well continue the role.

"I'm the client," she said, narrowing her eyes, "and *I* want you to try this wine." She handed it to me, and I had to accept.

It was so fuckin' tasty. *What do I say now?*

"Well?" she asked.

"Well, I think it tastes delicious." Shrugging my shoulders, my confusion must have shown on my face, my cock wasn't even hard at all.

Her gaze moved to my suspenders. "Does your boss make you wear suspenders?"

"No, that's my touch," I said, placing my arms across my chest. Did I seriously have to stand? I was beginning to realize I wasn't exactly getting off on this whole Dom/sub relationship. And that was because I wasn't a sub. Epiphany moment!

"Oh, that's your *touch*," she said seductively but in a way that didn't excite me in the least. I wasn't feeling this role-playing at all, but I still wanted to fuck her. "Theodore, why don't you have a glass of wine with me? There is no one in the restaurant but you and me."

I pretended to look around confused. There wasn't? So, it was an empty restaurant. She should have explained the scenario in more detail. Hopefully this dreadful scene would be over soon and we could get on with the fucking.

At least I could finally sit down.

"Yes, Miss Bella." My sarcasm must have been evident by now. I'd play her game. Why the fuck not?

Maybe if my enthusiasm changed, I *would* get excited by playing this role, because up to this point, my eyes were on the door, looking to bolt out of there and stop these fucked-up mind games.

I gripped the bottle tightly and poured myself a glass.

"Wait, Theodore. I didn't tell you to pour yet." A spark of anger appeared in her eyes.

I put the bottle back down. What the fuck did she want now? I wasn't a mind reader.

"Okay, now you can pour," she instructed.

I poured the wine, then sat down and almost finished the whole glass in one gulp. She watched me, looking unimpressed. Did she think I had to ask her to drink too? Fuck that.

"Now what?" I was so eager to get the show on the road.

She pointed to the door. "There's the door if you want to leave the restaurant."

"I'm not leaving," I said angrily. I'd made up my mind to do this. I was in. All in. Poker face.

"Why, Theodore, are you mad at me?" she asked as she drank her wine. I felt her bare foot gently touch my calf. When had she slipped off her shoes? I must have missed that. She slid her foot up my leg, her eyes never leaving mine. I loosened up at the touch and quickly refilled our glasses.

"Theodore, can you bring the food from the oven? There are two plates ready. They should be a little warm, so use the oven mitts on the counter," she said while tickling my balls with her toes, making my cock jump all sorts.

She removed her foot from my leg and smiled

ravenously at me, then glanced at my suspenders.

"Oh, and remove your shirt and wear *only* the suspenders," she said in a severe voice, her eyes turning a wicked blue that made me want to run out the apartment for fear of what was next.

Take off my shirt and leave on my suspenders? She wanted me to look like a Chippendales dancer? I could do that, I thought, grinning, but did I want to? This scene still wasn't working for me—I wasn't even slightly hard—but I was curious as to where she was going with it.

I went to the kitchen and brought out the food. It was steak, baked potatoes, and green beans, evenly distributed on the two square plates. It looked appealing and smelled incredible.

Placing the food on the two placemats, I then unclipped my suspenders. Removing my shirt took a while because of its tiny buttons, and cursing under my breath, didn't change my foul mood. I put on my suspenders again. A slight chill touched my bare skin, and my nipples tingled. She watched me as if she wanted to seize me. Her eyes scared me as the lust in them devoured me, and my cock remembered how her pussy had sucked me into her vortex.

"Sit down, Theodore."

I obeyed and lifted the fork and knife.

"Enjoy your meal," she said, "and don't leave anything on your plate."

"Enjoy your meal too, Miss Bella," I said sarcastically, my hunger taking control of all my needs. She was controlling in some ways that didn't appeal to me at all. Peeking up at her, she was looking at me keenly with desire.

"Theodore, can you turn on some music, please?" She wanted me to stop eating? "In the kitchen, play my iPod on shuffle."

I remembered from yesterday exactly where everything was in her place—getting up and doing as she asked was annoying as hell to me now. After pressing the button on her iPod, a girl's voice came on loud and clear, singing an unfamiliar ballad. I recognized the voice as Avril Lavigne's. She actually liked this?

I came back to the table and finished my meal within minutes, then wiped my mouth with a cloth napkin and leaned back watching her finish hers.

She ate and drank with a healthy appetite. As soon as she was done, she said, "Theodore, it's time to pick up the dishes."

I stood up to continue playing her stupid game. Getting into this role was taking longer than I thought it would.

I placed the dishes in the sink, and she came up behind me. "Wash my dishes, Theodore." Her voice was suddenly softer and sexier, and I felt myself harden at its seductive timbre.

I turned on the faucet and let the hot water run, then poured some dishwashing liquid onto the sponge. Not looking behind me, my body anticipated something would happen. She came closer and rubbed my back, then wrapped her cool hands around my waist, inching up to my chest—and snapped the suspenders against my bare skin. It shocked me a bit, my reaction didn't show. The motion of my hands continued to wash the dishes and place them on her dish rack as she lowered her hands to my dick and squeezed it hard.

"Do you want to *serve* me now, Theodore?" she

asked, close to my ear, her sensual voice sending slight shivers down my body and directly to my cock, which sprung forth in her hands. She turned off the faucet and took my wet, soapy hands out of the sink. She was still behind, her body touching mine. "Turn around," she whispered, letting go of my hands.

I turned to face her, and she started to play with my hair in an affectionate way that was enjoyable. She stroked my head and brushed my bangs away from my face.

"Now I can see your beautiful green eyes, Mr. Theodore Neros."

I rubbed my hands on my jeans to dry them before clasping her waist.

"You have such beautiful hair, the kind that drives women crazy. It's just the perfect length." Now she was stroking my hair with both her hands. Florence and the Machines started to play "Lover to Lover," and her eyes began to glow. "This is my song." She looked at me. "Theodore, kiss me now."

Now we're talking…

"Oh," I mumbled, getting harder.

I bent my head toward hers, and we kissed passionately. The song started off slow but progressed to a rapid beat while the singer sang about going from lover to lover and how "*there's no salvation for me now*." How come I'd never listened to this song before? It was apparent that Melina had a thing for music. The first night it was "Crazy on You," and now, this song…

It was actually pretty cool making out to music. She wasn't letting me breathe; her tongue was making these twirls and somersaults in my mouth. Tasting the wine on her tongue and sucking it while she roughly pulled my hair back, finally aroused me to move my hands from her waist to up high on her back and pulled down the spaghetti straps of her dress. Her nakedness was on my mind now.

"Not yet," she said, placing the straps back on her shoulders. The song ended, and the next one began with that same sweet voice singing.

"She has a really incredible voice," I mumbled, kissing her neck, "but you are even more incredible." As I listened to the song, I was losing myself in the moment, in the song, in the wanting of another... As we stood facing each other, "Never Let Me Go" played on.

"Dance with me, Theodore."

I detected a hurt in her voice that wasn't understandable at the moment. My arms wrapped around her tiny waist and I pulled her close. We held each other while swaying to the music. "*In the arms of the ocean*," Florence sang, and "*never let me go*," over and over again. As we danced, this feeling I couldn't explain came over me—it was as if I needed to possess Melina.

But then the song ended and somehow broke the spell.

She took a step back. "Well, that was unexpected."

From her tone, it was not recognizable if that was a good unexpected or a bad one. Her eyes revealed nothing. My emotions were in a whirlwind. Bending to kiss her, she pulled back. What exactly had been unexpected? The dance? The emotions? How nice it felt to sway to the music? And now it was as if she didn't want to say anything more about it. My thoughts were all rattled.

"Follow me." She took another step back as a new song began, one about being "*hard to dance with a devil on your back, so shake him off.*" I followed, thinking she was going to lead me straight to bloody hell, but I didn't care. All I could think about was her taste on my mouth and my dick responding to the shake of her hips.

She entered her bedroom, and I followed close behind, eager to clasp her waist and throw her on the bed, but instead I waited. Was I still the waiter?

"Theodore, I'm not happy about the wine," she said, turning around, a nasty look in her eyes.

The wine? Are we still on that? Fuck. My chubby went way down.

"What do you want me to do, Miss Bella?" I asked grumpily, standing straight and resuming the role.

"I want you to lie down on my bed and close your eyes for your punishment. When I ask for cabernet sauvignon, I want cabernet sauvignon, *not* merlot." Melina narrowed her eyes. "I'm the customer, and the customer has to be *served* appropriately."

Fuck, I brought cabernet sauvignon, but telling her that wouldn't do.

"Yes, ma'am," I said.

She turned around violently to face me, and her anger exploded, entwining me in this fucked-up scene. "Don't ever call me 'ma'am.' I'm not a 'ma'am.' I'm Miss Bella."

"Excuse me, Miss Bella." I faked a smile. "I didn't mean to offend you."

Her expression softened for a quick second, but then she went back to being a total bitch. She flipped her hair and caressed the side of her body, from her breasts down to her hips.

"Yes, you *did* mean to be a naughty boy, and I will punish you, Theodore. Now lie down."

I lay down on her bed and closed my eyes. What was she going to do now? If she took out a whip and a chain, I was going to run for the door. I peeked at her while she had her back turned, looking in her top dresser drawer. She took out a black rope.

I'm fucked! "Whoa. What are you going to do with that?" I sat up. "No way."

She put it back into her drawer and sighed. "Okay, Theodore. No ropes for now." She looked at me and smiled. "Calm down. We'll do verbal bondage instead. Intro to Bondage 101. I'm not saying I do heavy shit, like collars, leg irons, stocks, straps, restraint systems, and that type of bondage, but the occasional rope or cord does it for me, okay?"

What the fuck was she talking about? What were leg irons? Stocks? The back of my neck started to sweat.

"I think I have to go now…" I stood up.

"You're not going anywhere but *inside* me." She tapped her foot. "No physical bondage, I promise. Just verbal." She came closer to me, purring like a kitten. "Verbal means what we've been doing—talking. Okay?" She touched my hand. "Theodore, you do it for me, and I really want you. I won't hurt you." She stood straight and cleared her throat. "If you want to stop at any time, then say 'red.'"

"Red?"

"Yes. If you want me to stop, say 'red,'" she repeated, tapping her foot impatiently again. She let out a sigh, as if I was an idiot or something. "It's called a safe word."

I pretended I had heard that word before, and perhaps I had somewhere. I couldn't remember. Was it a compound word? "Safeword" or "safe word"? What the fuck was I thinking? I would be safe. It was a word that would keep me safe.

She was a fuckin' nut, and I had to get the fuck out of there A.S.A.P. My mind made up. I couldn't get into this type of sex. I didn't need any of it to get off. I just had to look at Melina's sexy, ready-for-porn body, and I was ready to come. I wanted to lift her dress and fuck her like a raging lunatic. She must have seen something in my eyes because suddenly she jumped me. She literally jumped on me, and I landed on her bed.

"Take off your pants," she said in an authoritative tone, her eyes shiny.

"By verbal, you *do* mean talking?" I asked, still thinking about what she had said to me. She nodded, and I started to calm down. Now *that* I could handle.

"I already told you that, silly boy," she purred.

She pulled off my pants but held on to the suspenders and looked at them curiously. "What can we do with these?" She snapped them in her hands.

Please do nothing with them.

She left them on the bed. "I'll think of something later." She smiled. "Now, are you ready for your punishment?"

Oh fuck, we were back to that story? I thought she'd forgotten about it. "What's my punishment?" I asked, ready to bolt out the door.

"You must fuck me so hard and promise to not come till I tell you when. It's called orgasm control."

"All this over a stinkin' wine?" I was totally confused. The part about fucking her was good, but for how long? And why would my cock want to control my orgasm? "Melina, I can't promise anything," my confession, sounding defeated.

"Neither can I," she said and pushed me back onto the bed. "Now hold still, Theodore." She stood on top of me with her legs spread open above my body. She placed her hands on her hips and peeked down at me, while my eyes had a perfect view of her pussy, and my dick grew hard, harder, and hardest...

Serena
Orgasms and safe words are making my heart jumpy

"It's called thinking off," Ben said. "Give me your hand." We were lying naked on the bed. "By the way," he said, smiling, "I fuckin' love your tattoo." He didn't even ask me what it was for. It was refreshing to be with a man who didn't ask twenty questions. It was like he got me even though he barely knew me.

I felt my insides move. The way he spoke made me so horny.

He held my left hand in his right one.

"Now, just look at me, and maintain eye contact. Don't turn away."

So I did. We stared into each other's eyes, our backs flat on the bed.

"Now, let's take deep breaths together," he whispered.

We took deep breaths, and my body relaxed. Looking into his eyes, I sensed my body reacting to no touch, just to the *idea* of touch. I felt my sex expand.

"Don't let go of my hand," he said, tracing tiny circles on my palm.

"But…you're…touching me," I said. My sex literally started to throb from his touching my hand in that circular motion.

"I said not touching your genitals, your pussy"—his eyes twinkled—"which is starting to heat up," he continued in a low voice. "I'm going to make you come without touching your burning-hot sex, just by my voice…my eyes. My hands will only touch your hands. I won't touch any other part of your body," Ben said, promising to do nothing yet doing everything.

I started to clench my pussy, imagining his cock entering me. Oh shit. Was this actually happening to me? Me, who couldn't come during sex? I could come like this?

"Breathe, Serena. Feel your breasts expand. Breathe harder, faster. Feel your pussy open, open… Let go."

His eyes got darker. His nose rings moved as he matched his breathing to the quickness of mine. I couldn't speak. I sensed my sex was in unfamiliar territory, for no man had ever made me orgasm without touching me. My body didn't know what was controlling it as Ben's voice continued its seduction…

"Serena, you are going to come so much for me," he said, his gaze on mine.

I began to let myself go and lanced my hips into the air, moving them as if I was getting fucked. My hips moved faster and faster, and this deep pleasure came over me. I don't know where it was coming from as I let out quick gasps of air. Ben's gaze was on mine as he clasped my hand tightly and continued rubbing my palm with his thumb in a senseless way that I felt everywhere in my body.

"You can do it, Serena." His voice was husky. I glanced down, and his cock saluted me. "Oh no you don't," he said, lifting my chin. "Keep your eyes on me." As I looked back into his eyes, I let out a sigh. "Breathe harder. Let's do it together." He breathed along with me, obviously excited just watching me. "I can't wait till you come and you're ready for me." His gaze penetrated mine, heavy with lust.

Then it suddenly happened. I exhaled a moan and allowed my body to be controlled by a force beyond my power. As the look in Ben's eyes hardened, I swung my hips back and forth and had an orgasm in the air. Ben's face glowed, and he smiled, grasping my hand tightly as I squeezed the shit out of it.

Wow! My insides trembled. I couldn't speak for a few seconds, letting out sigh after sigh while my pussy clenched. I was out of breath.

"You are incredible to watch," he said. "You are so intense."

He gazed at my lips now. I was still out of breath, coming down from that unbelievable climax, and then his mouth was on mine, his tongue desperately searching for mine.

After pulling back and giving me some space, he said, "Lie on your side, Serena."

I lay on my left side, not facing him, my body completely relaxed. If I had closed my eyes, I could have fallen asleep, but Ben didn't have sleep in store for me. He jumped off the bed—"Condoms," he said—and went into the living room, where he had left the box.

Oh my, here we go again. He wants to do it again? I closed my eyes for a second.

"Serena, you had better not fall asleep on me. You'll hurt my feelings." I opened my eyes in time to see him roll the condom onto his erection. The scarf was around his neck again, and he continued in the same comfortable voice, "I want you to compare and contrast"—he smirked—"like you're writing your report, which we'll get to soon enough. Compare and contrast your last orgasm and the one coming right up."

He quickly moved behind me, not even waiting for my reaction. I couldn't believe he was ready to fuck.

"Watching you come got me so hard I can't even begin to explain to you what I'm going to do right now. Just hold on, baby."

He grabbed my hips with his strong hands and placed one of his knees down on the bed. I lay on my side in fetal position, and he lifted my hips as he slid his penis inside me. It shocked me. Here I was in this twisted position, but I opened up to him immediately and moaned. He had a perfect view of my tattoo.

"Give me both your hands."

I put my hands behind my back, and he held them tightly while thrusting very slowly. He was fully inside me and I let out another slight moan. I felt the fabric of the scarf on my skin and peeked over my shoulder. He was tying my wrists with the scarf, concentrating on making a knot, and then he looked at me and said, "Now you're all tied up, Serena." And he immediately started pounding me hard.

He pounded me like a madman, fucking me like I had never been fucked before—fast, hard, sexy, my hands behind my back, and then he gently tapped my bum. At first it was a light tap that made me jump. "You like it?" His voice sounded rough.

"Yes," I said through moans and sighs, my eyes closed.

Then he slapped my ass. "You like it now, Serena?" His voice was rougher as his fucking intensified, and the pleasure was unbearable.

I couldn't speak. I didn't like the slap at all.

"Look back at me, and tell me you like it," he said,

"or I'll slap you harder." He moaned.

What? He confused me. Did I want him to slap me harder? *No.*

I still couldn't speak. Between the shock of the slap and his fucking, I didn't know what to do. What was I doing?

He stopped fucking me and caressed my ass. "Serena? What's it going to be? Tell me you like it. If you don't like it, then I'll slap you harder…"

His hand was on my ass and moving toward my anus. Where was he going? *No, not there.* His hand traveled to my clitoris, and I felt like I was at the wrong place at the wrong time. Something didn't feel right. My arms hurt, and the slapping hurt me more. I felt my body tighten up.

I couldn't say anything, which he thought meant I wanted it harder, so he slapped me harder, and this time I shouted, "Ouch! Pink!"

He immediately pulled out of me and untied my hands. "Are you okay? I'm so sorry if I hurt you."

He sat next to me, but I stood up, releasing my hands from his tight grip. "I don't know…if this is a good idea." I was embarrassed as hell because I couldn't take a little slapping of the ass. Seriously? *Get over it, Serena.* I looked at Ben on my bed and wanted to kick myself.

He got up and started to get dressed. His eyes were cold and distant. "I think this was a mistake," he said, looking down at his pants and avoiding my gaze. My heart tore into tiny pieces. "I don't know what came over me. I never wanted to hurt you." He rubbed the top of his head nervously.

"Ben, could you sit down, please?" I wrapped the sheet around me—as if he hadn't seen me naked before, but still—and told him the truth. "I feel too inexperienced. I've never been slapped before. I've never been made love to like this before. It's overstimulation. And then you tie my hands. It's just way too much. My brain and my body can't take it," I said in one quick breath, then paused for air. "I don't think I'm right for you." I looked down at my fingernails. "I think we're going too fast…"

How many orgasms could I possibly have? But I kept that thought to myself. I couldn't speak. Maybe I wasn't made for this type of sex, or maybe Ben was progressing things too quickly for me. I just had to stop.

"But you said 'pink.' I made you say 'pink,' which means I took it too far. I passed the limits. I'm much more low protocol. Safe words are about trust."

"What?"

"Low protocol, which means I'm more relaxed with terms used by Doms and subs. I don't care too much about the terminology, but I do care about hurting you and especially about you feeling you can't trust me. You used the safe word, and I'm upset with myself for not reading you well. I was too lost in my own pleasure."

"I couldn't speak. It was too much for me," I confessed. "Don't leave." *Please, don't leave.*

"I won't leave. I feel horrible. The last time…" He turned away. "Forget it."

"What happened the last time?" I needed to know.

"It's a long story."

"Tell me, please," I begged.

"I don't know… It's personal, and I don't like to go down that road." He looked confused.

"Ben, please tell me. I want to know about you too and why you are who you are."

He moved closer to me on the bed and studied me for a second.

Then he shrugged his shoulders. "Here goes nothing. I can't believe I'm actually going to tell you this." Ben took a deep breath. "This stays between us. When I was studying at London University, I was in medical school. I was such a whiz with numbers that I automatically applied to the medical field. But during that first semester, I couldn't take the sight of blood. It made me woozy, weak, and I would vomit. Obviously, the medical profession was not for me. I soon transferred into the English department."

He took another deep breath, and I was enthralled, listening attentively.

"There was a professor there, Mrs. Patricia Collins, who I had an affair with. She pursued and seduced me. She made me fuck her in her office, on her desk, after hours. In the library, in her car, in the stairwell…my naïveté got the best of me. Everything was kept secret. Our relationship was a secret. It was hard to not talk about it. My studies continued, but months later my work suffered."

He rubbed his head, looking at me nervously.

"One night she took me to this club where bondage was the theme of the party, and I saw things and did things that were all new to me. That was when I used our safe word and left the party. Your emotions right now are familiar to me. Even though the word is supposed to bring two people closer in trust, it had the reverse effect on me."

He looked directly into my eyes, hurtful memories invading our space, taking him back to another time. Maybe he did understand my feelings. He wanted to let me in on his life, which was admirable.

He continued in that same tone, and I wanted to cradle him in my arms and protect him like a small child. "Patricia convinced me to go back to her, and she continued her double life. She ignored me in class and made late-night rendezvous with me. The more sex we had, the more we wanted. I lost myself in her, making myself believe she cared for me, but she was my dominant, a term that made me laugh. I thought she was joking around but soon realized she didn't joke around. It was an intense few months, and when time passed and she became bored with me, she told me she was breaking up with me and that it was time to forget about her. She cut ties with me as if I were a dog."

He rubbed his head again, his eyes distant. My thoughts went to his pain and how he must have felt, so lost and hurt by all those emotions.

"I went to therapy because I couldn't function. Therapy made me realize it wasn't *her* who was the problem, but *me*. Why did I gravitate toward her? Why did my mind and body let her do those things to me? These are questions my therapist, God bless him, helped me come to terms with." He shook his head. "I can't believe I'm telling you all this crap."

"Go on, Ben. I want to know. Please, don't stop."

I took his hand in mine, and he examined our hands as if they were foreign and not part of his body or mine. He was in another time and place in his mind as he looked up at me with a look in his eyes that was unexplainable, but I could empathize with him.

"I liked being told what to do, and giving up my power. I liked when she handcuffed me to a bed and blindfolded me. That turned me on because her desire for me felt passionate, no one had ever needed me like this. The only other person who loved me and needed me was my mum. Granted, she was my mum, but she was the woman who taught me how to love. The therapist told me that Patricia's power over me made me feel weak, powerless. In a woman's arms, I wanted to be controlled. It was familiar territory for me, because through my therapist, I came to understand something I'd never ever realized before."

He looked away now, letting go my hand.

"Which was?" I asked delicately, trying to not ruin the moment between us and at the same time processing all this information.

"That my mum was controlling my entire life, and when I finally left her to move to London, Patricia was my replacement." He looked directly at me and gave me a weak smile. "So ever since then, I've done the opposite, consciously turned it around not to feel weak or powerless." He took my hand in his. "Hence, you see, I'm the one who needs to be in control, because when I'm not in control, I become another person that is dark, lost, headed on a road full of pain and disillusionment. And I don't *ever* want to head down that road again." He swallowed, and it suddenly dawned on me how nervous he was. "That's the reason I came to McGill. To start over…."

He was about to say something else but stopped himself.

I didn't want to push him any further. I merely sat next to him and studied his face. He avoided my gaze. He reached for his shirt and, still sitting on my bed, put it on. I stood up and got dressed too, following his lead. My brain was in overdrive, trying to understand everything he'd just told to me. He watched me get dressed, and his expression softened.

"I think it's study hall period," he suddenly said out of nowhere.

"What?"

"Your paper. Time to do your paper. This conversation is over," he said abruptly.

"Hold on, Ben. Your mom knew?" Control issues? Mother issues? I didn't know why I asked about his mom, but that was the first question that popped into my head.

"Well, not everything, but some things," he said reluctantly, slowly getting up. Where was he going? My head was spinning from his confession.

"I'll be in the kitchen," he said, and he walked away. I heard him opening cupboards and making himself at home. "Would you like a cup of tea?" he asked from the kitchen, concern for me in his voice.

I had already forgotten about the safe word and the spanking. I was still thinking about his confession, and now I had to write my paper? Impossible.

"No, thank you," I quickly replied. "I think I might need something stronger, like coffee, especially if I have to write."

I joined him in the kitchen, opened my pantry, and took out my jumbo-size Van Houtte Colombian coffee.

"Okay, I'll join you. Although I really need to have a cigarette."

"I'll make the coffee. You can go out on my two-by-four balcony. There's a view of a beautiful brick wall," I teased.

"I'll wait for you. I don't want to go by myself."

He stood next to me and leaned against the counter

as I pulled forth my coffeemaker and added the filter and a precise amount of tablespoons. *Four cups should be enough.* He folded his arms across his chest and watched me keenly.

"How did you like McGill?" I asked, the silence pounding in my ears and his body distracting me as I poured the water into the coffeemaker. *Last step, almost done now.* I was intrigued by imagining him having sex with his professor. I tried to clear my head.

"I didn't quite fit in." He grinned. "However, my marks fit in quite snugly. I was offered a writer's in-residence position after taking a creative writing course, and I refused."

"You refused?"

"I walk to the beat of my own drum, Serena. I did my doctorate on my time and without mingling too much with the professors and other graduate students. I had learned my lesson from London." He walked into the living room and put on his jacket. "Academia life is not for me." He pulled out his pack of DuMaurier. "Put on your jacket, and let's go see your room with a view," he said, changing the topic. He smiled, and his dimples appeared again.

"I can't believe you refused!" I said, putting on my jacket and walking back toward my kitchen to unlock my patio door.

"I'll get our shoes," Ben called out.

"Great."

He placed my shoes exactly in front of me and his in front of him, and my thought was that this paper would never get started. He was distracting me by just being around. My mind was more focused on his movements than on my assignment. The way he'd bent to put my shoes down was so sexy and thoughtful.

"A penny for your thoughts," Ben said, reaching out to unlock the door like he'd been doing it for years. He turned the knob to the left, and it unlatched.

"I'm thinking about my paper," I said, not wanting to tell him I couldn't think about it because I had to do the paper while really wanting to ask him more questions about his past, but he had cut me off.

"Don't worry. I'm here to save the day." He stepped out onto the tight balcony. "You weren't kidding about this balcony."

I stood next to him, inches away as he lit his cigarette and blew the smoke away from my face. I shut the door behind me and turned slightly.

"I told you, look at the lovely wall." I gestured in front of us. There stood another apartment building's wall, at a ninety-five-degree angle, not even five feet in front of us.

"I like small spaces," he said, looking at my ass as I turned. "You can get very creative in small spaces. It's very European."

I felt a hot flash between my breasts. There was no breeze here. He flicked his ashes over the balcony.

"I'll get you an ashtray," I said, flustered.

I went inside and quickly came back, catching my breath.

"Do you always follow the rules, Serena?" Ben inhaled his cigarette, his gaze on me like a hawk's, making me feel slightly self-conscious.

"Absolutely, Ben." I confessed my sin, holding the ashtray for him to flick the ashes in it.

He chuckled, and his nose ring moved. "I like that," he said. "I like that a lot."

He was so close to me, so I reached out and touched his nose ring, ignoring his racy comment and the way his gaze landed on my lips. "Did it hurt?"

He grabbed my waist and butted out his cigarette with his other hand. "No."

His answer sent a sexual charge to my brain as his touch enveloped me. I had that stupid ashtray in one hand and wanted to throw it over my balcony so I could grab Ben's back tightly.

"Let's go inside and put on our thinking caps, because all I want to do out here is put another cap on me, and it has absolutely *nothing* to do with thinking."

He had both hands around my waist, and pulled me toward his sex for a brief second, where I felt his fully erect penis against me. In a slight daze, I drew away and twisted to slide open the door. The aroma of coffee filled the kitchen.

"Would you like some vanilla ice cream?"

"I would like some vanilla something else." He grinned mischievously.

What did that mean? "How about chocolate?" I asked.

"Oh, I prefer vanilla." He sat down on my stool and waited.

"Okay, I'll go get it." I walked toward the freezer.

He immediately got up to stop me. "You're serious?" He pulled me toward the counter.

"I was going to get the ice cream, some dessert." I looked at him weirdly. What was his problem?

"Serena"—he smiled now, looking at me as if he was ready to tell a joke—"when I said vanilla *something else*, I meant vanilla *sex*. I figured you've read *Fifty Shades*." He smirked.

"No, I don't read erotica." I was annoyed at his smug attitude and condescending tone. "What's vanilla sex?" I had never heard of that before.

"It's straight sex. You know… No bondage shit, just plain old hanky-panky."

"Oh." Okay, so now would have been a good time to admit I was stupid, that I didn't know much about sex and couldn't possibly be with a man like Ben, whose lingo I didn't get.

I turned around to get the mugs for the coffee, not wanting to look at him in case I caught a look that signaled to me "are you living under a rock?" like my sister would be saying right about now.

I quietly took out the brown sugar cubes and the cream from the refrigerator. The sound of my *"oh"* echoed in the kitchen. I'd sounded like a five-year-old. I heard the beep of the coffeemaker and poured the coffee. Ben sat down on my stool again and studied me without another word. What was going through his mind? My insecurities had surfaced and were now floating around the room. I tried to erase one that read *"you're way over your head* and the *"he's too hot for you,"* but *"pink"* kept popping into my head like a sign at a rally that gets the attention above all else.

I sat across from him, refusing to get the ice cream now.

"Thank you," he said in a quiet voice, continuing to study me, holding the coffee mug firmly by the handle.

"I have to get something off my chest, or I'll explode," I blurted out.

He took a sip from his coffee and examined me closely, with interest in his eyes and something else that appeared to be a little humour, but I brushed that off. If he was laughing at me, that would have really pissed me off.

"I'm all ears."

"This whole submissive, safe word, vanilla terminology that I am not familiar with is sending me in a tailspin, quite frankly, and the fact that I had to use a safe word while you spanked me…I don't know if this…whatever is happening between us is for me. I'm not comfortable with most of it. Some of it I really like."

I took my first sip of coffee, purposely stalling for some time and ideas as to what to say. I was babbling. I didn't know how to tell him. He seemed to be enjoying my squeamishness, and he grinned from ear to ear while sipping his coffee, probably gathering his thoughts.

"Which parts do you *like,* Serena?" His voice had switched to that sexy tone he used in bed, and my sex suddenly woke up.

Shit. Not now. He somehow sensed my body react, and his eyes seemed to turn a darker brown.

"Um, you know…the vanilla parts," I said quickly, nervously focusing on my point. What was my point? I was totally distracted again. "I could do without the safe word stuff and the spanking and the pain…"

He stood up, his expression blank again. "How about we make a truce?" he asked, sounding sincere.

"Okay." I liked the sound of that.

"We don't talk about sex for the rest of the night. We finish your paper and call it a night?"

"Okay." I nodded, trying to cover up the hurt I felt.

That wasn't the truce I was hoping for, wanting him to tell me he never would spank me or use safe words again. This whole sex thing made me uneasy. Yet it was as if he had this magnetic string I wanted to pull and pounce on.

He started to talk about Virginia Woolf and what he thought about her style, and I just nodded, still thinking about vanilla sex and how hot and cold he was. I went into the living room and brought out my laptop and the book *To the Lighthouse*. When I opened my computer, his webpage popped up on the screen. Shit.

He smiled in a dangerous way that made me nervous all over again.

"Okay," he said, changing the subject, "it's time to show me your manuscript. While you write about stream of consciousness"—I looked at him blankly—"I'll simply read." He held Virginia Woolf's book in his hand and glanced through the chapters, already engrossed in it.

"No."

"The first chapter?" He looked up.

"No."

"Don't say 'no' like that, or I'll fuck you right here and now."

My insides jiggled.

"No," I repeated, waiting, my breath starting to quicken.

He beamed. "We have to work quickly, Serena, if our truce must change. First the paper, then the fucking." His voice was tranquil, but his eyes sent sexual signals to my insides, and poof, just like that, I was no longer focused on writing.

I clicked out of his website and started a new document. Trying to concentrate, I typed out the title. "The Use of Stream of Consciousness in Virgina Woolf's *To the Lighthouse*," while my brain was still stuck on the fucking, the truce, the manuscript. No way was he reading it!

"This is going to be so much fun," he said, elated as I typed.

Was he serious? I looked at him, and he was already into the book, just like that, unaware of my insecurities.

A few hours later, after I finished typing like a madwoman, over-stimulated by his beliefs and philosophy, turning them into mine, he turned to me and said, "Serena, it's two in the morning. I think you need to sleep now." He stretched out his legs and then put down the book. "It's time to leave. You look exhausted."

Shit. I must have looked awful.

I got up. "Okay, I'm tired. Thanks for your help." I was actually exhausted. I couldn't keep my eyes open.

"It was my *pleasure*."

I didn't know if I could ever be completely honest with Ben, because everything he said alluded to sex. He made me want to agree with everything he said. He made me want to do things I didn't want to. He made me crazy, but he also made me write my term paper.

"I'm still waiting. Don't think I forgot."

"About what?"

"Your first chapter."

Should I? After spending the last few hours writing my paper with his helpful insight, I knew it would benefit me to show him my manuscript. I hated people judging my writing, but Ben was different. He could probably help me. He was the first writer I had ever met.

"If you promise to be honest with me," I said reluctantly.

"I promise."

I walked into my bedroom, and he was right behind me.

"Now we're back to the scene of the crime," he jested, taking off his shirt.

I opened a drawer and pulled out my wrinkled manuscript. I ignored his naked chest and hastily handed him the first chapter. He took it from my hands and placed it on my dresser.

"Since your paper is finished, I was wondering if, before I read your first chapter, you would mind very much if I tasted you."

Anxious, I swallowed hard.

"It's lesson number two: oral pleasure."

He removed my garments slowly and with care. Shocked and tense, I gaped at him, trying to remain unaffected as he undressed me so tenderly, wanting to please *me*.

I'd told him I didn't think I could be his submissive, and now he was all over me, as if I'd never voiced my concerns. Had I gotten through to him, or did he just want what he wanted, when he wanted, how he wanted?

I lost all reason as his lips met mine, and my questions were flung on the floor along with my underwear.

Teddy
Ironic how sex blurs your sanity

Melina picked up the bottle of wine I had brought, glanced at it, and chuckled. "Cabernet sauvignon, Theodore? Isn't that ironic?"

"Next time I'll buy merlot," I said sarcastically.

"Not if you don't want a spanking." She placed the bottle on the kitchen counter and then looked at me from across the room. "I'm just kidding. You should see the look on your face."

"Ha-ha. You're a real comedian." More sarcasm.

It was time for me to mosey on out of there. She had said she needed to sleep. My phone buzzed as I placed it in my jacket pocket. She heard it and took quick strides toward me, as if it was for her, and stood next to me, hovering over my shoulder. I slid it open and clicked on Text Messages. Stephanie's name appeared. It was 11:50 p.m. What did my sister want? It had to be an emergency. I read her message quickly, feeling Melina's gaze on me.

"Who's Stephanie?" she asked angrily, accusingly.

I didn't look up. I was reading Stephanie's text message, sent at 11:00 p.m.: *Where r u? I need Tylenol for Margie, please, she has a fever and I just ran out. ASAP.*

Then the second message was sent 11:10 p.m.: *I called ur house. Roberto is still working. Call me.*

Roberto worked late. He was a hell of a husband

when he was around, but that restaurant ate him alive.

I clicked on Contacts and dialed her number. I had shut off the sound on my phone. I should have checked my messages right away.

"Steph?" She answered the phone on the first ring.

"What the fuck, Teddy? I texted you. I called you. Margie's fever is getting higher. I have her in the bath now."

"Okay, okay. I got the text. I'll go get the Tylenol, and I'm coming right over." I hung up before she said another word.

Melina eyed me suspiciously.

"Where's the closest drugstore?" I asked. "My niece is sick." I zipped up my jacket and quickly put my shoes so she would get the picture and stop looking at me like that.

"Who is Stephanie?" Melina asked again, still sounding suspicious.

"You got to be fuckin' kidding me..." I was so pissed off. "She's my sister!"

"Oh." She looked down. "Well, then, you won't mind if I come with you." She walked toward her closet, took off her dress, put on a pair of pants and a top, and took out her jacket, then grabbed her keys. "I'd love to meet your sister."

Yes, I do mind you coming with me. Margie was sick, and Melina wanted to meet my family?

"I don't think tonight is a good night for meeting the family." I couldn't help the sarcasm in my voice. My niece was sick, and it was late. "You're the one who told me to leave so you could sleep. I'm not going to drag you all across town and back again."

It didn't make any sense, but by the hurt look on

Melina's face, I guessed it made perfect sense to *her*. Now she was acting like the victim again. I swear she could get an Academy Award for her performance of a bitch one second and an innocent the next.

"You're so heartless," she said, clearly upset. "I really thought you had more of a sensitive side than other guys I'd met." Her jacket was still on, and her keys were swinging in her hand as she waited and pleaded. "C'mon, I know this *dépanneur* that has everything and is open at this hour of the night. It's not far from here. I could take you there, and you'll be in and out in literally two minutes. The closest pharmacy is on Saint Laurent Street, and you'd end up driving farther. Where does your sister live?"

"She lives in NDG."

"Great, it's on the way, and we have to go west anyway. Trust me, Theodore, I know what I'm talking about." She walked into the kitchen and shut off her lights, and I was left speechless as she opened her door and said, "C'mon, what are you stalling for? There's a sick child waiting for you."

There was mistrust in her eyes. I guessed she had to see for herself if I was bullshitting her, which really angered me further. Why did I have to prove to her I was honest?

"I think you coming with me is really *not* necessary," I said, following her out of her apartment and feeling ridiculous that I was actually listening to her.

She pressed the elevator's button to go down and tapped her foot. "Why, is there something you're hiding?" She pressed the button over and over again impatiently.

"What would I be hiding? An imaginary girlfriend

and child?"

Her eyes opened wide as if she hadn't thought of that. "Nothing would surprise me," she said as the doors opened.

She had that hurt look on her face again, the one that made me weak, that made me want to grab her and whisper that everything would be okay. Instead, I stood tall next to her and nudged her immaturely.

"Melina, seriously, you gotta trust me," I said gently, trying to ease the tension.

"Why?" Her gaze penetrated mine. "You have to prove yourself first."

"So, I'm not innocent till proven guilty, but guilty until proven innocent?"

"When you put it that way, yes. That's my motto."

As soon as we stepped out of the apartment building, we got soaked. "I hadn't realized it was raining," I said.

"Me either," she said, and we ran toward the car.

We got into my car, brushed the rain off our clothes, and then she guided me to this tiny corner *dépanneur* a few blocks down the street.

"Right there," Melina said, pointing to it.

I found a parking spot right in front of the store. As I opened the door to my car, a man ran out of the store, passing me, and I almost knocked him over with it. He was so close to the street, clutching a small grey bag. Running full speed in the rain, he didn't even turn back. I watched him run, thinking he looked exactly like Bald Guy model, but shook my head. Just because he was bald didn't mean it was him. Where was he going in such a rush? Then I thought of Serena and the way she looked at the bar, and I felt a tug at my heart. Fuck, not now.

I quickly got out, slammed my car door shut, and

walked to the front door of the store, my mind preoccupied. Could he have been going to see Serena? Did she live around here? The bell above the door announced my presence, and I looked around the store in a daze, searching for Serena. A tiny Asian man behind the counter gave me a look. It was neither friendly nor nasty. Rather, he looked completely bored, yet he seemed to have an inside joke going on.

"It's raining cats and dogs," he said with a heavy accent.

I nodded at him, then walked up the first aisle and then the second, looking for Tylenol. They *did* have everything here. I found it, glanced at the rip-off price, and headed to the cash.

"Sick child? You live around here?" he asked, looking at me directly in the eye as if he were a reporter.

"No, my sister's kid, and no, I don't live around here."

He studied me a moment, then nodded and punched in the amount plus the tax. "Nine fifty-nine," he said, seemingly eager for conversation.

Wait up. Maybe…

"Let me ask you, do you know that guy who was just in here? I think I know him. Does he live around here?" I asked, throwing all the questions and suspicions in my head at this little man.

He smiled now, ready to talk.

"Funny you should ask. I ask him too, 'You live around here?' He say, 'no.'" Then he winked at me in that secret man code way. "But he have fun time tonight."

I pulled out a ten-dollar bill from my wallet and smiled back, acting the part. "Ah, big fun," I said, joking too but not exactly sure where we were going with this conversation. Inside I felt uneasy and ready to scream.

"Yes, he came running here fast, grab condoms, and run back." The cashier laughed, seeming to want a long-drawn-out conversation. "Rainy night, good sex," he added, handing me my change.

Fuck. Could it be that Baldy was having sex with Serena? How coincidental could that be? Impossible. I was driving myself crazy over this shit. I needed to think straight. How could I possibly know it was her? I couldn't. That guy could have been anybody. I left the store in a daze, while the little Asian man made a lewd gesture with his hands, having his own good time.

Baldy could have been fucking Serena. She must live close by. I was fucking Melina, so I suppose both Serena and I were indulging ourselves. I wanted to run up and down the street to find him and follow him, but it was too late. I looked down the street and saw only the hard rain slapping the pavement, drowning my fantasy of living happily ever after with Serena. Plus, Melina was in my car. How could I explain to her that I was looking for a bald guy who could be fucking that girl from the club the other night who was not my ex? I would have sounded fucked up. And Melina would go running for the hills or paranoid or possessive or all three, and rightly so because even though I was having a hell of a sexual ride with Melina, I knew it wasn't going anywhere with her.

I couldn't be with Melina—she wasn't the type of woman I could spend time with and enjoy myself. She always put me on edge, and she was too unpredictable. My feelings for Serena were still solid, still there, and seeing Baldy and knowing he was running with such fervor with condoms to Serena… At least in my mind he was. But maybe it wasn't true…

Fuck it! Forget it! It was as if nothing had changed. I still wanted Serena to come to me, to enter my world and take me away from this crazy life. I opened the car door and tossed the bag onto the back seat.

"You found the Tylenol?" Melina asked, sounding concerned.

"Yes," I replied, my mind on the other tidbits I found out too. Like the perverse positions Baldy could be fucking *my* Serena in—my ideal woman, my soul mate—while I was in a car with a whacky girl I was taking to meet my sister, of all days, the day my niece was sick, in the middle of the fuckin' night. And there she was, all calm and polite, suddenly transformed into the school teacher she personified by day.

I glanced at Melina. *What the fuck am I doing here?* Was I driven by the twists and turns of her pubic hair, of which she didn't even have? There was a Greek expression my dad would tell us when he wanted to describe how much he loved my mother but couldn't remain faithful to her. It kind of went something like this: A piece of pubic hair can pull trains. *I triha travai traino*, he would say in Greek to me, and I would nod, trying to imagine pubic hair pulling trains or ships. He would change the mode of transportation when he felt like it, but I got what he'd said. I would chase a pussy just about anywhere, to any place, and fuck the consequences…destroying everything *en route*, such as our family. It was as if he was saying I couldn't help it. It was the pussy that had all the power.

"Daddy is a womanizer," Stephanie's young voice would whisper in my ear so Mom wouldn't hear.

When I heard that word as a young boy, I imagined my dad surrounded by women and their pussy hair entwined around his head. It was a sick visual, especially for a little boy of eleven years old or so, who should not have known any of this, who should not have been subjected to any of it. Weren't parents supposed to hide their deep secrets from their kids? It had been such a part of our lives that "womanizer" became the word Stephanie and I would mouth to each other in secrecy when other siblings would mouth swear words to each other. It made us feel like we knew what was going on when Mom sent us upstairs to talk to Dad. Otherwise, we were floating in this space of the unknown, in which children had no idea why their parents were fighting and tended to blame themselves. Well, we knew way too much to do that.

I drove to my sister's house in a daze.

My dad had been having affairs left and right when my mom decided to leave him. Stephanie and I would huddle in the corner of the room we shared, using our flashlight to read *Charlotte's Web* just loud enough to drown out their arguments, the questions my mom threw at my dad nightly and daily—*"where were you?"* was one she always repeated—or her comments, *I smell perfume, I know what you're doing, I hate you, I'm going to leave you.* We'd pretend to not hear my dad beg and plead his way out of it. He would be noble for a few months, and life was blissful again for a while. Then bam, just like that, he wouldn't come home, he wouldn't call, and Mom would cry in her room for hours, then come out with a fake smile, her tears wiped away, her brilliant blue eyes lost in the dullness of her suffering. Stephanie and I would cuddle with her, scared to death we would be abandoned and placed in a foster home, like that girl Jessica in our school, who never had anyone come to any functions or Christmas shows. She said her parents had died in a car accident, but we overheard the teacher tell her to not lie.

Melina and I listened quietly to a CD I had made of some new music. The volume was low, and Soundgarden's new song, "Live to Rise," was playing. I sang along, thinking of Serena again and pushing the childhood memories away. Right now, she could be in the arms of the bald model, and I suddenly felt sick to my stomach. I ran my hands through my hair. What was wrong with me? I opened the window, but when the rain fell inside, I quickly shut it again.

I glanced at Melina. She was looking out the window, engrossed in her own thoughts. I had this beautiful, volatile, sexy woman next to me, and I was pining for someone I'd met only twice. At least I could say twice, now. Better than once. This song was putting me on a downer. I really wasn't up for any conversation. The hard rain was pounding on the window, and the next song was by Seether. The rain and the song required my full attention; I wanted to raise the volume to full capacity and blow the speakers. As my hand reached over to the radio, Melina spoke.

"Do you actually *like* this music?" she asked as if I had no taste.

"Yes, a lot, *actually*." Obviously, I did. I lowered the volume instead of blasting it, though I was really irritated now.

"Oh, okay then." She looked at me. "What's wrong, Theodore?"

"Nothing," I said blandly, keeping my temper at

bay.

"Typical," she said, and I glanced at her just as she rolled her eyes.

"What's typical?" I asked, aggravated by her tone, her gesture, her observations.

"Your answers to my questions," Melina stated without looking at me.

I didn't reply, but when the next song, "Wait for Me" by Rise Against, came on, I cranked up the volume as if her comment didn't bother me at all. I blasted it just to infuriate the fuck out of her.

"You look disturbed," she commented again.

Did she ever let up?

"Seriously? It's raining hard. I'm just watching the road and trying to enjoy the music," I replied, being completely dishonest. I wanted to say, *I think you're the one who is disturbed*, but I kept my mouth shut and my eyes hard on the road.

Her attitude about the songs had gotten the better of me. I didn't know why I had this arrogance about music when I'd never even played an instrument. Music had been a constant in my life. If I didn't have anything else, at least I had that to change my mood, or to give me hope, or to depress the fuck out of me, or to make me want something I couldn't have, or to make me dream of being in a band, writing lyrics, singing onstage in arenas. Music grabbed me. It was as if it understood the complex workings of my mind. This song made me want to open the door and say, "I want you out of my car." But no, I had to drive downtown and back home to Town of Mount Royal, which was fifteen minutes from Melina's apartment. I was tired and felt wasted, and sleep seemed hours away.

"Whatever," she said, loud enough for me to hear.

This had to be the dumbest idea of the night. Stephanie didn't even know I was arriving with a girl. Oh well, what was the big deal anyway? I couldn't text Stephanie now. I was driving, and Melina was watching me keenly. We both were on the defensive; the tension in the car palpable. It was the complete opposite of the last time we were in the car together. I let myself go there for a few seconds and felt a rush of blood to my balls. My mind raced…Apparently, I looked *disturbed*. If Melina knew my thoughts, she would let herself out in the rain and never see me again, if she knew what was good for her. But she didn't know much about me, and I didn't even care to tell her. That was the gloomy part of how she made me feel—defensive, and horny, all combined in one.

Melina had no idea I had made a pact with myself at the age of fourteen, when my parents split up, to *never, ever* cheat on a girl, or I'd end up like my dad. I saw what it had done to my mom, and the most riveting exchange between my parents rolled in my mind like the worst part of a movie you couldn't stop replaying over and over again…

Mom was at the door, and Dad was a few steps down, looking up to her, his short brown hair and green eyes, my replica, full of tears. Stephanie and I were upstairs, shoving our ears to the screen, trying to catch a word here and there, shushing each other in the dark and fighting for space.

"I'm sorry, Despina. I promise I won't do it again," Dad said, an overnight bag and his keys in his hands. He was wearing those brown pants I detested and a black T-shirt that read "I love New York." He looked a mess.

"One day, Nick, your looks will fade, and you will regret everything!" She shut the door angrily on him, ran upstairs to her bedroom, and cried all night. She changed the locks the next day...

Thinking of Serena again, I turned down Stephanie's street.

"Your taste in music is awful," Melina remarked.

"And that's coming from someone who listens to Avril Lavigne," I retorted, exasperated.

I parked the car in front of Stephanie's driveway and shut off the ignition. Not waiting for a response, I got out of the car and didn't even wait for Melina. I heard her footsteps behind mine, and the front door opened immediately.

"Finally!" Stephanie's flushed face appeared, looking all worried, and she was out of breath. She peered at Melina before I could say a word, and rearranged her hair, becoming aware of how tired she looked.

"Stephanie," I said, "this is my friend Melina." Feeling ridiculous, I avoided my sister's gaze.

"Oh. Hi, Melina." Stephanie moved back. We stood uncomfortably at the door.

"Hi," Melina said, clearly feeling the awkwardness of the situation.

I offered Stephanie the bag. "The Tylenol is inside. Do you need anything else?" I asked, prepared to leave out of embarrassment.

"Well, I kind of needed your help, but I didn't realize you were busy. Why didn't you tell me?" Stephanie's aggravated gaze locked onto mine. "Margie is in bad shape."

"I'm coming in." I changed my mind like the wind,

and Stephanie stepped aside.

"Where are my manners? So sorry." Stephanie looked at Melina. "Come in."

"It's okay," Melina said in a low voice, following me inside.

Ignoring Melina, I removed my jacket and hung it on Stephanie's coat rack. "Where's Margie?"

"She's in her room. I'm putting cool compresses on her head." Stephanie opened the Tylenol and started to read the instructions. "I'm going to get a teaspoon. Would you mind going upstairs to see her? I told her you were coming over."

I ran upstairs, then glanced back at Melina, who looked mortified. "Come," I hollered after seeing that are-you-just-going-to-leave-me-standing-here expression.

"You guys look exactly alike," Melina said as we walked into my niece's bedroom.

I nodded absentmindedly and focused on Margie.

I walked over and sat on her bed. "How are you doing, sunshine?" I pulled back her short brown hair, took the compress from the tepid water, and reapplied it to her forehead. Margie gave me a weak smile. "The compress is getting warm," I said. "Maybe we should change the water."

"I'll change it," Melina quickly offered as Stephanie appeared at the door.

"I told you, sweetie, *Theo* Teddy is here." Stephanie turned to Melina. "The bathroom is to your right."

Melina went to empty the basin and refill it, and Stephanie took the opportunity to tell me off in a low whisper while the faucet ran in the bathroom.

"Teddy, who is that? How could you bring a girl

here at a time like this? You could have prepared me at least! I'll deal with you later." She scolded me as if I were one of her kids. "Open your mouth, Margie," she said and held the back of her head while I held her back up, opting to not answer any of her questions. Where would I even start?

"I know," I mumbled and smiled at Margie, whose eyes were closing and then opening.

"*Voilà*," Melina said as she walked into the bedroom, holding the basin. "Hi, cutie," she said as Margie swallowed the medication, grimacing.

"It's cherry flavor," Stephanie said. "You'll feel better soon." She touched Margie's forehead again.

"Did you try giving her a bath?" Melina asked, clearly not realizing how condescending her tone was as she put down the basin first and stood with her hands on her hips.

Stephanie swung around and looked at her. "Yes, I did." She turned back to Margie and wiped her mouth with a tissue. Her tone was softer as she spoke to her daughter and consoled her.

"Who's that?" Margie asked. "Is that your girlfriend?" She looked at Melina curiously.

I almost choked on my saliva. *No, she is so not my girlfriend.* "She's a—"

"Yes, I'm your uncle's girlfriend," Melina interrupted, placing her hands on my shoulders and standing above me.

Stephanie threw me a look that I knew only too well, and I avoided everyone's eyes, examining Margie closely and changing the subject.

"So, I guess you're lucky, sport. You get to stay home tomorrow," I said aiming for one of her winning smiles. Margie's green eyes sparkled from underneath her pain.

"Yes!" she cried, trying to force herself to speak.

"I think we should let her sleep now," Stephanie said, standing up. "Thanks for bringing the medication, Teddy."

I kissed Margie on the forehead, and Melina bent to rub her hand. "Next time we'll play with your Barbies." Melina pointed to Margie's basket of dolls and the playhouse in the corner of her room. Margie's face lit up. Melina was actually friendly and sweet with Margie. Surprised, I glanced at her for a split second.

"Can you show yourself out? I don't want to leave Margie alone or wake up Maddy."

"Sure." I stood up. "Let's go," I said to Melina.

Melina extended her hand to Stephanie. "It was nice meeting you," she said politely to my sister. "Bye."

"Yes, it was very nice meeting you too. Maybe next time it could be under better circumstances," Stephanie added, giving Melina a wry smile.

When we got into the car, I shut off the radio. I was on edge, the word "girlfriend" darting through my mind. I placed the car in Drive and waited as we put on our seatbelts.

I had to nip this in the bud. "Melina, why did you say you're my girlfriend?"

"Well, what are we, then? Did you want me to tell your niece we were fuck buddies?" Her eyes cold and dark. "I do have feelings, you know."

You could have fooled *me,* I thought. "I know you have feelings." *Fucked-up ones, but they are quite evident.* "I've known you for only two days."

"Three days, actually."

I glanced at the clock on the dashboard. Fuck, I had to be up in six hours, and she was counting the days.

"I have to be up early too, Theodore." Did nothing get past her? "You could at least thank me for accompanying you and finding the store and keeping you company." She folded her arms across her chest. "I didn't *have* to help you."

"I didn't really *ask* for your help," I retorted, outraged as I drove off.

"I know, but aren't you glad I came? I met your sister. You guys could be twins. And your niece, she is so adorable." Melina seemed excited now. "Is your sister younger than you?"

"Yes, we're fourteen months apart."

"Do you look like your mom or your dad?" She sounded like a fuckin' reporter questioning me.

"Whatever. Who cares? I asked you a question, and you utterly ignored it. Why did you tell my sister you were my girlfriend?" I turned to her as I pressed the brakes at a red light. "You're moving too fast for me, Melina. Let's take it a little more slowly."

"Because I want to be your girlfriend." She reached over and grabbed my dick, squeezed it gently, and said, "Do you want a blowjob while you drive?" Her eyes were no longer emotionless but warm and needy as she rubbed me up and down in that way that would drive any man off the road and into a ditch.

Whoa! My foot was still on the brake, and I felt a sensation from the tip of my dick all the way to the tips of my toes. Obviously, my answer would be yes—yes to the blowjob but no to being my girlfriend.

"Well, what's your answer?" She continued rubbing my cock, which was now throbbing.

"Yes." I sighed as the light turned green, omitting the "no" part of her being my girlfriend.

"Yes, it is," she repeated.

I wanted to say no, stop, but I couldn't speak as her mouth sucked me hard, and I felt such immense pleasure throughout my body while trying to focus on driving.

And just like that, in her eyes, Melina became my girlfriend.

Soon enough I would tell her it wouldn't work out, but for now, after three days of knowing her, fucking her madly, and arguing with her, of not liking her, of lusting after her, and wanting her desperately, of hating her taste in music and of thinking she was a porn star come to life, I moaned and sighed all the way to her house, coming in her mouth and thinking she was going to be the end of me.

Serena
Who would believe my sex life now?

"What have you been doing?" Connie's message rang in my ears.

After I stumbled out of bed, almost late for class, I'd caught the bus and was listening to my voicemail while rereading my paper one more time, which I should not have been doing, in case I found a mistake and got upset because I couldn't do anything about it anyway. I thought of last night and blushed. If you only knew what I was doing, Connie. Meanwhile, I had about five texts from Elsa, wondering if I was okay, and then there was my mom's daily text message.

The first person I called was Connie. I sat in the middle of the bus, and for some reason, I felt all eyes were on me. Stupid sensation came over me that they all knew I had been screwing a beautiful man who had tied me up. Was it written on my face? Everyone around me was texting, and I was using a cellphone to actually *talk* on—maybe that was it.

"Hello?" Connie answered after the first ring.

"Hi, I didn't know if you'd answer."

"I was in my office. I have a meeting in five minutes. What's up? Are you knee-deep in writing papers? I know the end of the semester is around the corner."

"I met someone," I said, covering my mouth, trying to remain anonymous, but I felt the stares immediately after saying that sentence. "He's gorgeous, smart, and I really like him." Thoughts about last night and how he made me come with his mouth popped in my head. Ben had gone back to the compare and contrast exercise, and I was stumped as to which orgasm was better. They were all mind-blowing; his tongue was like a magician's. And his cock...

"Hello? Are you there, Serena?"

"Sorry, I got distracted."

"I want to hear everything! Coffee tonight at seven. Second Cup. I want details. Have to run."

* * * *

"So...spill it," Connie said. "I've been dying to hear about this guy all day." Smiling and attentive, she crossed her legs.

Where do I begin? "Connie, he is different."

After I told Connie the story, skipping a few details that were too embarrassing to talk about, she took a deep breath.

"That's pretty intense. Wow."

"I know." I leaned in a little closer to her. "I had an orgasm," I whispered.

"What?" Her brown eyes widened. "During intercourse?" she asked, a little too loudly.

I shushed her. "Quiet! I don't want the whole café to hear about it."

"If I were you, I would be shouting it from the rooftops." She laughed. "It's never happened to me," she whispered.

"It's so different with Ben. He knows so much. He has so much sexual experience, and I feel so alive. Even when I'm just walking, I feel sexier somehow. He's opening up all these sexual feelings in me that I never knew I had."

"They're called orgasms," she joked.

"It's not just the orgasms. It's how he makes me want it, and beg for it, and give a part of myself to him. It's a power thing."

Saying it out loud helped me to think about it more clearly and to understand it was all about power. It was about my giving up my power to him, and I started to wonder whether I really could be in a relationship this intense for long. Could I really give Ben so much power?

"Power is deadly," Connie warned. "Be careful, Serena. Men like that could eat you alive."

"What do you know about men like this?" I asked, annoyed. "You've only ever been with one man."

I saw the hurt in her eyes. "Fuck you! You are sexually inexperienced," she said matter-of-factly. "What I know and don't know is not relevant."

"I'm sorry, Connie. I didn't mean to offend you."

"It's okay. I'm not offended. It's just that I don't want to see you get hurt. And you don't want to get some kind of disease."

"We used safes, for Christ's sake! I'm not sixteen."

"Okay, okay…" Connie smiled. "Good for you, Serena. Now is the time to have fun. You surely can't experience that when you're married like me."

We giggled and ordered another round of lattes, then talked for another hour.

When I got home, I found Ben waiting for me on his bike, a scowl on his face.

"Where were you? I've been trying to reach you."

I searched my purse for my phone and saw that the battery was dead. It must have died just after I saw Connie at the café. I hadn't realized the battery was low.

"The battery died on my phone."

"You could have at least called me," he said, clearly angered. I hadn't even saved his number on my contact list. He narrowed his eyes slightly. "I tried to call you, and then I came here, rang your bell, and decided to wait. Where were you?"

Why was he acting so possessive? I didn't like it at all. I took a step back from him.

He took a step closer. "I need to know where you are at all times, Serena, or else I can't sleep or eat… My mind gets…I just need to know!"

"Why?" I asked incredulously.

That was not normal. Mind you, he had said he wasn't a normal boyfriend, but I didn't like the way he was making me feel right now at all. I wanted to run away from Ben as fast as possible. I was so pissed off.

"I was with my friend, and I don't have to explain myself to you after knowing you only three days!" I shouted. Was he serious? Was he the possessive, jealous type of guy? Obviously.

He took a step back and a deep breath. "Which friend? A guy or a girl?"

His leg shook nervously, and I felt anxious just watching him as if I had to defend myself when I wasn't doing anything wrong.

"You don't know any of my friends!" I said, exasperated.

"What's your friend's name?"

"This is ridiculous! I think you need to leave now."

I *knew* he was too good to be true. I hadn't seen this

side of him before, and it scared the living shit out of me. I felt like I was in danger. What was he accusing me of? Being with another man? I didn't want to look at his angry face anymore, so I spun around to enter my building.

"I'm not going anywhere, Serena." He appeared in front of me in five seconds. I had just taken out my key, my hand trembling. He glanced at my hand and grabbed it to stop the shaking. I looked at him, and his expression softened. "I'm sorry. I don't know what came over me."

Great. Now he was apologizing for acting like a psycho.

"I…Ben…I need to go home—*alone*." And I really meant it. I didn't want to be around him right now. I was pissed off at his whole attitude.

"Were you with a guy or a girl?" he asked again, not letting up, his eyes now expressionless.

"My *girl*friend," I said angrily.

With that, he took another step closer, and I could breathe in his scent now. Uneasiness hit me. If I had been with a guy friend, would he have been so relaxed? I doubted it. He didn't trust me, and I'd known him only three days. What the fuck?

"I need to see you. I can't stop thinking about you." His eyes darkened with every word. A sensation spread all over my body as if he had just released a sweet liquid from his eyes into my body, and my mind began shouting loud and clear: *No! Don't do it!*

Then for some reason, Teddy's face and the sad way he had looked at me at the bar came to mind, and I suddenly felt like I had made a mistake that night. Why hadn't I gone over to Teddy and talked to him? Probably because I had just met Ben. But Teddy had told me he hadn't stopped thinking about me all this time either. I felt this whole Ben thing was getting out of control and turning into something I didn't like at all.

"I really need to be alone now," I said firmly.

Ben pulled back, gave me an odd look, and turned on his heels, muttering "okay" as he walked off.

Appalled, I stared at him. Was he seriously giving *me* attitude? He had given *me* the third degree, was waiting outside my building for God knew how long, and now *he* was the one storming off? No way! I had prepared myself for a fight, but he just left.

Without another word—not even a goodbye or a look my way—he sped off. I stood there, motionless. He had some fuckin' nerve acting so possessive and then so nonchalant. Was there no middle ground with him? It seemed like it was all or nothing, and I didn't like how that made me feel—insecure, lost, confused.

More thoughts of Teddy invaded my mind as I opened my front door, charged my phone, then cried for no reason at all. I couldn't understand my tears but sensed Teddy wouldn't act like this. Something inside told me that Teddy was The One I should be chasing after. Tears continued to roll down my face as thoughts took control of my emotions.

Something told me Teddy was still out there, calling for me, thinking about me as I thought about him.

I knew Ben was going to be complicated. I knew our relationship had *already* become complicated. Three days, and he was demanding to know my whereabouts— angrily!

It was all up to me now. This need to find Teddy consumed me, the good thing was I knew where to look. My soul was saying *go* try or feel dead inside. *What if would haunt me if I did not pursue this.* Lust would invade the molecules of Teddy's skin—under his skin and around his skin—laying naked with him would be heaven; fluttering my eyelashes coquettishly at Teddy, flirting with my one true love, and he would respond like a man in love. How this longing for a man to protect me, to take care of me, once and for all, kept me alert.

My phone buzzed, and I walked over to it. I knew it was Ben. I shook myself out of the heavy daydreaming mode I was seriously in.

Ben: *I'm sorry.*

Me: *I don't think this is going to work.*

Ben: *I think it will. I won't do that again. I promise.*

Me: *I need some time.*

Ben: *I'll make supper tomorrow night. Pick you up at 7. Relaxing dinner. I read your first chapter, and I loved it. Let's just talk.*

Me: *I don't know.*

Ben: *No sex, just talking. I'll explain. There's more I have to tell you about.*

Me: *I'll think about it. I'll text you tomorrow.*

Ben: *Okay. I can't wait.*

I didn't reply; I left it at that. I couldn't say yes or no. Plus, he'd read my first chapter, which put me more on edge. I wanted to know more. His place? I felt terrified to go there, but I had seen a softer side of him when he told me about his past, and the fact that there was more to the story intrigued me. I couldn't let it end like this either.

I decided to read his book and opened up my e-reader. I sat up most of the night, enthralled by the story. I couldn't put it down. The sex itself excited me, but the fact that Ben had written it made me even hornier. I wanted to see him.

I slept soundly and was woken up at eight a.m. by my phone buzzing again. My class was at ten, so I still had some time. It was Ben again.

Ben: *So what's it going to be? Chinese or Italian? I need to do my grocery shopping for tonight.*

I stared at the message for a minute, not sure how to respond. He either knew my answer would be yes, or he wouldn't take no for an answer. This had to go down tonight. I had to see him to find out more, and I was so excited from reading his book, my thoughts were all mixed up.

Me: *Chinese.*

Ben: *I hoped so. I'll pick u up @ 7:00.*

Me: *See you later.*

Ben: *Thanks for giving me another chance. I promise I won't let you down.*

Me: *I'm still pissed.*

I closed my phone after reading the messages over and over again, dizzy from Christopher Hawk and Izzy's story, all the sexual positions vivid in my memory, but at the back of my mind, I thought about how I should not be going to his place after his angry reaction yesterday. Could it be that Ben already had some kind of control over me I couldn't say no to? Could it be he knew how to control a woman without her even realizing it till it was too late? Was it the sex?

I was more curious as to what Ben thought of my writing of my first chapter; after all, he was a writer who could offer me some sound advice. What if he hated it? Also, his personal story left me hanging as to how his story ends. That was my motivation to see Ben again.

Teddy
All tied up…

Fuck, I was late. I was driving down the highway, headed to Laval at one hundred and twenty kilometres an hour. I hadn't even brushed my teeth. From my condo in Montreal to my work took twenty minutes. I was already halfway there in five, and still wearing the same clothes from last night. I'd crashed on my bed and slept soundly, and when the alarm clock rang, I shut it off instead of pressing Snooze.

I reached the exit, and glancing around for cops first, maneuvered out of some traffic illegally. Luck was on my side. I entered the school parking lot, noticing that no kids were outside. The bell had already rung. I ran to my office to grab my paperwork. Dave's voice surprised me. I hadn't even noticed him hunched over his desk, correcting papers.

"Teddy, what the fuck? You look a mess." He glanced at my clothes.

"I know."

"Rough night?" He smirked.

"You could say that." I thought of how Melina had sucked me dry, and I grinned. "Gotta run."

"Classes started five minutes ago," he said smugly, staring at me. "Maybe you should fix your hair."

I patted down my bangs and the rest of my hair then headed off with a nod to Dave.

I walked into my classroom, which was noisy as hell, and when Mean Girls got a look at me, they looked at one another, smiling.

"Mr. Neros," Chantal said, "I love your hair."

All three girls giggled. I placed my paperwork on the desk and acknowledged the class, ignoring her wisecrack.

"Good morning, class. Settle down. We have work to do." I proceeded to write on the board, not apologizing for being late.

I was totally off that day. My mind wasn't there at all. I kept going over the night before and how I had a girlfriend I didn't want. I had to break up with her. It didn't make any sense. When I was sitting at my desk both the bell and my phone rang.

"Hello?"

"Well, hello there." It was Melina.

"How did you get this number?" She called me at *work*? I didn't like this at all.

"Is that how you greet your girlfriend?" she purred into the phone, her voice turning sensual and sending thrills through me as I, forgetting how pissed I was at her call, imagined her in twenty odd positions on my cock.

"Um, Melina, I'm kind of busy. Can I call you back?"

"No, don't call me back. I just wanted to tell you I want you to come over for supper at seven."

"Why didn't you call me on my cell?" I asked.

"See you later, Teddy, and please don't bring a cabernet sauvignon—if you know what's good for you." And she hung up.

She was fuckin' nuts. *Fatal Attraction* nuts. I started to sweat. I was going to see her again tonight? How was

I going to keep up with her? My cock was sore and my body exhausted. I was too tired to even run.

I didn't like her calling me at work.

I turned to Dave, who was staring at me. "Dude, you look awful. Who is Melina?" he asked, grinning from ear to ear.

"None of your business," I said, and that was when the bell rang and I got the fuck out of school in a rush.

I went home and slept again. All I seemed to be doing was taking naps, having sex for hours at a time, and taking a nap again. I didn't even have any milk in my fridge. I needed to go grocery shopping and wash some clothes. After my shower, I searched my wine collection for a merlot and found one tucked away in the corner. I didn't even want to go to her place. I wanted to sleep until tomorrow morning, but at the same time, I wanted to fuck her like a porn star. I imagined there was a camera somewhere and we were being filmed. She would make any man come in seconds with her moans and groans and pillow talk.

I liked when women talked during sex. I found it very erotic and hot, but Melina took it to another level. She didn't shut the fuck up, and then she'd want me to talk, and I really wouldn't have much to say. I wasn't the talking kind of guy during sex. I liked to thrust and throw out the occasional *do you like it?* and *you're so hot*, but it had to be in the moment, and I had to feel it, not be told what to say and *how* to bloody say it. I knew I wouldn't be able to take much more of this whole sex thing with her. Either it was going to fizz out, or I was going to burn out.

I thought of Serena and regretted not going over to talk to her that night I met her at the bar. What had I been thinking? She had met a guy. So what? I could have asked to speak to her for a bit, or at least tried. *What a wimp.* And now look at the mess I was in. I had to break up with Melina. I couldn't go through with being her boyfriend when my mind was constantly on another girl and the what-if factor. I had to find Serena again.

I went to my closet and chose my brown, pin-striped suit with charcoal and baby blue stripes and my blue shirt. No tie. The pants and jacket were tight fitting and showed off my muscles. I rubbed some gel into my hair and let the bangs fall to the side. I wore my dark brown shoes to match, grabbed the bottle of wine, and locked the door to my condo.

Driving to Melina's house, I was nervous again. What was her plan tonight? Were we going to do another scene? Was I even up to it? Part of me was; part of me wasn't.

She buzzed me upstairs, and when arriving at her door, it was wide open, and the aroma of onions and garlic filled the apartment.

"Come in," she hollered from the kitchen. "I'm cooking."

She was in the midst of cutting some sweet potatoes and carrots and adding them to a hefty piece of beef roast. Norah Jones played in the background, and I grimaced because her voice and music didn't do anything for me. *Just turn it off.* Everyone loved her, but I didn't get the big stink about her. No one knew who she was until she won that Grammy. I shut the door behind me and removed my shoes. Melina was wearing an apron with a print of Bart Simpson on it, but under it she was completely naked. I swallowed hard as she smiled up at me. I placed the bottle of merlot on the kitchen counter.

"Hi, sexy," she said, glancing up and down my body. "I love your suit." She looked briefly at the wine. "Thanks."

"Hi there." I tried to focus on her face. "I like your birthday suit. Is it your birthday?"

"Actually, Teddy, it is."

"What?" Was she fucking serious?

"I didn't want to tell you over the phone or obligate you to get a gift for me. I don't like gifts."

"Seriously?"

"Yes."

"Well, Happy Birthday." Feeling utterly hopeless at this new surprise and attitude of hers once again. I approached her.

"Don't ask me how old I am," she said dead seriously.

My phone buzzed. I looked down and saw Dan's name on the screen. Fuck it. I'd read it later.

"Who's that? Your sister again?" she asked mockingly.

"Actually, it's my friend Dan. The one you met the other night, who's seeing your friend Jenny now." I must have sounded a little irritated.

"I know. She's told me *all* about him." She had just finished chopping, and she turned around to rinse her hands, exposing her nudity.

"What's that supposed to mean?" I asked, completely weak at the sight of her ass.

"Don't get so defensive, Theodore. Who cares anyway? I'm sure Dan and Jenny are having their own good time. Aren't you going to give me a birthday kiss?" She turned around to face me, and I kissed her on the lips.

"Happy Birthday," I said again.

"Thank you."

"You could have mentioned it was your birthday. I would have at least brought some flowers."

"It doesn't have to be my birthday to bring me flowers," she said, placing the dish with the vegetables and meat in the oven. She turned up the heat. "Let's have some wine before the festivities."

"What festivities?" I felt my stomach turn.

"The festivities I have planned for my birthday celebration, silly. Why do you think you're here? I invited my family, and they'll all be here in one hour and fifteen minutes. I told them I have a new boyfriend, and they're dying to meet you. My mom, dad, and brother will be here."

"What?" I was ready to bolt out of there like a bat out of hell. Meet her family?

"Are you okay? You look kind of pale. Well, the food is in the oven, and I've prepared everything else." She came up close to me, her apple scent taking control of my senses and body. "Follow me," she said and walked toward her bedroom.

"For my birthday, I want you to put on the handcuffs and the blindfold," she said as I scanned her bedroom and noticed the handcuffs already attached to the bed, waiting for my wrists, which were sweating profusely and not ready for this at all. "We don't have long," she continued, "and I've been wet all day just thinking about what I'm going to do to you."

"I don't know if I'm comfortable with this," I muttered. Why was her family coming? Soon? And she wanted to handcuff me? I probably should have been excited, but the idea just made me think she was insane.

"Didn't you hear what I said?"

"Yes, but don't I get to have an opinion?"

"No. Now lie down, and stop wasting precious time."

She looked crazy. Fuck, her front door was completely open when I walked in. Had anyone seen her like this?

"Wait up. When I got here, your door was wide open. How long was it open?"

"When you rang the bell, I opened it for you. What do you think? It's a free for all in here?" With her blue-eyed gaze on my body like a hungry wolf, she licked her lips. "Now, stop fretting, teach, and allow me to remove your clothes. I want to see your beautiful cock."

Something inside me went *boom*. My cock soared, and my body melted as she reached over and undid the buttons on my shirt while looking at my lips, thoughts of leaving long forgotten.

"Don't touch me yet," she instructed.

She took off my suit jacket first then my shirt and ran her hands up and down my chest and back, giving me small kisses all along my neck. Then, with both her hands, she reached down and rubbed me hard and strong. I let out a small sigh. The blood rushed to my balls, and I swayed back.

Melina undid the button and zipper of my pants in a quick sweep, her bangs falling in her eyes as she looked down and leered. "Let's let your big, juicy cock out, shall we?" And she hauled down my pants, bending low, wrapping her arms around my legs, placing her head between my thighs and smelling me. "You smell delightful," she said in her provocative voice. She kissed my thighs, then let her tongue travel up to my balls. She licked them rapidly, sending erotic sensations throughout my body and mind.

Melina stood up and grabbed my dick, rubbing it as it expanded in her hand. Her mouth locked onto mine, our tongues colliding in strokes and swirls. She pushed me onto the bed, my pants still wrapped around my ankles. She removed them and threw them on the floor with a violent fling, then tossed her apron in the same fashion. The sight of her breasts and her sweet body exposed made me sigh again.

"Higher," she said, then went over to her top drawer and removed a red silk scarf. I slid my body high enough on the bed to hit the headboard, where I eyed the handcuffs uncomfortably. "Close your eyes, Theodore," Melina coached me, her eyes light as the summer sky and needy.

I did as she wanted, driven by her voice and the heat of the moment. The thrill of doing something so crazy, something I never even imagined or ever fantasized about, excited me now.

She placed the soft silk over my eyes and tied it snugly at the back of my head, then took my arms and placed the handcuffs around my wrists.

"They'll be a little cold," she said as though talking to a child.

"I figured as much," I replied.

"You're a real wise-ass, you know."

The cold of the metal shocked my body for a split second, but not being able to see her or anything else left me in limbo—not in a good place. I hated it, actually. Nothing was happening. Then I felt something soft tickle my inner thigh.

"What the fuck is that?" I jumped and moved

around. I abhorred being tickled.

"It's a feather," she said. "What did you think it was?"

I felt the feather moving up and down my legs now, and my boner was going down.

"Are you okay, teach?" She obviously sensed my uneasiness. "It's only a feather. It's not a whip."

"I know. I'm fine." I really wasn't fine. Was this going to get any hotter? I didn't like the idea of not being able to see anything, and that feather was making me itchy.

"Well, then, let's see if we can get you hard for me," she said mockingly. She trailed the long end of the feather down from my chest to my cock and tickled me.

"I don't like being tickled, Melina," I finally said.

"Oh, I know you like being sucked, and we don't have much time…"

I felt her open mouth on my shriveled dick, and then it started to grow, and my body relaxed. This, I liked.

She got me so hard I was ready to fuck her. She knew it too, moaning and groaning and saying things like "You're so big. You're so strong. You're so fuckin' hot. I want to feel you."

She'd suck and talk, driving me wild. I didn't care if I couldn't see her anymore. I sighed loudly and said, "I want to feel you." It was driving me nuts with my hands tied. I wanted to touch her so badly.

"You can't touch me," she whispered.

She rubbed her sex on my cock, and then I was deep inside her. I moved my hips, but she said "Don't move" in a tone that made me stop, and then I was pissed. I wanted to fuckin' go with the flow of my body. I hated this constant stopping and teasing. She started to fuck me violently, and I let out a loud moan when she squeezed and pulled my nipples, which sent electric jolts straight to my dick. I was ready to shoot my load all over her.

"I'm going to come! Take off these fuckin' handcuffs!" I shouted.

She jumped off me, sighed, and said, "Stop that, Theodore."

"Stop what? Take this fuckin' blindfold and handcuffs off." Then I remembered the safe word. "Red!" I screamed, my dick wilting like a flower in the rain.

She pulled off the blindfold and produced a key to unlock the cuffs, her hand shaking slightly, her eyes serious. I was mad as hell and ready to scram out of there.

Once my wrists were free, I picked up my clothes and quickly got dressed, my heart pounding. I refused to look at her.

"I'm leaving!"

I was upset at the fear I was showing her and confused at my reaction. I thought I could handle it, but I guess there were limits. I was going with the sex, but once I let myself go, she wanted to control my reactions, and I couldn't handle that. I wanted to do whatever I wanted to her. I wanted to fuck her. I wanted to control her. This wait-then-stop shit wasn't what I wanted. In the beginning, it excited me, but I felt like it was a one-way street with Melina.

I was dressed and at her bedroom door, my thoughts racing a mile a minute, when I turned to her. She glared at me, refusing to speak.

"Just go," she said, looking down again, already half-dressed and putting on her stockings.

I told myself to not look at her glorious body and the

way her leg was positioned on the bed. I told myself to walk out, but I couldn't leave without an explanation. I had to be honest with her because up to now, I wasn't honest at all. It was my cock that was responding to her and not any other part of my body—namely, my mind.

"Melina, I can't leave like this. I have to tell you the truth."

"What is it?" she asked angrily as she pulled up her stocking, her bra already on. She stared at me.

"I can't do this anymore. This sex thing is not for me."

"You could have fooled me, Theodore. Perhaps I took it too far, but if you can't handle it, then there is no point. I'm not apologizing. If you want to leave, then just leave."

"There's more," I admitted, thinking about Serena. "I'm in love with someone else, and I can't be with you because I'm waiting for her. It's that girl at the club the other night."

"Your ex?" She looked hurt.

"She's not my ex, for Christ's sake! Listen to me. I've never even been on a date with her, but I haven't been able to stop thinking about her for years now. I can't be with you because of her, because of how she makes me feel, and because I don't want to have sex with a blindfold on or pretend I'm a waiter. You're beautiful, but I want more. And I don't want to hurt you." I ran my hands through the hair that had fallen on my face. Her blue eyes were expressionless as usual. "I think what we have is too much for me. And not enough. I'm sorry."

"Get the fuck out!" she screamed, bending to get her shoe. She threw it at me with full force. "You're a real fucking prick. You're hung up on a girl you haven't even screwed…choosing her over *me*!"

The shoe hit my forehead and stunned me.

I turned around and left in a daze, listening to her curse and shout at me and say something about her birthday, but all I kept thinking about was, why had I just told her about Serena? Why the fuck didn't I keep my big mouth shut? It was like some compulsion had come over me, and I couldn't stop it from escaping my lips.

If I continued to explore this crazy sex thing with Melina, then what about Serena? I had to focus. I texted Dan in the elevator and met him at a bar close by on Saint Laurent Street.

I turned up Jeanne Mance Street, running the whole scene over in my head again when out of the blue a familiar figure caught my eye. Bald Model guy stood in front of an apartment building, smoking a cigarette, and I was in such a rage, I wanted to ram right into him. Was he waiting for Serena? *Is this where she lives?* This drab building that I'd passed hundreds of times throughout my life when going out with friends or to university, spending my time in the city? Fuck, one of my university buddies had an apartment in the building right next to it!

My insides rumbled—butterflies in my stomach like a love-struck teenager—and then absolute and total wrath took over me at Baldy's composure, his casual stride and then his relaxed stance on the bike. He was the type of guy I couldn't compete with. I parked my car off to the side in a spot on my far right, and peeked at him through my rearview mirror, feeling like a stalker. I ducked a bit and pretended to text, the phone in the palm of my right hand. I looked at the clock on the dashboard; it was seven thirty exactly. Only half an hour had passed since I was at Melina's? It had felt like an eternity.

Every shady minute I had been with Melina felt equal to half an hour. The time went by slowly in that dark, unknown world of hers. How could I give myself to Melina or any other woman like that? Tied and bound, denying my orgasm…

There was Serena!

Fuck. She looked like the Serena I had first met. She was dressed like an average girl who shopped at American Eagle, not like a rocker chick from Foufounes. That was very interesting indeed. I studied her as she got onto the bike. She seemed aloof and cold, didn't even kiss Baldy on the lips. I watched them leave, but at the last second, right before she passed my car, I opened the window and looked at her when I knew for certain *he* was concentrating on driving ahead. She caught my gaze. She saw me, swerved her head toward me, and smiled incredulously. Then she mouthed something to me I couldn't understand. I was in such a state of shock I didn't even follow her. I should have. I watched her pass by me and tell me something. I shrugged my shoulders at her, then lost sight of her as a car came close behind the bike, and I felt desperate and lonely again. Desolate, jealous it was not me she had her arms around.

I should learn to ride a fuckin' bike, I thought.

Dan and I drank till three in the morning, taking cabs to every bar we felt like drinking in. My downward spiral had begun; I was hopeless, ignorant, misguided, unlucky, lucky, misunderstood. I couldn't believe I broke up with a porn star to wallow over a girl who was obviously fucking a male model. I was definitely calling in sick tomorrow. I couldn't teach a class in this state of mind and body.

"You're a real piece of work," Dan had said in a drunken stupor when I spilled the beans. "Any guy would die to be in your position, and you're running away?" He looked at me hard. "You're too pretty, you know that? That's your fuckin' problem. If you were ugly, you wouldn't have these problems."

"You're a fuckin' idiot. I don't even know why I bother asking for advice from a hack like you!"

"Now we're back to where you started from—pining for and obsessing over Serena. Are you happy now?" He smirked, and I wanted to punch his face because he was absolutely right. I was miserable, but it was a familiar miserable. One I could control.

And then it dawned on me… I liked being in control. I liked calling the shots. If I wanted to yearn for someone for years on end, who was anyone to tell me I couldn't? Who would stop me down that wanting road? Melina, and now she was out of the picture.

Now that I knew where Serena lived, it changed everything.

Serena
My decision is made…or maybe not…

At seven twenty-five I went downstairs. I had on my jeans and a plain black top that looked conservative. I didn't want to give Ben the impression I was coming over for sex. I wore just a tad of makeup and had straightened my wavy hair. When I got outside, Ben was smoking a cigarette, and I approached him with an indifferent attitude.

"Hi," he said warmly.

"Hi," I replied flatly.

He handed me the helmet, and I put it on. He took off rather quickly, looking straight ahead. I glanced off to the side when a man in a black jeep caught my eye. My heart pounded in my chest because I knew who he was.

Teddy.

He was staring right at me as if he had been looking at me for a while, and in that split second, our eyes met, and I knew—I *knew*—I had to see him again. No way was it a coincidence that he was just sitting in his jeep. I spontaneously mouthed to him, *I'll see you soon.* He probably couldn't read my lips from that distance, but I wanted him to know I was thinking about him too, that I knew he was there.

How Teddy found out where I lived didn't bother me as much as it should have. I realized he was still waiting for me, and I wanted to acknowledge that and him. Our hearts and souls were bonded. I didn't know why or how, but somehow it was inevitable. Seeing Teddy confirmed that not continuing this relationship with Ben would be the best thing for me to do, no matter if I was sexually attracted to Ben.

As I breathed in Ben's scent and thoughts of Teddy consumed me, I knew I was at the right place at the right time, so this was meant to be.

My heart ached. I wanted to turn back, and when I did, I had lost sight of him. How ridiculous to want someone so much.

It was as if I knew Teddy would think my feet were perfect, the swing of my hair a complete and utter turn-on, my quirks undeniably adorable. The fluttering of my eyelashes would pound in his heart, and my perfume would spread through his senses, marking my spot in his brain, penetrating deep within his psyche so that every time he smelled gardenias, I would come to mind. Teddy would know how to read my silence. He would understand my love of the space between guitar riffs, of melodic pieces and pounding drum beats reflecting my heartbeat. He would appreciate my love affair with words, lyrics, sentences, adjectives, verbs, synonyms, antonyms, paragraphs, chapters, that guide me through the reckless nights of sleeplessness and cold sweats.

As for Ben, even though we had a lot in common, it wasn't a spiritual connection or an understanding of each other's souls that connected us. It was more of a sexual awakening. I knew Ben had so many issues that they stopped me from giving myself to him. I felt like I had already given myself to Teddy a long time ago.

"You're awfully quiet," Ben commented as we

stopped at a red light on Sherbrooke Street.

"It's hard to talk while on a bike," I said. I was off on a tangent again, in my own word world, wishing I could remember half the things I think about so I could use them in a story or in my manuscript, which, shit... Ben had read.

"I know. We're almost there," he said, continuing for another five minutes and then slowing down in front of an apartment building that had been converted into condos a while back. So *this* was where he lived.

He touched a button on his keychain, and a garage door opened, revealing a massive underground parking lot with reserved spots spray-painted in yellow on the asphalt. We rode slightly downhill and entered a wider parking floor, then veered toward the back and parked at number 882. Ben shut off the engine, and I got off the motorcycle, a little bit chilled, and removed the helmet. My hair was again tangled. Why had I even bothered straightening it? I peeked at Ben and noticed his light blue jeans and a yellow T-shirt. He unzipped his leather jacket, and the words "FUCK THE MEDIA" screamed out at me. I quickly turned away. I supposed he was taking a stand against the media, but I didn't want to comment and get into a debate over it. My thoughts were already all over the place, seeing Teddy like that and knowing he was there for me.

"Serena, I know I've upset you, but are you going to give me the cold shoulder all night?" He seemed unsure how to handle me—for once.

"Ben, I'm preoccupied. Thinking about school," I lied.

"That explains it. Did you hand in your paper?" he asked as we walked toward the elevator.

"Yes."

He pressed the button to go up, and we waited silently. I could feel his stare on me and sensed he wanted to say something, but I deliberately avoided his gaze, because if I saw any trace of desire for me in his eyes, I would turn into putty in his hands. The doors opened, and a sharply dressed, older couple stepped out. We walked into the elevator, and he looked straight ahead, ignoring me.

Why the hell was Ben acting like he didn't even want me when I was the one who should be mad? He pressed the button for the eighth floor, and then he turned to me, his brown eyes no longer icy but the complete opposite. He bent and whispered in my ear, his voice so low that I struggled to listen to it.

"I know I said no sex, but all I want to do is fuck you in the elevator." He took a step back and watched me squirm.

I wasn't the type to go from cold to hot in seconds, but his words got the better of my senses. There was complete stillness in the elevator. I said nothing, not trusting my words. Every second felt like an hour. He slowly looked over my body, and I couldn't help but feel his hot gaze and respond to it. He hadn't shaved his head, and the stubble on his face looked fantastic. I wanted to rub my hands on his head.

"It doesn't matter what you wear or how your jeans drive me mad. All I know is what's underneath," Ben said quietly, licking his lips in that seductive way that made my nipples harden, and that was when the doors opened.

We exited the elevator, and he guided me to his apartment door. He removed the key from his jacket pocket and bent slightly to unlock it. When he opened the door, and gestured for me to walk in first, I saw the most luxurious apartment I had ever seen. It looked like something you'd see in those *Architectural Digest* magazines my mom used to buy and salivate over.

"Wow! Your place is gorgeous."

"Thanks," he said, offering to take my jacket when I hadn't even removed it.

The condo smelled like chicken, garlic, and soy sauce. I hadn't realized how hungry I was until I smelled that aroma and unconsciously said, "Mmm, it smells delicious in here."

"I made General Tao chicken and some rice with chop suey. No big deal," he remarked as I removed my jacket.

He glanced at my body, then looked at me closely. His gaze roamed up and down, from my face to my legs. His eyes darkened, and my insides clenched incessantly. Regardless of how I wanted to run away, he had this sexual grip on me I couldn't explain. Well, maybe I could explain, duh. Ben was the only man who made me come over and over again and who finally made me feel like sex was good—really fuckin' earth-shattering good.

"It sounds like a big deal to me," I replied. Did he think I was Rachael Ray? The closest I got to cooking anything out of the ordinary was shepherd's pie. Coming from a Greek household, almost everything my mom made was exotic to the rest of my friends.

"First you have to try it, and then you can decide for yourself," he said, hanging up my jacket in his perfectly arranged closet with wooden hangers that all faced the same way. His shoe rack was unusual. Before he shut the closet door, I noticed at least twenty pairs of shoes. Did he wear all those? He must have had that California Closet collection.

I glanced at his kitchen and couldn't believe he had two gas stoves like he served hundreds of people dinner. He had no cupboards but white shelves with a minimal number of white plates, white cups, platters, and bowls, and everything else was stainless steel. Glass tiles lined the walls, and the counter was the size of my entire kitchen. Ten silver bar stools were set up along the counter, which was adorned with ten small, white votive candle holders, one for each bar stool place setting. They added a touch of femininity to the room.

The first pieces of art that caught my eye were the Corno paintings the size of the two walls they occupied. The vibrant red, black and turquoise colours and the wicked shapes of the naked bodies took me aback.

"I love the Corno paintings. They're outstanding."

I stepped closer to them and marveled at the brushstrokes and brilliant artistry. I knew they were worth hundreds of thousands of dollars.

"This one is from the Art and Desire Exhibit in 2011. I bought it in Old Montreal at her art gallery," he said casually as if everyone had a hundred thousand or so in small change to buy a real painting from a famous French-Canadian artist that would be worth millions one day. I just hoped he had a tight security system.

"Oh."

I felt intimidated and tiny in this environment. Without ogling, I checked out Ben's attire and noticed he wore no brand names. He had mentioned when we first met that he didn't need them. Thank God, because right now I could never afford name brands.

Ben didn't dress like he could be living in this

luxury.

He approached me from behind and studied me while I stared in awe at the paintings, lost in a million thoughts. His place felt like a museum and I wasn't sure if I liked it or disliked it. One thing for sure, it didn't make me feel at ease.

"I met her at the exhibition. Her name is Joanne Corneau. She now lives in SoHo, New York. She is the ultimate success story, but what a talent. I bought this one for thirty-four dollars. I bargained for a while." He stared at the naked body. "I love looking at the female body. I'd pay just about anything…" He looked at me. "But I especially love it when it's free." He grinned and headed to the kitchen. "Wine, Serena?"

"Sure." I needed something to calm my out-of-control nerves, his sexy voice, the paintings, the kitchen, the *white* leather couches.

"Would you like to have a seat?" He looked at the couches, which I was scared to stain. He opened a bottle of wine with ease and expertise, his lovely hands twisting the bottle opener and making me slightly uneasy imagining them all over my body, slipping and sliding.

Stop it. No sex.

I sat on one of the couches and leaned back. It looked more comfortable than it actually was. He walked over to me, and I caught his dimples coming out, teasing me, saying, *here I am.* "I hope you like merlot," he said gently. "It's my favorite." He handed me the thin-stemmed wine glass and sat next to me with his.

"Of course." I nodded, knowing absolutely nothing about merlot. It sounded like the wizard's name in *Lord of the Rings*, but I kept my mouth shut and smiled politely. "Thank you."

I took a sip, and then he glanced at me. "What, no cheers?" His eyes darkened.

"Sorry. How rude. Cheers," I said, and we clinked glasses. He swirled the wine in his mouth for a few seconds.

"Well?" He waited, and I had no idea what his "well" was intended for. Did he want me to tell him something? I thought he was going to talk to me.

"Well what?" I asked.

"The wine, silly. Why are you nervous?" He moved closer to me, and his eyes held a warmth once again.

I tasted the wine again and let it travel down my throat, warming me up. "I like it. It tastes like rich berries."

He smiled, but then his expression suddenly turned serious. He took a long sip of his wine, almost finishing it. His strong legs were close to mine, mere inches away.

Don't stare.

"Serena, we need to talk about yesterday." Ben's face was no longer warm and friendly like it was just a few seconds ago when he called me *silly*. "I'm a jealous guy. I'm a possessive man, and I can't apologize for that. That's who I am, but I have to tell you a few other facts about me, and…"

He took another quick sip, and watching his throat move as he swallowed, I felt an urge to touch his neck.

Focus.

"And if you want to be with me," he continued, "then you must know about them."

"Okay," I said slowly, drinking the wine and trying to focus on his words and not his body being so close to mine.

"When I left London, I was a mess. I got accepted at

McGill on a partial scholarship. Even though I had ended it with Patricia, the repercussions were still there, and my therapist had told me to stay away from *any* relationship for a *long* time. When I met a fellow student, Nancy, I was still trying to resist temptations and triggers. She had all the triggers that sent me back over the edge. She was domineering, sexy as hell, and into an alternative lifestyle. It was Patricia Collins all over again. Nancy was a Domme and had led me back into that world."

He looked far away for a split second as if remembering something.

"And then she started to show me a part of herself that scared me. She confessed that she was bipolar. When she was on her medication, she was fine, but when she went off it…"

He raised his glass to take another sip of wine, but it was empty. He got up to get the bottle. I anticipated what would come next. He could make a movie out of his stories, I thought. He came back with the bottle. I took another sip and finished my glass.

As he refilled our glasses, he peered at me, then looked away. "She killed herself."

"Oh my God!"

"I was never in love with her. After I found out she had a mental illness, I drew away and then broke up with her. But Nancy couldn't accept the break-up. She would show up at my condo, drugged and acting crazy, yelling that she loved me… When I didn't see Nancy for one month, I thought she had given up, but I found out she had swallowed a bottle of pills and died in a hotel room not far from my condo. I was devastated. I felt guilty that I didn't help her enough, that I was a prick."

He stared at me intently, but I could tell he was off

in another place and time.

"Which I had been. I was a complete asshole. Unsympathetic to her problem."

He got up and paced for a few seconds.

"Sorry. Just talking about it is making me nervous."

"It's okay, Ben. Take your time," I said patiently, feeling bad for him but dying to find out more and why he felt so weak.

"I vowed to myself I would never be with a dominant woman again. And that's where I am now." He looked directly into my eyes, his showing a neediness I hadn't seen in him before, but then he quickly recovered. "I can't make any promises to you, Serena. I'm still learning who I am. I'm fucked up, I know."

Ben was clearly very nervous now, avoiding my gaze. He lifted his wine glass and stared at the drink. My head spun from his story, and I looked away, trying to absorb all this new information and at the same time trying to sort out my feelings, which were all mixed up. Then Teddy's eyes appeared in my mind. I mentally shook away the image.

"Are you okay?" Ben asked, compassion in his voice. "If you want to leave, there's the door. I just had to get that off my chest because, Serena, I really like you."

"Ben, thanks for telling me all this. It makes things clearer, but I don't know if I could be with—"

"With someone like me?" he interrupted, finishing my sentence, his voice and eyes betraying his disappointment.

"Yes."

It was true. Did I truly need this? Yes, the sex was…phenomenal, but all the other baggage weighed me down, and I felt that in time, it could drown me.

Ben stood and changed his whole demeanour, now displaying his twinkling dimples. "How about we don't let all this food go to waste?" His brown eyes pleaded to mine. "Let's eat."

I wanted to listen to him, and I wanted him to stop talking. I didn't want to hear any more. I didn't want his story to become my story. I felt I could never understand his world. Teddy's world was probably less complicated. Inside, in my heart, I knew Teddy was the one for me and that Ben was so far removed from my world. Ben needed me to understand so much, to feel so much. On the edge of his world, trying to understand what I couldn't, what I didn't want to…

"Ben, let's eat." The conversation made me completely uncomfortable.

He went straight to the kitchen and prepared the food on identical white platters.

"Do you need any help?" I offered, thinking how I didn't want to stay much longer.

"No, sit down, please," he said forcefully.

I hugged myself, rubbing my arms, sensing the air in the room had turned icy. On his counter, I spotted a tiny, little box David's Gourmet Green Apple Soft Licorice with pictures of tiny green licorice, and out of nervousness, I wanted to try one right away. But instead, I sat down and waited for Ben, trying to concentrate on nothing in particular.

He arrived with one platter filled with General Tao chicken, which smelled fantastic, another platter of white rice, and yet another with chop suey.

"Dig in," he said as he sat down and added the appropriate utensils to the platters. His expression was unreadable.

I filled my plate with food, and he did the same. My stomach started to growl at the aroma, and I couldn't believe I was still hungry after his disclosure.

"I gather you're hungry." He smirked.

"Yes," I said, slightly embarrassed. Then this cool singing voice came blaring through the speakers. "Who is this?"

"Niki & the Dove. It's called 'DJ Ease My Mind.'"

It had a calm beat, and the singer's voice got the better of me. It was so clear I could understand every word.

"*Bon appétit*," Ben said.

"*Bon appétit*," I repeated, listening to the music and wanting to dance. From a slow, haunting voice it became a dance song that made my legs move in time to the beat.

"It's a great song," Ben agreed. "This is the satellite station Chill, but this song isn't exactly chill."

"No, it makes me want to dance."

I took a few bites of the food and spontaneously moaned. He gave me a fierce glance as if I had committed a crime.

"This is delicious," I said.

"Thanks," he said, though he still seemed offended by my reaction.

I guess I should have saved my moans for the bedroom. What was I thinking?

We ate in silence while one great song came after another, and then I thought, I shouldn't be in his apartment. I wanted to run. I wanted to see Teddy again. Had he managed to read my lips when I mouthed *I'll see you soon* to him?

Ben quietly chewed his food, glancing at me every

once in a while, oblivious to my inner turmoil. I wanted to get out of this messy relationship with this complicated man.

"Your first chapter was really captivating. I loved how Maria and Jack met and the way you described Saint Tropez," he suddenly said. "Have you ever been there?"

"No, although I would love to go one day," I admitted shyly. He did like it! "What else?" I asked, curious, wanting feedback and focusing on him again.

"I like your writing style. It's quick and to the moment. You don't really beat around the bush."

"Oh." I took a bite. "I read your book too," I said quietly.

"Which one?" He peeked up at me.

"Volume one of *The Dark Angel* series. I thought it was very good."

"Which part did you *like*?" He stopped eating, placed his utensils down, and looked intently at me.

"Can't say…" I looked down.

"Which sex part?" he asked bluntly, his expression straight and serious.

"Um, the part on the…roof…" That was a fuckin' hot scene that got me all excited.

"Especially the rain?" Ben smiled wickedly.

"Yes." I couldn't eat anymore. My insides were shaking again with the way Ben was looking at me, thinking of how Christopher and Isabella had sex on the roof, the rain not stopping them… "It was very…sensual."

Ben got up and came around to me, leaving his plate half-full, and extended his hand. "Come here, please," he said, and I did exactly as he bid, as if I were under a spell, all thoughts of running away vanishing.

"Let's go to my rooftop." His eyes were heavy with desire. "Too bad it's not raining tonight."

"Um, I don't know…" My legs wobbled as I stood up. "I thought you said no sex." My voice was wobbly too.

"I did, but…I can't. You're near me, here in my apartment, and I'm smelling the gardenia scent, and you look like a sad puppy, lost. I want to take you and make you completely…mine."

His voice faltered at the last line, and he seemed lost as well, holding my hand in his, inching closer to me, and staring into my eyes with a need I knew only too well.

"I want to hold you tight." The song "You Don't Know How Lucky You Are" by Keaton Henson came on, and he grabbed me close. "Let's dance."

The singer sang about lips beginning and whether you know who you are, do you love—a beautiful guitar melody and a soft male voice singing about knowing.

Does he love? Does he know who you are? Does he know not to talk about your dad? Does he know when you're sad? You don't like to be touched, kissed, does his love make your head spin? And I thought about Teddy singing this song to me. I wasn't thinking about Ben at all. I wanted Teddy to sing this to me. I wanted to be dancing with Teddy. I pulled away.

"I…have…to go…"

The singer continued to sing *Does his love make your head spin?* over and over…

Ben looked bewildered, and then it was like he had an epiphany. He stepped back, hurt.

"Serena, what is it?" But he looked like he knew—he knew exactly what I was thinking. "It's your ex,

327

right?"

"He's not my ex." I searched for my purse. He had put it with my jacket.

"I have all your things in my hall closet. I'll get them." Ben's voice was serious, his eyes cold.

"I'm sorry, Ben. I just can't do this," I said as he handed me my jacket and purse. "It's too much for me. *You're* too much for me."

He lifted my chin with his fingers. "Never say that, Serena." He still had that confident look on his face. "I'll take you home, but don't say *I'm* too much for you because you are absolutely perfect for me, and I am exactly what you need. You just don't know it yet." Ben's eyes darkened, and he took out his keys.

"I'll take a cab." I felt awful and guilty leaving like this and thinking maybe he was right—that he was exactly what I needed and that Teddy was just a figment of my overactive imagination…

"Bloody hell you will. I'm a gentleman, Serena." He rubbed the back of his head nervously and shifted from foot to foot. I leaned in and touched his right shoulder.

"I'm really sorry, Ben."

"Don't be sorry." He placed his hand on top of mine and squeezed it. "I'm not letting you go that easily." And he leaned down and kissed me on the lips. It was an unexpected kiss, taking me by surprise—a sweet, tasty surprise.

His tongue immediately met mine, and he pulled it into his mouth and sucked it hard. Then he sucked my lower lip and gently kissed my upper lip. He dropped our jackets to the floor and ran his fingers through my hair, holding my head tightly with both hands and then cupping my face as his tongue continued its magic.

I let out a moan and forgot the world, forgot Teddy, forgot my dreams, forgot his night-mares, forgot the reason I was standing at the door, forgot the song... I only remembered how Ben's kiss made me float into another galaxy. How his hands, now removing my shirt, made me weak with desire. How his lips, traveling down my throat, my breasts, my stomach, made me shiver. As he neared my sex, it began to pump with lust, silently shouting out his name. *Ben. Ben. Ben.*

And just like that, my intention to leave was thwarted by Ben's convictions. I wanted to possess his body as he did mine, but my soul floated away, looking elsewhere for a connection. In the middle of this heated moment, a thought hit me: Could Ben possess my soul? I knew the answer before I asked myself the question. I wanted to not care about the answer; I wanted to go with the moment. Carpe Diem.

But a tiny voice inside me spoke, and I listened.

Part Three

Souls Never Forget
Love is written in places you can't see.

Teddy
Do you know your mouth quivers when you're sad?

I knew what I wanted. I only hoped Serena wanted the same things I did. Identical needs flowing from me to her, as I sat there on my couch in the middle of the night, trying to decipher her words, picturing the movement of her mouth, and coming up with nothing.

She would soon come to me. She told me so. I knew that must have been what she had told me. Even if I couldn't make out the words, I'd gotten the message. It didn't matter what she'd said, only that she had said *something*. Deep inside I knew that was the real deal. I couldn't wait to see her again. My soul needed her desperately to make it bright, to open it up, and to finally be loved.

I got up and paced. I had to be up in three and a half hours. How was I going to teach my class? I was a fuckin' wreck.

Melina had done things to me these past few days that most men never experienced in a lifetime. I knew I wasn't exaggerating. And there I was, craving her touch, just because it was a familiar one and not for any other reason. She knew the right buttons to push, but she was fuck-in' nuts. I knew it; I knew it like I knew I needed Serena. Melina was all wrong for me. We didn't fit like a glove; we just fit because we needed to fit. The sexual attraction would have dissipated eventually, and where would that have left me? Plus, the sex was not the kind of sex I wanted. It was too controlled, too needy, too planned. But man, she was hot as hell.

To clear my head, I went to the kitchen for a glass of water, before I popped a boner just thinking about how Melina's body was my wet dream.

I brought my glass to the living room, propped my feet on the coffee table, and knew I had to wait for Serena. But what would stop me from going to her apartment building and finding her? It was three thirty in the morning. This was crazy. How would I find which apartment she lived in?

What if she wasn't home? What if she was? What if she was doing exactly the same thing I was doing?

Serena
Do you know your eyes blink when you're sad?

I didn't know who I was fooling. I guess just myself. I glanced at the clock on my nightstand. Shit, it was three thirty in the fuckin' morning, and I seriously should get up, because the bed was sucking me in and ready to spit me out. I sat up, grabbed my robe, and then headed toward the kitchen. Turning on all the lights, I grabbed a bottle of water, thinking about what went wrong with Ben.

At first, he made all the right moves, pressed all the right buttons. He had me weak, out of control, desperate for his kisses, his mouth, his tongue, his cock… Up until I realized that, even in my horniness, he had me exactly where *he* wanted me, not where *I* wanted to be.

I wanted Teddy, body and soul, not Ben…

Ben had me half-naked on his couch and kissing my neck when I reached down to get my bra.

He looked perplexed. "What are you doing?" His voice was heavy.

"I'm leaving," I said weakly. "I have to go now."

He stood up, and I quickly put on my bra and shirt, avoiding his gaze.

He stepped back. "You're a strong woman, Serena." He rubbed his head and shifted from one foot to the other. "I admire you." He lifted my chin, forcing me to look into his dark eyes that were devoid of emotion. "I'm too fucked up. I understand. I would probably do the same in your situation."

He held my chin gently and caressed my cheek with his other hand, sending waves of desire through me. It was going to be hard to reach that front door. He traced my cheek with his thumb while he slid his other hand down my neck, making my nipples hard.

"One thing you can't deny, Serena, is this." And he bent to kiss my lips softly, gently.

I closed my eyes, trying to find the strength to push him away, when he pulled back first and led me to the door, took his keys and quietly led me down to his bike. We didn't say another word till we stood in front of my building.

"Thank you for the lovely supper," I said politely.

"Fuck the supper," he said angrily. "We both know you don't ever want to share another supper with me, so cut the crap, Serena, and tell me to fuck off, because if you don't, I swear I will not stop calling you and texting you and wanting you. I haven't had my fill of you. We've just gotten started."

Ben's gaze hovered over me, penetrating mine and speaking his truth. Not necessarily *my* truth. He'd confused me when he kissed me, but if I felt the same as he did, then I wouldn't be thinking about Teddy.

"I'm not going to say that to you," I replied, avoiding looking into his dizzying eyes.

"You want me to call you? Fuck you?" He came closer to me.

I took a step back, feeling every word he said in my body. "No, I didn't say that. I just can't do this."

I headed for my front door without another word and without my body betraying my mind. I wanted him too, and that was not good. Not good at all.

"Then this is not good-bye," he said as I unlocked my front door.

I didn't turn back or reply, because I was scared to— scared to death, scared to lose myself, scared to be myself, scared about Teddy, scared about the unknown…

I hadn't slept a wink since then…

I unlocked my balcony door and opened it to get some fresh air. I couldn't breathe in my apartment. I looked down on the street and felt a gaze on me. Not dark piercing eyes, but light eyes. Green, the colour of my dreams, looking directly at me from a familiar black jeep. I didn't pull my gaze away, and neither did *he*. The windows separating us didn't matter.

He opened his car door and pointed to my apartment building door. I didn't care about the time. I didn't care about the fact that he was there in the middle of the night. I didn't question his motives, because I knew them, just like I'd felt he was near. I couldn't sleep because he was outside my window. I couldn't dream because he was waiting to dream with me. I nodded, opened my apartment door, and headed downstairs. I didn't shut the door to my apartment. I didn't put on any shoes. I didn't tie my bathrobe. I didn't fix my hair. I didn't say no.

I took the stairs down to get there quickly, urgently. As my bare feet struck the cold steps, I knew my soul was leading the way. I knew my soul had control over my body and not my body over my soul.

My soul remembered. My hair flew in my face, my bathrobe flapped at my sides as I stood in front of the glass doors separating me from the love of my life. I held on to the handle as his green eyes met my violet ones, and our souls spoke to each other: *Open the door, and let me in.*

Teddy
I'm the one who really loves you, baby

I didn't know why I was still wearing my Joe Boxer pajamas and my Converse T-shirt. I hadn't changed; I just grabbed my shoes and my jacket and knew I had to go to Serena's in the night, in the dark, so no one can see me waiting—waiting for her to see the light. Lenny Kravitz's song "I'll Be Waiting" was playing on one of my CDs I'd popped into the player, and I thought, how appropriate to hear this song on the night I was going to her.

More like stalk her…

It could have been for naught. I could have been wasting my time. Perhaps I could have caught a glimpse of her…

Or she was sleeping right now, and I was a fool, as usual. It took me less than ten minutes to get downtown and park across from her building to have full view of all the windows. At this time, there were only two lights on in the whole apartment building.

Lenny was singing *I feel your pain, can I make it right? I realize there is no end in sight, but still I wait for you to see the light…* I was singing loud now, glancing from one window to the next, until suddenly I saw movement behind a patio door, and I knew as I shut the car's engine and met Serena's gaze in a quick second that she was searching for me too. Sounded crazy, but I felt this energy pull me toward her.

As long as I'm breathing, I'll be waiting... I gestured for her to go to the building's front door. She nodded, and I ran across the street, not even looking for speeding cars, although one honked at me.

I was at her door, awaiting her presence like a groom at an altar. The exit door opened, and I saw her hair flowing behind her, her robe off her shoulder, her lilac nightgown clinging to her every curve, and her beautiful bare feet running to the door.

Her violet eyes met my green ones, and I wanted to know if she wanted to marry me. What a crazy thing to think about, but that was the thought that surged through me. I shook my head for a second, studying her face. It was perfect in the middle of the night. Not a trace of makeup, not a trace of sadness...only hope in her eyes. I was home. She pushed the lever and let me in from the cool night, and then breathlessly said exactly what I wanted to say.

Nothing.

She took me by the hand and led me up the stairs in silence, glancing back and smiling every once in a while. Our words traveled from my soul to hers and back, communicating. I followed her up the staircase quietly, and she'd turn every once in a while, to make sure I was there. I wouldn't turn my eyes away from hers, not even for a split second. Scared this was all a dream, I waited to meet her gaze. She didn't care that I was outside in the middle of the night like some creepy stalker. She knew that was the farthest thing from the truth.

Our souls met and sang songs to each other while

we took the steps two at a time. She led me through an open door, and I removed my shoes, then noticed I was barefoot too. Serena looked down at my toes and smiled.

"How is it possible?" her soul asked.

"It was meant to be. You are meant to be. I am meant to be. We are meant to be. Together. It is possible," my soul replied.

Serena
We speak in silence and in words…

Teddy followed me into my apartment building, and I shut the door behind us. I led him to the couch without a word. He removed his coat and flung it on the side of the couch. He removed his shoes, and I smirked at his naked feet. They were perfectly aligned.

We sat opposite each other for the longest time, our eyes memorizing each other's lines and smiles. No words were needed. The silence spoke for us; it was as if we were under each other's spell.

I stared at his face, examining every detail. Teddy had an olive complexion with clear, small pores. His eyes were a deep green with hazel lines around the iris. He had a straight nose that was slightly wider at the bottom. He had dark eyebrows and dark brown hair that fell on his face as he shook his head to the right to get his bangs out of the way. His hair was messy, and I wanted to run my fingers in it endlessly, tirelessly, and not fix it, but to feel it, to feel the texture on my fingers. Did he have soft hair? Thick hair? Coarse hair? I wanted to know, but I didn't dare touch him. I preferred to stare at him. I discovered he had three tiny brown moles—one above his eyebrow, just under his bangs; one close to his left ear; and one under his lip that I wanted to kiss. He had a perfect chin with a dimple that reminded me of a young John Travolta. My gaze traveled to his ears, which

I could see only half of, as his hair covered them.

Suddenly he broke the silence with a voice that seeped straight into my heart.

"Would you like to go out with me this Saturday?" The sound of him was sexy, calm, straight to the point, and I wanted him to say my name.

Saturday was only three days away, but it felt like an eternity.

"Yes," I whispered, searching for my voice. "But why do we have to wait till Saturday?" I spoke the truth with Teddy. It was natural.

"I don't know," he replied. "Let's make it Friday night instead."

"That sounds better."

We continued studying each other's face.

"Do you usually walk around barefoot?" he asked, his gaze never leaving mine.

"Never," I replied. "You?"

"Never."

His eyes were round and full, but when I studied his lips, I felt his gaze on mine, and I nervously bit the inside of my mouth. He had a full lower lip, plum colour, and a smaller upper lip. He smiled, and I noticed the whitest teeth ever.

"Do you whiten your teeth?"

"It's the toothpaste, Arm & Hammer. My dentist recommended it."

"Baking soda does wonders for sinks as well," I said. "My mom told me to add vinegar to it to unclog sinks."

He had a graceful neck, a small silver cross on a black leather string gracing it. I guessed he slept with it on.

"Really?" He held on to his cross, playing with it, moving it back and forth as my eyes followed his hands, and I realized how big and strong they were, with long, lean fingers, well-groomed nails. I imagined those hands on my body...

"Yes. Um...natural ingredients are better than chemical products."

I felt his gaze on my neck, my arms, and then he quickly looked back into my eyes.

"Would you like some tea?" I asked.

"Yes, tea sounds perfect."

I got up to go to the kitchen, feeling my heart beat strongly as my feet took one step at a time. The apartment was silent, but I swear I could hear our hearts beating together. I prepared the mugs and took out my herbal teas while waiting for the kettle to heat the water.

"Would you like chamomile? Orange-passion? Mango?" I asked from the kitchen.

"Chamomile sounds fine," he replied.

I couldn't see him, but I could sense his presence near me. I wanted to run back into the living room and ask him a million questions, but it seemed the questions were flowing between us, and the conversation had its own rhythm, its own natural flow that I never felt with anyone before.

"Do you like Avril Lavigne?" he asked out of the blue.

"Not really. I like her style, but I never got into her music all that much. Why?"

"Because I met a girl recently who liked Avril Lavigne, and I don't like her at all, so I wanted to know if you felt the same way. Stupid, really. It feels like you and I like the same things. It feels like you and I like the same songs. I have no idea if this is true, but in my head, this is what I've believed. Do you think it's true?"

I couldn't see his face from the kitchen, but as he spoke, I left the kettle and approached him. He was searching me out, and as our eyes met again, I knew exactly what he was saying.

"Do you want to see my CD collection?"

His eyes lit up. "I'd love to."

I bent to reach under the coffee table, removed two dark wooden chests, and opened them. "Here are a few of them. Help yourself."

He bent down on his knees and skimmed through them. I heard the water boiling and the light pop up to announce it was ready and headed back to the kitchen. I poured the hot water into the mugs to let the tea bags steep. I brought the mugs into the living room. Teddy was still in the same position.

"Teddy?"

He turned his head and smiled. "I like my name on your lips. Say it again, please."

"Teddy," I said, feeling slightly dizzy at the tone of his voice and at the feel of his name vibrating off my tongue and body.

"Serena, I absolutely love your selection, and you know what I love the most?"

When he said my name, I almost fainted. This was too surreal. Too much to take. He was in my living room, and we were sitting here in the middle of the night, talking. Was this real? Was I dreaming?

"What?"

"There is music in here that I've always wanted to listen to, to buy, but never did for one reason or another. Sometimes I select a CD based on a review or on the feeling I get from one or two songs or from the front cover. I think you do the same."

"Venom Blog?" I asked.

"Of course!" He smiled. "Hear You downloads?"

"I don't know that one." I placed the mugs on the coffee table. "Be careful, it's really hot."

He was holding Ellie Goulding. "I really like her voice."

"I went to buy that one specifically the day before yesterday. The song "Lights" blew me away the first time I heard it. She is incredible to listen to. Her music is dark, romantic, and her voice sends shivers down my spine, especially this one song, 'Don't Say a Word.'"

"Put it on, please."

I took the CD from his hand and almost ran to the kitchen.

"I want to hear that song," he shouted.

I brought the radio into the living room so it wouldn't be too loud and wake up the neighbours. I plugged it into the socket near the television and pressed Play.

"Do you know what's odd? Her music is considered electronica. I consider it magical," I said.

Her voice traveled through my apartment, and I sat on the couch next to Teddy. We quietly listened to the song and sipped our tea. It started off slow, and then it ended with the pounding of the drum and her voice again.

"Wow," he said at the end of the song. "I loved it. Let the whole CD play."

"Okay. That was the first song."

"What a song to begin with."

"It only gets better and better."

"That's the way it should be."

I lowered the volume and let Ellie Goulding do her magic as we continued our stare-down.

He opened his mouth to sip his tea, and I caught a glimpse of his tongue. I almost flung my mug to the floor to kiss it, to suck it passionately. I turned away, blushing.

"I love a girl who blushes." He tilted his head slightly, peeking up at me from the mug.

"You don't want to know what I was thinking."

"I think I could guess. I'm pretty much thinking about you too, only I don't blush." He smiled, and those eyes lit up, etching themselves into my memory to remain there forever.

"I feel like I could tell you anything," I said.

"Are you sleepy?" he suddenly asked, downing his tea. He was already finished?

"Not at all."

"I have the same problem."

"What shall we do about it?" I joked.

"Chamomile is supposed to help, only I'm not sleepy at all. I'm so excited to be here with you, in your apartment. I don't think I'll sleep for days…"

"I'm in the same boat."

"I really want to take it slow with you, Serena."

"Me too."

"I don't want to leave yet."

"I don't want you to leave."

"Can I just stare at you for a little while longer?"

"If I can do the same."

So we faced each other, and I noticed a tiny scar above his eyebrow. "How did you get that scar?"

"I fought with a bully in the schoolyard, and he cut me with a rock. He called me Theodore the whore one too many times."

"Theodore is your real name?"

"Yes."

"I prefer Teddy."

"Me too."

"What's your last name?"

"Neros. You?"

"Photine."

"With an f?"

"No."

"I love that. You are my light."

"I've been waiting for you for so long."

I finished my tea, my heart pounding. The conversation was like playing word Ping-Pong.

"I knew you were Greek too," he said, his eyes bright.

"I'm half Greek. My mom is Greek and my Dad was English. You?"

"I'm full, purebred Greek-Canadian."

"I can't wait to hear about your parents."

"Not tonight."

"I'm not ready for that conversation either." I smiled.

"I knew you had violet eyes, just like Elizabeth Taylor."

I laughed, and suddenly I yawned. I didn't mean to. I didn't even want to, but I felt my eyes getting heavy.

"I think the chamomile is taking effect," he said and yawned too. "Although I don't want to leave *ever,* I must, but not before I get your phone number." He stood and smiled.

I went into the kitchen and jotted down my number on a piece of scrap paper.

Teddy was going to call me! I gave it to him, and with an undeniable wide grin, he clutched it close and pressed it to his heart. "I'll never forget this CD," he said. "She is magical. You are so right. What time should I pick you up on Friday?"

I loved that he asked me that. "How about six thirty?"

"I'll be downstairs." He held onto the paper tightly. "Serena, I'll never forget this evening."

Suddenly, the sun beamed through the living room, sending blasts of light throughout the room, and I wanted to see Teddy's eyes in the natural light. I walked over to him.

"Yes, your eyes are perfect. Exactly as I'd imagined them in the dawn's early light."

"Me too," he said, studying my eyes closely too. "'Even better than the real thing.' Now I understand what that means. I never got that line before, but now, staring into your violet eyes, I understand exactly what that means, and I thank Bono for the words to express them."

I lost myself in his eyes again, not giving any thought to tomorrow or to yesterday, when suddenly I started to recite a poem.

"Let me not the marriage of true minds. Admit impediments. Love is not love—"

"Which alters when it alteration finds," Teddy interjected and his eyes twinkled. "Sonnet 116."

"Or bends with the remover to remove: O no! It is an ever-fixed mark," I continued, and he joined me, and together we recited the rest of the poem, our voices united…

"That looks on tempests and is never shaken. It is the star to every wandering bark, Whose worth's unknown, although his height be taken. Love's not Time's fool, though rosy lips and cheeks Within his bending sickle's compass come: Love alters not with his brief hours and weeks, But bears it out even to the edge of doom. If this be error and upon me proved, I never writ, nor no man ever loved."

We didn't even ask how we both knew that poem as we looked at each other and recited one of the greatest love sonnets ever written. We both felt the air in the room between us was moving, flowing back and forth like waves in an ocean, like sand on a beach. We understood each word in the sonnet, its meaning, and felt the words erupt inside us.

When two souls meet, they speak a secret language.

We hugged briefly, my arms wrapped around his waist, and I smelled Teddy's scent for the first time. I couldn't wait for the multitude of first times with him. I closed my eyes and inhaled his scent. Indescribable how that scent became a part of my cells within seconds. I felt his heart beat strongly against mine while his arms were wrapped around my shoulders.

I heard him inhale deeply, and he whispered, "Gardenias."

I couldn't think of anything to reply, so I spoke his name. "Teddy," I said as I caught a whiff of his shampoo, and instantly added, "wood sense," whatever that meant.

"Axe." He smiled, looking down at me, his face inches from mine, and it took all my energy to pull back.

"Till Friday," I said, my heart pounding.

"I have to tell you, Serena, this has been one hell of a week."

"For me too," I confessed, my thoughts starting to be invaded by Ben.

"I can't wait till Friday," he said, light-hearted and soul-warmed.

I nodded, scared to say anything else, as sexual positions with Ben ran through my mind, and I became skittish. *Is this the same week?*

I nervously looked down at my bare feet. "See you then." I looked up.

He caught something in my look and brushed his hair out of his eyes. "I feel like I could read your mind."

"This is a crazy feeling," I admitted, not knowing what else to say.

We gazed at each other again. I knew he didn't want to leave, and I didn't want him to leave.

"Can you stay a little while longer?" I asked gently.

"I thought you'd never ask. I wasn't sure if you wanted to sleep or not."

"I can't sleep."

And so we sat there on my couch, talking and talking till it was time for breakfast, and we made coffee, and then he left to get ready for work.

"I have so much energy. I don't know where it's coming from," he said, putting on his jacket and then his shoes.

"I feel the same way." I wrapped my robe around me nervously.

"See you Friday." He turned to go.

"Bye."

I shut the door behind him and placed my back against it, exhaling a deep breath, listening to his movements in the corridor. I ran to the window and waited to see him outside. As I saw his form leave my front steps, he turned back and waved at me. Our eyes met again, and my heart pounded uncontrollably.

This is what it feels like. This was what love was supposed to feel like.

We weren't waiting for anything magical to happen, because the magic was right in front of us. He stood in front of his car, his gaze holding mine, and as much as he struggled to leave, I struggled watching him leave.

I welcome you, Teddy, to the deep, complicated workings of my soul. I am ready for you. Let the adventure begin.

At six thirty sharp, Friday night, Teddy rang my doorbell. I buzzed him upstairs.

A word about the author…

Christina Strigas is an author and poet. She has written five novels, four poetry books, and one self-help book based on her popular quotes on Twitter. She writes romantic love poetry in a stream of consciousness narrative. Her novels vary from paranormal fiction to erotica and romance. She holds a BA in English Literature and a Teaching Degree. She teaches English and French in an elementary school and is a part-time Course Lecturer at McGill University. http://christinastrigas.com/

Thank you for purchasing
this publication of The Wild Rose Press, Inc.

For questions or more information
contact us at
info@thewildrosepress.com.

The Wild Rose Press, Inc.
www.thewildrosepress.com